CRITICS PRAISE *ONCE A PIRATE*

"This is a sure-fire, five-hearts-five-star . . . five-galaxy read. . . . Please don't miss it!"

—*Under the Covers Book Reviews*

"Passionate and captivating! . . . This is a must read for all lovers of romance!"

—*The Bookworm*

"*The Star King*, Susan Grant's second novel, proves that her first terrific romance, *Once A Pirate*, was no fluke. . . . If you're looking for some excitement and adventure, *The Star King* will provide it—in spades."

—*All About Romance*

"This book literally blew me away. . . . I eagerly look forward to more, more, more from Susan Grant."

—*Kathy's Faves and Raves*

"Ms. Grant cranked up the sizzle factor for this story."

—*The Romance Journal*

A TRUSTING OF THE SENSES

Jas leaned into his warm, roughened palm, her eyes drifting half-closed. She couldn't shake the feeling that she'd waited for this man all her life, that fate somehow bound them together. "I'm analytical," she whispered fervently, "levelheaded. Things like this don't happen to people like me."

He cupped her chin, silencing her. Then, slowly, reverently, he brushed back her hair, his fingertips skimming along the edge of her ear. She held herself completely still, certain that a single move would shatter this dream.

Her breath caught as he pressed his lips to her hair, then her cheek. "Trust your senses, my angel," he murmured, nuzzling her throat. "What they reveal is not always what we expect." Weaving his fingers through her hair, he guided her to his mouth.

Other *Love Spell* books by Susan Grant:
ONCE A PIRATE

The Star King

Susan Grant

LOVE SPELL   NEW YORK CITY

A LOVE SPELL BOOK®

December 2000

Published by

Dorchester Publishing Co., Inc.
276 Fifth Avenue
New York, NY 10001

ISBN 0-505-52413-9

Printed in the United States of America.

Visit us on the web at www.dorchesterpub.com.

For my parents, Davis and Isabel
Your unconditional love gave me the wings to fly

ACKNOWLEDGMENTS

It is with awe and gratitude that I thank the following individuals: Kelly Bloom, to whom I owe this gorgeous cover; Christopher Keeslar, for the priceless gift of "creative elbow room" in letting me write the book of my heart; Catherine Asaro, a true Renaissance woman, for her generosity, and her eagerness to brainstorm space battles; Major Sean Bautista for his dogfight advice and the de-wimping of my heroine; Julie Hughes Ryan and Karen Morgan for their expert cyber-navigating of Andrews AFB; the Lollies (my pod-sisters) for always being there for me; the staff at Borders Books in Roseville, CA, who provided the chaos and coffee I needed to write this book; Stefanie Hargreaves of Amazon.com for giving this "newbie" the chance to shine; Theresa Ragan, writing partner extraordinaire (I couldn't have done it without you); Maudeen Wachsmith, an infinite well of ideas; Carolyn Stahl, for being "mommie"; and finally, Morgan's grandma, Mary Alice Gibbons, a woman wonderful beyond words. Thank you, all. You've helped me more than you will ever know.

"A dream not understood is like a letter unopened."
—*The Talmud*

Chapter One

The missile pursued Lt. Jasmine Boswell's fighter jet across the sky with heartless accuracy. Fear-fed adrenaline pumped through her veins. *No time to be scared.*

"Thunder Flight, break left! Bandit in your six!" Her wingman's warning roared inside her helmet. "Harder left!"

Jas gripped the control stick in her gloved hand and pulled. Nine times the force of gravity crushed her into the seat. Her oxygen mask slid lower on her sweaty face as she struggled to suck in enough air to fill her compressed lungs.

"Bandit right—seven o'clock. Two miles."

Damn it. Her thoughts spun in a whirlpool of fear, denial, and anger. This was Saudi Arabia, the no-fly zone, for Pete's sake. Who had fired at her? And how could she not have known they were there?

"Take it down! Reverse right!"

Jas shoved the stick the opposite way and forward. Her seat belt and shoulder harnesses kept her bottom firmly on the seat, but the effect of negative gravity propelled her insides upward, as if she'd just crested the highest hill on the world's biggest roller coaster.

"Missile in your six, less than a mile. Thunder Flight, break right, hard right!" Urgency slipped into her wingman's tone. "*Harder* right!" A heartbeat later an explosion bleached the cloud-starved sky.

Aw, hell. Teeth-rattling vibrations shook her against her harnesses while warning lights in her snug, single-seat cockpit flashed like a Christmas tree gone berserk. Then the F-16C began a slow sideways slide, barreling crookedly along—pulling left like her grandfather's old pickup truck.

"I'm losing hydraulics . . . and fuel," she said, wrestling with the stick and rudder pedals. "Can't keep her level." She glanced outside. Hundreds of miles of barren desert yawned beneath her. If she lost control, then—

The horizon plunged as the jet tumbled. The sudden violent acceleration pinned her head and shoulders to the top of the canopy. Distantly, she heard "Eject, eject, eject" in her headset. But she couldn't. She tried to stretch her left arm to reach the ejection handle below her, but her limb felt as if it weighed hundreds of pounds. She gasped past clenched teeth, battling to move her hand while her trusted stoic inner voice scrolled through a litany of options. If she bailed out trapped in this awkward position, she would likely break her back. But the fighter was out of control—if she stayed inside, she'd surely die.

She slid her hand lower, lower. *Please.* Her arm trembled and her shoulders burned. Sweat stung her eyes.

Oh, God. One . . . more . . . inch. Her gloved fingers closed over the handgrip and she pulled for all she was worth.

"By all that is holy, no!" Romlijhian B'kah vaulted from his starfighter cockpit to the ground below. Propelled by urgency and dread, he raced from his ship to a massive furrow littered with rocks and slag. Long-ago wars had ravaged Balkanor, turning the planet into a lifeless desert of coarse, shifting sand. Rom grimly acknowledged it was a fitting base for Sharron, the fanatic he'd come here to kill.

Where the ditch ended, the wreckage began: his brother's starfighter, a once beautiful now broken bird, vapor hissing from vents torn in its hull. Although the breathing apparatus in Rom's helmet did not draw upon outside air, he could well imagine the stink of leaking propellant.

"Lijhan!" Rom scrambled up the handgrips. At the top, he cracked open the cockpit, reaching for the man inside. "Get out! *Now*." He yanked open the fastenings crisscrossing his brother's chest.

Lijhan shoved at his hands. "Go without me." His voice was hoarse, impassioned. "I—I can't move my legs."

Rom jerked his attention downward. Glittering shards from what had once been the navigation panel snagged Lijhan's trousers like teeth. "*Crat*." He sagged on the handgrips. A sudden, soul-deep weariness threatened to overtake the adrenaline rush of combat. Freeing his brother's legs would be a delicate, time-consuming job. If he rushed, he risked puncturing Lijhan's protective suit, and his brother could die of radiation poisoning before they made it off Balkanor. Conversely, if he took the time the chancy procedure demanded, he'd erode the advantage of surprise he'd gained by evading Sharron's defense forces undetected.

Rom's fists tightened over the handgrips. Too many months spent and too many lives lost weighed on his conscience to risk failing today. He had to continue on.

"I'll return for you," Rom said, his voice flat. "Propellant's leaking; don't turn on the power."

"No, sir."

"Be mindful of sparks when you detach the panel."

"Yes, sir."

Rom clenched his jaw. How could he in good conscience leave his brother behind? "Show me your weapons." His brisk tone camouflaged his inner turmoil. "I must know you can protect yourself, if need be."

Lijhan showed him a laser pistol and a sheathed blade. Uncharacteristically solemn, he squeezed Rom's shoulder. "Follow your senses, Rom. Trust what is revealed to you, as our ancestors did, and the Great Mother will guide you to your destiny."

Rom covered Lijhan's hand, glove over glove, and stared into his brother's black-and-gold helmet visor that reflected his own equally unfathomable visage. "To victory," he whispered. Then he jumped to the sand.

Lijhan thrust his fist in the air, the warrior's gesture for victory. "Crush the darkness!"

Bouyed by the war cry, Rom ran toward his objective: a cluster of caves housing a vast underground labyrinth of tunnels, from where he would penetrate Sharron's compound. But his body was depleted from the hours of space combat preceding the invasion, making every stride feel like twenty. He'd barely reached several monolithic boulders, a landmark his spies had given him, when static erupted in his helmet comm link. He slowed, scanning the sky for enemy craft. It was empty. The hair raised on his neck. *Lijhan.* He spun around.

His brother's starfighter was on fire. "Lijhan!" he bellowed, bolting forward as flames spread over the fuselage with horrific efficiency. Before he took a second step, the heat detonated a propellant tank, and the starfighter exploded in a blinding fist of orange light. "No!"

Pop-pop-pop. The sand around him began percolating in erratic little puffs. Shrapnel! He dove away from a whirling projectile. It glanced off his chest, slicing through fabric and skin, searing him like a molten blade.

Pain squeezed his lungs in an invisible vise and almost clamped off the flow of air. His legs buckled. Gasping, he fell to the sand, holding closed the tear in his protective suit. Lijhan had been his virtual shadow since childhood, his devoted ally and closest friend. More than brothers, they'd shared a friendship forged by blood and love, the kind of bond broken only by death—which was supposed to come long after they had both lived full lives and aged into feeble old men.

Hoarsely, Rom shouted at the amber-hued sky, "Great Mother—why this! Why did you not take me?" Dizzy with agony that was far more than physical, he doubled over and nearly blacked out.

The good of the people outweighs the concerns of an individual.

The oft-recited words invaded his delirium. Drawing strength from the age-old maxim, he regained control slowly, blocking out his grief over Lijhan's death to focus on his mission. When the tremors in his hands stilled, he removed his gloves and assessed the damage to his body with the cool objectivity he employed when inspecting his starfighter after combat. Blood saturated the frayed, bloodied cloth across his chest. But the wound was the least of his worries. He'd been exposed to radiation; if it didn't kill him, it would likely render him sterile. If he couldn't produce an heir—his responsibility to his family as the Crown Prince—there would be no marriage. And now, with his younger brother dead and unable to take his place, Rom might have single-handedly obliterated his eleven-thousand-year-old family line.

"I will not have it!" He winced at a particularly vivid memory of his father storming toward him, the man's golden eyes dark with uncharacteristic rage as he'd forbidden Rom to fight. But Rom had defied him.

Even now the memory of that insubordination, the first in his twenty-three standard years, alternately exhilarated and sickened him. His pacifist father refused to see the reason for this war. He'd scoffed at Rom's claim that Sharron's ideas threatened the age-old mores of fidelity and family, and that the renegade religious figure was swiftly growing in both power and influence. Rom had hoped to prove him wrong. But in the wake of this disastrous invasion, he doubted his father would see anything but his firstborn's failure as heir and the shame it would bring upon their family.

The sun settled toward the horizon, flooding the valley with shadows of russet and gold, reminding Rom of the planet Sienna, his ancestral home. Somehow, he had to return to the palace there, to inform his family of his brother's death—and his own accountability for it.

He attempted to sit up, but his muscles disobeyed him, and blackness appeared at the edges of his vision. Groaning, he laid his head back, but did not go willingly when unconsciousness claimed him. . . .

"Don't move," said a female voice in a language Rom had never heard, but somehow understood. Long before he'd heard her, he had sensed her presence in the darkness, coaxing him to awaken, to not give in.

To not die.

Rom's eyelids grated open over eyes as gritty as sand. He propped himself on his elbows to better discern whoever it was who was calling to him. The rocks beneath him bit into his back, but inexplicably, the sickening pain in his chest and ribs was gone. As was his helmet.

He did not recall removing it.

Rom stared dumbly at the apparition walking toward him. By the heavens, he had never seen anyone like her in his life. Her skin looked as pale and soft as sea-swept sand, contrasting vividly with her hair, silken strands cropped below her jaw in an impossible shade—the color of deepest space.

Such an extraordinary vision could mean only that he was hovering between life and death. The borderland at the edge of eternity was a world all its own—or so said those rare warriors who returned to describe it.

"If you're the angel dispatched to bring me to the Ever After," he said under his breath, "perhaps it will not be so bad to die."

She halted. "Move again and I'll shoot you in the balls and stitch you up from there."

Certainly she sounded more like a soldier than a heavenly being. Yet her uniform was not one he recognized, nor was it of a design to shield her from radiation. A muted green one-piece garment covered her arms and

19

legs. Black patches filled the places where insignia might normally be worn, and a primitive helmet dangled from one gloved hand. In the other was a gun just as crude—and she was aiming it at his head.

He curled his fingers around his own pistol. She fired. A single shot plowed between his knees and sprayed dirt in all directions. Great Mother, he thought, swallowing his cough of surprise.

"The next shot will be higher, pal. A lot higher. Now drop that weapon," she said, weaving slightly. Her breathing appeared rapid and shallow, though from injury or agitation, he couldn't tell. She indicated with a curt flick of her arm that he should lay aside his laser pistol, but an inner warning stopped him. She might be one of Sharron's minions, a scout dispatched to investigate the crash. No. Her gaze was too discerning, too intelligent, nothing like the glazed-over eyes of Sharron's cultist followers.

He set his pistol on the ground near her feet. "I have no reason to harm you."

"We can debate that when you're unarmed."

She used the toe of her boot to slide his weapon out of his reach, but as she did, thunder erupted. A series of explosions flared on the horizon, while rumbling beyond the hills heralded more of the same. Her jaw dropped. Four delta-winged craft soared through the twilight sky.

"What in the blazes are those?" she asked.

"Starfighters," he said simply. "Ours."

Starfighters? Jas's heart lurched. Like all combat pilots, she'd memorized images of scores of aircraft; it minimized the chances of firing on a friendly target dur-

ing battle. But these incredibly sleek jets didn't resemble anything she'd ever seen.

They looked like spaceships.

She swerved her attention back to her captive—the soldier or whatever he was. An iridescent blue, silver-trimmed uniform covered his long, well-built body from neck to boots. The bronze, almost amber skin of his face and hands matched his hair color, but his gold eyes were dark-lashed and disconcertingly pale. "You're not Saudi, are you?" she said in what had to be the understatement of the year.

A sharp blast shook the ground beneath her boots.

"Take cover!" The man lunged for her, yanking her down onto his chest. Her .45 discharged into the air. A massive detonation and answering ground fire drowned out the sound.

He wrenched the gun from her hand, dragging her backward to an outcropping of reddish boulders. Her world narrowed to a need for survival—her own. She fought back. Aiming the heel of her palm, she jammed it upward to shatter his nose. With deft agility he blocked her, twisted, and the knee she'd aimed at his groin slid harmlessly past his thigh.

They rolled over the dirt. Sharp pebbles scored her exposed skin, but she continued to grapple, pummeling him with her fists and knees. Then he flipped her onto her back—expertly, easily. Damn! *Humiliation and surprise at being so handily defeated blossomed into fury. Gasping, she tried to wrench her wrists from his big hands, calculating how best to ram her knuckles into his larynx from such an awkward angle.*

"Cease your struggles!" he commanded, equally breathless. "There is far greater danger to you than me."

As if to underscore his words, another pair of inconceivably futuristic ships flew overhead. Shielding her head with his hands, he protected her with his body while debris rained down from the sky. Jas swore, a muffled exclamation against his torn uniform, and tried to push away, but he held her close. When the fighting had stopped, he released her.

Dazed, she pushed herself to her knees, combing fingers through her damp and gritty hair. To her horror, the sand where she had stood only moments earlier was charred and steaming. Her discarded gun was a rapidly congealing blob of molten steel.

She fought to slow her breathing. "You saved my life."

"No," he said. "You saved mine." Oblivious to her confusion, he eased himself to a sitting position. "I felt myself slipping away. But I heard your voice, and I followed it back." His face contorted with pain, and he jammed his fingers into his hair. "Though I don't know why." Angry eyes accused her. "You should have let me die."

"I have no idea what you're talking about." Her tone turned brisk, defensive, as if she were already at her court-martial, explaining why she'd fraternized with the enemy in the midst of an alien invasion. "I must have hit my head. None of this is real, including you. Watch, this time I'll touch you and you'll disappear like a bubble."

To her dismay, the man offered his hand. "Please."

Countless heartbeats ticked by as they observed each other within the deepening shadows. Kneeling beside him, she hesitantly touched her fingertips to his warm palm.

"I'm still here," he said.

"Yes," she whispered.

Their gazes locked. Her hand flattened against his, as if of its own will. Her awareness of him intensified. But before she could distance herself, the floodgates opened. Curiosity . . . wariness . . . and unmistakable, flattering interest—the thoughts—his *thoughts*—flowed into her mind, swirling with hers.

A cry of bewilderment lodged in her throat.

Reveal your purpose, *his eyes beseeched her. Guide me.*

She helplessly shook her head.

Please.

Jas snatched her hand away. She didn't know what disturbed her more, being able to "hear" his thoughts, or not knowing how to give what he so clearly asked of her. Her gaze dropped to his bloodstained uniform. "Are you in pain?"

"I was. But I don't feel a thing now." He lifted his hand to touch the swelling bruise on her forehead, then stopped and clenched his fist. "Do you?"

"No, but I—" Gasping, she pressed her knuckles to her mouth. "I can feel your grief."

Great Mother. The knot Rom had cinched around his emotions nearly unraveled. He fought for control, barely regaining it before he answered, "My brother is dead." The four tersely spoken words did little to convey the enormity of his loss. "I shouldn't have left him in the wreckage; I should have freed him while I had the chance."

"No." The woman's eyes closed. "Crush the darkness."

"What?" he asked in a harsh whisper.

23

"You must crush the darkness." She was paler now. "I hear that in my head. What does it mean?"

"My enemy, Sharron, is the darkness," he said in a growl. "A monster of matchless evil whose death will mean the end of this war. My troops cry 'crush the darkness' before we go into battle. It was the last thing my brother said"—his voice softened—"before he died."

"Then you must do it," she said with conviction, moisture glinting in her eyes. "Kill Sharron."

All doubts as to why she was here scattered like dust. Those few words gave him the determination, the heart to go on.

"This was your purpose all along," he said. "To guide me. To set me back on my path." He risked smoothing his hand over her cheek. Consternation flickered in her eyes, but in the way of dreams, she accepted his brash caress. The feel of her soft and disturbingly real skin set off alarm bells in his head. To be so moved by this woman, even if she was a vision, was unfortunate and improper, especially given—should he survive physically unscathed—his impending arranged and very necessary marriage.

Jas leaned into his warm, roughened palm, her eyes drifting half-closed. She couldn't shake the feeling that she'd waited for this man all her life, that fate somehow bound them together. "I'm analytical," she whispered fervently, "levelheaded. Things like this don't happen to people like me."

He cupped her chin, silencing her. Then slowly, reverently, he brushed back her hair, his fingertips skimming along the edge of her ear. She held herself completely still, certain that a single move would shatter this dream.

Her breath caught as he pressed his lips to her hair, then her cheek. "Trust your senses, my angel," he murmured, nuzzling her throat. "What they reveal is not always what we expect." Weaving his fingers through her hair, he guided her to his mouth.

Her eyes closed and her lips opened under the soft, warm pressure. Lovingly, his tongue stroked hers. Passion scorched through her, heightening the sensitivity of every square inch of her skin. Out the door went her inner warnings and anything else resembling rational judgment. *He's not real, and this isn't happening,* she chanted silently.

Desperately.

He was a stranger, a wounded soldier whose courage and integrity mirrored those of the knights of old; a handsome, golden-eyed warrior whose briefest kiss left her breathless, whose pain and grief she had taken into herself as if it were her own. His familiarity, her depth of feeling for him, and the way she could read his thoughts—it defied logic, and baffled her, for clear-headed reasoning was a trait she had valued and cultivated since childhood, just as she had trained herself to suppress strong emotion.

Until now.

They kissed deeply, fully.

Rom rolled the woman onto the coarse sand, careful to cushion her head with his hand. He surrendered to her taste, her scent—whiffs of exotic blooms from lands he had never seen mingled with the harshness of smoke and blood and dirt. He needed her with a desperation born of his precarious position at the edge of death, wanted to make love to her while he possessed the strength and passion of life.

25

Her pleasure would be his salvation.

But the blackness returned too quickly, flickering specks at first, and then billowing clouds that blotted out his vision. He prayed for more time, prayed that this ethereal being would prevent him from slipping from his mortal life into eternity.

"Wake up!"

Rom sucked in a breath as the toe of a booted foot jammed into his abdomen and wrenched him back to reality with stunning cruelty. The laughter of at least half a dozen helmeted men echoed off the hills, and he was again a wounded pilot lying on his back on a battlefield. Drawing his knees up to his chest, he seized his weapon. The booted foot kicked it out of his hand.

"Dreaming about your last pleasure servant, eh?" one of the soldiers inquired with a muffled sneer. "By the looks of it, she must have treated you well." More laughter. "It's B'kah. And he's hard as a rock. Kick him again." Rom twisted to one side, deflecting the vicious strike from his groin to his hip.

"Enough," a deeper voice ordered. "There's not much time. Sharron wants him now."

The soldiers hauled him to his feet. Pain rocketed through his chest. He was burning alive, couldn't fill his lungs with air. He gritted his teeth, struggling to stay conscious, but his legs swayed like ribbons. He prayed for strength, for discipline, for focus, so he could complete his mission. And he clung to the vision of the woman—the angel—to keep him awake, remembering the words that would keep him alive long enough to kill Sharron: *Crush the darkness.*

They dragged him down into the caves, humid caverns

ripe with the stench of suffering. There was laser-lit darkness, the sound of distant weeping, then blessedly cold, crisp air in the decontamination chamber.

"He will see you now," said one of the three muscular guards who propelled him along a corridor that stretched on forever, rivaling in size the hallways of the palace in which Rom had been born. Home. Sienna. But that grand architectural showplace emanated goodness, not this . . . evil.

"The prince, my lord."

Rom was all but dropped onto a chair. Struggling to maintain some semblance of aristocratic poise, he sat up straight. You are the B'kah heir, he reminded himself, gritting his teeth as his battered ribs scorched his insides like white-hot pokers. The guards had been fools; out of respect for his status, and the presumption that his injuries had rendered him helpless, they had not bound him with shock-cuffs.

Sharron stood tall, serene, as he contemplated a floor-to-ceiling painting of the black hole at the galaxy's center. He had the pale hair and perfectly formed features of his well-regarded merchant family. Generations of loyal men preceded him. What had happened? What had changed him?

Sharron turned, facing Rom. A medallion engraved with a rising sun above two clasped hands dangled from his neck. Rom recognized the metal: an empathic alloy. Disgust curled his mouth. Medallions such as these had been banned since the Dark Years, when they were used by warlords to influence behavior. He was surprised Sharron hadn't already ordered one hung around his neck.

"Romlijhian B'kah, the wayward prince," Sharron

said pleasantly. "How I wish our meeting were under better circumstances."

"Frankly, I'd envisioned sifting through the wreckage of your headquarters, searching for your worthless remains."

"Please, no harsh words. This is the chance to smooth over our differences. Most of what troubles you stems from not understanding what the Family of the New Day is and what we stand for."

"You're a butcher. You and your chosen elders impregnate your female followers, then send them on a one-way journey to the center of the galaxy after they give birth."

Sharron's smile was magnetic. "Baseless allegations."

Rom gripped the sides of the chair. That had been his father's response, too. If only he *had* proof, other than a few dozen holo-images recordings of women being loaded onto ships, perhaps he could have gathered support from his father instead of fighting this war with only his own trusted men.

Sharron projected genuine empathy. "Since infancy you've known only the brainwashing of the *Vash Nadah*. It's extraordinarily difficult to see past that relentless indoctrination, Romlijhian. But you must endeavor to do so. You are a powerful young man, one of the few influential enough, intelligent enough to make a difference." The man took another step, coming near enough that Rom could reach out and grab him. "Innocent lives have been lost, on my side and yours. Let us stop this killing."

"Sign the agreement of surrender. It is the only way." His muscles tense and ready, Rom peered at his enemy through half-closed lids. "Capturing me changes nothing."

"True." Sharron clasped his hands behind his back and paced across the room, away from him. Rom swore under his breath. "I miscalculated. Force was not the path to take. Not yet. I did not anticipate you'd drum up such support so quickly, and without your father's blessing. Yet, in a way, my mistake has garnered good results."

A sudden malicious delight flared in the cult leader's eyes. "You were exposed to the radiation many long hours. Too many, don't you think?"

Rom masked his fear of what Sharron implied, that he had rendered himself sterile, ending his family's unbroken lineage of kings.

Animosity slipped into Sharron's light tone. "A rather amusing situation, had either of us been men blessed with a sense of humor. Look at you—scion to the richest, most powerful family of the *Vash Nadah*, the undisputed rulers of all known worlds, damaged beyond repair in the only way that truly matters." He flicked his broad palm up as if tossing grains of sand to the wind. "Your seed is undoubtedly ruined. No hope of sons—or even daughters, for that matter."

Clutching the sides of the chair, Rom let his chin bob forward. Just as he'd hoped, he heard Sharron move closer. "You're going to die on me, aren't you, Romlijhian?"

"The hell I am." Arching upward, Rom shoved the heels of his boots into Sharron's midsection, throwing him off his feet. Then he was out of the chair and on his prey before Sharron had any chance to beg for his sorry life. They skidded across the floor and slammed into a wall. A painting crashed to the ground nearby. Broken glass crunched under Sharron's back as his head hit the leg of a table with a muffled thunk. To his credit, the man did not cry out.

Rom felt his chest wound reopen. He knew the bright crimson blood smeared across Sharron's face and over the white-tiled floor was his own, but fury obliterated his pain. He wrenched the frame from the fallen painting and jammed the jagged metal edge up and against Sharron's throat with both hands. It cut through tendons and flesh. Blood spurted across the wall. Sharron gurgled, clawing at his neck.

"Die, bastard, *die!*" Rom used the last of his strength to hold Sharron's shuddering, dying body in place. He had to be sure, or this monster's matchless evil would spread to the farthest reaches of the galaxy.

Sharron went limp. Rom's vision grayed, and the buzzing in his ears grew louder, muting the sound of approaching boots and screaming men. "Our security has been breached!" he heard someone nearby shout. "Evacuate!" Hands pried his arm from Sharron's neck. A burst of light stunned him. *No!* Rom groped blindly about him. *Where?* Crawling, then dragging himself across the floor, he pursued the sounds of the retreating soldiers.

Rom knew that his own men had found him by their gentle, deferential handling. He forced his dry mouth to form words. "Sharron . . . dead. They took the body." As his troops lifted him, he urged hoarsely, "Don't let them escape!" The roaring in his ears covered his soldiers' response. The walls careened around and around, and he squeezed his eyes shut to blot out the tilting room. Someone slit his uniform open to the waist, exposing his wound. His teeth chattered; his heart faltered, then continued its odd, shallow flutter.

You're not going to die.

The Balkanor angel. He recognized her sweet, husky voice in his head.

"My beloved," he whispered. No longer able to open his eyes, he felt her warm arms around him, comforting him, filling him with a bliss he never imagined, holding him to this side of life.

Her presence wavered.

"*No.* I don't know how or where to find you," he cried, his pride secondary to having her at his side. "Don't leave. I need you." But she slipped from his grasp. Great Mother, he'd lost his brother, and now the woman. "I will find you. I swear it." Someone—his surgeon, perhaps—laid a cool cloth over his forehead and soothed him in worried tones. Despite the doctor's ministrations, Rom chanted his promise until he could speak no more. "I will find you."

I will find you.

Jas tightened her embrace. "I'm right here." She pressed her cheek to his, relishing the prickly roughness of stubble on his otherwise smooth, tawny skin.

Don't leave.

"I won't," she assured him in his language. But in a rush of hot, dry wind, his presence evaporated, draining her heart of its newfound joy. She clutched the air, crying out, "No, don't leave!"

"Hey, hey. No one's going to leave you, Lieutenant."

Someone clamped a mask over her mouth and nose. "She's conscious! I need the C-collar—now!"

With an enormous effort, she opened her eyes, blinking to clear the shadow floating in front of her, squinting until the blurred shape became a young black medic

Susan Grant

dressed in U.S. Air Force combat fatigues. "Oh—" The
world roared back. Chaos. The rhythmic thunder of
chopper blades. Saudi desert heat. Turbulence. Pain
streaked outward from the right side of her forehead as
she fought rising nausea.

The medic leaned closer, patting her on the cheek. His
voice eased into a honeyed Southern accent. "That's it.
Keep those gorgeous eyes wide open for me." He lifted
the oxygen mask from her mouth and clamped a neck
brace over her throat. Peering at his watch, he held her
wrist between his fingers. Then he pressed the microphone attached to his headset to his lips. "Say again?
Yeah, blood pressure's ninety over fifty. *Fifty.*"

"I bailed out, didn't I?" Her words were slurred.
"Don't remember."

"Shot down . . . friendly fire." His voice was drowned
out by the incessant drumming of the rotor blades.

She tried to sit up, but was strapped firmly to a litter.
"I saw someone out there. A man. He's hurt—we have
to go back." The medic pressed his hand onto her shoulder and squeezed. "No," she persisted. "We talked . . .
and he said . . . and then we—" She swallowed hard.
How in the world was she going to explain that he
needed her, that she needed him, when she hardly understood it herself? "Just don't leave."

"Lieutenant—"

"*Please.*" She beseeched him with her eyes as he settled the oxygen mask over her mouth and nose, silencing
her. *No!* she screamed silently.

"Ma'am, we circled the site. If there'd been anyone
else, we would've seen them." His tone was gentle, not
condescending. "Breathe deep and slow. There you go.
You'll feel better in no time."

"Don't need to feel better," she mumbled into the mask. "Don't want to forget." Groggy, she closed her eyes.

Don't go. I need you. The lyrical, exotic words swirled like dust motes in the hazy place between wakefulness and sleep. Then the blackness closed in, and she was helpless to stop it.

Chapter Two

Nineteen years later

"True love? Oh, spare me." Jas pulled her hand away from the palm reader only to have the woman yank it back. "Isn't there a money line?" she asked brightly. "Ought to be, Tina. Much more practical, I think. Tell me about the big collector who'll walk in and buy out my paintings so I can live in Sedona like Betty here."

"Open your hand, dear."

The adobe walls of the softly lit art gallery radiated coolness and muffled the street noises so that all she heard was her own pulse—and the drumming of her fingers as Tina made her way back to her love line. "I could use a weather forecast," Jas ventured. "My son and I are going camping next week."

"Mrs. Hamilton . . ." The aged fortune-teller pursed her lips, the mirth in her eyes magnified by her thick spectacles. Then she lifted her exasperated gaze to Betty, Jas's friend and agent, and the owner of the chic gallery. "Artists are supposed to be intuitive, open-minded, and *receptive,* are they not?"

"Supposed to be." Betty winked at Jas, then turned her mischievous brown eyes back to the palm reader. "I simply don't know what to say about this one. But her paintings sell, and sell well, mind you. So"—she sighed—"I put up with her." Chuckling, Betty arranged a tray with chocolate biscuits and a pot of espresso and carried it to the table, while Tina resumed her study of Jas's palm.

"Your love line runs steady and does not branch out. A rarity. It means one man, one love. A love everlasting." Tina's voice dropped lower. "He is your soul mate, you see. You have loved him in the past and will love him again, for your souls are forever intertwined."

Every muscle in Jas's body went rigid. The chimes near the entrance tinkled as the wind hissed down from the surrounding hills, whispering over her bare arms with a lover's touch. *I will find you.* Swamped by an inexplicable feeling of déjà vu, of longing, Jas inhaled and exhaled several times through her nose to calm herself, a technique she'd learned from yet another one of Betty's octogenarian New Ager pals. Instinctively her eyes sought an enormous painting, her most recent, into which she had poured all the passion of her wounded soul. It held hues of gold, amber, rich sienna. Sand. Sky. The hush of deepening twilight as the first stars of evening glittered in cool desert air.

The mysterious dream had awakened her the night she'd painted it, and she'd worked through the following day and night, trying to re-create the harsh splendor of the landscape, while lingering desire thrummed deep inside her, more powerful than ever, along with the sense that she'd left someone behind. But whom? Upon waking, she sometimes recalled a man with enigmatic golden eyes, but his features were always blurred, as if she were viewing him through frosted glass.

It was the only aberration of her otherwise wholly rational mind.

"Jasmine." Tina tapped a roughened fingertip on the heel of her palm. "Pay attention."

Jas blinked at the mild rebuke. "Yes, ma'am."

She spoke gently. "There has been heartache and disappointment in your past, yet this pain will continue to make you stronger, strength you will need for your true love. He will require the full power of your spirit, your faith . . . your flesh."

Jas snorted. "Tell *that* to my one and only"—she glanced at her Marvin the Martian wristwatch—"who happens to be in Las Vegas, as we speak, honeymooning with his new pregnant twenty-year-old wife."

"Jock was not your true love."

"Yeah. I finally figured that out." She no longer loved Jock. And she certainly didn't miss him. It had been six months since they divorced, and over two years since they'd last slept together, had sex, or whatever that joyless coupling that had characterized their marriage was called.

Jas spread her free hand on the table. "True love's a myth, a fairy tale."

"You did not always think this way," Tina said softly. "You *believed.*"

Jas clenched her hand into a fist. She'd let magic derail her life once. Once. She was smarter now.

As calmly as she could, she stood. Bewildered, Tina let her shake her hand. "Thank you, really," Jas said, pumping the elderly woman's arm. "I'm open to palmistry and all that, but love's not my favorite subject these days. Why don't you join Betty and me for lunch later at Tomasita Grill?" She kept up her chatter as she helped Tina up and escorted her to the front entrance. When the door closed, she leaned her forehead against the cool, smooth wood.

"I'm sorry," she heard Betty say.

"Don't be." Jas walked back to the table and helped herself to another biscuit. "I hope I wasn't too rude."

"She didn't think so." Betty regarded her tenderly. "She knows it's been tough for you lately—the twins off to college, the divorce. Before you know it, life will be back the way it was before." She squeezed her shoulder. "Have another espresso."

"What I need is a shot of tequila. Hold the lime and the salt. Shoot, hold the glass. Just pour it down my throat."

"Your show's opening brought in thirty-five thousand dollars and an invitation from the governor's wife to paint a mural in their dining room. If you want to drink yourself into a stupor, you may do so with my blessing. I'll celebrate with you—in spirit, of course."

Jas grimaced. Problem was, the thought of drinking herself into a stupor was actually appealing. She hadn't had herself a good drunk in nearly twenty years, an inhibitions-be-damned, bed-spinning drunk—not since her air force fighter pilot days, and that seemed like a hundred years ago. Even without imbibing a drop back then, she'd been drunk on innocent, youthful exuberance, the joy of believing the rest of her life stretched gloriously ahead of her.

I'd do anything to feel that way again.

She shoved aside the dangerous and unexpected yearning. She had a nice life: friends, a job she enjoyed. Two healthy children. She was happy—or at least she was supposed to be, she thought guiltily—and she refused to waste another minute longing after some elusive sense of completion that existed only in her imagination. Concrete goals, not wishes, were what kept her life nice and orderly.

And uninspired.

Jas groaned. "I think I need a vacation."

Her statement left Betty speechless. Heck, it left her speechless, too. She never took vacations. *You're indispensable; everyone needs you.* That mantra had echoed inside her since childhood. She'd practically raised her three sisters, while her parents had buried themselves in research at the university.

"You certainly deserve a vacation," Betty said carefully. "Take as long as you like."

Jas mulled over her half-finished canvases propped up at home in Scottsdale, the ones she hadn't had the heart lately to complete. The thought made her stomach burn. She had a responsibility to produce. "I'll let you know what I decide," she said quietly.

A trilling invaded the silence. "Darn phone again," Betty said, and hurried into her office, leaving Jas alone with four walls of her own paintings. The colorful canvases magnified and reflected back her most intimate passions, her fears, her pain and frustration, as if she were seeing herself turned inside out. The crash had done this to her, she thought. Turned her inside out, made her art, her dreams, more vivid than her life. She wasn't sure where or when she'd hit her head that day, but by the time she had come to in the chopper, everything had changed.

The brass wind chimes above the front entrance tinkled, drawing her out of her thoughts. "Hey, Mom!" Jas's son strode across the gallery. Grinning, his dark brown hair damp against his forehead, Ian swept her up into a high-spirited, one-armed hug.

She inhaled his warmth and life, and the smells of motor oil, dust, and leather, the result of his newly acquired and sporadically running 1984 Harley. "I didn't expect you, sweetie."

"I snagged an earlier flight, dropped my bags at home. Sorry I missed the opening," he added with genuine regret.

She ruffled his hair. "You'll catch it next time." She feigned nonchalance, for Ian's sake, but it hurt that Jock had scheduled his wedding on the weekend of the opening of the most important show of her career, forcing Ian and Ilana to be with him, not her. "So did you have a good time?"

"You mean in Vegas?" His hazel eyes clouded over. "Dad's wedding?" He looked as if he'd rather talk about something else, anything else. "It was okay. For a Las Vegas quickie."

"Jas!" Betty hung up the telephone and hurried toward them. "That was Dan."

Jas smiled with a mental image of Dan Brady's easy grin. The man was good-hearted, nice-looking, and Ian's former economics professor. He'd also been the one who'd gotten Ian avidly interested in finance after a failed air force prescreening medical exam ended her son's dream of becoming a pilot. Grateful, she had cautiously let Dan into her life—on a wholly platonic level. He patiently assumed that her reluctance to date him stemmed from the recent breakup of her marriage, and she didn't correct him. It was as close to the truth as she dared get. "I thought he drove home last night," she said. "Since he's still here, let's invite him to lunch—"

"He called from Tempe, Jas. He wants us to turn on the radio."

Only then did Jas notice that Betty's skin looked unusually pale against her gray-threaded black hair. A quiver of worry tightened Jas's stomach. "Why? What's wrong?"

"Just turn it on." Clearly agitated, Betty gripped the edge of the table to steady herself. Mystified, Jas exchanged glances with Ian and flicked on the radio, wondering who had died, or what plane had crashed, or where a major earthquake had struck. Her heart sped up. Grace, her little sister, was visiting San Francisco—

"This is Kendall Smith, live at the White House with this breaking story. President Talley will now address our stunned nation."

"My fellow Americans," the president's voice cut in. "Today is a day we will remember for the rest of our lives, the day that changed the course of human history forever, the day we were given undeniable proof of our neighbors in the galaxy."

The president was briefly drowned out by a crackle of static, drawing Jas's gaze to the cloud-sprinkled sky outside. Her emotions swirled in a storm of skepticism and disbelief—and raw, primitive fear. On the heels of that eerie vulnerability, her long-ago, discarded dream of going into space flared to life in a burst of unadulterated, almost childlike excitement. Out of breath, she turned up the volume to hear the president over the hammering of her pulse, then joined Betty on a Navajo-print settee.

"This morning at three-fourteen A.M. Eastern Standard Time, as most of you slept, the United Nations received a transmission from an individual stating, in English, that he was the commander of a fleet of spacecraft. Extraterrestrial spacecraft. Every listening post around the globe, both civilian and military, has confirmed that the transmission originated from a craft in orbit around the planet Jupiter. I repeat, the transmission has been confirmed."

Outside, a car roared out of the parking lot; another slammed on its brakes. There was muffled shouting, a woman and a baby crying, dogs barking.

Ian wore a look of intense concentration, but the usually unflappable Betty appeared stricken. Jas took her friend's icy hand in her own and squeezed it.

"As a result of the commander's conversation with me, my military advisers, and the other world leaders, I have approved his request to pursue a formal diplomatic and, I emphasize, a nonadversarial relationship with Earth. Negotiations will commence with utmost vigilance. I have placed our military forces on the highest state of alert. In light of this, I ask you, as your president, to remain calm, to set the example for the rest of world. Let us see this as a glorious new beginning." Obviously moved, the president cleared his throat. "The beginning of an era of promise and prosperity beyond our greatest hopes, for all the people of Earth . . . and the generations yet to come."

Jas shot to her feet. How her fellow human beings might react to this news troubled her far more than the headline itself. "Betty, where's your gun?"

"Locked in the office."

"Give me the key."

Jas ensured that the handgun and bullets were in the drawer Betty indicated, then carefully, methodically locked each window and the rear door. As she flew past Betty's telephone, she snatched it off its base and punched in her daughter's number in Los Angeles, praying the call would go through. Endless ringing. Her sense of helplessness skyrocketed.

"Mom, Ilana's still with Dad in Las Vegas."

Jas shot her son a grateful glance and returned the telephone to its cradle. *Stay with your father,* she willed her daughter. *Stay safe.*

"I think it's best we go to your place," Jas told Betty. She herded the woman and Ian into her Range Rover, then drove to the ranch in the forests above Sedona, while she rather guiltily wrestled with her exhilaration over what clearly alarmed the rest of the world.

That night, they watched the news: scenes of fear-fed hysteria and jubilant celebration, a pair of mass suicides, evangelists proclaiming the end of the world was upon them, and those who preached acceptance and love, even of the aliens—or *Vash*, as the extraterrestrials referred to themselves.

By morning, President Talley had declared martial law, which included a dusk-to-dawn curfew. The ensuing footage of National Guard tanks rumbling down Fifth Avenue in Manhattan and along the Highway 1 in Santa Monica was almost surreal. And the images were daunting enough to keep her independent and headstrong daughter Ilana in Las Vegas, rather than risking a return to her UCLA dorm.

At the end of the second day, when it appeared that

the roads were safe for travel, Jas made sure Betty was secured in her home and left with Ian for Scottsdale. Traffic was horrendous, with fender-benders, stalled National Guard Humvees, and roadblocks slowing progress every few miles. Once home they immediately headed for the couch and CNN.

"In a stunning announcement this afternoon," an exhausted correspondent rasped, "the ten astronauts stationed aboard the international space station offered to meet with the *Vash*. The lone woman on board, Japanese scientist Keiko Takano, delivered the following statement: 'Because Earth must be protected from unknown diseases and unintentional contamination, we humbly ask to act as Earth's emissaries by meeting with our visitors face-to-face.' "

Intense debate and speculation ensued. "A noble and visionary sacrifice," some called it. "Suicide," others said. In the end, the request for the gathering was approved, and the astronauts were picked up by one of the *Vash* ships and whisked farther into space than any human had ever been.

"Approximately ten hours ago," the reporter announced, "the astronauts boarded the *Vash* command vessel for a historic summit. The transmission sent back to Earth was viewed by world leaders, military and intelligence experts, and selected members of the United Nations before being released." A checkerboard of NASA publicity photos popped into view—nine men and one woman of various nationalities. On the screen, the reporter held his hand to his ear and nodded. Then journalistic poise fled as his eyes lit up. "The pictures are coming through now."

Jas stared, unblinking, at a video, both ordinary and

43

extraordinary, of a group of people smiling and shaking hands. *Shaking hands!* "My God," she murmured. Tears of disbelief and joy blurred her vision as she struggled to distinguish between the astronauts and the *Vash*. When the differences sank in, they weren't in any way like those she had anticipated. In fact, she was a bit embarrassed. Dressed in ill-fitting, standard NASA-issue jumpsuits, Earth's astronauts looked like their hosts' poor country cousins. The *Vash* wore sumptuous, silver-trimmed indigo uniforms, and their bronzed amber skin and fair hair imparted an air of prosperity and robust health.

"Mom, they look human," Ian said, his voice full of wonder.

Jas squinted past the congenial group in the foreground to a tall figure in the back, a *Vash* man dressed in casual clothing. He wore a loose shirt tucked in form-fitting pants, and knee-high boots that appeared broken-in, as if he actually worked in them, unlike the shiny boots of the others. His arms crossed over his chest, he was viewing the proceedings with a look of vague disdain and aristocratic boredom, as if he knew he could run the show better but chose not to interfere. He came across as arrogant as hell. Or maybe he was just confident—or possessed of some kind of inner strength.

She had to laugh at herself, at what she was thinking, but he was so damned good-looking that she couldn't pull her gaze away. He had great cheekbones, and a long, straight nose. His hair color was strange, though—nutmeg, yet not quite, and several shades darker than that of the blond Scandinavian types surrounding him. Amusement softened his countenance as one of the indigo-clad diplomats veered in his direction. Remarkable, but the closer the approaching *Vash* officer came to the tall man the less godlike he appeared, turning shorter, stockier, and coarser-featured in comparison. Judging by the uniformed man's ill-disguised intimidation, he too, sensed the other man's superiority. The *Vash* officer's spine was stiff when he spoke.

The space rebel cocked his head to listen. At the same time, he glanced directly into the camera with eyes as pale and brilliant as gold. Jas froze. The air whooshed out of her lungs. Her skin tingled and her pulse kicked into overdrive. She knew that man, those eyes. He was the man from her dream.

Impossible. She'd never been able to see his face.

She leaned forward and took a closer look. At the very edges of her mind, memories teased her—memories that felt as if they belonged to someone else. She heard whispers, *his* whispers, his breath hot against her ear: *I want to make love with you.* Her entire body screamed, *Yes, yes, yes,* though she knew he hadn't actually spoken, and that she had never known his touch.

A fact with which her heart vehemently disagreed.

The group on-screen now resembled players in a game of musical chairs as the uniform-clad *Vash* and the astronauts took seats, leaving her spaceman with none. His warm gaze turned to ice. Shoulders squared, dignity intact, he turned on his heel and left. Gasping, she battled the ludicrous urge to find a way to follow.

"Mom? Yo, Mom!" Ian's voice came to her, as if from the other side of the ocean.

Inhale . . . exhale . . . inhale. She frantically massaged her temples.

"Did you zone out, or what? Are you okay?"

She dropped her hands. "Frankly, Ian, I'm not sure."

Clinging to wisps of magic, savoring the last shreds of desire, she tried in vain to recall the last time she'd felt this alive without a paintbrush in her hand.

"No! I will not allow it, B'kah!" Commander Lahdo slammed his sizable fist onto his desk, tipping an empty vase onto the environmental control console. The lights dimmed and hot air began blowing down from the vents. "Hell and back!"

Still in dress uniform from the meeting with the Earth delegation, Lahdo unbuttoned his collar with one hand, while his other danced with remarkable dexterity over the blinking lights on the panel, returning his quarters aboard the merchant ship *Lucre* to normal. "I repeat, you have broken our most holy covenant. You are in violation of the Treatise of Trade, article four—"

"Paragraph nine, third line down, I believe." Rom B'kah settled against the wall opposite the commander. Propping one booted foot behind him, he folded his arms over his chest and recited: " 'No organization other than the *Vash Nadah* or its duly appointed representatives may conduct transactions for profit or other such gain.' "

Lahdo's expression said, *Need I say more?*

"Commander, if I may clarify—it so states in the appendix that if no formal agreement is in place, the Articles of Frontier Trade apply, meaning independent merchants such as myself cannot be excluded." Rom peered out the viewport at the rainbow-hued gaseous giant with its odd red eye. *Jupiter,* the locals called it. "And I do believe this remote little system qualifies as the frontier."

Lahdo exploded. He punched the comm button, shouting, "Dram, call up the Articles of Frontier Trade—"

"Page twelve, subparagraph four," Rom offered blandly. He'd been reciting the like since he was a child. "My ancestors wrote the damned thing, Lahdo. But have your man look it up, if it makes you feel better."

The commander closed his eyes, his lips fluttering as if he were counting silently to calm himself. "Disregard, Dram." He pushed himself to his feet. Gripping his hands behind his back, he paced the length of the room. "You have the audacity to maneuver your vessel into my fleet. Uninvited. Then you announce your intent to follow us to the new planet. *Now* you barge into my quarters spouting some obscure regulation that says you can trade with them."

Rom lifted his palms. "I didn't barge. I knocked."

"This is your most brazen ruse to date, B'kah!"

"Another gem in a long string, eh?"

"What brings you here? And why now? No one's heard from you in over a standard decade."

"I'm looking for a little adventure," Rom replied candidly. "This is the first new territory discovered in years. The frontier is shrinking. And what used to be the frontier is now entirely *Vash Nadah* controlled. As it should be. But that does make earning a living a challenge, if not outright impossible for independent entrepreneurs."

"Entrepreneurs? Bah! Profiteers, the lot of you."

"I have a ship to maintain, Lahdo, a crew to feed."

The commander rolled his eyes, and Rom bit back his urge to bait the older man. The man was intimidated, understandably, for few men of his station ever had the chance to cross paths with a B'kah, let alone speak with one. But Rom was no longer heir to the most powerful family in the *Vash Nadah*—he was no longer capable of being anyone's heir, for that matter. But the prestige still followed him. Romlijhian B'kah—the unrepentant pariah, the legendary war hero, depending on whom you asked. By his father's decree, he was forbidden from involving himself in *Vash* affairs. For that alone, his presence here made Lahdo and the others uneasy.

They'd get over it.

"All I am stating, out of sheer courtesy, Commander, is that my ship will trail the fleet when you are invited to land."

"But Earth will not let us land! They are suspicious. They fret over disease, or that we will attack. I have never seen such a backward, dark-minded, pessimistic little ball of dirt."

"Give them a ship."

"A ship?" Lahdo repeated blankly.

Rom offered a gentle reminder. "The inhabitants of Kaaren Prime were suspicious, too. We gave them a class-four merchant ship, a vessel far beyond the technology they'd had in place. It whetted their appetite for more. They all but begged us to land."

Lahdo returned to his desk. He called up something on his viewscreen studying the text thoughtfully. "A ship . . ." He was now oblivious to Rom's presence. "Class twos and threes, only. No fours. Perhaps the cruiser? No, that won't do. Too old, needs repair . . ."

Rom fought to keep his temper in check. Was this officer the best the *Vash Nadah* could find for this delicate mission? He found it easier to believe the rumor that the discovery of Earth had been made by accident. It would explain how this narrow-minded bureaucrat had been thrust into a once-in-a-lifetime opportunity. Unless Lahdo made an unholy mess of the initial proceedings with Earth, he'd be promoted, ensuring status and a life of ease for his family. No wonder he wanted to shoo Rom away.

Crossing his arms over his chest and drumming his fingers, Rom gave a sidelong glance past the partition separating Lahdo's quarters from the bridge. The *Lucre's* engineer was in the midst of explaining the ship's propulsion control panel to the group from Earth. The one woman, Keiko Takano, was animatedly asking the translator one question after another, her black chin-length hair swinging with each movement.

Something long dead inside him stirred.

Rom cleared his throat and averted his eyes. He had been stunned when he'd first seen that woman, finally realizing through a haze of shock that she was not the angel from his long-ago vision on Balkanor. Three of the men in her party shared that hair color; it was common on Earth, if nowhere else, the shade he'd thought belonged solely to the ethereal being who had saved his life. *Only to lead to your complete ruin.*

But was that her fault or his? He'd chosen to remain under her spell when he should have sought refuge from the radiation—squandering precious minutes to bury his fingers, his lips in those strands of midnight, reveling in the tousled silk, inhaling the fragrance that was her. He'd been driven half-mad by her sheer responsiveness, the way she'd sighed when he kissed the tender place under her ear, moaned when he'd whispered his need for her, how he would bring her pleasure, all the ways he would love her.

She deserted you ... when you needed her most. Vanished without a trace.

"Great Mother!" He shook himself out of his trance He was exhausted, pushing himself and his men too hard. Only once had he allowed himself to succumb to his imagination, and look where it had gotten him. By all that was holy, if that woman from his vision ever dared take the form of living flesh, she'd better make damned sure she didn't find herself in his path.

He took his irritation out on Lahdo. "I cannot waste time lolling about while you catch up on your trade history lessons. I will take my ship to Earth when the fleet goes in. It is my right." Tempered by the man's expression of abject dismay, he assured him, "I do not seek to cause you trouble. While on Earth, I will conduct my business apart from yours. I will not interfere. And when my transactions are complete, my crew and I will leave."

The besieged commander sighed, then closed his viewscreen. "Very well, B'kah. I'll need your ship's name and registry number. Earth has requested the information. I must pass along yours, as well, since you will be accompanying us—*if* Earth allows us to land."

"Ah, of course, Commander. Name and registry number." Rom's mood ratcheted up a few notches. He was going in with the fleet.

Chapter Three

Aboard the *Quillie*, his muscles tense, his combat instincts pulsing in readiness, Rom turned in a full circle, slowly, holding a sens-sword in front of him in a sure, two-handed grip. "It's over for you, Gann." His voice echoed dully in the cavernous room. "Give up now and I might show you a bit of mercy—you sniveling whatever-the-Earth-dwellers-call-those-subservient-furry-creatures. Ah, yes, you sniveling little *dog*."

Rom froze. He was certain he'd heard a muffled laugh. Quelling his own, he stared wide-eyed into a wall of complete blackness. "It's over. I see you."

Though not with his eyes.

The neurons in his body hummed, pointing to his prey. Honed to a nearly infallible sensitivity from years of training in Bajha, the age-old game of warriors, Rom's senses guided him. Following their ancient, mysterious direction, he trusted his body in the way warriors must, inching closer. Listening.

Though not with his ears.

He relied on the blood coursing through his veins, his tingling pores, and the tiniest hairs on his body, while he clutched the blunt sens-sword in his fists. Ah, he loved this aspect of the sport: the thoroughly arousing anticipation of a victory not yet realized. *Show yourself, Gann.*

His opponent attacked, the rounded blade of his sens-sword passing so close that the wind sang over the tops of Rom's bare hands. Rom arched his back, ducked. Whooping in joy, he whirled, swinging his own weapon in a brutal arc from above his head and sharply to the right. He heard a grunt of surprise as the sens-sword vibrated in his hands, signaling a hit.

"Ah, hell and back," he heard Gann mutter.

"Lights," Rom said. The illumination came up, revealing his second-in-command on one knee. He pointed his weapon at him. "Give?" he inquired, breathless.

"Give."

Rom offered Gann his hand—a show of respect for the man he trusted as much as he had his brother, and the only member of the *Vash Nadah* willing to follow him into exile. Gripping each other at the wrist, they inclined their heads, formally ending the match.

Fealty, fidelity, family. Like him, Gann was devoted to the ancient code of the warrior, one that stressed control and self-discipline. It was an honorable way of life, one that set the example for the lower classes—unlike the habits of most current rulers.

Fools, Rom thought, wrenching open the fastenings on his collar. Certainly eleven thousand years of peace was an accomplishment worthy of awe, but many of the *Vash Nadah* were using pacifism as an excuse for apathy, caring more for personal power, pleasure, and riches than the foundation of their civilization. If that foundation were allowed to crumble, the chaos and death of long ago would return. The Dark Years. Already there were signs of deterioration—terrorism, the destruction of supply lines and ships, previously unheard-of riots on essential planets across the realm. Had Rom not killed Sharron with his own hands on Balkanor almost twenty years before, he would have sworn the acts bore the mark of the monster and his cult following.

Rom's stomach muscles knotted up. The politics and future of the *Vash Nadah* were no longer his concern. He was estranged from his family, banished in disgrace. If the *Vash* wanted to wallow in ignorance and inaction in the name of peace, so be it. He was quite content to live out his life on the fringe, meandering along the ancient routes in the stars with his loyal crew, trading for baubles on backwater frontier planets.

Gann interrupted his decidedly dismal thoughts. "What was that you called me?" he asked, unfastening his white Bajha jumpsuit. "A *dog?*"

"Yes. A *dog.*"

"I can match you epithet for Earth epithet, B'Kah: *A-okay-have-a-nice-day.*"

Rom said dryly, "Not something I'd care repeat to my mother, I take it?"

"Wouldn't risk it."

Chuckling, Rom draped a towel over his shoulders and squeezed half the contents of a bag of drinking water into his mouth.

"Zarra's volunteered to serve as translator," Gann said. "The lad boasts he's fluent."

"I've no knack for languages," Rom admitted. The fact had never posed a problem before. *Vash* Basic was used galaxy-wide; it was the language of commerce. Nevertheless, during the two months he'd wasted waiting for Earth's governments to decide whether to welcome Lahdo's fleet, Rom had been memorizing what little English he could, a guttural and oddly familiar tongue. It lessened the chance of being cheated in trade—should there be those on Earth who'd dare try.

He packed away his sens-sword, stripped off his Bajha suit, then stretched and flexed his muscles. He felt sated, alive. The game had heightened all his senses. A fleeting image of a bath—a real bath, not a timed hygiene shower—flitted through his mind. Next appeared a woman, offering him the gift of herself for a long night of lovemaking, yet another one of life's sacred pleasures he'd had to go without on the long voyage.

"Bridge to Captain B'Kah." His engineer appeared on the viewscreen positioned near the soundproofed ceiling.

Rom rubbed his head with a towel, then draped it over his shoulders, combing his fingers through his damp, spiky hair. "Go, Terz."

"Fleet Commander Lahdo is on the line, sir."

Rom exchanged surprised glances with Gann. "Mr. Composure, himself," he said under his breath. "Put the commander through, Terz."

Lahdo appeared on-screen, looking harried but triumphant. "Earth has cleared us to land."

"Well done, Lahdo, on keeping the Earth astronauts happy and healthy. Am I correct in assuming the quarantine experts on their homeworld have concluded we won't infect the general population?"

Lahdo's face fell. "No. Until an establishment they call the Center for Disease Control completes its final study, we will be placed in quarantine. A restricted area designated"—Lahdo squinted at a viewscreen on his wristband—"Andrews Air Force Base."

"Andrews . . ." Rom committed the odd-sounding name to memory.

"I will forward the coordinates," Lahdo continued. "Earth's astronauts will pilot the lead vessel, the class-three ship I gave to them. I want you to move into position and follow the fleet." He thrust out his chin. "Now remember, B'Kah, I expect nothing short of full compliance from your ship and crew."

Rom lifted his palms and smiled reassuringly. "No worries, Commander. No worries. You can depend on us to do our part."

The viewscreen went blank, and Rom whooped heartily. "Frontier time!" Lighthearted for the first time in—by all the heavens, he'd lost count how long—he snapped his towel against his friend's solid back. "All right, Gann, let's find ourselves a nice bit of cargo while we're there. I'm in a profit-making mood."

Jas slid onto a bench seat next to Dan Brady, making sure she had a clear view of the big-screen television in his microbrewery, a side business he operated out of sheer entrepreneurial enjoyment. Fortifying herself with a swallow of beer, she watched a replay of the arrival of eleven huge but sleek delta-shaped spacecraft. Trailing whirling ribbons of condensation, they floated out of the sky like exotic petals, settling onto an unused runway of Andrews Air Force Base, the installation near Washington, D.C., that housed Air Force One. Even the smallest interstellar vessel was larger than a 747 airliner, but the command ship *Lucre* was said to be as big as five U.S. Navy aircraft carriers. It had stayed behind in an orbit around Earth because no one had been able to figure out where to put it. "This is incredible—*spectacular*," she said, vainly searching for words worthy of the event.

Abruptly the scene changed to an aerial view of the highways in and out of Maryland, backed up for miles in each direction. Tens of thousands of people were fleeing what they called an alien invasion, but an even greater number were flocking to get a glimpse of the spacecraft. "And *that's* chaos," she said to Dan out the corner of her mouth.

"I pictured worse, considering how fast this was approved."

Two months of worldwide protests, bureaucratic snarls, misunderstandings, and emergency orders had ended abruptly in a unanimous invitation extended to the *Vash*. The decision had rocked the planet. "Our backs were to the wall; only idiots would risk losing a light-speed starship and the cure for cancer."

Dan's eyes lit up. "The *Vash* knew that from the start. I doubt we're the first technologically inferior planet they've 'discovered.' They understand the power of gifts."

Thoughtful, Jas tucked her jean-clad legs beneath her. "A ship and some shared medical tech—small potatoes compared to the minerals they claim permeate the asteroids between Mars and Jupiter." The rights to which the *Vash* wanted badly. "But they'll have to give us more technology if they want us to run the mining operation ourselves."

"They will," Dan said with confidence. "We get free start-up equipment and a built-in clientele. They get cheaper minerals. It's a win-win situation for both parties. Their trading federation is immense, Jas. The potential for profit is staggering."

"Unless they offer to pay us in salt," she quipped— unbelievably, the stuff was a rare and costly luxury for much of the rest of the galaxy. "In which case you'd better up your shares in the Morton company."

He spread his hands on the table. "Done."

Laughing, she raised her glass of Red Rocket Ale. "Here's to the only other person I know who shares my obsession with our visitors from space."

"Not obsession, Jas." He clinked his glass against hers. "Demonstrative intellectual and entrepreneurial fascination."

Whatever Dan might label her absorption with the *Vash*, it had taken over her life. Although she hadn't again glimpsed the handsome spaceman who'd so unsettled her, she was channeling her preoccupation with him into a far more sensible pursuit: learning *Vash* Basic, the language of intergalactic trade. Night after night, she logged onto the U.N. Web site to practice Basic and study *Vash* history and culture.

"Now I wonder what *this* could be," Dan muttered.

A special report headline was scrolling across the TV. Jas lowered her beer glass, praying it wasn't a reinstatement of the curfew, a return to squeezing her life between dawn and dusk, battling it out every third day for gas, and having to put up with the crowds at the supermarket. But the footage showed a gathering of newspeople. Flashbulbs flickered as a distinguished-looking African-American man strode up to a podium, looking more like a young boy with his excited grin than a fifty-seven-year-old senior correspondent for CNN.

An odd mix of yearning and envy squeezed her chest. "So Kendall Smith's the lucky winner," she said. The competing networks had chosen Smith from an impressive pool of candidates after the *Vash* had offered to bring a correspondent into space to tour their main cargo depot. Afterward, if Smith wanted, he could continue on, traveling and reporting back indefinitely.

"A *Vash* public-relations stroke of genius," Dan remarked, "like the 'go west, young man' posters of the eighteen hundreds."

Unexpectedly, Dan's words painted an image of a new life, of starting over. What would it be like to do what Smith was doing, to set out into the unknown, to feel *alive* again?

The way she had before the crash.

Longing struck her with surprising force, and the ache in her chest tightened to where she could hardly breathe. She thought of all the adventures not yet taken, of all the dreams she hadn't envisioned since before obligations and heartache had stolen them away. Quietly, she said, "I'd give anything to be in his shoes."

Dan contemplated her with an understanding smile. "Within a couple of years I'm sure we'll all have the chance."

"Right." *A couple of years.* What should have been a deflating statement of fact unexpectedly became a challenge. Was there was a way to circumvent such a long wait? Nervously she twisted the silver bangles on her right wrist. Adrenaline made her hands tremble. At the age when most women were ensconced in their nests, she was suddenly buoyed by the overwhelming urge to spread her wings.

As the sun reached its zenith over Andrews Air Force Base, Rom, Gann, and young Zarra, their trusty but untried translator, climbed into the backseat of the automobile. It was an antiquated vehicle, one not capable of flight, Rom noted with some relief, for he didn't relish the prospect of traveling any great distance wedged in its cramped interior. Like Gann, he struggled to fold his long limbs into a comfortable position, pressing one knee into the seat in front of him while angling his other leg toward Zarra, who appeared quite content, nestled between his two larger companions.

Gann said under his breath, "Great Mother, this is worse than the cattle hold of a Tromjha freighter."

"The lower hold." Rom recalled in vivid olfactory detail—the two hellish days that he and Gann had spent trapped in one during the campaign against Sharron.

A cheerful female voice called out from the front passenger seat, "Buckle up, gentlemen." Rom winced as the last door slammed.

"She means the waist harnesses, I think," Zarra said, holding up one black strap in his hand as he fumbled rather intimately behind Rom's rear end for the other. "Sorry, sir."

Their escort, one Sergeant Mendoza, scooted around to watch their progress. She was dressed in a crisp, dark blue uniform, her black hair twisted and gathered at the nape of her neck in a clawlike contraption. Rom stared. Though he refused to dwell on what had happened that

59

long-ago day on Balkanor, Mendoza's tresses evoked an undeniably erotic yearning for the woman tied to his worst memories. He continued to study the sergeant, wondering idly what her hair would look like brushed loose, whether it was long enough to fall below her shoulders.

"Would you like some assistance, sir?" she asked, a flirting lilt to her accented Basic.

"Not at this time, no." He snatched the harness from Zarra.

Her gaze meandered from his face to his boots, and her brown eyes glittered with an invitation that was unmistakable on any planet, in any culture. "I'll keep the offer open, sir."

Rom masked his lack of interest with a polite dip of his head. To his relief, she turned her attention to a folder in her lap. Gann observed the exchange with a speculative gleam in his eye. "Shall I make alternate arrangements for your transportation back to the ship?" he inquired in Siennan, their native language, one few outside their class knew.

Rom frowned. "Don't be a fool. It's the hair color again. Damned distracting."

Ever tactful, Gann said no more. He knew more about Rom's battlefield vision than anyone else, recognized what its aftermath had done to his friend's life.

In a torrent of incomprehensible English, Sergeant Mendoza gave the driver instructions. The vehicle lurched forward. "What did she say, Zarra?" Rom asked.

"Out the north gate to the capitol, sir. For Commander Lahdo's address."

His thoughts tied up in the day ahead, Rom only half watched the landscape whir past. He anticipated success.

After all the time wasted waiting to arrive on Earth, and then two more months spent sitting on the Earth base Andrews while the planet's politicians fretted over disease, he deserved a round of satisfying negotiations, salt trade heading the list. This planet's seas were laden with the expensive, sought-after commodity. The inhabitants actually *swam* in the precious liquid and thought nothing of it! Ah, it was easy to envision the *Quillie*'s hold filled with blocks of salt. Perhaps, too, he could buy a stake in one of the mines opening on the asteroids. That would be a unique opportunity, for most mining was under strict *Vash Nadah* control, making it nearly impossible for unaligned traders to buy an interest. If he could purchase a claim while here, he'd make a handsome profit selling it once they reached the Depot—enough to buy that trading post he'd had his eye on. It was a tiny, remote moon, but it had a nice port. In no time, he'd have a small but efficient operation up and running. Not that he'd give up his nomadic life for good, but it wouldn't hurt to put down some roots.

Rom clenched his jaw. Dreams were one thing, but today had been a near disaster. If not for the quick-thinking officer monitoring the viewscreens of the cameras mounted on the exterior of the *Quillie,* Rom would have been excluded from the day's events. Vehicles had been picking up delegations from the other ships all morning, and would have skipped theirs had his bodyguard not blocked one of the automobiles with his sizable bulk. Oversight? Rom doubted it. It was subterfuge, and most certainly Lahdo's doing. Rom would waste no time locating the impertinent commander at the gathering, and looked forward to sharing a few choice words of wisdom on the subject of violating the Treatise of

Trade. By the time he was done with Lahdo, the buffoon
would never consider such traitorous behavior again.

Poised on the edge of her bed, Jas waited for the broadcast to begin. Applause signaled the *Vash* diplomats' arrival. The president, the members of both houses of
Congress, and heads of state from around the world
stood as the *Vash* delegation filed in. Dressed in their
beautiful indigo uniforms, they greeted their audience
with their distinctive handshake, gripping each Earth
diplomat's forearm and wrist. But they saved most of
their enthusiasm for the secretary of commerce, whom
they flocked around until she was lost behind them.

After a spirited introduction from President Talley,
Commander Lahdo stepped up to the podium. His res-
onant voice boomed, while a translator relayed his hopes
for partnership, understanding, and, to no one's surprise,
profit. To test her grasp of Basic, she concentrated on
Lahdo's voice. Here and there a phrase eluded her, a
few words that she didn't recognize, but she could understand him. A talent for learning languages was something she'd inherited from her linguist mother, but it had
never proven useful until now. Not that Basic was complicated. Throaty and to the point, it was designed to
facilitate dialogue between inhabitants of countless
worlds. Other languages existed, but they were evidently
never used in commerce.

To hearty applause, Lahdo relinquished the podium to
the secretary of commerce and rejoined his delegation,
basking in their adulation, their handshakes and smiles,
until a tall *Vash* stepped in front of him, blocking his
path.

A *Vash* dressed like a futuristic buccaneer.

Jas sucked in a breath. It was the devilishly charming space rebel. His lean body radiated strength, purpose, and a powerful, masculine self-confidence that made her head swim and her body respond with a deep, aching yearning.

Then he turned his back to the camera. His hands were fisted behind him and hidden from Lahdo, his fingers clasping and unclasping, betraying the intensity of his anger.

Lahdo's uneasy delegation began gathering around their leader, while dark-suited Secret Service men hovered closer, drawn by the *Vash* leader's discomposure. A microphone placed nearby was picking up the argument, barely. Jas grabbed the remote, punching up the volume. The tall *Vash*'s tone was low but intense. "The Articles of Frontier Trade state that I may trade with whom I please. You cannot exclude me, Lahdo, as you tried today. I will commence contact with the merchant leaders of my choice."

Lahdo fidgeted. "The agreement will be signed next week. Earth will no longer be a frontier planet then, and your articles will not apply."

The tall *Vash*'s hands closed into fists. "But until then, Commander, they do."

Lahdo's tawny skin gleamed with perspiration. He tugged at his collar, and his clipped Basic took on a pleading tone. "It would be best if you and your companions leave the planet. I trust that one Earth week will be enough time to prepare the *Quillie* for departure. Shall my crew assist you in gathering the supplies you need?" Applause exploded and in the foreground of the screen, the secretary of commerce relinquished the podium to the British prime minister. More heated words were exchanged between the Lahdo and the other *Vash*, but because of the noise, Jas missed them.

"One Earth week," Lahdo said, louder.

The tall rebel gestured to two similarly dressed men standing nearby. One was tall and muscular with hard and handsome features like him; the other was much younger and had hair of a lighter blond. With glowering faces, the rebel and his friends strode out of camera range, trailed by a battalion of Secret Service men.

Jas flopped backward onto the bed. Her *Vash* man had just been unceremoniously and undemocratically kicked out of a joint session of Congress. For Pete's sake, he'd been kicked off the planet, too, if she'd heard Lahdo correctly. Her thoughts plunged ahead. The trade commander wanted to exclude him. Why? He apparently was not part of the delegation. She'd assumed all the *Vash* were, but if he wasn't, it would explain why she hadn't seen him in any of the previously aired interviews. In fact, she'd begun to think she had imagined him.

Without warning, a memory of the rebel's golden eyes evoked a shivery, erotic echo of the way she'd felt when she woke from the dream of him. But she clenched her teeth against the unbidden image; she'd endured too many years of unbidden images, fantasies that were more vivid than life. Common sense told her that this flesh-and-blood man had nothing to do with her dreams. She couldn't fathom why he affected her so profoundly, but maybe somewhere in his world was her answer.

His world.

She sat up, her elbows on her knees, her chin in her hands. She wasn't wealthy, and she wasn't a dignitary. Average citizens like herself would have to wait many years for the chance to travel into space. And even that was only conjecture. She massaged her temples and concentrated. It looked as though her only way into space was though the back door. But short of thumbing a ride on one of the *Vash* ships, how would she do that?

Thumbing a ride . . .

Yes, she could hitchhike. Her heart sped up as she analyzed the plausibility and risk of such a scheme. It was a rash idea. Insane.

Electrifying.

She lurched off the bed and began to pace. All her life she'd been praised and rewarded for making sound, logical choices. Even her unconventional desire to become a fighter pilot had been driven by a sense of duty to her country. Dependable, do-right Jas. Well, except when it came to her love life, but she was smarter now. Her thoughts circled back to the *Vash* rebel. He was the key. If she could somehow make it worth his while, he might be willing to take her along. She'd even bet that he didn't play by the rules, as did Lahdo and the others. He was an outcast, or better yet, an outlaw—exactly the kind of individual she needed for her plan. Yep, he was her ticket out of here. And she had one short week to prove it.

Chapter Four

Jas lurched to a sitting position in bed. Her silk robe fell open in a sensual glide to her elbows, exposing her breasts and thighs to the cool, air-conditioned breeze. Still dazed from her dream, she reached for the bedside lamp and fumbled for the switch. Hugging a pillow to her chest, she stared unseeing at the TV she'd forgotten to shut off after watching Lahdo's address. She'd dreamed of the desert again. Only it hadn't been this intense, this real, since the days immediately after the crash. As always, she found herself wandering through the twilight in a barren but lavishly hued landscape. But this time the charismatic *Vash* rebel was waiting where only the blurred image of a man had been before. When she knelt at his side, he'd splayed one hand on the back of her head and pulled her down to his warm mouth. Every nerve ending in her body throbbed with the echo of their passion-filled embrace. If she hadn't woken, she might have made love with him. *A joining that would have meshed our hearts and souls forever.*

Jas flung one arm over her eyes as if she stood a chance of smothering the almost poignant yearning that flared inside her. In the weeks following the crash, these dreams had visited her nightly, leaving her with the same futile longing. Little wonder she had been overcome by a sense of destiny, of magic, falling in love at first sight when Capt. Jock Hamilton, armed with roses, wine, and apologetic eyes, came to visit on her first day home from the hospital. Convinced that their meeting was meant to be, certain that Jock *must* be the man from her dream, she'd thrown aside the reason that had guided her all her life and went to bed with him. Without protection. And after learning she was pregnant, a consequence of that one night, they'd done the right thing. Only it had turned out so wrong. Never in a million years would she regret having Ian and Ilana, but the marriage? She winced. What did she expect, playing dream interpreter, believing a man she'd never met was her one and only, her true love, who had transcended the dreamworld to be with her?

She'd learned her lesson. Never again would she mistake fantasy for reality. The *Vash* man was real, but the man from her dream wasn't. Any similarity between the two was coincidence and nothing more.

Jas extricated herself from her tangled sheets. It was nearly six-thirty A.M., later than she'd thought. As she finger-combed her hair into a ponytail, she stared bleary-eyed at a basket of clean laundry sitting by the bed. Her socks were wrapped one inside the other in matched pairs; her panties were tidily folded; her running shorts were stacked one atop the other. So neat and ordered.

So unlike her immediate future if she went ahead with her plan to hitchhike into space.

She dressed in a pair of jeans, an apricot silk blouse, and a pair of socks decorated with little Halloween pumpkins. Then she picked up the telephone and called Dan Brady. Of all the people close to her, no one was better equipped to help.

By nine A.M., the coffee shop near the Arizona State University campus was crowded. She told Dan about the tall, rebel *Vash,* the argument she'd overheard in Congress, and what she wanted to do. As she'd hoped, he listened with interest and respect. "In other words," she concluded, "I've found the vehicle and the driver. Now I need the incentive."

Dan cradled a cooling latte in his hands and regarded her soberly. "I'd be lying if I said I wouldn't rather keep you here."

You're indispensable; everyone needs you. Jas let out a breath. She was leaving her children behind; she was disappointing Betty, her family, and now Dan. Steeling herself against a resurgence of doubt, she replied more harshly than she intended. "The plan is only for six months, Dan. *Six months.* For God's sake, people take cruises for longer than that."

"Hey." His expression gentled. "That wasn't said to make you feel guilty. I'll miss you, that's all."

Her fists clenched convulsively. "Sorry," she whispered.

He relaxed in his seat and stretched out his legs. "Now explain how it is you think I can help."

"It sounds like he expected to make money while he was here, but the others won't let him. That's where we come in. You've served on or headed up every major business association in town. You have plenty of contacts."

"I know the governor," Dan conceded. "So do you."

"I know his wife. We need more than that. And we don't have much time. Lahdo gave him a week to pack his bags and get out. And we've already lost a day. That leaves us six more. And there's the weekend to consider."

"No problem. I do quick work. Everyone seems to have their eye on space these days. If it's resources our *Vash* friend wants, he won't be lacking in Arizona economic and leadership support by the time we're through." He picked up the pad and pencil she'd laid on the table and began writing out a list. Flooded with gratitude, Jas stilled his busy hand. Dan must have seen the question in her eyes. "Yes, I'm doing this for you," he replied frankly. "But naturally I'm very, very interested in the outcome."

She shared his slow grin. "I can tell. Your capitalist heart is beating hard."

"Oh, yes," he said. "No doubt about that."

Jas wrapped her son in a fierce hug. Ian's Harley-Davidson T-shirt blotted the tears she tried to hold back. "Call Ilana," she said huskily. "Once a week. Make sure she's not burning the candle at both ends."

"I won't forget to call her."

"Remember, the house payment and the other bills will be paid automatically—"

"I know, Mom."

"Betty will make sure there's always money in your account. Your father manages Ilana's finances, so there's no problem there. And of course Dan will be here to look in on you every once in a while—"

Ian grasped her shoulders and moved her back. "Mom, I'm going to be fine. You can't worry. Just go on your trip. Paint lots of pictures. And tell me all about it when you get back."

She smoothed her hand over his cheek. "I love you."

His lips compressed as his eyes reddened. "Love you, too."

"We have to leave in ten minutes," she said softly. There was no room for error. If she missed this flight to Washington, D.C., she'd miss her chance to leave earth. The reporter who'd won the flight into space had departed days ago. According to CNN, two more ships were lifting off at midnight. She was betting one of those was the *Quillie,* the rebel's ship. "Help me check my gear one more time."

Ian read from the checklist she handed him, and she inventoried the contents of her waterproof cylindrical travel bag. In addition to the floral skirt and lavender twinset she was wearing on the plane, she'd packed three black microfiber jumpsuits and a jacket that a seamstress had created from her sketches—clothing suitable for both a spaceship journey and sightseeing. Next to the jumpsuits was her old air force flight suit that she'd use as a disguise at Andrews Air Force Base. There were the barest of toiletries, her watercolors, a pouch containing every piece of real jewelry she owned, and all the boxes of Morton's table salt she'd been able to cram into the remaining space. If the rebel captain required a down payment for her trip, she was prepared. On top of it all she laid the slim leather folder that Dan had given her. Inside were promises and statements from a dozen of the most powerful CEOs in Arizona, from aerospace firms to mining operations to banks, and, of course, beer, where Dan had typed the name of his microbrewery at the bottom of the list. "It's all here," she said, opening her wallet to check her cash and credit cards.

Her cell phone rang, and her heart sank. She'd already endured all the bittersweet farewells her emotions could handle. Everyone but Betty, her children, and Dan was under the impression that she was taking a long vacation, but if she successfully boarded the spaceship, Betty would call the rest of her family and pass on the news.

Ian hoisted her travel bag onto his shoulder. "I'll put it in the trunk," he said and disappeared into the garage.

She snatched the telephone off the foyer table and sailed through the town house, checking one last time for any items left behind. "Hello?" she said breathlessly.

"You're acting like a dammed teenager, Jasmine—taking off on a joyride and leaving our kid alone in the middle of the school year. What the fuck's gotten into you?"

She squeezed her eyes shut. *Not Jock, not now.* "It's no longer your business where I go or what I do."

"Oh, yes, it is if it concerns my son."

"Who's grown, in case you hadn't noticed." Her stomach roiled. "Listen, I'm on my way to the airport. If you feel like fighting, go find your wife."

"Oh, I'll find her in a minute, Jasmine," he shot back, "but I guarantee it won't be to fight."

Inhale . . . exhale . . . inhale.

"Self-absorbed as always, Jas," he went on. "Vain and irresponsible. When we had infants at home all you wanted to do was hop back into the cockpit. Fortunate for all of us the docs said no. But you won in the end,

71

didn't you? Made those kids go through a divorce because you were too self-centered to put out any effort in bed."

An invisible fist squeezed her, and shame heated her cheeks. The man had the knack of knowing where she was most vulnerable. And somehow he'd figured out a way to make her feel responsible for his failures, using her built-in sense of obligation to justify his behavior.

But if you leave, he won't be able to punish you for his sins, and that scares him.

The realization slammed into her with the force of an explosion, and she grabbed the edge of the nearest table to steady herself. So much was becoming clear about her life. "This isn't about Ian at all, is it?" she said. "You're desperate. You can't let me go. If you do, you'll have no one to blame for your mistakes." Why hadn't she seen it before? Why had it taken so long? "*You* shot me down, Jock, and that got you booted out of the air force. *Remember?* But you hated the fact that I was still in, so you told me I'd do a lousy job of raising our kids if I returned to flying. I stood by you through everything—the Saudi incident, the court-martial. Even when Glen accused you of sleeping with his wife." Her voice shook. "I must have been blind! Every time you failed— as a soldier, as a husband—*I* paid the price." There was silence on the other end. Her voice gained strength and purpose. "Guilt was your weapon of choice. Used quite effectively, I might add, when I found out you'd been fooling around on me for years. That's my fault, too? Go to hell, Jock. The reason I was lousy in bed was because *you never could find the target.*"

Jas jammed the off button with her finger as Ian

popped his head through the garage door. "Ready, Mom?"

Her heart thundered and her hands shook. "Yeah, sweetie."

She climbed into the Range Rover's passenger seat. Clutching her hands, she stared straight ahead as he backed out of the driveway. "I don't care how you do it. Just get me there in time for the eight-ten flight to D.C."

"You got it." Tires squealing, they were off.

Ian gave her a sidelong glance. As if sensing her disquiet, he joked. "So, madame. Is this trip for business or pleasure?"

With that, a surge of pure excitement swept through her, along with the calming sense that what she was about to do was right. With a sigh, she relaxed against the leather seat. "Well, now. I suppose I'd call it a little bit of both."

Andrews Air Force Base Flight Operations sat next to the flight line—an asphalt field of taxiways, hangars, and runways. Jas ignored the FLIGHT CREW ONLY signs on the building's automatic doors and found the women's rest room. Hurriedly, she changed into her flight suit, combat boots, and standard air force–issue brown leather jacket. Facing the mirror, she donned a flight cap; it was a dark blue hat worn many times, with her former officer's rank pinned to the right side. After positioning the cap two fingers' width above her eyebrows, she headed out into the cold, damp night, hoping no one noticed that she was a bit mature-looking to be wearing the silver bar of a first lieutenant. But everything else so far had gone smoothly—including the lift she'd gotten from a former colleague of Dan's, a Pentagon employee happy to do a favor for his friend. Their admission onto the base proceeded with little more than a cursory wave, and the man was unaware of the crucial role he'd played in dropping her off. Without the coveted sticker he had on his windshield, she would have needed a visitor's pass, which meant forms to fill out, delays, questions—attention she did not want.

Jas strode along a well-lit road paralleling the flight line. To her left was a barbed wire–topped chain-link fence separating her from the runways. Jet engines thundered in the distance. Her muscles tensed as she watched green and red winking lights soar skyward. It was a cargo plane, not a spaceship. So far, so good—all air traffic would be stopped long before a spaceship was allowed to depart. Yet she couldn't keep from checking her watch.

Ninety minutes until launch.

Quickening her pace, she ignored the pounding of her travel bag against her thigh, and the way her lungs tightened in the jet fuel–scented autumn air. The moon floated behind a tattered curtain of clouds, painting the shadows of two hulking vessels ahead in a hazy, fog-touched glow. They loomed, foreboding and ominous, and she wondered fleetingly whether she was out of her mind.

One block to go.

From behind, Jas heard a car approach. Then came the unmistakable sound of a police radio. Gravel popped and headlights hit her in the back. She fought an irrational urge to run toward the ships, to freedom. *You have no ID,* her conscience screamed. *You're impersonating an officer.* But fleeing would be an admission of guilt, so she lowered her bag. Perspiration prickled her forehead despite the chilly air. Then slowly, reluctantly, she turned around.

Rom's boot heels clicked over the *Quillie*'s alloy flooring. "Begin the prelaunch sequence," he ordered his bridge crew. But he did not settle into his command chair to watch the proceedings, as was his habit. Instead he paced, as if the mindless exercise would burn off his anger, his frustration—and the deeply personal sense of shame. He'd been forced to leave Earth without completing a single act of commerce. It was his own fault, too, for thinking he could best the *Vash Nadah*. And now the men who trusted him would suffer for it.

At the far end of the bridge, Rom turned on his heel and tramped back. *Months!* He'd wasted months on this jaunt to Earth, only to be sent away with no more regard than was used to flick away a Centaurian morning-fly. The barest of supplies graced the larders; a pitifully small cargo of salt lay in the hold—and *that* was booty left over from the system visited before this one. *Hell and back!* Shoving the fingers of both hands through his hair, Rom sat heavily in his command chair, his forearms balanced on his knees. From his position behind the six men preparing the ship for launch, he observed the proceedings in sullen silence. Nothing less than a million standard miles between the *Quillie* and this miserable backwater planet would improve his mood.

Zarra called to him from his station in front of the sweeping navigation console. "Sir. The prelaunch checklist is complete."

"Call the tower," Rom said wearily. "Tell them we

75

want an early launch approved. I see no reason to pro-
long our stay, do you?"

"No, sir!" cried Zarra. The bridge crew chorused in
hearty agreement.

A young security police officer rolled down his window.
"Evening, Lieutenant," he said to Jas.

She forced her mouth into a casual grin. "How's your
night going so far?"

"Quiet. Just how I like 'em. Where you headed?"

She gestured with her chin. "The *Vash* ships."

He chuckled and lowered the volume on his radio.
"You and every other pilot on the base. Can't get enough
of them babies, huh?"

"What I wouldn't give to fly one."

"I'll bet." He propped his arm on the door.

Jas relaxed a fraction. He sounded like a bored cop
looking to chat. But that could change in a heartbeat if
he asked her for ID. She'd better take control if she
wanted to win him over. She took a breath. "You know,
you're my one lucky break all night."

He grinned. "How's that?"

"I'm beat. Have time for a lift?" Criminals didn't ask
policemen for rides.

He unlocked the back door. "Hop in. I can drop you
off in front of the checkpoint."

"Perfect." She hopped into the backseat, clutching her
bag with shaking hands. "I need to run some paperwork
out there. Then I'm headed back to the VOQ," she explained, using the lingo for the building that housed visiting officers.

He stopped in full view of the checkpoint, establishing
her much-needed credibility with the two MPs sitting

inside. Weak-kneed with relief, she thanked the young cop profusely.

Inside the cramped trailer the odor of cigarettes and coffee hovered in an interior illuminated by overly bright fluorescent lights. Jas slipped the leather portfolio from her bag and set it on a dented metal desk next to the radio. "This is for the *Quillie*."

The stockier MP reached for it. She blocked his hand. "Actually, I'm supposed to deliver it in person. Governor's orders. The Arizona state governor," she emphasized. She opened the portfolio and smoothed her palm over the creamy white cover letter. "He promised the captain of the *Quillie* he'd have these here yesterday, but"—her voice hushed—"all I can say is that it's embarrassing that these are so late."

"I don't know, ma'am. . . ."

A sharp hiss echoed from the vicinity of the two *Vash* ships. Then a rumbling began, increasing in volume until the linoleum floor vibrated beneath her boots. Jas's heart slammed urgently in her chest. She jabbed her finger in the direction of the ships. "We're running out of time. Radio the *Quillie*. Tell them their papers arc here."

But the MP picked up the telephonc instead. "I've got to check with the duty officer first."

"No time for that!" Jas flipped over the cover letter, revealing the first page. "Look, it's a trade agreement. A legal contract. A lot of work went into this." She watched him read thc governor's message and then scan the signatures and statements from the CEOs. "Can you imagine the repercussions if this doesn't get on board? Civilians get nasty, especially when the military screws up. My butt's already on the line. I'm sure Governor Goldsmith would love to roast yours, too."

The thinner MP piped in. "Jesus, Russ. Don't get anal on me. We're running stuff like this out there all the time." Grabbing the radio transmitter, he lifted the mouthpiece to his lips. "*Quillie*, this is Alpha Five," he said in painfully mangled Basic. "Alpha Five to *Quillie*. Please respond."

There was static, then a curt, unintelligible reply.

The MP raised his brows. "Ma'am, what do I tell them?"

Jas grinned. "Special delivery."

Rom spread his hands in disbelief. "They want to *what?*"

"Trade," Gann replied, equally puzzled. "He—or she— claims to represent a consortium of powerful merchants. With supposed signed proof of their eagerness to trade."

Rom choked out a laugh. It was no doubt a bureaucratic blunder, a contract destined for one of the other ships. He raised his headrest and buckled his safety harness. "Send the Earth-dweller away. He can sort out the mess with Lahdo."

Gann returned to the bank of communications equipment that had received the Earth guard's call.

"Zarra," Rom demanded. "Where is my clearance?"

"Working on it, sir. The tower says the delay is with a higher aviation authority of some kind—Washington Center, I believe they called it. And they can't give me an estimated time of departure."

"Why doesn't that surprise me?" Rom frowned. More blasted minutes wasted sitting on this rock. In the lull that followed, he pondered the Earth-dweller's offer. Lahdo would be mortified when he found out that the *Quillie* had been contacted in error.

A grin slowly lifted one corner of Rom's mouth. The

launch was delayed, was it not? He might as well solicit a little entertainment to make the time pass faster.

He unfastened his harness. "Gann, disregard that order. What do you say we have ourselves a little sport?"

Gann laughed. "At Lahdo's expense?"

"Naturally. Summon the Earth-dweller. I ache to see his face when you tell him he's aboard the wrong ship." Rom walked to the railing that overlooked the cavernous bulkhead below. "I'll view the fun from here. Naturally I'll join you should the encounter prove amusing."

Jas's body hummed with awe and fear as she followed the MP to the rebel ship. The dark, smooth metal hull gleamed dully, punctuated by winking multicolored lights. Steam hissed from the craft's belly, adding to the chorus of whirring motors and intermittent mechanical clicking. Distinctly alien, it was at least as long as a Boeing 747, but much fatter, with stubby triangular wings close to the fuselage. A row of odd symbols decorated one side, resembling hieroglyphics—not the Basic she'd learned—likely the ship's name in an exotic, unknown language. A film of some kind coated the forward windows, preventing her from seeing inside. The hair prickled on the back of her neck. She had the feeling that she was being studied by those she could not see. Her suspicion was confirmed when a portal below the nose opened slowly, spilling warm, golden light onto the tarmac. Then the heavy ramp hit the pavement with a gravelly thud and there was silence, broken only by the sizzle of escaping steam.

"Go on in." The MP's throat bobbed, and he stepped backward. "I'll wait here."

Unable to see what lay beyond the steep ramp, Jas

inhaled and exhaled slowly, steadying herself mentally. Everything she'd accomplished in her life so far—the choices she'd made, the mistakes and the triumphs—were so that she could experience this one glorious moment. No matter what the outcome, tonight her life had reached a turning point. "Here goes," she said, and began the long climb.

Recessed green lights in the floor led her inside. Laden with the mysterious humidity of a cave, the air gradually warmed, and the lights began to alternate between gold and green. The tunnel was featureless. No graffiti, no trash cans, she thought in a frantic attempt at humor. No cigarette butts or Coke cans lay wedged, trampled and forgotten, in the space between the floor and the walls. There were no signs of life, though she could hear distant voices. And laughter. That unnervingly familiar sound coaxed her forward.

The ramp ended in a cavernous chamber, ringing with a metallic emptiness, reminding her of the interior of an aircraft hangar. A vibration rumbled beneath the floor, and she had to clench her teeth so they wouldn't chatter. The rattling ceased. She heard the muffled voices again, emanating from a room above, beyond a balcony with a double railing. She could see shadows moving, and lights of instruments and computers reflected in an enormous curving window at the front of the ship. Most likely the flight deck, or the bridge. Still, no one had shown up to escort her. Did they know she'd come aboard?

She was weighing the consequences of shouting "Anybody home?" when she spotted a *Vash* man waiting behind a low table that extended at a right angle from the wall. Good-looking and ruggedly built, the man was easily six-foot-three. Dim, bluish light illuminated the room, bleaching his tawny skin. If not for his startling golden eyes, he would have looked entirely human.

"You not the captain," she said in choppy Basic. Nerves were making it tough to speak the language she'd so recently learned.

He spread his hands, palms down on the table. "I'm Gann, the second-in-command. Show me the agreement."

She dropped her gear onto the table. Several lights blinked in protest. Quickly Gann flicked off a switch. His expression was downright forbidding, but his eyes glinted with laughter, pricking Jas's pride.

"My name is Jasmine Hamilton," she announced with cool professionalism, using words she had rehearsed a thousand times in the past few days. "I represent business leaders who want to trade with your ship." Opening the finely bound folder, she turned it so he could see. "This is everything the captain wants. Commander Lahdo said no to trade. But the state of Arizona says yes."

Gann examined the documents. "English," he said, pronouncing it "On-gleesh." With obvious dismay, he admitted, "I cannot read it."

Of course! Why hadn't she thought to make a copy in Basic? Sheepishly, resorting to unrehearsed Basic, she summarized what was on the papers, and who had signed them.

"This is the *Quillie*," he said. "No one is permitted to trade with us. Weren't you told this? Your agreement is meant for another ship."

"No. Yours."

He peered over her head and lifted his palms. She

glanced over her shoulder, following his gaze to the balcony, to where the shadowy form of a man stood. His face was hidden, but he was the rebel captain; she was sure of it.

She returned her attention to Gann. "I know he wants to see this. Exclusive deal. For very small price."

He appeared incredulous. "You want us to pay you?"

"Well, yes." She thought hard, struggling to remember the words she needed. "Small price, big reward. I give you this agreement. And you give me passage into space. That is all."

His nostrils flared. "We don't take passengers."

She rooted through her bag until she found her pouch of jewelry. She tugged open the silken cord and upended the bag, spilling out her beloved silver bangles and assorted gemstones. Her old wedding ring wandered in a wobbly circle before taking a suicide plunge off the edge.

The *Vash* caught it neatly in one big palm. Unimpressed, he smiled, as if charmed, which irked her some more. She'd bet that the South Pacific islanders of centuries ago felt the same when they climbed aboard Captain Cook's superior ship only to find that that their most valued offerings were considered trinkets. Again he glanced over her head. Her stomach squeezed tight. Any minute her apparent novelty would wear thin and they'd boot her off the ship. It was time to roll out the heavy ammunition. "Have salt," she said. "Many, many salts." She began plunking box after box of Morton table salt onto the gleaming table, making sure she left her personal supply hidden, what she'd estimated she'd need to purchase supplies and lodging.

This time when Gann turned his attention to his captain, his eyes widened slightly. Then his incredulous gaze lowered. "My captain says you may come."

Overcome by a torrent of conflicting emotions, Jas fought to keep them from appearing on her face.

"Quickly," he said. "We're ready to depart." He locked the salt and jewelry in a recessed cabinet. Then he lifted her bag onto one broad shoulder and gestured to a ladder that led up to a cutout in the ceiling. She was halfway up when more rumbling began, forcing her to tighten her sweaty grip on the ladder. On the bridge the crew stopped midtask to stare at her. Blond and healthy, they wore sensible, rugged work clothes. If not for their bronzed skin and odd-colored eyes, they could have passed for a group of Swedish sailors. "Greetings," she said, offering a half-smile.

"You. Earth-dweller."

Her insides quivered at the very timbre of that too-familiar voice. The rebel captain was glowering at her from the bridge. For countless heartbeats, they regarded each other in mute astonishment.

He spoke first. "It *is* you."

She braced herself. Now was the ideal time to kick her habit of transferring the expectancy of her dreams onto flesh-and-blood men. "I do not know you."

"I believe you do." His voice was low and deceptively calm, but his eyes were as hot as glowing embers. "I see it in your face."

The first tendrils of panic squeezed her chest. She wondered irrationally if she'd appeared in his dreams, too. "You are mistaken."

"Am I?" Clearly he was a strapping male in the prime of life, but in that moment, his eyes were those of an old man—a man who had lived long and lost much.

Inexplicably, her heart went out to him. He must have seen it in her expression, because his features hardened, and he strode past his crew and took her by the upper arm, steering her to a darkened corner. Her vivid physical awareness of every square inch of him rendered her speechless, while his gaze, reminiscent of a jungle cat's, meandered over her, from her boots to her face, pointedly lingering on her mouth. Her cheeks heated, and self-preservation kicked in. *The Vash religion is based on a feminine entity*, she desperately reminded herself. *In his culture, women are respected, motherhood is revered, fidelity and marriage are held in high regard.* He wouldn't hurt her—she gulped—unless, of course, he didn't care for those dictates any more than he had Lahdo's.

She inched backward, but the computer consoles behind her allowed no retreat.

"How did you find me?" he demanded under his breath.

"I watched Commander Lahdo's address. I heard name of your ship, so I know where to look."

"I see. Was that the technique you employed the first time?"

"The *first* time?"

"On Balkanor! Sharron's headquarters."

"Bal-kan-or. Sorry. New at Basic. Please repeat."

"Cease your games, woman! Why are you here? Is it because of my provocation of the *Vash Nadah?* Pointless it is, but satisfying as hell. Am I to retreat to the farthest reaches of the galaxy? Is that it? Is that what you want? So no one need be reminded of my existence?"

Rom gripped the comm console behind him with unsteady hands. The old fury boiled inside him, and he heard it in his voice. Little wonder she looked as if she wanted to bolt from the ship—or knee him in the groin. In either case, his prospects of learning anything from her were disappearing faster than salt in a sieve. "Well? What have you to say?"

She lifted her chin another defiant notch. "I have no idea what you talk about."

Rom scrutinized her. He considered himself a good judge of character; usually he could tell if a trader was lying to him, or holding something back. That was one reason he'd done so well on so little all these years. But he sensed absolutely no guile on her part. Either she was a master of deception, or she was ignorant of her fateful role in his life. But with the launch sequence well under way, there wasn't time to ascertain which one it was.

With an effort that cost him, he encased his turbulent response to her within an iron will. "So be it. We have many days of travel ahead—more than enough time to finish this conversation."

"Sir," Zarra called out before she could reply. "We have received the launch clearance."

"You may use my chair." Rom urged her across the bridge to his contoured command chair, from where he normally oversaw planetary departures. He drew two straps over her head and buckled them at her hips, then pulled two more belts from the sides of the chair and clicked the ends into the alloy receptacle between her knees.

"I have dreamed of this all my life," she whispered.

Startled by her candor, he met her gemlike gaze.

She spoke haltingly, as if searching for each word. "For you it is routine. But for me it is wonderful." Her eyes shimmered.

He clenched his jaw. He must not allow her suspiciously genuine emotion to touch him. He must not let his guard down. The last time he did, it had cost him everything. "When you see me get up that means it's safe to move around," he said briskly. She gripped the armrests and nodded. He strode to a seat close to Gann's and fastened his safety harnesses as the powerful plasma thrusters rumbled to life. But he could not pull his gaze from the expression of awe on her face, and tried to imagine what the launch must feel like to her. Wondrous, of course. One never forgot his first trip into space. He'd been little more than a toddler when he'd accompanied his parents on his first flight. It remained his earliest memory.

The vibration increased as the *Quillie* lifted off. He watched the woman clutch the armrests, the invisible force of gravity pressing her into the seat as the ship accelerated. Then the nose rose to a steeper angle. Her bright, keenly intelligent eyes sought the forward view window. The turbulence increased. Outside, clouds slapped wet fingers across the glass in a futile attempt to keep the great craft atmosphere-bound. Then the ship tore free and there were only stars, bright pinpricks against the vast backdrop of deep space. The exact color of her hair . . .

Rom swore under his breath.

"I see the woman has already captured your thoughts," Gann said in Siennan. "I envy you. Other men must hunt for their treasure, but not the B'kah." He chuckled. "To you the treasure comes willingly, a lovely, pale-skinned, black-haired Earth woman, who not only pleads to be taken as cargo—she pays you for the honor."

Rom scowled. "She paid for passage to the Depot."

"Ah, yes, jewels and salt. A simple act of trade."

"Jewels? Bah! Only a petty smuggler would take such cherished personal possessions. It's the salt I want."

"It does seem to be of excellent quality," Gann conceded.

"I'll allocate a quarter of it to the galley to pacify the crew. The rest we'll sell at the Depot, along with the documents—*if* they prove genuine, and *if* Zarra can translate them."

"And meanwhile, you'll enjoy her charms."

The ship continued to accelerate, pressing him into his seat. Rom raised his face toward the air rushing down from the ceiling vents, wishing he could cool his dangerous and foolhardy attraction to the woman as easily as he did the perspiration on his brow. "Our culture places much import on dreams, so perhaps I am predisposed in this regard, but I believe she is the incarnation of the Balkanor angel."

Gann gave a bark of laughter. "Ah, yes. Back for a visit after all these years, eager to toy with your destiny a second time? Armed with orders from the Great Mother to divert you from your chosen path?"

"I did not choose this path! *She* did!"

"By all the heavens, Rom, enchanting as she is, she is not your angel. You've stared at every black-haired woman we've met since coming to this system. And there are billions more you haven't seen. How can you say she's the one?"

"I swear to you, before the voyage is out, I will have my answer." Rom's attention shifted from Gann to the Earth woman. All at once he recalled his first years in exile, the loneliness, the guilt, how thoughts of the Balkanor angel had kept him from giving up entirely. "By the heavens!" he muttered, and averted his eyes. The woman whipped up painful memories like a sudden sandstorm dredged up grit. Their encounter on Balkanor had preceded the worst period of his life—and yet he was drawn to her. He had yet to understand why. If she had answers locked inside her, he wanted them. Only then might he resolve the loss of his family and his birthright.

Chapter Five

The clamor of conversation and laughter emanating from the crew dining area sounded more like a party than a morning meal, Jas thought, pausing in the corridor to work up the courage to join them. As in the other common-use areas she'd seen, the walls were adorned only with rivets and control panels. The crew sat on bench seats next to tables made for family-style dining. Brightly colored jars decorated the tables, and the men eagerly scooped out generous helpings of their contents, spilling it onto their food. Next to trays stacked with loaves of flat bread were steaming crocks of something that smelled wonderful.

Lured by the savory aromas, Jas walked inside. The hush in conversation was immediate. Then the sounds of chair legs scraping, boot heels scuffing, and spoons clattering ricocheted off the metal walls as the entire crew, thirty of them at least, stood. They inclined their heads in an obvious show of respect, then sat just as quickly and, with gusto, resumed eating and talking.

One man remained standing: the *Vash* captain. Her heart skipped a beat. The heat in his intense, searching gaze made her toes curl, but she held her head high and faced him. Okay, so he had incredible eyes. And he was handsome as sin. But she'd be damned if she'd reveal her attraction to him. She had hitched a ride on his ship for one purpose only: to get to the Depot, from where she intended to taste enough adventure to knock her life back on track before heading home to the people who needed her. Anything more would be a distraction. And a mistake.

Pasting what she hoped was an expression of cool objectivity on her face, she greeted him with the Basic equivalent of "good morning."

Equally stoic, he said, "The *Quillie* is a merchant cruiser, not a tourist vessel, but I trust your quarters are to your liking?"

"Yes." Well, except for the timed three-minute application of soapy spray that passed for a shower. But he probably didn't care that she'd had to choose between shaving her legs and shampooing her hair. "Again, I thank you for allowing me on board your ship."

He opened his mouth as if to speak. Then he shut it, scrutinizing her. Finally he said, "I never knew your name."

That implication again that they had met before. It unsettled her further. "Jasmine Hamilton. Jas, most call me."

"Romlijhian B'kah." The polite dip of his head contrasted with the wariness in his eyes. "I prefer Rom. It's less formal. And better suited to my current state of affairs, wouldn't you say?"

She was sure that any answer she gave him would be the wrong one. Fidgeting, she glanced past him, searching for an empty spot. "I must find a place to sit." Preferably somewhere on the opposite side of the dining hall.

"Join us." With a gracious sweep of his hand, he indicated an empty place opposite him and next to Gann, who was obviously entertained by their awkward exchange. Amusement crinkled the other *Vash*'s eyes, yet she got the feeling that he was assessing her at the same time. She'd bet that fierce loyalty was as much a part of his nature as humor.

Still in a mild state of shock from the crew's display of homage, she settled onto the bench seat. "Rom, Gann, you are very polite"—she used her hands to fill in the gaps of her halting speech—"but it is not necessary for all to stand for me."

Rom replied, "You are a woman, and thus deserving of such respect. Since I insist that my crew adhere to the warrior's code, no doubt you will grow accustomed to our traditions by the end of the voyage."

So the rebel trader valued etiquette. She hadn't expected that, and it intrigued her.

"*Lar*-bread?" He reached for a tray and held it in front of her until she chose a pita-thin slice; then he continued his deferential behavior by filling her empty bowl with hot stew. There was only one utensil—half spoon, half fork—and she dipped it in the bowl, stirring gingerly, releasing steam that smelled vaguely like a grilled ham-and-cheese sandwich, along with other scents that were unidentifiably exotic but not unpleasant. Rom and Gann used pieces of the flat bread rather than utensils to dig out clumps of stew. The spicy fare burned her tongue, but the only thing available to wash it down was the greenish hot beverage Rom had poured into her mug.

"*Tock*. It chases sleep away," Gann supplied when she lifted the steaming mug to her lips. She grimaced. It tasted like licorice. She missed coffee already. "I see that this is one more thing I must get accustomed to. But I am happy to do it."

Rom continued to watch her intently, as if evaluating her—or waiting for her to make a mistake. That was understandable. She was a stranger, a possible security risk. As the captain, he had a responsibility to protect his crew. "You speak Basic quite well for an Earth-dweller," he said.

"I am lucky. Languages come easily to me. But I have nowhere near the skill of my mother. She speaks fourteen."

Rom raised his brows and leaned forward. Lacing his fingers together, he murmured to her in a foreign tongue. The language was soft, lilting, and lyrical, the way Italian or French sounded when spoken in intimate tones. She cocked her head, concentrating. Something about the cadence sounded familiar, but she couldn't grasp a single word. "I do not understand." This time he spoke more slowly, but she spread her hands. "I do not know this language."

"No," he said quietly, "I see that you don't. It is Siennan," he explained. "The language of my birth. Few know it outside my homeworld. I apologize."

She'd swear he had just put her through a test. And she'd passed.

The table tipped, then righted itself, and a blond man of gigantic proportions took a seat next to her. He was the biggest man she had ever seen, three hundred pounds, at least—and not an ounce of it fat. But his smile was friendly as he extended a paw that could easily grip a basketball. "It's my honor to meet you, Earth-dweller."

"Jas Hamilton." She clasped his wrist in the *Vash* handshake as his powerful fingers closed around her own wrist gently, as if he thought she'd break as easily as an eggshell.

"I am the B'kah's bodyguard," he said.

Bodyguard? Her gaze swerved to Rom, who remained inscrutable. Why would he need protection?

"Muffin is my name," the big man went on, releasing her arm.

"*Muffin?*" Jas suppressed a smile. "Please. Basic is new to me. What is your name, once more?"

"Muffin."

She pressed her lips together. The man was at least six-foot-eight. His shoulders were as wide as a football player's with full padding. Anywhere else he'd be named Thor . . . or Conan. "Muffin—" Her eyes were tearing up.

"It's an old-fashioned name," he insisted somewhat defensively. "But still popular on my homeworld."

"In my language a muffin is . . . a little sweet cake."

Both Gann and Muffin roared in delight. Rom's eyes shone. Jas's heart gave a little twist. He looked like a different man when he was happy. Inexplicably, it brought out a playful urge in her to tease him, just to see him laugh.

Gann leaned forward, propping his elbows on the table. "What does my name mean?"

93

Jas tore her bread in half. "You are lucky. There is no word that is the same."

"And Rom's?" he asked.

"Ah, Rom." Their gazes met, held. "I am sorry to tell you that yours is not as interesting as Muffin's. Rom sounds like the Earth word *CD-ROM*." She mentally searched for the right translation. "A data storage disk. A receptacle for bits of information."

He almost smiled. "I have been called worse."

"Good morning!" The young man who had escorted her to her quarters the night before hopped into a seat vacated by another crew member. Zarra greeted her hurriedly before pouring stew into a clean bowl. Then he upended one of the brightly colored jars and shoveled several hefty spoonfuls in as well. Jas rose slightly to peek inside the jar. "Is it a seasoning?"

Gann looked appalled. "By all the heavens! Where are our manners? Jas hasn't partaken yet, Zarra. Salt her stew."

"No, thank you." Jas blocked Zarra's arm with hers, spilling half the contents onto the table. The men gasped. Within seconds, Muffin and Zarra were wiping their stew-soaked bread over the table, only to pop the revolting morsels into their mouths with relish.

Muffin patted his belly. "Haven't enjoyed salt of this grade since we raided the stores on Parish Three, eh?"

Gann mumbled in agreement, his mouth full. Zarra was too busy eating to add anything at all. Rom oversaw it all with resigned, paternal amusement.

Bemused by the crew's antics, Jas propped her chin on the heel of her palm and watched them eat. It appeared that her adventure had already started.

*   *   *

The corridors in the aft section of the ship were narrow and dark, and she wasn't sure if she was headed in the right direction. After leaving Terz, the engineer who had given her a tour of the gravity generators, she'd made two right turns, then a left. Now should she go left again ... or straight? The click of her boot heels hitting the floor echoed down the long passageway and joined the sound of other footfalls coming her way. She rounded the corner and collided with a warm and very solid body.

Rom grabbed her forearms to keep her from stumbling. His sensuous mouth spread into a lazy grin, and every pore, every nerve ending in her body flared to life. "Are you lost?" he inquired. "Or merely out for a stroll?"

"Lost," she said somewhat breathlessly, and clamped down on her reaction to him. "I am trying to find the bridge."

"I'll escort you. We'll be making the jump to light speed within the hour. You'll find the procedure interesting, I'm certain." He pointed the way and they walked side by side, boots clattering in unison, while he chatted in a comfortingly rational and professional way about what she would be observing on the bridge. Once there, he left her to confer with several crew members studying an array of monitors. Jas stepped around them, drawn to the enormous curving window at the bow of the ship. The air was cooler here, redolent with the faint tang of electricity. As a periodic clicking tapped against the soles of her boots, she stood in front of the thick glass, compelled to silence by sheer awe. Distant stars gleamed, icy and impossibly ancient. One, tinged faintly green, glowed brighter than the rest.

Rom joined her. Eyes narrowed, he folded his arms over his chest, his demeanor reminiscent of an experienced sea captain. *The places he must have seen,* she thought. *The adventures he must have had . . .*

He followed her gaze to the ocean-hued star. "It is the eighth planet from this sun, I believe."

"Neptune," she whispered. Gooseflesh pebbled her arms. Images of the people she'd left far behind squeezed her heart. *You're indispensable; everyone needs you.* She braced herself against the onslaught of guilt. Six months away from home wasn't forever.

Rom was regarding her strangely, as if he sensed her pensive mood. "Would you like to sit in the pilot's chair while we await the jump?"

"I would like that very much." The chair sat behind a bank of what she surmised were flight computers. In front of the glittering, alien equipment was a hearteningly familiar-looking control yoke. Yearning swept through her. "I used to be a pilot," she said wistfully. "Many years ago." She strapped in and rested her hands on the controls.

Rom climbed the six stairs to the engineer's console, where Gann was overseeing Terz as the engineer prepared for the transition to light speed. From there he took advantage of Jas's captivation with his ship to study the woman. Her hair tumbled over her shoulders in silken waves that reached to the small of her back. She had the curves of a mature woman, with limbs sleekly muscled from physical activity. But it was the vivid expectation in her eyes, as if she believed something wonderful was about to occur, that would have drawn him to her in any setting.

Hope.

Surprise sparked inside him. Yes, her luminous gaze

radiated hope. He had become so damned jaded that he'd forgotten what it looked like.

"You two are getting along better, I see," Gann said.

Rom thoughtfully stroked his chin. "She informed me that she was once a pilot."

"Hmm. A rather odd vocation for a heavenly being."

Rom ignored the amused lilt in his friend's voice. "Perhaps." Yet he couldn't resist the urge to catch Jas Hamilton in a lie, any lie. "I say we test your theory. Of course," he said glibly, "a more diplomatic man might warn her before handing over full manual control of the ship."

"B'kah—"

Rom ignored his friend's warning and switched off the automated flier. Jas yelped, then launched into a muttered stream of Earth epithets. Both men grabbed hold of whatever they could as the ship pitched. It was a stomach-wrenching ride for a moment or two, but Jas gained control and maintained a straight course for the *Quillie* with nary a ripple. Stunned by this newest unexpected dimension to the woman, Rom turned the automated flier back on.

Gann grinned smugly.

Rom set his jaw. "Point made; she told the truth— with regards to the flying, at any rate." Arms folded over his chest, he paced along his usual path in front of his command chair. Jas's obvious truthfulness may have cooled his anger, but not his determination to decipher her role in his long-ago vision—and in his life. "From this point forward, I will proceed assuming she's simply forgotten our meeting." Slowly he began to walk away, then turned and headed back. "The obvious course of action is to make her remember."

Gann appeared doubtful. "How?"

"I'll seduce her."

His friend slapped his hands on his thighs. "An ambitious and daring undertaking, B'kah. The sign of a true warrior."

Rom refused to allow Gann to bait him. "On Balkanor, she and I never finished what we started. This time we will." He climbed down the gangway to where Jas was unstrapping herself from the pilot's chair.

As Rom approached, Jas smiled. "I did not expect what you did. Thank you for the chance to pilot your ship."

"You fly like a seasoned space jockey."

His compliment brought her an unexpected jolt of pleasure. "Thank you."

"You continue to astound me," he said with candor. "I would like to learn more about you. Perhaps we can chat further over dinner this evening." His voice dropped to what seemed a meant-for-her-ears-only pitch. "A private meal. My quarters."

Awkward and out of practice in the spotlight of his flirtation, she twisted her bangles around her wrist, desperate to come up with a witty response before the silence became too awkward. She hadn't gone out on a single real "date" since being divorced. She hadn't wanted to—hadn't felt ready. Was she ready now? Dinner for two with the *Vash* hunk? "We can discuss the commerce agreement," she ventured lamely.

"Ah, yes, the list of merchants who wish to trade with us," he said as if it were the last thing on his mind.

Tell him. Warn him that you're not like other women, that he ought not to get his hopes up. She gave her head a quick shake. She'd come here seeking adventure, hadn't she? Besides, it wasn't like she was intending to jump into bed with him.

Flustered, she spoke quickly. "I do not know why I did not make the contract in Basic. But I translated it after the morning meal. It should be transparent now"— she tapped the heel of her palm against her forehead— "no, *clear*. The agreement will not expire—ever—if you have that concern. But everything we can review tonight."

The ends of his mouth lifted in the barest hint of a smile. His voice was low and earnest. "Yes, we have much business to discuss. Both finished and unfinished."

"Right." And then she'd be able to get him out of her system and finish this voyage without worrying that she'd do something she'd regret.

To her relief, she heard Gann call out, "Thrusters to max."

They were diving into hyperspace, a place beyond the relentless passage of time, achieved only by speed. The sheer physics of it baffled her, despite her technical inclinations.

"Thrusters to max," repeated Terz. "Three . . . two . . . one."

The ship shuddered, and distant metallic components moaned. A fleeting magenta-orange glow suffused the bow of the ship. "Light speed," Gann confirmed. Ordinary stars elongated into cometlike objects, trailing threads of light behind them. Excitement danced with her accelerating pulse. "Look at the stars," she said to Rom.

"A temporary distortion," he explained. "They'll appear this way until the end of the voyage. When we slow approaching the Depot, the stars will look just as you remembered."

Thoughtful, she gazed out the forward window as the *Quillie* streaked farther away from Earth and all she'd ever known. Rom said that the stars would be unchanged at the end of this journey. But she doubted she'd be able to say the same about herself.

Rom prepared his quarters for dinner with the same meticulous attention to detail he'd use readying a starfighter for battle. The laser-candles were lit, bathing the room in a warm, romantic glow. Incense gently sweetened the air. The ancient music of Sienna—cymbals and cascading bells—floated down from the sound vents. The table was set in the traditional *Vash Nadah* way. Bowls of every size held the few delicacies left on the ship. Some vessels were covered, with steam wafting from beneath the ornate lids; others contained morsels that were iced, salted and dried, or preserved with liqueurs gathered from around the galaxy—some acquired through legally recognized means, most not. It had been years since he'd enjoyed a meal presented entirely in the old way, and he found he was looking forward to the evening.

If only you weren't as apprehensive as a young man on the night of his marriage rites.

He cinched the tie on his robe and poured himself a tiny glass of rare and quite illegally obtained star-berry liqueur. Eyes closed, he let the sweetness glide over his tongue. Fleetingly, it numbed his throat before warming his belly, leaving behind the barest hint of its notorious intoxicating power. Tonight he would partake sparingly, so he could apply the time-tested erotic skills he'd been taught at the palace in his youth, along with the more subtle techniques he'd gleaned as a man, to give Jasmine the most exquisite pleasure imaginable—if she allowed him to make love to her. Heat pooled in his groin as he pictured ways to arouse her before bringing her to fulfillment, and he chose several that he was certain would inspire her to give up her secrets as easily as star-berry blossoms fell in the first snow.

"Open." The doors to his personal-items repository slid apart and he chose his attire prudently, skillfully, as a warrior might select his weapons. Lifting his best shirt from a protective wrapper, he fastened the coppery Nandan silk tunic from left to right across his chest, and then tugged his dress boots over a soft pair of Nandan trousers—procured years ago, and worn but once. In texture, and in feel against bare skin, the luxurious fabric had no equal. He poured a few drops from a golden flask into his hand, rubbed his palms together, and massaged the oil into his scalp. Peering into the mirror, he combed his freshly trimmed hair back from his face. This was not preening, he assured himself, but a hunter's meticulous attention to setting his snare.

His viewscreen chimed. He flicked it on. Jas was standing in the corridor outside his door, her arms wrapped around a packet that looked suspiciously full of paperwork. The soles of her shoes sported cylindrical protrusions that raised her heels off the ground. With surprised pleasure he noted that her skirt, decorated with blossoms of some sort, reached only to her knees. It was not the custom for women—other than the pleasure servants who advertised their wares in the sex markets—to wear short dresses, so Rom treated himself to a leisurely perusal of her bare calves. "One moment," he said into the comm. The doors swished open. She cast an admiring but nervous gaze around his quarters. Bowing, he beckoned her inside with a sweep of his hand. "I'm pleased that you came."

"I look forward to this. We have much to talk about." Her tone was purposeful but pleasant. "I can tell you more about the agreement now."

"Care for a drink?"

She tucked a strand of hair behind her ear. "Yes. Thank you."

He filled two thimble-sized glasses with star-berry liqueur and touched his glass to hers. "To adventures not yet taken."

Her mouth curved. "Perfect."

He waited until she'd almost lifted the glass to her mouth before he stopped her. "Wait. This is star-berry liqueur, a very special drink. It is to be shared in the traditional way." He dipped his finger into his glass and dragged his moistened fingertip along her warm, pliant lower lip.

She stiffened, her nostrils flaring. They maintained eye contact long enough for him to see her alarm. Then, glancing away, she said dryly, "That is some tradition."

"Thousands of years old. Now you anoint my lips with star-berry liqueur. Methods vary. Be as inventive as you please."

She gave him a long look, color rising in her cheeks.

"Perhaps another time," he said under his breath, relenting. He couldn't remember the last time his words alone had made a woman blush. Her unexpected innocence captivated him as much as her spirit and intelligence. "Go on. Sample the liqueur."

Self-consciously, she licked her bottom lip. "It is delicious"—her eyes narrowed—"and alcoholic."

"Very much so." Rom clinked his glass to hers. "Now we empty our cups." When she finished, he asked, "What do you say we have dinner? Perhaps we can get to know each other better over a good meal." He motioned for her to follow. They paused several times to peruse the artwork adorning the walls. After explaining the history behind the Centaurian weavings in his collection, he led her to a nest of pillows surrounding the dinner table.

"No salt?" she asked warily.

"I have some if you wish to add it to the food."

"No. Thank you." She grimaced. "The crew ate a year's worth at breakfast. Do you have a doctor on board? Has he checked your"—she searched for words in a way he found surprisingly endearing—"blood pressure lately?"

He laughed. "The salt is a rare treat. I thought the crew deserved it after the months wasted in your system. By tomorrow, what I gave them will be gone, and they'll be back to normal fare. In the absence of salt, we spice our food differently." He waved at the festively set table. Dropping gracefully to the floor, she slipped off her shoes. Above her left heel was a tiny, fresh cut. A similar wound marred her ankle.

"Have you encountered sharp edges in your quarters?" he asked. "I'll call Terz for repairs."

She dropped her face into her palms and groaned.

"What is it?" he asked worriedly.

She lowered her hands. "I showered too slowly this morning. Since you do not allow more than one shower per day, I had to shave my legs with lotion." Her cheeks colored further.

"You shave the hair from your legs? The way a man removes his beard?"

"Yes, I do."

His loins tightened. He had a dozen related questions he wanted to ask her but didn't know where to begin.

As if she sensed the direction of his thoughts, she said in accented, carefully worded Basic, "I hope you do not mind if we talk about something else. Surely there are more engaging topics than my poor leg-shaving technique." With a supple flex of the muscles in her calves, she pointed her toes, then curled her legs to one side, eliciting in him a sharp, erotic image of those strong, long legs wrapped over his hips, squeezing him as he made thorough and delicious love to her.

"For instance," she said, splintering his reverie. "I want to know about your clothing. The workmanship is lovely. All the clothes I have seen here are this way. Not manufactured, like on Earth. May I?" She reached for his shirtsleeve and rubbed the material between her fingers. "So soft . . . I am an artist—I paint. But I often wonder if it is not the wrong medium, because I have always loved fabrics."

"This is not a surprise. As an artist your senses are tuned to a higher level. Smell and touch, sight and sound, and, of course, taste." His gaze lingered on her throat, then her mouth. "They affect you more than other people."

Jas snapped her hand back into her lap. It was new to her, this kind of deep and meaningful eye contact. Flattered, self-conscious, and despising her lack of sophistication, she studied her clasped hands. "Are your pants of the same fabric as your shirt?"

"Yes. Nandan silk."

"Nandan silk." She savored the exotic name, pictured delicate, amber-skinned women using looms on a distant tropical planet. "From plant or animal?"

"Plant. The strands are made from the sap of a willow found on the planet Nanda. The trees aren't grown anywhere else. It's forbidden to take the seeds off-planet, making the cloth rare and beyond the reach of all but the very wealthy."

"Business must be good for you to be able to afford such luxuries."

He gave a soft laugh. "Not that good." Plucking at his trousers, he told her, "The clothes were a gift from a grateful seed-stealing smuggler sentenced to death by the Nandans. Since Drandon and I had a nice little business supplying non-*Vash* plantations in the frontier, I facilitated his escape from a rather dismal dungeon."

At the end of his explanation, Jas caught herself leaning forward, thoroughly fascinated. In those few moments, she had lived the adventure right along with him. "You have more stories," she prompted.

"A few."

"I want to hear them all."

He appeared pleased. "I'll bore you."

"No," she said with a sigh, "you won't."

"Very well. Then you will tell me your tales afterward."

She waved her hands rapidly. "Which will take all of five minutes."

"That I doubt," he said, a grin transforming his profile. His nose was too long to be perfect, but she loved the way it came that extra, sexy fraction of an inch closer to his mouth, giving him the look of an ancient Greek statue. His long, lean athlete's body was muscled just enough to keep him from being lanky. The candlelight warmed his hair to a honeyed cinnamon, a shade or two darker than his skin, and she wondered whether the strands were as soft as they looked.

If he was aware of her fascination with him, he didn't show it, and busied himself preparing the meal. Steaming savory aromas rose and mingled in the air as Rom uncovered various crocks, choosing from among the dishes to adorn a plate with a colorful array of food. Jas's stomach rumbled.

"Let us begin the meal." Rom settled onto the pillows. From across a corner of the triangular table separating him from her, he selected a morsel from his plate. Holding it carefully between his thumb and index finger, he offered it to her. "Tromjha beef," he explained. When she reached for it, he drew his hand back. "In my culture, on occasions such as these, we feed each other."

"Oh." The thought made her dizzy—and not only because of the liqueur's subtle effects on her brain. The act screamed of intimacy. *Oh, just do it.* It was one reason she took this trip, wasn't it? To embrace new experiences, to remember what was like to feel alive.

She parted her lips.

His three lower fingers, those not touching the meat, brushed against her jaw. Whether it was by accident or design, she couldn't tell, and didn't care, because the feel of his warm, dry fingertips was as delicious as the tender beef he fed her. Blotting his thumb and forefinger on a napkin, he watched her intently as she chewed, savoring the delicate citruslike flavoring. And then it was her turn.

Her heart slammed against her chest as she raised a piece of meat to his mouth, holding the food the way he had, between two fingers, leaving the others clean and free . . . to touch. His lips were warm and surprisingly soft.

When he had finished chewing, he murmured the name of the next delicacy, then fed it to her, his fingertips sliding along her jaw as he withdrew his hand. Goose bumps rose on her arms. As he watched her, she crushed the tart-sweet marinated fruit with her teeth, then selected one for him, lifting it to his parted lips. This time she dared to let the heel of her hand linger on his cheek, and his whiskers, too pale to be seen, pricked the tender inside of her palm. The temperature inside the room skyrocketed, but she suspected it wasn't due to a faulty environmental-control system.

"I could get used to this," she confessed.

His mouth curved as she paused to clean and dry her fingers. She glowed inside with his smile, and felt her belly contract when she entertained the insane thought of kissing him. Not that he would waste his time with a rookie like her. He was a man of galactic experience. If she were a male guest, he'd be regaling her with tales of conquests and sexual prowess. "I think you must have had adventures to fill ten lifetimes," she said.

"Twenty."

She laughed softly. "Tell me some." She lifted her glass of liqueur. "Like this. Why is it so special?"

He settled onto his side and balanced one arm across his upright knee, a move steeped in lazy, graceful sensuality. "Star-berries grow in only the most inhospitable locations. The berries in this bottle came from a planet that sits between two red-giant stars. It knows only eternal sunset and freezing temperatures, except for a very brief summer. When the snow melts, the star-berry

Susan Grant

bushes bloom. Magenta flowers stretch to the horizon. And the fragrance"—his pale eyes glazed over with the recollection—"some say it's as intoxicating as the liqueur itself."

Without a second thought, Jas dipped her fingertip into her glass of pink-tinged fluid and stroked the essence of that frigid, faraway land across his lips. His eyes darkened. Seeing his response elicited a shivery, long-forgotten yearning. A tiny alarm sounded inside her, a warning, but she chose to ignore it.

"The flowers are extremely fragile," he began again, watching her intently. "They fall with the first flurries. The ripe berries must be picked shortly thereafter, because within days they'll be buried under hundreds of feet of snow."

Basic feet measured longer than Earth feet, making it even harder to picture so much snow. "Does anyone live there?" Jas asked.

"Butterflies. And the harvesters who fly in for the summer. All vanish with the first snow. But it gets cold long before that." He glanced away. "You can't imagine how cold."

She thought she saw him shudder, but she couldn't be sure. Astonished, she spread her palms flat on the table, leaning forward to scrutinize him. "You were a harvester?"

"For a time." His eyes flashed with something she couldn't define. Secrets. She would bet he was full of them. And contrasts. His self-assured, aristocratic grace implied good breeding, yet he was a trader and part-time smuggler. His crew clearly worshiped him—his mere presence commanded a room—but his cocky attitude and disregard for *Vash* rules gave the impression that he

108

didn't give a damn what others thought. "You are not what you seem, Rom B'kah."

His voice was quiet, frank. "Nor are you."

They offered each other more food. Jas found that the ever-changing tastes, the nuance of textures, the heightening of the senses, made every touch and smell and murmured bit of conversation incredibly erotic. Warm fingertips lingered. Hands caressed. It seemed so natural when, at last, their lips came together. She didn't know who reached for whom first, but she was in his arms and he was kissing her, almost lovingly, and she couldn't catch her breath. Honeyed warmth spread through her. She wrapped her arms over his shoulders and angled her head, allowing him to deepen the kiss. His tongue was velvet, stroking hers in an endless caress. Desire coursed through her with an intensity she'd felt only in her dreams.

She never imagined that a kiss alone could be this blissful . . . this arousing. Fingers skimmed across her throat and collarbone, and she longed for them to reach lower.

He lifted his mouth from hers and kissed his way to the hollow under her earlobe, lingering there. She hunched her shoulders. No man had ever lavished such attention on that spot, one she never knew was so sensitive. Toes curling in delight, she arched her neck and bit back a sigh, twisting restless fingers into his thick, mink-soft hair.

Again his mouth found hers. This time his kiss was hotter, and hard with passion. Distantly she sensed that his ardor was intensifying. Unease flickered through her as he expertly maneuvered her onto her back, his lean, powerful body molding to hers, his muscular thighs holding her in place. Only now did he begin to explore below her neck and shoulders. His fingers glided up her thigh, slipping past the elastic band of her panties, kindling a breathless carnal urgency. Suddenly she understood that his technique of limiting his touches had been a cleverly erotic way of teasing, of intensifying her need for more intimate caresses. "Oh, Jas . . . my sweet angel," he whispered, his breath hot against her ear. "Now we will make love."

Chapter Six

For reasons Rom could not fathom, Jas stiffened. Instinctively he transferred more of his weight to his arms and nuzzled the side of her throat, murmuring her name and sweet, soothing endearments until she relaxed. Closing her eyes, she answered his whispers with breathy sighs, reacting to the simple caresses as if they were his most expert moves. Her unschooled response, her genuine appreciation of his every touch, aroused him beyond anything in his experience. She was no pleasure servant, of course, and was not raised as a *Vash Nadah,* so he hadn't expected her skills to be honed. But her apparent innocence in the ways of lovemaking unsettled him with a soul-shaking carnality.

Perhaps that is her intent, an inner voice warned him. *To drown your wits in pleasure before you gain the answers you seek.*

It was a risk he'd gladly take.

Rom molded her bottom to the curve of his palm, felt her warm, pliant flesh. Utter heaven lay between her thighs. Groaning softly, he raised her hips and eased her legs apart, fitting himself, swollen and aching, against the inconsequential wisp of her undergarment. Her moist heat embraced him, and somehow seared him through the fabric of his pants. Eager to remove any barrier between them, he tugged on the undergarment. Again she went rigid, grabbing his hand. "Don't."

An Earth word, but there was no mistaking its meaning. One thing a *Vash Nadah* man did not do was force himself on a woman. Though he had little to do with his old life, the teachings of his ancestors guided him to this day, and would remain with him until his last breath. Dazed, he sat up, untangling his limbs from hers.

She almost stumbled as she stood, studiously avoiding his gaze as she yanked on the hem of her wrinkled skirt. Bewilderment dampened his thrumming desire. Frantically he reviewed the past few moments in his mind. Had she found his embrace distasteful? Clumsy? Surely not. He prayed not. Most likely her uneven grasp of Basic had caused her some confusion. He patted the rumpled pillows next to him. "Sit. The evening is not over."

"Oh, I think it is," she said crisply.

"Ah, just as I suspected, a translation problem. Lovemaking is the traditional end to a fine meal."

Nodding, she clasped her hands primly in front of her. "Like dessert?"

He nodded. She rolled her eyes. "Rom, I came here to show you the benefits of the commerce agreement. I hoped you would find it useful, if not of great value. I thought that was what you wanted, too. Or did you invite me here only to . . . to—"

"To make love to you," he finished helpfully.

She fixed him with a narrow-eyed, contemplative gaze. "You are honest. That is a point in your favor. Good night, Captain B'kah," she said with sardonic formality. "I enjoyed your hospitality. And your food."

He opened his arms in invitation. "The most exquisite delicacies are yet to come."

She made a small squeak. "You are amazing."

"Some have said that, yes."

Her gray-green eyes flared with inner fire. For a moment she looked as if she were struggling for inspiration. She opened her mouth to speak, then closed it. Finally she threw up her hands in frustration. "Basic! Totally useless. A million words for an act of trade. And not one to put you in your place." Spinning on her heel, she marched past him.

He went after her. She stopped at the double doors, and he tipped his head to peer into her eyes. Ah, how her spirit and independence invigorated him. "You don't need words to 'put me in my place,' Jas. I'm already there." He lifted a tendril of her hair and tucked it behind her ear. "For tonight I am with you."

Almost imperceptibly, her pupils enlarged. An untrained observer would have missed the subtle signal. He did not. An odd sense of longing filtered through him— for her reaction to be one of attraction, not fear. He hadn't realized until that moment how much he wanted her to feel as he did. "Stay," he said quietly.

"I can't."

"Why not?"

"Many reasons." The fleeting anguish in her haunted

eyes pierced his soul. "None of which you would understand."

"How can you be so certain?"

She turned slightly, revealing the rapid pulse flicking
in her throat. "I have dreams . . . dreams that haunt me,
and leave me exhausted for days afterward. I am walking
in the desert, searching, never finding . . . and when I
wake, I feel empty, as if I left someone behind."

Great Mother, Rom thought. Could she be reliving
their encounter in her sleep?

"I have so much in my life," she said with feeling,
her accent even more pronounced. "Yet the emptiness
does not go away. I do not want to spend the rest of my
life feeling this way. So I came here, to space, to maybe
find what I am missing. I want to feel alive again. I want
adventures—like you've had."

"I suppose I've been around the galaxy a few times."

"I envy that." She studied him, her gaze contemplative. "I *want* that." Slowly, deliberately, she flattened
both hands on his chest. Her husky voice mellowed into
a somewhat uncertain but nonetheless seductive murmur
as she tilted her chin up. "Kiss me, Rom," she whispered. "Just kiss me."

His heart leaped at her blatant longing. Weaving his
fingers through her dark, silken mass of hair, he covered
her mouth with his. She made a muffled cry and locked
her hands behind his head, kissing him back with a soul-
searing sensuality. It was a fiery, desperate mating of
hot, hungry mouths and searching hands, and his senses
spun gloriously. *Precisely the kind of uncontrolled passion you were trained to rise above,* warned the com-
bined voices of his father and the generations of men
before him. *She's undisciplined. Dangerous.*

And all he'd ever wished for.

She pulled away before he could react to the explosive revelation. "I'm sorry. I'm not as adventurous as I thought." Tears in her eyes, she hit the entry control panel with one shaking hand. The double doors coasted open, revealing a darkened corridor. Then he watched her disappear into the shadows, her pale, bare feet a silent blur atop the alloy flooring.

Gann inquired the next morning, "Tell me, old friend, was your night with the Balkanor angel everything you hoped it'd be?"

Rom frowned at the bowl of breakfast stew in front of him.

Gann gave a quick, astonished laugh. "No! Tell me it isn't so."

Rom ground his teeth together. "Tell you what?"

"She exhausted you!"

"Control yourself," Rom implored under his breath. "These are private concerns, and not for the crew's ears."

"Or the woman's, I take it." Gann waved his arm at the emptying mess hall. "Don't worry. She's gone. I joined her for breakfast as she was finishing. But I couldn't wrest a scarran's seed of information from her about last night. She seemed to be in good spirits, though. Very talkative." He gestured to his cheeks. "Her color was high, too. The look of a well-satisfied woman. A *Vash Nadah*–satisfied woman." He peered at Rom speculatively.

Rom glared back.

Gann smacked his open hands onto the table. "Hell and back! She refused you. A first, eh, Rom?"

It was, but Rom would be damned before he'd admit

it. The men sitting nearby rose. With a clatter of utensils, they handed their dirty bowls to the day's assigned kitchen crew before leaving the room to attend to their duties. Mulling over last night's fiasco, Rom stirred a hefty spoonful of dried Mandarian pepper flakes into his stew. The evening had taken a toll on him emotionally and physically. Command of his body and emotions was bred into his very bones. But with Jas, he'd fought— and nearly lost—his ability to maintain it. Just as he had on Balkanor. The knowledge shamed him.

A warrior must never allow his desires to take precedence over those of a partner.

Gann broke into his sullen thoughts. "You have the look of a man obsessed."

"Finding out why that woman helped me live when I was better off dead is good enough reason for obsession," he snapped.

"Give it up, B'kah. She has nothing to tell you."

"I was beginning to feel the same. Until she mentioned having disturbing dreams. Within them, I think, lies my answer. I must switch tactics."

Cradling a cup of *tock* in his hands, Gann asked, "To what? Other than wrestling her out of her clothes."

"A game of Bajha."

Gann choked. "You're joking."

"No. In fact, I intend to hunt her down this very morning and invite her to the arena."

"This is one match I'll be content to watch."

For the first time that morning, Rom smiled. He looked forward to joining with Jas on a level far more intense than simply physical. "My regrets," he said, swallowing. "But for this I cannot allow spectators." After a purposely drawn-out pause, he folded his arms over his chest and leaned forward. "Some games, Gann, are best played in private."

After breakfast, the solitude of her quarters brought Jas no peace. She worked on her upcoming travel itinerary, adding to her list of questions to ask the men at the next meal. Many concerns were still unanswered: how to get transportation once at the Depot; what types of accommodations were available; how to exchange her salt for currency.

She threw down her pen. Most of the time making lists soothed her. But not today. Not after last night.

As was her habit at home, she sought electronic distraction. Using a keyboard that was a flat, touch-activated surface labeled with radiant Basic runes, she logged on to the ship's computer, just as Terz had taught her. A display of current mechanical anomalies sprang up. A balky gravity generator, a couple of seized air-circulating fans, a broken cargo panel—she skimmed the items and found nothing to interest her. Moving on, she navigated through a vast realm of knowledge, until she came to a file entitled *Trade History*. She read further. If she knew more about *Vash* history, then maybe she could better understand Rom and his effect on her.

The first passages described the galaxy eleven thousand years in the past, on the eve of a cataclysm known as the Great War.

Eventually technological evolution outpaced spiritual evolution. Societies that had existed for eons crumbled. Disease, endless famine, and fear caused by selfish warring kingdoms spurred a complete collapse of civilization. Warlords took control by renouncing spirituality and the Great Mother, and by condemning those who embraced sexuality for reasons other than procreation.

The account smacked of propaganda, but even pondering the events objectively, she knew that the distant past had been dark and dangerous.

Eight brave warriors banded together and vanquished the evil. Their vow to never again bring war to the galaxy formed the basis of the Vash Treatise of Trade.

" 'Motherhood is revered,' " she recited from the excerpt in a hushed voice. " 'The family is holy. Sexuality is to be celebrated, for sacred is the joy found in pleasing, consensual sexual relations between a man and a woman.' " Closing her eyes, she thought of the way Rom had touched her, held her. . . .

Shuddering, she pressed two fingers to her lips, recalling the kisses they'd shared, so enthrallingly tender and passionate that the mere memory made her long for the more intimate ways he could give her pleasure. Most shocking of all was that she'd responded to him with *instinctive* carnality, almost as if such passion had been inside her all along.

But she'd run away, frightened by that discovery and the feelings Rom evoked in her. Magical. Like her damned dreams.

And dangerous.

The one time she'd let magic cloud her reason, she'd acted rashly, and it had spelled disaster. Embracing logic was the only way to keep from getting hurt again.

She pushed away from the desk. By now most of the crew would be gathered on or near the bridge. She was in need of a little distraction, some company; she would even brave Rom's company—she swallowed—should he be there. She walked confidently through the darkened corridors and emerged into the brightly lit area alive with the sounds of conversation.

"Ah, Jasmine," Rom called to her. "I have something for you." Rising from his usual seat, he opened the bottom drawer of a console crammed full of computer hardware and produced two excruciatingly familiar, black suede high-heeled pumps. Holding them easily in one of his big hands, he announced, "You left these in my quarters last night."

Heat rushed to her face. Mortified, she glanced at Gann and the rest of the bridge crew, then expelled a hiss of breath. "I do not believe you."

Rom appeared genuinely taken aback. "It is the truth. Regretfully you left with everything else intact."

"*That* is not anyone's business."

"I most certainly agree." Spreading one broad palm on the center of his chest, over his heart, he said, "Commerce would pale in the blaze of your kisses."

Six pairs of light-colored eyes watched her expectantly, diluting the effect of Rom's compliment. Flashing a stiff smile at the men, she thrust out her hand. "Give me the shoes."

"You are not pleased. Tell me why. You are a woman. I am a man," he recited, as if quoting the teachings she'd read earlier. "And everyone knows that the traditional end to a fine meal is—"

Jas made a small choking noise.

"—making love. Sex in its myriad forms is yet another form of sustenance."

I was only snacking, doll. Look, I came home for the main course. Jas flinched as Rom's words brought back the bitter memory. As Jock's admission of that first affair echoed inside her, every fiber of her being wanted to flee the bridge. But she stayed, riveted in place, exposed, while that scene played out inside her: Jock's teasing attempt at making up; how she'd stubbornly dammed her tears to avoid upsetting two inquisitive five-year-olds in the middle of a fast-food restaurant. But Ian had known somehow, recognized the pain his father's dismissive words had brought her. She'd never forget how Ian looked, a little boy with a cardboard Burger King crown propped crookedly atop his head, a knight-in-shining-armor look on his face. He'd been her champion.

"Jas?"

Rom was wearing that same look. Her heart twisted, and longing blanketed her eternal loneliness. Oh, how she wanted to believe in magic—*his* magic.

No!

She lashed out in a harsh whisper. " 'Holy pleasure,' 'sacred sex.' Garbage! You are no different from my . . . my . . ." What she intended to say stuck in her throat. Nothing translated to *ex-husband,* so she blurted out the next best thing. "From my husband!"

"Your *husband?*" Rom exclaimed, equally shaken.

"Yes." Her voice throbbed with pain. "Intimacy meant nothing to him, either." She snatched her shoes out of his hand and stormed off.

"Children?" Gann inquired mildly as she passed by.

"Two." Head held high, Jas disappeared into the corridor.

"And so the story unfolds," Gann said cheerily. "Boys or girls, I wonder?"

Chapter Seven

Misery loves company, Jas told herself, seeking refuge that evening with the crew in the *Quillie*'s common room, where Kendall Smith, the reporter from Earth, dominated the oversize viewscreen. The image was clear and bright, as if the correspondent stood in Washington, D.C., and Jas were watching from her living room at home. Thanks to Terz, chief engineer and sought-after handyman, she'd now be able to see all of Smith's broadcasts.

The group of rowdy crewmen made for a perfect distraction. They found the idea of a "frontiersman," expounding on tourist attractions while being wined and dined by the *Vash Nadah*, entertaining. And that, in turn, gave her a humorous insight into their world. So far they'd told her how to book passage on tourist shuttles, the best vacation spots, and that the Romjha Hotel was *the* place to stay when she arrived at the Depot.

Setting aside the pen she was using to take notes, she reached across Muffin's lap to a hammered copperlike bowl, scooping up a handful of the crispy little question marks that passed for chips. They were spiced with something savory instead of salted . . . and she couldn't get enough of them. "My thighs hope that shimmer crackers don't taste better than these. I could *live* on these toppers—or rather, poppers." Jas dusted crumbs from her hands with a napkin. "That isn't it. What do you call them?"

"Positively addictive."

She stiffened at the sound of the familiar voice. Arms crossed over his chest, one shoulder propped against the door frame, Rom was watching her intently. She fought the urge to dive for cover, wishing she were anywhere else but beneath the stare of those unwavering, hauntingly familiar golden eyes.

"Croppers is the common name," he said pleasantly. His devil-may-care exterior didn't fool her. And that expression of practiced boredom was a mask. She'd bet her bottom dollar that the muscles tensing in his jaw indicated barely contained fury. "You'll see them again and again. They're a staple in drinking establishments from the galaxy's heart to the frontier." He looked her over with something akin to contempt. "Surely you're looking forward to socializing during your, ah, unfettered travels . . . *Mrs*. Hamilton."

Nodding, she choked down the suddenly dry wad of croppers that had stuck to her tongue.

"Ah, Rom, glad you could join us," Gann sang out as he returned, two large bowls brimming with peculiar glittering crackers in his arms. He set one bowl close to Jas. "Shimmer crackers. Freshly baked."

Rom followed him into the room. Hastily she camouflaged Gann's empty spot with pillows, but Rom stopped in front of the couch, towering over her. Everything about him looked bigger, stronger. Threatening. She could hear his slow, even breaths, could smell the broken-in leather of his work boots, the laundered fabric of his loose-fitting silvery shirt, and his skin—warmly scented with hygienic shower soap—mingled with something exotic, musky . . . and distinctly male.

The way he tasted.

She gulped. Rom gestured to the cushions stacked between her and Muffin. "Any claims on this spot?"

Jas beseeched Rom's tall friend with her eyes. "Gann, I saved your seat."

Gann waved demurely. "Sit, B'kah. Rank before beauty."

"That's *age* before beauty," Jas corrected sourly.

"Rom wins on both counts then." Gann tipped his head toward his captain, then settled onto a pile of pillows on the floor. Rom sat next to her. The viewscreen's muted, multicolored image behind him made his perfectly sculpted profile look as cool and impenetrable as marble.

He spoke in hushed tones. "I would have thought it impossible on such a small ship, but aside from glimpses here and there, I haven't seen you all day."

She could barely hear his voice above the background noise of chitchat and laughter. Leaning closer, she unintentionally brushed her arm against his. His biceps went taut with the contact. "I have been painting," she said uneasily. "And reading."

An emotionally charged silence pulsed between them.

"Tell me, Jasmine, do you intend to avoid me until the end of the voyage?"

"I did not have a plan one way or the other."

"I see. A vague reply to blunt your deceit."

She bristled, whispering harshly, "Explain what you mean."

The small creases etched on either side of his mouth deepened. Disturbingly calm, he pressed his fingertips together, flexing them. "I cannot stomach adultery."

"What?"

"I made a grave error in assuming you were free to make love with me. Because I was so sure that you were the incarnation of my vision, I did not consider that you might be a wife. Had I known this I would not have asked you to make love. Never would I take a woman who has spoken the sacred vows with another."

"Rom," she said softly. "I am not married."

There was no mistaking the relief in his eyes. "You are a widow, then."

"No. The marriage was"—she hunted for the best words—"legally severed."

"Why didn't you tell me on the bridge?"

"I tried. But there is no Basic that means 'broken marriage.' " He looked so bewildered that she rushed her explanation, stumbling over the simplest Basic words as she told him how her marriage had officially ended almost a year ago, and how they'd lived apart even longer. Still, she skirted any mention of how they'd ceased to have a real marriage long before that.

"Jock." A hint of a grimace curved Rom's lips, as if the name itself left a bitter taste. "He left you without a protector? When you had children?"

125

"They are grown. Nineteen in Earth years. Duplicates."

Rom raised one nutmeg-colored brow. She could tell from his expression that she'd chosen the wrong word. "Twins?" he supplied, almost smiling.

She nodded. "A boy and a girl." Her voice mellowed. "I miss them. . . ."

He gazed at her with open and respectful admiration. Then his expression darkened and he jammed his fingers through his hair. "You could have clarified this earlier."

"I was furious," she reminded him.

He jerked his palms in the air. "*This* I don't understand, either."

"You embarrassed me. You announced the private details of our dinner. It . . . it made what we shared trivial and cheap."

"You misunderstand!" Under the scrutiny of a dozen curious stares, he lowered his voice and took her hands in his, studying her fingers as they lay nestled in his wide palm. "There is much between us, Jas. None of it trivial or cheap."

Quietly, he added, "You may not accept this, but I do: we've met before, you and I. If not in the flesh, then in the realm of dreams. On a battlefield . . . on a planet called Balkanor. I was badly wounded, grieving for Lijhan, my brother, who was killed there. I didn't care if I lived or died. . . . But you did."

Her mouth tightened. "It wasn't real. It did not happen."

"Are you certain?"

Her doubt must have been obvious enough to give him his answer, for he gentled his tone. "My culture places great import on visions, on dreams. Hence, I'm less inclined to dismiss what happened to me on Balkanor as mere hallucination—or disregard your resemblance to the woman I saw there."

She stared her clenched hands. "In my dream there is a man with eyes like yours. But I always wake before I walk close enough to see his face."

"*My* face, Jas. You dream of the desert. Balkanor is a desert planet."

She lifted her eyes. "Coincidence."

"There are no coincidences, Jas. Nothing happens by accident, nothing. Including your appearance on my ship."

A sensible person, like herself, knew that what he suggested was impossible; but, good Lord, he made it sound so reasonable. In less than three days he'd intimidated her, awakened her desire, embarrassed her, and angered her. Now he claimed he could interpret her dreams. Yet instead of fleeing the insanity of it all, all she wanted to do was wrap her arms around him and kiss that sweetly sincere face of his. Never had her emotions been on such a roller-coaster ride. To gather her wits, she focused on Kendall Smith's broadcast, vaguely aware of having missed half the show.

". . . I'll spend two full days there," the reporter was saying. "After that I'll take you to a land of magical beauty."

An image of a glowing, picturesque, almost iridescent forest of tall, feathery conifers appeared behind him.

The crew grumbled appreciatively.

"Sureen," Rom murmured in her ear. His warm breath raised tingles along her neck.

"Sureen," the reporter's voice echoed distantly. "A popular tourist destination for thousands of years . . ."

127

Susan Grant

Rom's velvety lips brushed over Jas's ear, fanning her tingles into a bonfire. "Been there a dozen times," he whispered, his iron-hard thigh pressing against hers. "The trees there are phosphorescent, and at night they glow so brightly it never becomes dark."

"—producing a unique phenomenon I liken to stepping inside a rainbow," the reporter said in a narration nowhere near as fascinating as Rom's very personal one. "Heightening the effect, the inhabitants incorporate the substance responsible for the phosphorescence into their architecture and artwork."

Jas's fingers ached to grasp a brush soaked with the lush hues. She lifted her chin, nearly meeting Rom's lips. Only because of the decided lack of privacy did she inch away from the tempting possibility of a kiss. "They paint with the substance? What color is it?"

Everyone answered her at once.

"Turquoise and lavender," Zarra declared.

Muffin waved his big hand. "Not at all. It's as green as jampala jam."

"Don't buy any trinkets painted in the rainbow colors," Terz cautioned.

"Or the paintings," Rom added. "Beautiful as they might be."

Gann chimed in. "The merchants make a hefty profit selling them. But once you leave the planet, they all turn gray."

"Because the phosphorescent substance can exist only there," Jas said thoughtfully. Sureen would be one of the places she visited, if only to paint in the extravagant shades.

A loud, female-sounding, computer-generated voice

pierced her reverie. "ALERT, ALERT. SMOKE DE-TECTED IN SECTION SIX B."

Terz groaned. "Blasted gravity generator. It's over-heating again."

Jas's stomach flip-flopped, and she blinked away a vague dizziness. Then she floated off the couch. She laughed in shock and delight, levitating amid clouds of liberated croppers and shimmer crackers.

"To your stations," Rom commanded. The men re-acted calmly, as if they'd been through similar situations before. In a wildly incongruous picture, they streamed out the door, some headfirst. "Gann, stand by on the bridge to bring us out of light speed, should that become necessary."

Forgotten while Rom conversed with Gann and Terz, Jas pointed a shimmer cracker at a whirling empty *tock* cup and flicked it with her thumb and index finger. It missed the cup and spun into the other crackers, creating a ripple effect across the room. Chuckling, she snatched another cracker out of the air and took aim, but Rom grabbed her by the ankle and yanked her toward him.

"We've had trouble with the generator ever since we had it serviced by that no-account mechanic on Gamma Nine," he said. "I guarantee I'll be making a return visit."

"I recall seeing a reference to the gravity generators on the maintenance status page on the computer. But I never imagined it meant *this* could happen."

Rom appeared surprised and somewhat troubled. "You've accessed the computer?"

"Terz showed me how. So I could plan my travels," she added, in case Rom was worried that she was a se-curity risk.

"ALERT, ALERT. SMOKE DETECTED IN SECTION SIX B," the computer droned.

Rom laced his fingers with hers. Using the bolted-down furniture for leverage, he steered her into the corridor. "How long will we be weightless?" she asked.

"Varies. Hours, perhaps. I want you go to the bridge and wait it out. Find a chair and strap yourself in. Gravity might come back at any time. When it does, it'll—"

They plummeted to the floor. Rom twisted so she fell onto his body instead of the unforgiving metallic surface. Nonetheless, her left arm glanced off the wall. Gritting her teeth, she tucked her smarting elbow to her chest. Rom eased her to the floor, cushioning the back of her head with his hand. Concern shadowed his face when he noticed how she clutched her arm. "You're injured."

"Just bumped it." She gasped, sitting up, still startled by their sudden fall. He tugged her sleeve almost to her shoulder and examined her arm, gently probing the bruise.

"ALERT, ALERT. SMOKE DETECTED IN SECTION SIX B."

He brushed the back of his hand across her cheek. "There are cold packs stored in the medical kit on the bridge. Ask Gann. I have to go below, or I'd tend to you myself." They floated off the floor again. "Bucket of bolts," he muttered, and guided her to a row of metal rings on the wall. "Handgrips. Do you think you can pull yourself to the bridge?"

Jas flexed her arm. The twinge of pain faded as she flexed her elbow. "I think everything is in working order." To prove her point she grabbed two handgrips. The motion caused her lower body to arc upward. She gave quick, surprised laugh, stopping just short of a giggle. "Hey, this is fun."

Rom pointed toward the bridge. "Go. And no acrobatics along the way."

"Not even one . . . ?" She didn't know the word for *somersault* so she rolled her hands one over the other.

"Absolutely not." Planting his boot heels on the wall, Rom pushed away with the agility of an Olympic high diver. "You never know when the gravity will come—" He plunged to the floor and landed with a resounding thump.

"Back?" she supplied.

Rom propped himself on his arms. "Precisely." Even sprawled on the floor, he managed to maintain his noble demeanor, as if it were bred into his bones.

"ALERT, ALERT. SMOKE DETECTED IN SECTIONS SIX A AND SIX B."

"Two sections now." A trickle of unease ran down her spine. "It's spreading."

Rom's tone turned serious. "Go to the bridge." The change in his mood told her all she needed to know. She nodded, her heartbeat accelerating. Rom climbed to his feet and limped into a jog. Gravity fled and he'd lifted off the floor even before rounding the corner.

Favoring her sore elbow, Jas drifted one-handed, peering down the darkened corridor. It was a long way to the bridge, particularly if she had to use the handgrips. The generator room was closer. She'd lived through more than her share of aviation mishaps. Surely she'd be able to offer some help to Rom and the others down below.

"WARNING, WARNING. FIRE DETECTED IN SECTIONS SIX A AND SIX B." This time an earsplitting klaxon followed the honeyed computer-generated voice. Curiosity paled with the thought that the men were in danger. And Rom . . .

Adrenaline surged through her, accompanied by the need to protect him, a force as elemental and instinctive as ensuring her children's safety. She decided not to analyze it, but to act. Hand over hand she made her way to a ladder that descended into the cold, echoing bowels of the ship. Though the air recyclers hummed loudly, an acrid stench of burning wires stung her nose and throat, and a white haze billowed near the ceiling. Gravity returned. She dropped to the floor, landing on the thick soles of her boots, and sprinted toward the bright lights at end of the corridor. The dancing reflection of flames and what she figured was an extinguishing agent flickered over the metallic flooring. The ship gave a long, controlled shudder. She stumbled. Righting herself, she kept going. Rom must have given the order to come out of light speed. Not a good sign. Finishing the voyage in zero-g was one thing, but what if the fire damaged the ship? Would they limp along until supplies ran out? Or worse, be marooned in space?

Whatever experience Rom had at squeezing out of tight situations, she hoped he would use it to get them out of this one.

To her right were two widely spaced doorways leading into the smoky generator room. Shielding her nose and mouth with her sleeve, she glimpsed Rom, Muffin, and Terz about thirty feet farther down the hall, across from the first hatchway. Animatedly engaged in a discussion, they were gathered around a panel with blinking green and red lights mounted on the wall, a larger version of the door control panel in her room. Relief washed through her at the sight of Rom's muscled, athletic frame and confident stance; yet her nauseating dread lingered. She'd best distract herself, or risk going crazy.

"PURGE SEQUENCE ACTIVATED. TWO MINUTES UNTIL DEPRESSURIZATION," the computer intoned.

It sounded as though Rom was going to open the outer hatch doors to space. The resulting vacuum would suffocate the fire in an instant. But wouldn't he have to close the inner corridor hatches first? If not, everyone and everything not bolted down would be ejected into space. The handgrips looked more enticing than ever. But as she opened and closed her hands, fighting the impulse to grab on for all she was worth, the urge to reach Rom was stronger. Awash with an unsettling vulnerability, she scrutinized the two closest doors, praying they'd hold tight during the imminent depressurization.

Zarra skipped backward out of the hatchway closest to her, blocking her path. His exposed skin gleamed with perspiration despite the chilly temperature, but his hands were steady as he gripped a bulky fire extinguisher. Squinting, he aimed it into the generator room, shooting a powerful stream at a tall metal cabinet. Smoke poured out of the charred housing, hissing as it made contact with the spray. Though the enormous overhead vents quickly sucked it away, the residual odor reminded her of burning plastic.

"Zarra, how can I help?" She shouted to be heard above the intermittent fire alarm and the sound of men's voices boomeranging off the metal walls. He looked startled to see her. His face was flushed, his pale, whiskey-colored eyes bright. It hit her then how young he was, and what a grown-up situation he'd been placed in. The spray dissipated and he lowered the extinguisher.

"Empty. Here, hold this." He handed her the dripping hose and heavy tank. "There's one more inside, I think."

"PURGE SEQUENCE ACTIVATED. ONE MINUTE, THIRTY SECONDS UNTIL DEPRESSURIZATION," Jas heard the computer warn.

"In *there?*" Jas shot a wild glance into the room. An antifire mist rained onto glowing flames and coated the floor. On the far side, half-hidden by smoke, loomed a pair of outer doors ready to open to endless, deadly space. "They're going to seal the room," she warned him.

"Some of the most expensive equipment we have is in that housing."

"Zarra, in less than two minutes they will depressurize."

"A lot of damage can happen between now and then."

Jas resisted the motherly urge to snag him by the collar. Masking his face with his sleeve, Zarra assured her, "Two seconds, that's all I'll be," and darted inside.

A commotion dragged her attention down the hall. Muffin was waving at her, while Rom cupped his hands around his mouth and bellowed, "Jasmine, back away! We're sealing off the room!"

Her anxiety skyrocketed. "Zarra is inside!"

Rom looked stricken. "Terz," he said brusquely. "Cancel the sequence."

"Sir, it'll take time—"

"I *know*. Do it anyway or we'll lose him." Rom sprinted her way. "Stay where you are, Jas! Do *not* go in after him!"

"PURGE SEQUENCE ACTIVATED. ONE MINUTE UNTIL DEPRESSURIZATION. CLOSING INNER HATCHES."

Terz wheeled around and ran to the control panel, his hands a blur as they moved over the touch screen. Extinguisher in hand, Zarra reappeared as a vague outline in the mist on the far side of the room. Jas cried out in relief. "Hurry!" His eyes widened at her urgency, and he tried to comply, but his feet flew out from under him. Spinning over the slippery floor, he slammed hard into a post and collapsed onto his side.

There was a deafening boom and a prolonged hiss as the inner hatchway farther down the corridor slammed shut. Then the thick double doors in front of Jas vibrated and began to glide closed.

She rammed the empty fire extinguisher lengthwise into their path, keeping them apart. Muffin wedged his enormous bulk between them, and Rom drove through the narrow opening, after Zarra.

"DEPRESSURIZATION INITIATED. SECURE HATCHES. SECURE HATCHES."

Jas had never felt such terror and emotional agony in all her life—because she could do nothing to help. "Rom!" She crushed her hands into fists and pressed them to her mouth. Her stomach muscles cramped in a painful spasm. *She was going to lose him.* Seconds extended into eternity. Then she saw Rom again, and her knees almost buckled.

Skidding over the wet floor, struggling to keep upright, Rom had one arm wrapped around an unconscious Zarra. Muffin seized Rom's shirt, yanking him into the corridor so violently that Rom lost his grip on Zarra. Tumbling, Rom managed to recapture Zarra's hand. Then all hell broke loose.

An explosive roar obliterated all other sounds. Fog formed. Jas's eardrums wrenched painfully. The outer doors had opened, and with the inside hatch still partially open, it had created a ravenous, tornadolike vacuum. Jas dove for a handgrip as Rom, on his stomach, his fingers wrapped around the boy's hand, hurtled headfirst toward oblivion. A scream of horror lodged in her throat.

From her spot, all Jas could do was watch as, flailing one-handed for a grip on the smooth surfaces of the wall and floor, Rom tried in vain to stop his slide.

Nearby, Muffin braced his muscular legs against the wall, grabbing on to his captain's shirt. It tore. He clawed for Rom's arms and missed, hampered by the frigid white mist Jas knew from her old training accompanied all rapid depressurizations. Battered by the loose tools and bits of paper that sailed past, Rom blindly reached for Muffin, still maintaining his hold on Zarra, but at last the strain proved too much. Zarra's fingers slipped from Rom's hand.

The boy disappeared behind the closing doors, and Rom gave a cry of anguish that Jas felt resound through her heart.

Chapter Eight

"Rom . . ." He heard his name being called as if from a long distance away. "Can you hear me? Wiggle a finger, blink your eyes, something. Anything.

"Please."

This time the plaintive voice fully penetrated the blackness. A woman's voice. Husky, familiar. Accented. He fathomed that she'd been talking to him for some time, but only now could he focus on the words. Warm hands smoothed his hair off his forehead over and over, tender yet insistent stroking.

"Heads don't do well against doors, you know," the voice continued. "You are lucky you didn't crack your skull wide open. Though I think this will be one ugly bruise." There was silence for several moments. Then the voice's owner patted him on the cheek, beseeching him once more. "Rom, do you feel me? Hear me? Come on, I know you're a fighter."

His stomach twisted ominously, but an onslaught of pain centered in his head and neck shattered his queasiness. His hands clenched involuntarily, and he felt the fingers wrenched from his grasp all over again. *You shouldn't have left him in the wreckage; you should have freed him while you had the chance.* A groan slipped from his throat before he could stop it.

The comforting hands stilled. "Muffin! He's awake! Rom! Do you hear me?"

Rom opened one eye, then the other, squinting through a haze of pain at a blur of dark hair framing a pale face and glittering intelligent eyes that saw and understood every nuance of his soul. *The Balkanor angel.* His heart swelled with joy and wonder.

But hadn't she abandoned him? Hadn't *he* left there, too? Bewildered, he searched the sky above. It was dull, metallic . . . no stars.

Ten firm fingertips pressed lightly into his jaw. "Try not to move your neck." She resumed her soothing caresses, her face closer now.

He heard a male voice then, and it bewildered him. "Momentum threw you into the hatch. We're getting a stretcher to bring you to sick bay."

"You will be fine," the woman whispered in her accented voice. Rom raised leaden, shaking hands to cradle her face. Entranced by her sweetly curving lips—tempting, full, made for kisses, *his* kisses, and a hundred other erotic activities he envisioned all too easily—he pulled her down to him. She locked her arms to keep him away, her hands splayed atop his chest. "Oh, now look who is feeling better."

"But this is where we kiss." He wrinkled his brow,

concentrating hard. "Yes, I'm certain it's what comes next."

"No, my sweet, confused man. Wrong script." Then she smiled through her tears. *Tears?* He dabbed at the moisture with his thumbs. Shame wrapped around his scattered wits. Of course. He'd disappointed her, failed her, as he had his family. How could he expect her—or anyone—to abide by his impulsive abdication of responsibility? "I shouldn't have let my brother come. He should have stayed home—safe—not here."

She stared at him blankly for a moment, then made a soft cry. She grabbed his hands and crushed them to her lips. "No, Rom; it was Zarra. *Zarra.* Not your brother. Do you understand? He's fine—banged up like you, but you saved him."

The male voice said, "The gravity generator's on backup power, and Terz's crew is working on repairs to the hull. Gann called from the bridge—the structural integrity's intact."

Rom knew that what he'd just been told was significant, but for the life of him, he couldn't figure out why. The woman laid her angel's hands on his stomach. She spoke slowly, her speech somewhat halting. "You're on the *Quillie*. A spaceship. You're her captain . . . a very heroic captain."

A hero? How could this be? Her statement so diverged from his view of himself that he let his eyes drift closed to hide the burning hope he feared lurked there. Agony thundered in his skull with each beat of his heart, but he floated, buoyed by an odd giddiness of spirit, something he was certain he'd never felt before.

There was a clattering, the urgent murmur of deep voices. Supporting his neck and shoulders, several men lifted him. Pain rocketed from one side of his head to the other, ending in a strange, icy tingling in his neck, fading when a medicine patch was pressed under his chin. The woman's magical, healing hands skimmed over his face and hair once more, then withdrew. Bereft, he tried to call to her, but the drug was too powerful, and all that emerged was a hoarse mumble. *This is where she abandons you without so much as a backward glance.* He clamped his mouth shut before he displayed anything else that might be construed as neediness.

"I'll see you when you wake up, Rom."

He stiffened upon feeling her breath moist and hot against his ear, laden with promises he knew she wouldn't keep.

"Yes, I'll stay with you. . . ."

The inevitability of her betrayal kept him company as he began the long slide back into darkness.

He woke to an ethereal world where pain and time did not exist. A soft mattress had replaced the cold, hard floor beneath his back. Someone sponged his face and neck with a damp cloth, scented with a fragrance he recognized—one used for healing the body and the spirit, reminding him of the cloudless melon-colored skies and cool sands of a Sienna dawn. He drifted for a while amid a thousand memories, saw himself as a teenager playing Bajha with his father, then, much younger, sitting nestled with his beloved sister in his mother's lap while she read to them. He would have laughed, had he been able, as he recalled scampering over the sands with his younger brother Lijhan, eager to catch one of the planet's elusive green-banded turquoise quillies. The images left him with a longing so great it that took his breath away. He missed his family.

In a jolt of self-awareness, he faced the emptiness inside him. For all his success as a smuggler, and his solid, if somewhat disreputable, standing in the frontier, he was no different from the shiftless space drifters he despised—lonely, resentful, and suffering from an inherent lack of purpose.

Perhaps his father had been right about him.

A sound distracted him from his dismal epiphany. The woman ministering to him began half singing, half humming a song in a hushed voice as she pressed a cool, damp cloth to his brow. *The Balkanor angel!* Drugged lethargy held his eyes shut, so he listened to the soft song. It sounded maternal, yet at the same time deeply sensual, and was in a foreign language that sounded familiar. Earth words.

The images of the angel and Jas Hamilton coalesced. She said she'd stay   and she had. She hadn't turned her back on him, as his father and his family had. Astonishment and piercing relief plowed through him, as if he were a man who'd just plunged to his doom only to be unexpectedly caught.

What if she had been equally helpless within the framework of the vision? He had never considered the possibility that her departure might not have been of her own choosing, that, perhaps, she'd been allowed to stay only to give him the will to finish his task that day. Instead he'd blamed her for what might have been beyond her control.

As he succumbed to drugged slumber, he released a long-held-in mental sigh. For the first time in countless years, his dreams held hope.

*　　*　　*

Rom blinked rapidly. His sight was blurred and his eyes gritty. Hell and back, he felt like he'd spent a month drinking in a frontier bordo bar. He swallowed against a scratchy throat and eased his head from side to side, then flexed his arms. Stiffness, but no pain. No light-headedness, either, which indicated that he'd been weaned off healing drugs and painblockers, meaning he'd most likely recovered. He wasn't alone, however.

He heard a long and languorous snuffle followed by a full-fledged snort. "Jasmine?" he queried in a raspy voice. The woman snored like a Taangori dragon.

Rom propped himself on his elbows to look around, then gave a hoarse chuckle at the sight of Muffin, out cold, slumped in a chair at the foot of his bed. The man's head had tipped back, and his dinner plate–sized hands were splayed, one on each thigh, propping him upright.

Another shuddering snore, then a lusty sigh. Rom settled against the pillow and laced his fingers behind his head. "Muffin, if the sounds coming out of your mouth are any indication of your need, I suggest you hire a pleasure servant as soon as we dock at the Depot."

His bodyguard jerked awake. Instantly alert, Muffin swept his cool gaze around the room. Focusing on Rom, he brightened, breaking into a grin. "B'kah."

Rom snorted. "Some protector."

Muffin's smile spread. He leaned back in his chair and hooked his thumbs in his waistband, drumming eight thick fingers against his massive upper thighs. "Odds were against your being murdered in your bed on your own ship. Besides, you know I feel out of sorts if I miss my midday nap." Rom also knew how quickly Muffin

142

could transform from contented napper to lethal combatant. The giant pushed himself off the chair. "As for the Depot, I'll be employing two pleasure servants there, not one. Three if I can afford it."

Rom inquired mildly, "All at once?"

"One after the other after the other." Impervious to Rom's chuckle, Muffin wedged another pillow under his captain's shoulders to help him sit up. "With all due respect, B'kah, you've kept me away from port too long this time." He poured water into a glass.

After Rom drank his fill from it, Muffin lumbered to the environmental control panel and adjusted the settings to those more suited for a healthy man than a sick one. Once satisfied with the lights and temperature, he related the events leading to Rom's injuries.

In light of Muffin's gory description of his severe concussion, Rom made a cautious but thorough inventory of the rest of his body parts. Everything was still attached and seemed to be functioning properly.

Muffin refilled his glass. "Ever since Zarra returned to duty, all he talks about is how you saved his life."

The water Rom had just swallowed plummeted into his belly like a cold stone.

"Captain B'kah this, Captain B'kah that," Muffin mimicked in a singsong voice. "Like saving a drowning ketta-kitten. You've won yourself an ally for life."

"Redirect the boy's gratitude. If Terz hadn't closed the hatch, he'd be dead now."

"But you—"

"Facts only, please," Rom snapped. *I am no hero.* "How long have I been out?"

Muffin eyed him with something akin to pity. Rom clenched his jaw and turned away. "How long?"

"A standard week. I saw to your personal needs. Jas was with you the rest of the time." Muffin poked his thumb at a nest of pillows piled near Rom's bed. They held an indentation in the shape of a body, revealing that Jas had indeed stayed with him day and night. Like hunting for beads from a broken necklace, Rom retrieved the scattered images remaining from a week of drugged semiconsciousness. What few memories he could salvage formed a fragile strand of tender caresses and caring words—Jas's. His chest squeezed tight. "Where is she?"

"On the bridge," Muffin said casually. "Gann intended to bring the *Quillie* back to light speed this morning, but Terz wanted to inspect the door repairs first. Not the one you dented with your head, B'kah, the other one. He's got four men suited up and outside. Then Jas asked if she could replace the pilot on duty."

"What! She's flying the ship?" Rom sat bolt upright. "Right *now?*" Muffin grinned, and he sagged against the pillows, muttering, "I've got men tethered to the outside of the ship, and an adventure-seeking, cropper-popping mother of two at the controls. A frontier woman, no less. What did I expect after sleeping for a week?" Rom peered around his quarters. There was no adverse pitching or rolling. And nothing was tipped over, as far as he could tell. "I see she had the good sense to keep the ship on the automated flier."

"Actually, she's manually flying."

Rom let out a laugh of pride and surprise. The gentle, nurturing woman who had cared for him for a week was upstairs flying his ship on manual control like a seasoned space veteran. It sparked his longing to see her again. Unfortunately, his body lagged behind his spirits as he struggled to free himself from the blanket. His muscles wobbled from lack of use as he headed into the hygiene shower with a distinctly unsteady gait. As the water hissed on, Muffin moved next to the enclosure and remarked, "I take it you'll be making an appearance on the bridge."

"The moment I'm presentable." Rom aimed the sprayers at his shoulders, arching backward into the water until the kinks eased out of his knotted muscles. "It seems I've been tossed aside for a crate of metal and bolts. Time to size up the competition and see if I stand a chance at winning back the lady's affections."

"As if you ever had them."

The big man was out the door before Rom had the chance to react.

After a fruitless search of the main part of the ship, the aft cargo storage areas, the midlevel corridors, and the Bajha arena, Rom paused by the ladder leading to the lower deck. He couldn't fathom why she would be down there, but he sensed, somehow, that she was. His legs protested the strain of climbing down the ladder. It would take some time to bring his strength back to what it had been. As his eyes adjusted to the dim light, he leaned his back against the gangway and listened to the thumps of the gravity generator and the incessant purring of the air recyclers. They were the sounds of a healthy ship.

Unaware of his presence, Jas was cross-legged on the floor across from the hatch to the generator room, vigorously sketching something on the pad of paper in her lap. The sight of her, so serious, so absorbed in her artwork while sitting in the middle of the floor of a cold and impersonal hunk of trillidium, kindled something inside him, something fundamentally warm and needed, and not unlike the yearning he experienced upon recalling his childhood. The zippers of her baggy black coverall and her silver bracelets glinted in the meager overhead light. Each time she leaned over her drawing, her long, unbound hair spilled forward like a veil. Only when she flipped it back behind her shoulders did she allow him a glimpse of her profile—a soft, expressive mouth nestled perfectly between a strong, straight nose and that stubborn chin. Her face was a study in contrasts, like everything else he'd discovered about her so far.

Carefully he crouched in front of her, and she dropped her pencil. With her flushed cheeks, darkened eyes, and lips parted in astonishment, she resembled a woman who had been interrupted in the middle of lovemaking. The imagined sight of her beneath him, their bodies intimately joined, conjured a dull, hot throb in his groin. He tried his damnedest to ignore it, and scooped up the pencil rolling across the floor. "What, may I ask, lures you to the coldest, darkest part of the ship?"

"You." Her smile was infused with warmth and welcome, and her eyes held none of the wariness of the days before his injury. "Muffin told me the drugs would wear off today, but I didn't expect you to be up so soon. I want to show you something, but I need a few more minutes." Her Basic had become remarkably smooth and colloquial. "Do you mind?" she asked. "I'm almost finished."

She searched through a pouch, chose another stubby, soft-pointed pencil, and went back to work with an intensity that awed him. Her left hand whisked over the page, two fingers hugging the pencil, while the others were engaged in making shadows and smudges.

This was passion in its purest form, he thought. Not patently rehearsed, as he'd suspected of the skilled palace courtesans of his pre-Balkanor days, or modified to suit a partner, as one expected from a pleasure servant. No, this passion arose from her soul, and it humbled him.

Jas's hand slowed, then ceased moving. She scrutinized her work, then him, massaging the small of her back. "You look better," she said. "How do you feel?"

"Like the morning after a long night of over-indulgence. Only without the benefit of having had a good time."

She laughed. "If anyone deserves a good time, it's you. You dove through that hatch without a thought to your own safety. It's all the crew's been talking about." Her face glowed with unmistakable admiration.

He recoiled, and a rush of dismal memories plowed into him—his father's fury the day he discovered that his only remaining son couldn't sire a child, his mother's anguished weeping, and the feel of his sister's frantic embrace moments before the doors were slammed behind him upon his expulsion from the palace—the only such episode in eleven thousand years.

He'd failed his family, his people. He was not a man deserving of such esteem.

"Makes me wish I had the paints I left at home," she went on. "Not that I have the skill to truly capture what happened." Almost shyly, she placed the pad in his lap. "A rather inadequate representation of the single greatest act of bravery and selflessness I have ever witnessed."

Rom's mouth went dry. It was an illustration of two men joined in a life-or-death struggle. One man, sprawled on his stomach, had a face that looked like his—Great Mother, it *was* him. He was gripping Zarra's hand as if he refused to let go, the strain evident in the sinewy muscles rippling the skin of his forearm. His teeth were bared, his eyes dark with pain and purpose. Whirling debris framed the entire scene, one that held all the emotion and drama of life.

Except that it depicted a lie.

"You do exquisite work." He set the portrait on the floor. His weariness had returned, and he settled onto the floor, his legs stretched out in front of him as he supported his weight with his hands. His pulse battered his temples, threatening to turn the pressure there into pain. "However, a more accurate representation would show me releasing him." She cocked her head, as if she wasn't certain she'd heard him right. "I let go of Zarra's hand," he clarified.

"But you held him for those critical seconds. It delayed his slide across the generator room floor. That gave Terz the chance shut the hatch. The only reason he's alive is because you held him as long as you did."

"Don't make me into a hero." *You left him; you should have stayed.* "I let the boy go."

"Irrelevant."

"Unforgivable," he answered.

Jas stared in disbelief as one end of Rom's mouth tipped into a smirk. Gone was the man she'd begun to know. In his place was the cocky smuggler, a man who smiled while his eyes held an unknowable grief. "This isn't a simple case of modesty, is it?" she asked. Shaking, her heart racing, she crouched next to him. "You're a hero, Rom. And no matter how hard you try to convince me otherwise, that's how I see you. And that's how your men see you. Why don't *you* see it, too?"

A tiny scar above his upper lip stretched as he drew his mouth into a tight line. "Almost twenty standard years ago, I fought in a war—the first true conflict in eleven thousand years. My younger brother joined me . . . without my father's permission. But he was a good fighter, a superb pilot, and so I let him come. Balkanor was the crucial battle, one we planned for a full year. It was a full-scale invasion, the culmination of much courage and hard work." Quietly, he finished, "We won the war that day. But I lost Lijhan."

Her heart twisted. "I'm sorry," she whispered. "But he followed you into battle because he wanted to. He was a soldier. Soldiers die."

"You don't understand! His ship took damage during the space battle. He survived the crash, but he was trapped inside. I chose to go on, intending to return for him. But—Great Mother—his starfighter exploded. I should have freed him while I had the chance! I shouldn't have left him alone—"

"You're a warrior, Rom. You did what you had to do."

His gaze went cold. "I had a choice, Jas. I made the wrong one." He pushed himself to his feet. "Now, if you're quite through with your inquiries—"

"I'm not."

Surprise flickered over his handsome features, and he lifted one brow. Folding his arms over his chest, he drummed his fingers against his biceps in an agitated rhythm. But she refused to let him intimidate her; she knew what it was like to feel desolate inside and not know why. "I figured out why you and Gann are so different from the rest of the crew. Why your skin and hair are darker, and your eyes are lighter."

His fingers stopped drumming.

"You're *Vash Nadah,* a member of the ruling class. You were raised with a rigid code of ethics only a god could follow perfectly. I know how strict they are . . . I've read them!"

At her words, Rom jammed his fingers through his hair. Then he strode to the ladder leading to the upper deck. There he stopped, head bowed, shoulders hunched, his fingers curled over one of the rungs.

Jas followed him, praying her instincts were right. "But maybe you *are* a god. After all, you don't make mistakes."

He turned around, his honey-colored eyes flooded with anguish. Her own eyes burned in response. The depth of empathy she felt for this man she'd so recently met overwhelmed her.

Ruefully, he said, "I've made many."

"Aha! You *are* a mere mortal, just like the rest of us. But instead of accepting that, you punish yourself over and over. It's been years! You have more than paid your penance for Lijhan's death! Let it go," she beseeched him.

Could he? Rom wondered. Could he let it go? He'd been running, choosing the most dangerous, the most frenetic pastimes, avoiding anything that smacked of contentment and stability. He thumped two fingers on his chest. "I fear that if I let this void close up, I'll forget all I've lost. And I will not make a waste of my brother's sacrifice."

She spread her hands. "I'm not asking you to. But maybe there are other ways, better ways, to honor his memory, than by carrying the pain of his death to your grave."

They stared at each other until the very air resonated with emotion. Rom felt bruised inside as well as out. "Perhaps," he answered at last.

That seemed to please her. Depleted, he instinctively sought the tenderness she so generously imparted, and drew her close. Brushing his lips over hers, he stroked her hair with his palms. "Why do you trouble yourself with my concerns?" he murmured.

"Because I care about you," she whispered, and lifted up on her toes to kiss him—lightly, and with obvious restraint. Her body was another matter entirely. It played traitor to her lips, pressing against him, the lush feel of her full, soft breasts and gently swaying hips making him instantly hard. The kiss melted into a breathless hug before they moved apart.

Gently gripping her upper arms, Rom felt the heat of her skin through the fabric. Her faintly floral scent drifted in the air between them. She said she cared about him. Hadn't his father once said the same? He succumbed to the irrational urge to test her, for when she found out who he was—"Do you have any idea who I am?"

In that sometimes unsettling, sometimes exhilarating, intuitive way of hers, she studied his face. "Yes. I do."

He plowed one hand through his hair.

"You're Romlijhian B'kah—"

Great Mother.

"—and you're the only son of the richest, most powerful man in the galaxy."

Chapter Nine

Rom took a step backward. Adrenaline pumped through his veins, and his hands shook, but he drew on years of discipline to maintain his composure.

She shrugged. "No wonder you need a bodyguard."

He jerked his hands in the air. "That's it? That's all you're going to say? No wonder I need a bodyguard?"

"What am I supposed to say?"

"Surely you can find something. I'm the biggest stain in an eleven-thousand-year family history. By all the heavens, the only stain!"

"Don't believe it. I'd bet my last grain of salt your esteemed family founder was considered a troublemaker, too, when he and the other warriors stood up to that crazy warlord."

"The eight original warriors—troublemakers!" he roared, incredulous. A giddy sense of freedom flooded him, and he laughed, actually laughed, shaking his head.

"Jas, only you could take something as vain and ponderous as Trade History and make it thoroughly entertaining."

She stared at him, perplexed. She did not understand the humor of it all, he guessed. But then she hadn't the fortune—or was it misfortune?—to have been raised as he was. He sagged against the wall and folded his arms across his chest. His temples pounded, but he ignored the pain. "Who told you about me?"

"The ship's computer."

"Hell and back. What led you there?"

"I was using it to plan my trip—and to study galactic art and history. But I didn't find out about your family until I figured out how to read your signet ring."

His left hand closed involuntarily, causing the ring to bite into his flesh.

"I took it off after you were hurt because I was afraid your finger might swell," she explained. "I tried to read your family crest, but I couldn't. So I looked it up in the language-translation data bank and matched the symbols: 'fealty, fidelity, family,' the warrior's code. That directed me to the history of Sienna, and that's where I found the list with every firstborn B'kah son. At the bottom was yours. I figured out the rest."

"How long have you known?"

"Almost one standard week."

"And yet you said nothing?" he almost shouted.

Her chin jutted forward. "It doesn't change how I feel about you. If anything, I respect you more. You sacrificed everything for a cause you truly believed in. I find that incredibly heroic."

He stared at her. She admired him for the very things

others disdained in him. A strange sense of wonder filled him, and more. He searched for the right words to express his appreciation for the unaccustomed lightness of spirit she'd evoked, but found none. "Thank you," he said, knowing the statement was wholly inadequate. "I am in your debt."

She waved away his gratitude.

He caught her hands, smiling gently. "Commerce lesson number one: an honest trader always repays his debts." He curled his hand behind her head and brushed a lingering kiss across her lips.

Her chin remained tilted upward after he pulled back. She said, "Hmm. And lesson number two?"

"Recognize the talents in others." He touched his finger to the tip of her nose. "You, for instance, are a woman of many. Flying, to name but one."

"Who told you?"

"The captain is all-seeing, all-knowing."

She laughed. "Right. Who turned me in?"

"Muffin. When I woke."

"Don't blame Gann for letting me fly," she said quickly. "I harassed him until he gave in."

"Blame him? By all that is holy, I'll thank him. This brings me to lesson number three—take said talents and profit by them. I'd be a fool not to, Jas. Good pilots are hard to find. Now that I have, I must take advantage of my good fortune."

"Oh?" she asked, skeptical. "How?"

"You're hired."

Jas blinked. "I'm what?"

"Hired." Rom's catlike eyes watched her intently. "I'm offering you a position on the *Quillie*. Apprentice

155

pilot. Gann will train you. With your skills, you'll be awarded regular status within the year."

"You're serious."

He grinned.

"Thank you, but I can't—"

"Full benefits. A good salary."

She chuckled. "Retirement plan?"

"Ah, no. Unfortunately no one has lasted long enough in my employ to require one."

"Oh, *that's* encouraging. No wonder you're desperate to hire a pilot who hasn't flown in almost twenty years." She smiled at his enthusiasm.

"Come work for me."

"I can't."

"Why not?"

"Because . . ." *Because I'll fall in love with you.* Her cheeks heated, and she clamped her jaw shut, thanking her lucky stars that she hadn't blurted that bombshell aloud. If she let her heart steer her away from her goals, she'd be repeating the biggest mistake of her life. "Rom, I came here for adventure. To see and do things as far removed from my Earth life as possible."

"Ah, of course. Your vacation has barely begun. We'll travel first, then."

"We?"

His eyes sparkled. "I assure you that the travels we will experience together will be far more thrilling than those you'd complete alone."

Her skin prickled with excitement, the same feeling she had when facing a clean canvas, wet paintbrush in hand. She steeled herself against the sensation; she mustn't let her untrustworthy emotions chip away at her stone-cold logic.

Yet maybe a little craziness, a little impetuousness might help her come to terms with the frustrating emptiness inside her. From somewhere deep within, Jas scraped together a lump of resolve; she certainly hadn't achieved all she had in her life by taking the easy route.

"What about the *Quillie?*" she asked, eyeing him speculatively.

"I'll give my crew the choice of taking shore leave or continuing onto the Quibba System, our next stopover after Skull's Doom. Should they opt for profit over pleasure—which I suspect they might—Gann will take over in my absence. I see this as a perfect opportunity to test your theory that I ought to enjoy myself more. What better way than by showing you the galaxy?"

She met Rom's strangely perceptive gaze. Her heart leaped, and she felt vividly and utterly alive. Weren't the feelings coursing through her the very reason she'd left her home and family in the first place? Yes, a few months spent with Rom would be exactly the kind of adventure she needed.

She balled her hands into fists and blurted, "Yes," before she lost her nerve. "I accept both offers. Travel and the flying job—but not permanently," she reminded him—and herself, "because I promised my children I'd be home in six Earth months."

"I understand." Suddenly looking tired, Rom sifted his fingers through his hair, causing a few shiny locks to flop forward over his bruised forehead. Much of the color had leached from his skin. "Certainly there are more hospitable locations on this ship to plan our itinerary." Fatigue made his voice raspy and deep.

Her caregiver instincts roared to life. She grabbed his arm and propelled him toward the ladder. "You shouldn't be down here. You belong in bed."

"Yes. We do."

Hands on the middle rung, she looked at him askance. "Lack of persistence is not one of your faults."

Grinning, he climbed up after her.

"So what's Skull's Doom?" she prompted as they walked through the midlevel corridors to his quarters. "Sounds forbidding."

"It is, for the uninitiated. Doom is a nearly lawless outpost—two-days' round-trip from the Depot at sub-light speed. The Trade Police have mostly washed their hands of it, which conveniently makes it the only decent place to trade outside the frontier. I promised I'd run some goods out to a quirky little merchant there who says he'll negotiate only with me. Because of the risk, I'd much rather you waited for me at the Depot."

After punching in the code to the door of the room that had become more familiar to Jas over the past week than her own, Rom pressed his palm to the small of her back, guiding her inside. The gorgeous carpet covering much of the floor immediately muffled their footsteps. The rug resembled a Turkish kilim, dyed in rich tones and soft as sin. Rom lowered the lighting to a comfortable glow, then lit a laser-candle under a clear, shell-shaped bowl of scented oil. The heat released the fragrance she'd come to love. It smelled like early mornings at Betty's house in Sedona, where she used to bring her coffee outside to sip it on the deck as the sun rose. Jas had been told the scent was therapeutic, and she could believe it—spending the nights on a nest of pillows by Rom's bed, she'd never slept better.

As she watched Rom set his lithe warrior's frame to simple domestic tasks, she began to wonder why no one lasted long in his employ. Just how much adventure had she signed up for? She clasped her hands behind her back and casually rocked back on her heels. "So what happened to those men who didn't make it to retirement?"

"I'm tempted to weave tales of hungry serpents and murdering bandits that prey on women who refuse my job offers," he began, sitting on the foot of his mattress to tug off his boots. The scent of skin-warmed leather mixed with the incense. "But I don't have the heart." Affectionate mirth and candlelight turned his eyes the color of warm honey. She never imagined there could be so much communication between two people through eye contact alone.

"The men simply moved on," he said at last. "Found what they considered better opportunities. One fellow, my first engineer, saved his pay and purchased a small ship of his own. But most returned to the more populated parts of the galaxy to marry and raise children. The frontier's no place for a family."

"Haven't *you* ever wanted children?" she asked.

The muscles in his jaw clenched, then released. He twisted off the thick gold signet ring he wore on his left hand and carefully set it on a tray next to his bed. "Growing up, I didn't give much thought to whether I wanted them or not. It was expected that I would have them. The irony is that I never did."

She supposed he hadn't wanted to expose children to the dangers of frontier life. "Maybe you'll change your mind someday. I think you'd make a wonderful father."

Something unbearably sad flashed in his eyes. "I suffered radiation poisoning during the war. The damage was irreparable. There will never be any children."

"I'm . . . sorry."

Reflective, he rested his forearms on his thighs. "I killed Sharron. That is what makes my circumstances bearable."

"Sharron, a renegade religious figure. I read about him in a section entitled 'The Unauthorized Uprising.' "

"Is that what they're calling it now?" His mouth twisted in disgust and he shook his head. "I never understood why the families did not take action. Sharron had resurrected weaponry banned since the Dark Years. He championed everything the *Vash* despised. 'Sex is sinful,' he preached."

"But if no one under his control had sex, then how did they plan to . . ." She waved her hand, searching for words.

"Procreate?"

"Yes."

"Sharron and his chosen elders impregnated the women. Then, once the women completed their child-bearing duties, he rewarded them by sending them on a journey to the ever after."

"But isn't that your term for where you go when you die?" At his nod, the blood drained from her face. "He took their babies? And then killed them?"

He acknowledged her with a curt nod, then began undoing the top fastenings on his dark olive iridescent shirt. "After all the spying we did, after all the lives lost, I never did prove that allegation. If only I had, then perhaps I could have gathered the support I needed. Instead I was left with a few dozen holo-images of women being loaded onto ships and taken away."

"Why on Earth would anyone worship such a monster?"

"He was extremely magnetic and intelligent. And he offered what the *Vash Nadah* do not—the impossible promise of a classless society, and blanket acceptance for those who chose not to follow our stringent moral code."

"The Treatise of Trade," she murmured.

"No urging to have a family, no pressure to remain faithful to a husband or wife. No pressure to have a husband or wife, period."

She thought of their upcoming travels. "They're not still around, I hope."

"Perhaps some remnants of his cult remain. My soldiers never found the men who escaped with his body. I can only assume they fled to a remote world to bury him." Absently, his fingers brushed over his chest. "They wore medallions—an engraving of a man's and a woman's clasped hands below a rising sun." He stared off into someplace in the past. "I stopped tracking their activities after the war, when I returned home to recover from my injuries. But once the family surgeon interpreted the findings of the medical examination and announced them to my father, nothing much mattered anymore."

"Your inability to have children," she whispered.

He nodded. "My father wanted a functional heir. Because I couldn't be that heir, he sent me away."

"Where did you go?"

"To lose myself in what you called my adventures," he said wryly. "My brother—and best friend—was dead. The woman I was betrothed to wouldn't speak to me . . . not that I wanted charity or sympathy from the other seven families. So I wandered the galaxy, almost became addicted to painblockers for a time. After that," he said quietly, "I stopped living altogether."

Goose bumps tiptoed up her arms with his unexpected, heart-wrenching admission. After Saudi, she'd stopped living, too. "Maybe we both need to live a little."

"Agreed."

They exchanged weary smiles. Then he settled onto his back and tucked one flexed arm behind his head. Extending the other at a right angle to his body, he beckoned to her. "Keep me company."

She hesitated in the midst of plumping the floor pillows she'd slept on. She'd intended to stack them neatly and then leave for her own quarters. "Well, I—"

"I'm tired," he reminded her with gentle candor. "*Very* tired."

She admitted sheepishly, "To be honest, a little snuggling sounds nice." She'd used the English term, unable to come up with the Basic equivalent. It didn't matter; she'd translate using body language. She slipped off her boots, crawled over the mattress, and molded the length of her body to his, nestling her head in the warm hollow between his chest and shoulder.

His arms came around her. "Is this *snuggling?*" he murmured in a damned good imitation of English.

"Mmm . . ." She sighed against his shirt. As he pressed his lips to the top of her head, rubbing one wide palm over the small of her back, she shivered. It had been so long since she'd been held this way, cradled in tenderness, wrapped in a man's protective warmth, and, oh, did it feel good. Their arms tightened around each other. He let out a long breath and stroked her hair as if they'd been lovers for years. As her eyes drifted closed, she listened to Rom's heart thudding beneath her ear, reminding her of his inner strength and passion with every beat. Her body responded with a slow, spiraling heat as sexual curiosity replaced her drowsiness. And she weighed the consequences of adding a night of erotic abandon to her list of hoped-for adventures. Yes, the unthinkable—Rom's lean, powerful body entwined with hers, skin to skin, his hot kisses . . . his knowing hands. But she recoiled when she took the fantasy to the point of consummation. Rom was a man of galactic experience, and out of her league sexually. She wouldn't be able to fool him, pretending pleasure when there was only pain. The realization both terrified and intrigued her.

And aroused her.

Lovemaking would be as common and natural to Rom as eating and drinking. What if she were to approach sex in the same casual way? Might she stand a chance at putting the shame of her past behind her?

She felt Rom shudder, and she lifted her head. Good heavens, while she was contemplating lovemaking, her interstellar Romeo had fallen asleep! Disappointment, relief, and a dozen other emotions too jumbled to make sense somersaulted through her. So much for her grand plan for seduction. Besides, it made more sense to wait until tomorrow, the last day before they reached the Depot, to proposition him. That way, if the experience proved a disaster, she'd save them both from the morning-after awkwardness. When the ship docked, she'd simply say good-bye and disappear into the crowds.

* * *

Rom slid his hand over the rumpled, empty space beside him. She was gone. He jolted to full wakefulness. Lifting his head and shoulders off the mattress, he peered around the room and almost called her name, stopping himself at the last moment. Jas was crouched at the altar near the opposite wall, her hands clasped, her eyes squeezed closed in utter concentration. She was praying. It pleased him that she had faith—in her Earth God, naturally, but faith all the same.

It made him want her even more.

As she stood, she made a simple gesture with one hand, bringing it from forehead to breast, then shoulder to shoulder. Then she noticed that he was watching her, and her expression brightened like a T'aurean dawn. Odd, but she appeared somewhat nervous. And there was something else . . . something new. He'd swear she was assessing him, but for what he could only imagine. "You were speaking to your God," he said.

"Yes. I was praying—for my children, my parents. And my younger sisters, three of them, all with families of their own. So"—she rolled her eyes—"it takes a while to work everyone in. You're a religious man," she pointed out. "I don't know why, but I didn't expect that."

"I've had my moments over the years," he admitted dryly. "But faith is one of the few things I kept from my life on Sienna."

She absorbed the information with a casual, nonjudgmental nod. It was a singular pleasure to be accepted for who he was and not what he represented. Or *had* represented.

"Let me demonstrate," Rom said, crouching in front of the altar. He fitted his knees into the well-worn hollows in a woven floor cushion and lit laser-candles under half a dozen shallow bowls holding fragrant oils. "We worship a female deity, the Great Mother. The scents please her." He gave Jas a sidelong glance. "Pleasing a woman makes her more receptive."

Jas laughed softly.

"When you're ready to send your prayers to the ever after," Rom explained, lifting his prayer wand, "simply tap this against this." In an action he'd repeated almost daily since he was old enough to grasp the thin silver stick, he clinked it against an ancient brass bell. The single chime was crisp and clear. "Now your prayers are on their way."

"How lovely," she murmured.

He rose, stretching with a noisy groan. "Let's go the galley and see about our dinner."

"Too late for that. Or too early, depending how you look at it. You slept all afternoon and all night. It's morning."

"Morning!" Only then did it sink in that Jas appeared fresh from a hygiene shower. She'd woven her hair into a single gleaming braid, and had replaced the silver hoop earrings she'd worn yesterday with tiny purple gems. He muttered, "The medical technician must have fed me enough painblockers last week to kill a Tromjhan steer."

"That and exhaustion, too. I was just about to wake you. The stew's getting cold." She waved her hand at the dining table. Two covered bowls and a basket of bread sat next to a steaming pitcher of *tock*. "Breakfast is served."

After he washed and changed, they ate leisurely. "I had a cup of *tock* with Zarra in the galley earlier," she said. "Other than some temporary hearing loss, it's like nothing happened to him."

Rom gave a long-suffering sigh. "The resilience of youth."

"You had a severe concussion and a fractured skull," she reminded him. "Zarra was lucky to walk away with a couple of ruptured eardrums and a few bruises."

Rom hunched his shoulders and extended one quivering hand. "Don't contradict a feeble old man."

"Feeble!" She straightened her back and lifted her chin. "You have wandered onto sensitive ground, Captain B'kah. How old are you anyway? And it had better not be younger than me." They laughingly went through the conversions and concluded that they were roughly the same age. Lingering over their *tock,* she animatedly answered his questions about the provincial planet Earth, her children, and her friends—and her time spent as a warrior flying Earth fighter-craft.

"Tell me about your family now," she coaxed as she refilled his mug.

"We no longer speak to each other."

"I gathered that." She gave him one of her soul-searching stares. "You must miss them."

"I do," he conceded. The loss ached like a phantom limb. "I fought Sharron's faction against my father's wishes. The consequences of my actions cost me his respect. He called me irresponsible, disrespectful, and selfish. He said that I didn't care a whit about the traditions that bound our family and our society together. Rather than try to prove him wrong, I took the easy route. I became everything he said I was."

"But you aren't," she insisted softly.

"I will never be the man I was before Balkanor."

"Who's to say that's a bad thing?"

The question shocked him. She constantly found

points of view he hadn't contemplated. "Woman, you have a talent for turning me inside out and examining the contents. Furthermore, it's impossible to keep secrets from you."

Her eyes glinted with mischief. "Does that bother you?"

He snorted. "My sister had the same knack. So I suppose I should be used to it." The unexpected memory warmed him. "Growing up, we were very close."

"Maybe . . . we'll grow closer, too." Her cheeks turning pink, she smiled.

Rom stretched across the table to sip the poignant sweetness from her lips. It was a quick, light kiss, as he'd intended. But her hands were slow to leave his shoulders, and she kept her lips slightly parted and her eyes closed for long seconds after he pulled away: the look of a woman hungering for more. By all the heavens, he wanted more, too. A lot more.

He recalled his original plan to seduce her, and how he had discarded it. Whether or not she'd visited him in his vision, she did not remember doing so. Bedding her with an ulterior motive in mind was tasteless and pointless now. He craved more than a casual exchange of pleasure, however memorable it might be.

But how to proceed? She wasn't like any woman he'd ever known. She didn't respond to traditional advances, or anything that he'd been taught. Not that he could give her a *Vash Nadah*–sanctified marriage, or children, or even the comfort and joy of an extended family. Only physical gratification and the assuagement of loneliness . . . and his heart, if in fact he still had one to give.

He was startled out of his musings by the feel of her fingertip gliding down his arm. He focused on her face to find her regarding him with a decidedly flirtatious, if somewhat apprehensive, smile. "Rom, tomorrow we arrive at the Depot, and you haven't taught me how to play Bajha yet."

He looked at his wrist time-teller. "Gann and Zarra are likely in the arena. We can join them."

"A private lesson was more what I had in mind. And"—she tucked a loose strand of hair behind her ear—"an even more private dinner afterward."

The suggestive glint in her eyes left him speechless. This was no mere flirtation. Great Mother, the woman was trying to seduce him.

A warrior must always be prepared for the unexpected, he reminded himself while a slow smile spread across his face. "I would be most honored," he replied.

Rising, he made a courtly bow and extended his hand. Jas settled hers in his warm palm.

"My lady, I look forward to our match," he said, touching his lips to her knuckles.

"Me, too," was all she said in reply.

That afternoon, Rom escorted Jas up the stairs to spectator seats a dozen rows above the padded playing floor, where Gann was in the midst of his weekly practice session with Zarra, leading the boy through a merciless series of stretches and lunges.

She settled onto her chair, resting her boots on the footrest. Rom sensed an intense energy simmering in her, just below the surface, more than he'd felt in the entire time they'd been together. Her eyes were bright, and her lush mouth looked as delicious as a plump, ripe berry.

Sweetness that begged to be tasted.

He would have kissed her without a second thought, had that second thought not arisen in the form of a vivid memory of the day he'd returned her shoes in front of the bridge crew. She didn't care for public displays of what she considered private matters, and the last thing he cared to do was rouse her ire when she was acting so very . . . receptive.

Jas was watching the two men vaulting across the Bajha floor. Buoyed by her particularly agreeable mood, Rom followed suit. Gann too easily swerved out of the way of the boy's thrusts. "Use your senses, lad. Let them guide you."

"It would help if he could see," Jas said out the side of her mouth. "Why isn't Gann wearing a blindfold, too?"

"The game is based on intuition and instinct. We hone these skills to reach a higher state of consciousness. It helps us become better warriors, or more skilled pilots. Or"—his gaze lingered pointedly on her mouth—"more giving lovers."

Her eyes flicked away, revealing to him how uncertain she was in her role of seductress. Overwhelmed by a surge of affection and protectiveness, he said, "You must use senses other than the obvious ones, other than those you were raised to trust. Watch closely; Gann is teaching Zarra not to depend on sight, which tends to overpower the other senses. When the boy gains confidence, he will be able to fight without visual clues."

Jas twisted a strand of hair around her finger, tighter and tighter. "So we're going to wear blindfolds. . . ."

"Not today," he assured her. "A genuine match is played in complete darkness."

She released the lock of hair, and whispered what

sounded suspiciously like one of her Earth swear words.

By the time Rom returned his attention to the arena, Gann had cornered his young opponent. Rom shot to his feet, his hands cupped around his mouth. "Parry, Zarra, parry!"

Zarra's mouth twisted uncertainly. Gann shot an annoyed glance upward. "Is it my day to instruct the lad, Rom? Or am I mistaken?"

Rom held up both hands and sat back down. The combatants resumed their drill. This time Zarra missed Gann by a foot. Rom slapped his hands against his thighs. "Too early!"

Jas smothered a laugh.

"What is so amusing?"

"Men and sports. You're all alike."

"Is that so?" he asked dryly. "I'm delighted to know I'm no different to you from any other man."

She hesitated for a heartbeat. "No, you are different." Her cheeks colored. "Better."

Disarmed by her honesty, Rom searched for a suitable reply and found none. Such openness was surely an enormous step for her, given the heartbreak of her severed marriage.

Below, Zarra peeled off his blindfold. Gann spoke to him in private, then patted the boy on the back. After collecting the equipment and packing it away, Zarra left for the hygiene showers next door. Gann threw a towel over one shoulder and climbed the stairs to where Jas and Rom were sitting. "The lad did well. I was beginning to question whether he'd inherited any of his father's blood at all."

"Zarra's father is *Vash Nadah*," Rom told Jas. "A distant B'kah relation. His mother was of the merchant class."

Gann sat behind Jas. He unzipped his Bajha suit and tugged off his gloves. Then he brought his mouth close to her ear. "Why don't you have Rom teach you how to play?"

"He's going to." She stretched her arms and arched her back with the sensual, restless grace of a ketta-cat. "A *private* lesson," she practically purred.

Without missing a beat, Rom matched the seductiveness in her voice. "As private as they come."

Gann's head pivoted from Jas to Rom. He lifted a brow and eyed Rom with interest. "I shall leave you two to your match, then. But go easy on him, Jas," he cautioned, grinning as he headed downstairs. "I fear he's out of practice."

As the doors slammed behind him, leaving the white-walled, featureless arena silent but for the steady hiss of the air circulators, Jas smoothed her hair away from her forehead. "Whew. The last thing we needed was an audience."

Rom's grin became positively rakish. "Agreed."

"No, I meant—" She stopped, laughing. "Well, I don't disagree. But my point was that compared to me, Zarra is an expert. My ego might allow me to make a fool of myself in front of you, but not Gann. Or anyone else on the crew."

"Bajha is different from the sports you may be used to. Don't be concerned. I will show you what to do." He took her hand and led her to the playing floor. He appeared taller and more powerful in the arena, and his body radiated heat like a furnace. "Besides," he said, his

171

grin twisting into an inscrutable smirk, "had you not gotten rid of Gann, I would have."

They exchanged knowing glances.

She waved her hand at the somewhat intimidating array of gear taking up most of the shelf space on the wall behind Rom. "What do we do?"

"First we change. Dressing rooms are to your right." He took a folded Bajha suit off the shelf, handed it to her, and she carried it into one of the snug curtained cubicles.

Inside, she leaned against the wall and closed her eyes. She'd crossed an imaginary start line, where the game of Bajha was but the first lap. She was in Rom's domain, *his* area of expertise—now and for the rest of the night.

Thrumming with anticipation and nerves, she lifted the one-piece white suit from its clear wrapper. It was stiff and coated with a protective, rubbery substance on the outside, but silky soft against her skin on the inside. A series of fastenings similar to Velcro ran from each ankle to the neck. By the time she closed them all she was perspiring. "Think adventure," she said under her breath, and pushed aside the curtain. Rolling her shoulders back, she strode into the arena in her stocking feet.

Rom was already dressed, and when he glimpsed her black woolen socks decorated with fluffy white sheep, he choked out a laugh.

"What?" She wriggled her toes.

"You choose to adorn yourself with . . . farm animals?" His eyes gleamed with mirth.

She stood proudly. "*Sheep,* we call them on Earth."

"Do all Earth women wear such"—he waved one hand at her feet—"foot coverings?"

She baited him. "When they're not wearing ones with little hearts or ducks or happy faces."

"Happy faces," he repeated flatly. Then he blinked, bringing himself back to the task at hand. "You'll need these." He stooped to reach for a pair of boots on the floor. His Bajha suit faithfully followed the outline of his thighs and the tight curve of his buttocks. "Try these on while I ready the equipment."

Her flexible white boots were as comfortable as slippers. She stood on her toes and stomped a couple of times. "If it's dark we won't see each other. But with these on, we won't be able to hear each other, either."

"Ah, but we will. Though not with our ears and eyes."

Doubtful, she asked, "With our neurons, right?"

"I'll explain." With reverence, he unpacked two blunt-tipped, roundish swords, handing her one. It was roughly the same size and weight as an aluminum baseball bat. Assaulted by images of Little League practice, she tapped it gingerly against the floor, causing the green glow emanating from within to pulse like a heartbeat.

"It's called a sens-sword." Rom reached around her from behind, curving his tall frame around her. "Hold it with two hands."

She aimed the weapon away from her body. Placing his hands over hers, he gripped the base with her, moving it slowly from side to side. It was hard to concentrate with his breath caressing her ear and her bottom nestled against his abdomen. His physical closeness aroused her immediately. She recalled his last kiss, and craved the feel of his mouth on hers.

"That's it, Jas. Good. Now we will talk about the senses you were born with, but have never fully used." He continued, unaware that his words had temporarily

173

tamped down her urge to turn in his arms for a kiss. "Certain neurons act as sensors for different parts of your body. Some are activated by movement. Others through touch. When an object is placed near that part of the body, the neuron responsible for that alert flicks on." He tightened his hands around hers. "Once trained, your body does not forget." His voice became softer, more intimate. "This is how we locate our lover's mouth in the dark. Did you know that?"

Speech eluded her. She shook her head. By accident or design, his whisker-roughened cheek brushed over hers. "The neurons remember. Then the sensors associated with your lips guide your mouth to the kiss."

That was all her neurons needed to hear. They went wild. They screamed and danced in circles. *Kiss him, you idiot! Kiss him now!*

But she paused, and, all business again, Rom backed away. Disgusted with her cowardice, her neurons howled and fell to their imaginary little knees.

"In this way, we will sense each other's presence in Bajha. You will find, at first, that you'll have to stop often to listen to what your body is telling you. But you'll learn. Someday these instincts will come to you as easily as walking or reading. Are you ready to begin?"

"Yes," she said as confidently as she could.

He circled her. She remained rooted in place, her club-like sword clutched in hands that were getting more moist by the minute. Then he disappeared behind her. Her stomach quivered.

"Are you afraid, Jas?"

She hesitated. "No."

"Good. You mustn't be," he said. "Our code instructs warriors to be cautious, not fearful." He stopped, facing her, his sens-sword held in his two large fists. "Say that. It will help you. 'I will be cautious, not fearful.' "

"I will be cautious, not fearful." Damn, but her heartbeat accelerated when he moved behind her again.

"Lights," he said, and absolute darkness swallowed them both.

Chapter Ten

Jas's hands clamped convulsively around the senss-
word, her lifeline in the most complete darkness she'd
ever known. Deprived of sight, she was acutely aware
of her body. Optical fireworks danced before her wide-
open eyes. She heard and felt the blood coursing through
her veins.

"Raise your sword," Rom said in a quiet, even tone.

She lifted the weapon into the blackness, concentrating on his footsteps. Were they getting closer or farther
away? She couldn't tell. And why did the sword cast no
illumination in the dark? She had no time to wonder.

"Do you trust me?" he asked.

I want to.

"Good," he whispered in answer to her silence.

"How did you—"

"Not mind reading, Jas. Intuition. Instinct."

More footsteps. She bit back her moan of alarm. It

was dark. And painfully quiet. She was clothed from head to toe in a protective suit. Yet, she felt naked. Vulnerable.

"Now we will play."

Rom's voice carried from across the arena, disorienting her.

She whirled to face the direction from where his voice had come. Or from where she'd *thought* it had come. Waving the sens-sword in front of her, testing its weight, she tried to see into the wall of black, tried to hear above the thundering of her heart. Then she felt it: a breeze, the hairs prickling on the back of her neck. She gasped as the tip of Rom's sens-sword dragged across her lower back, leaving behind a mild pins-and-needles sensation. "That hurt," she blurted indignantly.

"It shouldn't have." Rom sounded defensive and somewhat worried. "My sens-sword is tuned to the lowest setting."

"It didn't hurt my back." She swung her sens-sword in the direction of his voice, heard him step out of the way. "It hurt my pride!"

He chuckled.

She bolted toward the sound. She'd get him now.

Her sens-sword jammed into something solid and slightly giving. A vibration shuddered up the weapon to her arm and into her chest an instant before she slammed into one of the padded walls. "Damn."

"Never act purely out of emotion," soothed Rom's deep voice from the far side of the arena. "Use your senses. Trust them. For they will bring you to me."

He's coming toward you, warned her inner voice.

She arched away. Rom stumbled past, and she cried out in delight.

177

"Excellent! However, triumph often leads to complacency."

To prove his point he tapped her on both kneecaps with his sens-sword. She briefly saw a green glow before a shower of hot tingles suffused her knees and calves. "Hey, you turned up the level."

He laughed at her accusation. "You're catching on too quickly. I had to raise the stakes."

"Thanks a lot. What's *my* sens-sword tuned to, by the way?"

"Seventy-five percent of maximum."

"Won't that hurt you?" she asked worriedly.

"A lingering sting," he replied, this time from well behind her. "Nothing more."

"Good. Prepare to feel that seventy-five percent in places you'd rather not."

She heard his bark of laughter—from the right. Sword extended, she spun slowly, around and around, reaching deep within her, tapping into a reservoir of what she sensed had always been there.

It came in a rush: the essence of Rom's generous and wounded heart.

My soul mate.

She sought him with her weapon, reaching instinctively, symbolically, for the love she'd always longed for but had never found.

He inhaled sharply. Her blunt sword skimmed along the fabric of his suit, but did not contact hard enough to signal a hit. She felt his surprise in her very bones. "Almost got you, Rom!" She laughed with the joy of it.

"Enjoying yourself?"

She lunged. "Very much."

His sens-sword slapped against the back of her thighs.

"Not so much." She winced at the brief pinpricks. "You'll pay for that."

"We shall see," he replied playfully.

Use your senses.

She paused . . . listening.

But not with her ears.

Saw . . .

But not with her eyes.

Hunting him in the darkness, she resumed the exhilarating and oddly arousing game of cat and mouse. Once more she grazed him, barely, only to receive a punishing whack in return on her bottom. She sucked in a breath and lowered her sens-sword. Tingling heat lingered between her legs. Suddenly the game lost its appeal; she hungered for Rom's touch, not that of a dispassionate, cybernetic weapon.

Setting her sens-sword on the floor, she slowed her breathing and stood still. If neurons could remember, then maybe hers could remember Rom's kisses. *She* certainly hadn't forgotten. She'd never been kissed the way he kissed her. It was more than his consummate skill; it was his tenderness, the intense passion she sensed he fought so hard to control, and his obvious enjoyment of the act itself.

She willed her lips to remember it all, and for his to remember hers. Then, with all the yearning in her soul, she willed him to want her as much as she wanted him.

She waited. . . .

Concentrated harder.

And waited . . .

Her lips tingled. Then she caught his scent, as if she were an animal in a primeval forest. Her nostrils flared.

So close now . . .

There. His lips, warm and smooth, brushed over hers. She let out the tiniest of sighs, magnified in the pounding silence.

He lingered, teased, sipped.

Arms limp at her sides, she opened her mouth in blatant invitation. Without touching her in any other way, he covered her mouth with his, kissing her deeply, passionately, the sensation of moist, searching heat powerfully erotic in the hushed darkness. She made a needy groan into his mouth. Anchored in nothingness by the kiss, wanting more, much more, she flung her arms over his shoulders.

He splayed one hand behind her head, crushing her to him. Her hands twisted in the fabric at his collar, teasing the ends of his hair, which was damp with perspiration. Pulling away, she dragged breathless, openmouthed kisses along his jaw and neck, tasting the salt on his skin, wanting to devour him.

"Jasmine, wait," she heard him say as if from miles away.

She was beyond language, beyond reason. With the tip of her tongue, she explored the precisely cut, silky hair by his ear. "Rom—oh, Rom." She worked her way from his ear to his beard-roughened chin, then suckled his tender lower lip.

He mumbled something and squeezed her shoulders, gently moving her back. "Lights," he said.

She blinked, as much from the sudden brightness as the disorientation of her arousal. Then she lowered her forehead to his chest. "I'm sorry."

"Great Mother, don't be. I certainly am not. But our privacy is not guaranteed here." He hesitated, tilting her head back, his thumb under her chin. "Privacy is what we want, isn't it?" His eyes had darkened with desire to the color of rich sherry. In their depths she saw a question far beyond the mere issue of being alone.

"Yes," she said on a sharp breath. "Privacy." *And more.*

She longed to feel like a real woman again.

His gaze was oddly perceptive, as if he could read her thoughts. If only he could, then tonight might be so much easier. Tightening her arms around his waist, she played with the soft hair at the nape of his neck. He arched into her kneading fingers ever so slightly, then seemed to catch himself. Pressing his hand to the small of her back, he steered her toward the dressing room. "I'll wait for you in my quarters."

"I'd like to shower first." Plucking at her damp Bajha suit, she felt her playfulness return. "How about it, Captain? My *second* of the day."

"Permission granted," he murmured, and settled his mouth over hers.

"It's me," Jas called to the tiny viewscreen above the entrance to Rom's quarters. The doors parted and she walked inside. Already the room was aglow and scented. Music played, barely audible, but loud enough to add to the atmosphere. Rom B'kah was a master at setting the stage for seduction. But then, unlike her, he'd had plenty of practice.

"Greetings, Jasmine." He crossed the room to meet her. His hair was still damp from his shower, and he'd combed it away from his face. His white shirt, glowing with a pearl-like iridescence, was tucked into a pair of snug buff-colored trousers, half-hidden by soft knee-high boots. His overt confidence and precisely groomed appearance made her stomach clench all over again. *Girl, you're out of your league.*

His appreciative gaze skimmed over her conservative floral skirt and lavender sweater, halting at the two bottles of Red Rocket Ale she clutched in her hands. "Since you introduced me to star-berry liqueur, tonight I thought I'd introduce you to my favorite drink."

He took the bottles and squinted at the label. "An Earth beverage?"

"Yes. Beer. My friend Dan Brady's Red Rocket Ale."

He peered at the lids. "Interesting. How are they opened?"

She dangled a bottle opener from one finger. "First get them as cold as you can without freezing them."

Rom opened the door to a small rectangular compartment in the wall, then punched a code into the adjacent control panel. The chiller hummed on. Seconds later he removed the frosty bottles and carried them to the triangular dinner table, where he had arranged a simple meal of cold meat, flat bread, salt, and two different kinds of preserved fruit. She tucked her legs under her and arranged some pillows behind her back. Crouched by her side, he watched her pry the lids off the bottles, staring at the five-dollar opener in her hand as if it were a wondrous and exotic marvel of technology. She chuckled at his boyish curiosity and placed a bottle in his hand. Vapor floated upward along with the tangy scent of ale. "Go on, try it."

His tone was pointedly suggestive. "Take your pleasure first," he said. "I'll watch you."

Her heart did a little flip. She sipped, trying hard not to look at his mouth. The single swallow of cold, crisp beer did nothing to cool her desire. He must have heard her overheated neurons rattling their cages, because he leaned closer and pressed his lips to the side of her throat. Shutting her eyes, she breathed in his exotic and distinctly male scent, while her hands rode the flexing of the muscles in his iron-hard thighs. When she lifted her chin and offered him the arch of her neck, he caressed her with his hot breath, nuzzling his way lower. She hunched her shoulders and shivered.

"Perhaps we should sample our beverages," he said softly. "For in another moment I doubt either of us will be interested."

"Interested in what?" she whispered dazedly.

Grinning, he lifted the bottle to his lips. His golden eyes flashed, and he tipped the bottle for a longer swig. "Ah! This is delicious. Tell me again what you called this."

"Beer."

"Beer," he said with reverence. "Salt, bah! *This* is reason enough to trade with Earth. Does the document you brought me contain a provision to obtain beer?"

"It sure does. Dan's beer."

"Good man, this Dan Brady." Rom closed his eyes and swallowed. Fascinated by the sensual pleasure he took in a simple bottle of ale, she propped her elbow on the table, her head on her hand, and watched him until he'd finished. "I want to taste you," she confessed, to her own utter amazement.

His Adam's apple wobbled. "Yes, I want you to," he said quietly and set aside his empty bottle. "Tell me, Jas: in what ways can I please you tonight? What are your desires?"

Her face heated. She was not used to verbalizing her intimate needs—no one had ever asked her. Long ago she'd grown used to burying them. But in the spotlight of Rom's patient gaze, the words came out easier than she expected. "Just make love to me. That's all."

"Know this," he said quietly. "I do not take your gift lightly. You offer me your woman's body, your mother's body. In this I am blessed." He dragged his thumb across her mouth, tenderly tracing the shape of her lips, immersing her in a kind of intimacy beyond her experience.

Spellbound, she saw all her tomorrows in his eyes. But she shoved aside the dangerous thought even as goose bumps covered her arms. This was exactly what had gotten her into trouble before. *Don't hope for a future with him,* she warned herself. *Just enjoy the moment, and you won't get hurt.* But a little voice, silenced for years, tugged on her mental sleeve. *This is different,* it insisted. *This time it's real.*

He reached into one of the bowls of fruit, plucking out what resembled a glistening black cherry. Holding it with two fingers, he offered it to her. A droplet of juice trembled on its plump underside, and she caught the moisture with the tip of her tongue. Rom's pupils dilated. Encouraged by his response, Jas placed her hands on his thighs and slid them upward. Hard muscles bunched beneath her palms. She skimmed her lips over the heel of his palm and the inside of his wrist before curling her tongue suggestively under the little fruit, taking playful bites until it was completely inside her mouth. Sweet heat pooled low in her belly, and her pulse quickened between her legs. It was astonishing how arousing food-play could be without further physical touching. Of course, the *Vash* had figured that out eons ago.

The tart, crunchy little fruit left her palate feeling

clean and fresh. Swallowing, she sorted through the bowl and chose another, lifting it to his mouth. Clearly the expert, he alternately teased his tongue over the glistening taut skin and suckled. Her nipples puckered under the sheer, tight fabric of her bra.

"I want to do this to you, Jas," he whispered, his eyes heavy-lidded. "Would that please you? If I kissed you like this? If I kissed you everywhere?" Mortified, she heard a sigh escape her.

His expression changed to one of satisfaction. Observing her from under his dark lashes, he took her finger fully into his slick mouth. His deft tongue rasped the underside of her finger. Her toes curled. It wasn't hard to imagine what his tongue could do to the rest of her.

When she withdrew her finger, he reached over and swirled his own in the dark crimson liquid pooled at the bottom of the bowl of fruit. As he had once done with the star-berry liqueur, he moistened her bottom lip with the sweet juice. "Another berry?" he inquired. She shook her head. "You've had enough to eat, then?"

"Of berries." She burrowed her fingers in his thick, silky hair. "But not of you."

A groan vibrated in his throat and he rose to his knees, pulling her toward him and into a kiss. His tongue was slow and sure, cherishing rather than demanding. She adored the way he took his time exploring her mouth. In fact, she adored the way he took his time doing everything. He so drugged her with his delicious kisses and skillful caresses that the feel of his warm and rough palm slipping under her sweater came as a shock—albeit a welcome one.

His mouth muffled her sigh. The kiss deepened with an increased mutual urgency, and he slid his hands upward to cup her breasts, lifting them, skimming her taut, sensitive nipples with the pads of his thumbs. "Beautiful," he whispered. "Beautiful woman."

Drinking in his words, she arched forward until she felt the ridge of male flesh beneath his pants pressing into her. Instinctively she rubbed against him, as much as their kneeling position would allow. His breath came faster and his arousal strained even more beneath his snug trousers.

"*Inajh d'anah,*" he murmured. "My sweet Jasmine." He tugged her sweater over her head, distracting her from the sudden vulnerability by kissing her throat and that wonderfully sensitive hollow just below her ear. By the time he lifted her to her feet and led her to his bed, she was putty.

Dazed and almost painfully aroused, she sat perched on the plump, silken coverlet while he crouched between her legs. He removed her pumps, then her skirt, leaving her dressed only in her lace underwear as he struggled out of his boots and pants. She glimpsed his arousal jutting against his undergarment—a flap of shimmering ivory silk wrapped low on his narrow hips—before he came to her again. More kissing, incredible kissing.

Running his hands appreciatively down the long, bare length of her legs, he spread his hands wide under her knees, stroking her, kneading her muscles, appearing to derive an inordinate amount of pleasure from the simple caresses. She leaned back on her arms, savoring the singular joy of this man's clear enjoyment of her body.

"So incredibly smooth," he said, massaging the long muscles under her calves. "Like Nandan silk. I've never known a woman to remove the hair here." Bending forward, lowering his head, he nuzzled, nipped, and tasted his way up her legs. Her eyes drifted closed with the pleasure of it, and she curled her toes behind his back.

She felt the slight roughness of his cheek on the tender skin of her inner thighs, then his thumbs slipping under the waistband of her panties. He eased off the garment, but did not touch her where she so desperately wanted him to, the moist place thrumming for his touch. She whimpered in need, and he seized her wrists, pulling her to a sitting position. He kissed her hard, and her thighs fell open to accommodate his swaying hips, setting up an exquisite friction against her sensitive flesh.

Her fingers clumsy with urgency, she unfastened the remaining closures on his shirt, slipping it off his broad, sinewy shoulders to revel in the feel and the scent of his hot, bare skin. He shrugged off the shirt, wadded it, and tossed it aside.

An ugly, jagged-edged scar marring his chest caught her off guard. It arched from his right nipple to where it ended below his ribs on his left side. "My God, Rom, what happened?" Embarrassed by her shocked reaction, Jas felt heat rush to her face.

He gripped her arms, his golden eyes burning bright. Sweat glistened on his forehead and chest. "Touch me."

Barely breathing, she lifted trembling fingers to the old wound, tracing the cool, bumpy flesh, an appalling contrast to the rest of his smooth, bronzed skin. He had so little body fat on his torso that every muscle, every tendon, every vein was clearly defined, perfectly sculpted, making the scar that much more out of place.

"What do you see?" he whispered.

Something tugged at her subconscious. She blinked, trying to decipher what she sensed she was supposed to remember. "You were wounded in the war. . . ."

His fingers pressed into the bare skin of her upper arms. "Yes." He appeared poised for some revelation. But it seemed she was incapable of supplying it.

"This should have killed you," she said as frustration swelled inside her.

"But it didn't, Jasmine. It *didn't*." His mouth came down over hers, hard and hungry, desperate and wanting, and his lithe, powerful frame drove her backward onto the mattress.

Chapter Eleven

He kissed her with the fierce tenderness of a warrior returning home to a lover. Jas's arms closed over his shoulders as she met his urgency with a consequences-be-damned hunger of her own. By the time his mouth moved to her bra, she had sunk into carnal oblivion.

She heard a muttered curse, then came a slight tugging at her bra. "I've never seen such an undergarment," Rom lamented irritably.

Her eyes flew open. Wearing a look of intense concentration on his face, he was fumbling with the front clasp. She swallowed a laugh of crazy relief and joy—even for this man of galactic experience, apparently there was a first time. "What do *Vash* women wear to support their breasts?"

"Not *this*."

"It's easier to open than a bottle of beer." That made him chuckle. "I'll show you," she said softly. They un-

189

fastened her bra together, and then her breasts were heavy and free, every flaw, every stretch mark exposed to his hot scrutiny. Suddenly she wished the lights were lower—a lot lower.

But he was gazing at her breasts in awe.

Awe?

This was crazy.

When he skimmed his fingertip over one of the faint silvery lines emanating from her right nipple, she wanted to die. She tried rolling into a position where she wouldn't be so exposed. He snatched her wrists and pushed her back down. "Don't look at me there," she pleaded.

His voice was husky and thick. "Please don't deny me this pleasure. These attest to your motherhood. You are a woman, a beautiful woman." And then he kissed her. . . .

There.

And there. Every silvery line.

This wasn't happening. She couldn't possibly be with a man who was turned on by stretch marks. Shifting position, he leaned over her, the sinewy muscles in his arms flexing as he took her nipple into his mouth.

The gentle, insistent suction reignited the heat between her legs, and a moment later two long, agile fingers slid inside her. She let out a strangled gasp. He rotated the heel of his hand over her sensitive core, bringing her swiftly to the verge of release. Mindless with need, she clutched at his shoulders, rolled her hips. Then her insides clenched.

At the first tremor, he almost stopped stroking her. She made a whimper of protest, but he murmured in her ear, "Not yet, not nearly yet," soothing her with kisses and lyrical words in his native language. Again, he worked his erotic magic and she climbed higher than before. Each time she was about to peak, he backed off until the moment had passed, then started all over again.

The hot, aching pleasure-pain built until it was almost too much, and she fumbled for his wrist to hold him close. She couldn't bear it if he stopped again.

"No, Jas," he whispered tightly, his breath hot on her ear. "We will go together." He knelt between her legs, his arm supporting one thigh, and raised her leg over his back.

Laser-light illuminated his golden brown hair and shadowed his face. As she clung to his broad shoulders, he began to push into her, thick and hard. Every muscle in her body went rigid. He sensed the change and paused.

She wanted him—oh, God, how she wanted him! But this would all go wrong; despite her desperate state of arousal, her muscles would clamp closed, as they had frequently during the last years of her marriage. If Rom managed to penetrate at all, her pain would ruin it for them both.

Eyes squeezed shut, she panted in both fear and embarrassment. The past had caught up with her—every bad memory. She'd thought she could run away, but it had kept pace with her every step of the way.

"Jas, open your eyes." Rom was whispering to her; maybe he had been for some time. "Come now, my angel, look at me." He kissed each eyelid in turn. "It's me. *Rom.* I won't let another man's misdeeds keep us apart. It will be good with us," he promised, stroking her hair. "You'll see."

"I'm sorry," she began, mortified for him, for her.

"Hush. Put your hands over my shoulders. That's it. Hold me. If at any time you don't like what I'm doing, tell me, and I will stop." He waited for her nod, then spread his hands on the rumpled sheets, supporting his weight, his shoulders rigid and gleaming with sweat. Then he dipped his head to kiss her, deep, incredibly erotic kisses, as he rubbed her intimately with the tip of his penis. Once again, the pleasure began to build. She pushed her hips against him, moaning softly.

"Trust me, Jas," he murmured, his gaze knowing, expectant, as if he understood every nuance of the doubt and desire warring inside her. "Let me love you."

At her barely perceptible nod, he slipped his arm under her left thigh, his splayed hand supporting her bottom. Then he tipped his pelvis and entered her.

Her body resisted him at first, but he drove slowly forward. There was an exquisite stretching, a delicious pressure; then he filled her completely, pushing until he could go no farther. They stayed like that for long heartbeats, his face buried between her neck and shoulder, her arms twined around him. She felt his heat, every ridge of his deeply seated flesh. Then he began to move.

And, oh, Lord, did he move: withdrawing halfway, he glided deep inside her, then out, angling himself so that he created friction over the precise center of her pleasure. She caught his hair in her fists, heard herself moan his name. Ecstasy washed over her with each roll of his hips. The heat and tension built . . . until at last she gave a shuddering cry and helplessly convulsed around him.

"Squeeze me hard," he said in a gasp. "It will delay you and bring you more pleasure." Eagerly she gripped him with her inner muscles. A ragged groan escaped his lips. "Yes, my *Inajh d'anah.* Yes." He ground himself against her, rotating his pelvis as they kissed, their embrace primal and raw.

She clung to him, overwhelmed by the force of their passion, the coming together of bodies and souls, an experience so new, so intense, that it brought tears to her eyes. Trembling inside and out, she ached for release. When she could hold back no longer, she pushed hard into his thrusts, throbbing around him, and found the most joyously vivid climax of her life.

Light exploded around her.

Enveloping her in a litany of exotic words—lyrical sounds infused with love and praise—Rom hugged her close and rolled them over. She landed on top of him, breathless and still dazed. He covered her mouth in a lush, openmouthed kiss, guiding her hips, coaxing her into a sensual, swaying dance that matched his continued thrusts.

"Jas," he said on a burst of breath. And then, as he gripped her upper arms, heat pumped into her—his essence, his glorious release. In that endless moment, the tension melted from his body. Amazingly, he didn't roll to his side and away from her. Instead, still inside her, he cradled her head in his hands and took his time exploring her mouth, then her face, affectionately nipping kisses along her nose and chin and brows.

She smoothed her fingers through his damp hair, enjoying its fragrance. *"Inajh d'anah,"* she said languidly. "What does it mean?"

"It's difficult to translate Siennan to Basic. Siennan is a language of love. Basic is the language of trade." Concentrating, he caught and twirled her hair in his fingers.

"The best I can do is, 'flesh of my flesh.' It's an endearment. Like 'beloved.' But more than that."

"It's a beautiful word, either way," she said softly. She eased off him to lie on the mattress, tucking her head in the scented hollow between his shoulder and chest, absently caressing his abdomen, the softness under his navel, the only softness on his entire upper body. She murmured, *"Omlajh anah,"* recalling more of the words he'd said during their lovemaking.

His chuckle grew into a full-fledged laugh. She leaned over him. "What's so funny? I'm sure I heard you say that a few minutes ago."

He wiped his eyes. "The phrase is said to a woman, not a man."

She pretended to glare at him. "Why? Is it condescending?"

"Not in the least. *Omlajh anah.* It describes . . . how good I feel when I'm inside you."

"You actually have words in Siennan that describe *that?*"

"Yes, and more, many more."

She cuddled closer. "What should I have said to you, then? When you were inside me and making me so crazy?"

Even without seeing his handsome face, she knew he smiled. *"Omlajh dah,"* he replied, lightly caressing her back.

"It almost sounds the same."

"Many of the words do. Siennan is a language of subtle differences."

"Must be difficult to learn."

He kissed her hair. "It was my first language, so I

wouldn't know. I'll teach it to you. Would you like that?"

She lifted her head. "If the rest of the lessons are as good as this one, you bet I would."

He pushed himself up to a sitting position. Mesmerized by his muscled torso gleaming in the laser-light, Jas watched him wedge several cushions between his back and the bedside wall. Then he beckoned to her, arms wide, his mouth curved into a grin that was inviting, devilish, and very male. "The rest of the lessons will be better," he said.

The safety and trust she felt in his presence brought out her playfulness. "If not, we'll have to repeat them."

He laughed softly. "One by one."

"Deal," she said, and smiled, wondering briefly when she'd last thought of sex as fun. Simmering with anticipation, she caught his outstretched hands and eased herself astride him.

A familiar chiming dragged Jas half-awake. Then she felt Rom's comforting heat slip from her arms. She groped sleepily for him, but when she opened her eyes, he was already sitting on the opposite edge of the bed, facing the viewscreen on the wall. According to the bedside clock, they'd been asleep for only a few hours. Who'd be calling this early?

Rom hit the answer panel. "Go."

"A very good morning to you, B'kah," a man's melodious voice said. "It took you long enough to answer." There was a pause, then, "Thought you would like to know we're three hours out."

Jas froze. The last traces of slumber evaporated. Gann's face filled the viewscreen next to the bed in the darkened room, and only Rom's shoulder blocked him from a full view of her nude body. If Rom moved . . .

He did. Propping his elbows on his knees, Rom groggily scratched his fingers through his hair. "Have we entered comm range yet?"

"Affirmative."

Jas's face heated. *Think, think.* The coverlet. It was twisted somewhere near her knees. She sent her left hand on a covert mission, inching it lower, lower . . . lower. *Contact!* She tugged hard and clutched the bunched fabric to her breasts.

"On my way," Rom replied, heedless of her embarrassment.

"Gann out."

The viewscreen went blank.

Jas made a wretched moan.

Rom's twisted around and stretched, his mouth curving into a sexy, sleepy smile. His hair was ruffled from sleep, his cheek creased from the pillow. "Morning, angel."

"Your second-in-command just saw me naked." As if to punctuate that fact, her breasts jiggled under the silken coverlet as she spoke.

"He wasn't looking."

"How could he not see? It's a viewscreen fact—if I saw him, he saw me. Being that I was sleeping when you answered," she added sourly, "tact would have dictated covering me up."

Rom rolled on top of her, and his body heat seared her through the thin blanket. Supporting his weight with one arm, he moved aside her hair and nuzzled her neck. "You haven't said good morning."

"You're changing the subject," she admonished tenderly. Wrapping her arms over his shoulders, she gave him a slow, sensual kiss.

"That will suffice," he murmured. "Now . . . back to your allegation. Let us assume that Gann noticed your state of undress. He is, after all, a man." Rom lifted a lock of her hair to his lips, then brushed it across his jaw, inhaling deeply as he did so. "But he's a man of discretion. He maintained eye contact with me the entire time we spoke."

"Didn't any of the others object to being caught in the nude? Or am I the only one?"

He tilted his head. "Others? What others?"

"The other women."

She tamped down on the hurt those words brought her. "If it didn't bother them," she went on, "then I won't let it bother me. My friend Betty told me I'm too old-fashioned. I'm trying to change that, really, but I've been away from home for only a few weeks. I expect it takes a while to blossom into a truly wild and wanton woman. But I've made progress, though. I mean, look at me now—"

Rom clamped his hand over her mouth. "May I say something?" Nodding vigorously, she mumbled something into his palm. He lifted his hand tentatively. "Apparently we are having a misunderstanding, language-induced or cultural; I'm not sure. But there have never been any other women."

She whooped in disbelief. "Oh, please. Am I actually supposed to believe that you were a virgin? I bet you're going to sell me some beachfront property in Arizona next."

"Rest assured, I am not a virgin." Further reminding her of that fact, he nestled his swelling member between her legs. Her eyes drifted half-closed, and she raised her knees. He sucked in a breath and clamped his teeth together. "Great Mother," he muttered. "I should have been at the bridge five minutes ago."

"Gann's used to this by now," she reasoned. "I'm probably the hundredth woman, or maybe the thousandth—"

"Thousandth!" Rom roared.

"But I don't care," she said with a sigh, "because last night was wonderful. Actually, it was better than wonderful and—"

This time he silenced her by covering her mouth with his, kissing her thoroughly. By the time he pulled away, they were both breathless. "You are the first woman I have had in this bed," he said huskily. "And the only one I have made love to on this ship."

"Really?" Jas asked softly. Then she narrowed her eyes. "How long have you owned the *Quillie?*"

"Ten standard years. No, it's been eleven now."

Her heard soared. She was used to being last in line to many. This was a lovely change. Everything about Rom was a lovely change. "Thank you."

Rom stroked her hair and slowly lowered his mouth to hers, loving her without words. Her breasts tingled, and she throbbed between her legs, both from last night's lovemaking and from the need he was now kindling within her. She molded her hands to his buttocks, and the kiss caught fire.

He made a rough sound deep in his throat. Pushing away, he held himself above her, arms extended. Passion had turned his eyes to molten gold, but when he spoke, it was with his ever-present discipline. "I'm needed on the bridge. There is much to do before we dock."

She toyed with suggesting something quick and hot, but instinct told her that Rom wouldn't settle for rushed sex. For him the seduction, the foreplay, and even the cuddling afterward, were all integral parts of lovemaking. "After I change and finish packing, I'll meet you there."

He gave her a light, affectionate kiss before climbing out of bed and walking to the shower enclosure. He stepped inside. The hiss of water filled the silence. When he emerged moments later, he looked wet, sexy, and delicious. Muffling a whimper, she watched him dry off.

She'd heard the term *good breeding* before, but she had never truly understood what it meant. Until now. Rom's whipcord lean, tightly muscled body was the product of eons of carefully arranged marriages, eleven thousand years of powerful warriors joining with beautiful women. His looks were the best of what the galaxy could offer. Yet it was his inner strength, his generous spirit and innate kindness, that drew her to him, beyond all else—beyond even the persistent familiarity that had compelled her since the moment she'd first seen him.

Wrapping the coverlet around herself, she hopped out of bed. "Being with you is magical, you know that? I don't trust magic, not at all. But"—she seductively lowered her lashes—"I'm enjoying every bit of yours."

He gathered her wrap in his fists, drawing her close to nuzzle under her ear. "Magic and dreams light our life's path. Trust . . ." He moved his mouth down her throat. "Believe."

Dreams come true.

The absurd phrase rang inside her. Believing in fairy tales and magic was frivolous, childish . . . dangerous. But damned if the man didn't make a convincing argument. It was as if everything she'd taught herself, for protection, was wrong. She hooked her fingers in the waistband of his pants and closed her eyes. He maneuvered the coverlet lower, baring her shoulders, following the ridge of her collarbone with his tongue. Her knees almost buckled. "How about we make some magic in bed?"

"I can't." He grazed his teeth over her shoulder. "I'm needed on—"

"—the bridge," she chorused impatiently and clutched the coverlet around her with prim determination. "Then go, will you? There's only so much a woman can take."

"Or a man, for that matter." He admitted. "Open," he commanded then. The doors to his clothing storage compartment parted. Shaking out a plush bundle of fabric, he drew it over her shoulders. "We'll need cloaks when we arrive. The Depot is cool and damp year-round."

The luxurious, deep green velvety wrap fell in a graceful swirl before settling just above her ankles. He fastened the heavy cape at her neck. The gold clasp was genuine, she suspected, weighty and engraved with the same symbols as Rom's signet ring.

Scrutinizing her, he lifted the voluminous hood over her tousled hair. "It's best that you don't call attention to yourself while awaiting my return from Skull's Doom. Your hair color will get you noticed, whether you want it to or not. Keep it covered."

What kind of wild and woolly world was she headed into? The reporter who had preceded her to the Depot, Kendall Smith, had black hair, and he hadn't mentioned anyone suggesting *he* wear a hat. She rubbed her cheek against her extravagant new garment's silk lining. "It's so soft. Nandan?"

He nodded. "The shell is Centaurian velvet."

"It's beautiful, thank you. I'll make sure it's still in the same condition in sixth months." *When I have to go home to Earth,* she left unsaid.

He waved his hand, casually dismissing her comment, yet for a moment his eyes held some deeper emotion. Briefly he smoothed his warm palm over her cheek, then turned away to fasten his pants.

Keeping the cape wrapped around her, Jas shrugged off the coverlet and let it fall to the floor. As she folded it and placed it on the bed, she reveled in the sinful feel of the Nandan fabric caressing her bare skin.

"You'll need this, too," he said, rummaging through the drawer of his bedside table until he found a narrow black leatherlike case. "My comm call." He pressed a gleaming metallic object the size and weight of a cheap plastic hair comb into her hand. "A thigh strap, too." He demonstrated, fastening its thin black strap around his upper leg like a garter belt.

"Rom, I'm going to be alone for all of two days—"

"What if I'm delayed? An unlikely possibility, but one nonetheless. Or what if you need to contact me for some reason?"

She spread her hands in surrender.

"Fit the comm call into the sling. It's preset to signal the *Quillie* from anywhere in the galaxy. Simply find a comm box, drop it in, and call."

Jas remembered the reporter mentioning comm boxes. They were everywhere, even the frontier, and were used as frequently as pay phones were on Earth. But the comm call he had demonstrated on television bore no similarity to this sleek piece of equipment. Nor did it have the kind of range Rom described. "I can't take this,

Rom. It looks expensive. What if it gets damaged? Or I lose it?"

He wrenched his boots on. "Yes, the device is costly, and yes, it's available to only a few." His mouth twisted. "A perk leftover from my days as the B'kah heir. I keep it for emergencies. But I want you to have it. Should you encounter any difficulties while I'm gone, use it to call me."

His tone was brusque, but the protectiveness underneath was obvious. And touching. "Thank you." She couldn't recall the last time anyone had looked out for her so thoroughly. That had always been her job—taking care of herself and everyone else.

Rom strode to the door. "We won't have much time. I'll have to escort you to your accommodations as soon as we dock if I'm going to make it back here by our scheduled departure."

"The Romjha."

"Correct." His mouth thinned in distaste.

She pondered the odd reaction. Was there something wrong with the Romjha? The reporter had stayed there, and everyone on the crew said it was luxurious.

The doors whisked closed before Rom could enlighten her further. Ah, well, she told herself, gathering her things, she'd find out soon enough, wouldn't she?

Chapter Twelve

"Stay close to the storefronts and avoid the alleys, particularly at night," Rom cautioned with a sidelong glance at Jas. Since they'd disembarked from the shuttlecraft that brought them from the *Quillie*, he'd recited all the advice he'd gleaned from a lifetime of frequenting gritty outposts like the Depot. Appearing mildly amused at times, shocked at others, she'd heeded his warnings of terrorists and anti–*Vash Nadah* protests, and listened raptly to his words on how not to be cheated when exchanging her salt for currency. Through it all, her eyes had glowed bright with anticipation.

He shook his head in exasperation. Had she any idea how difficult it was for him to let her out of his protection? She was a warrior once, he reminded himself, forcing himself not to construe her relative innocence as helplessness. Then why couldn't he shake his sense of foreboding?

He tightened his grip around her hand, drawing her closer until his cloak billowed around hers. It was a move designed as much to shield her from the crowd as it was to keep her near him a bit longer. He took the most direct route through the main business district, pointing out a gritty sprawl of aging brushed-silver buildings along the way. "Auxiliary Trade Headquarters," he explained. "Three thousand years ago they were built from a material that supposedly does not deteriorate over time."

Jas raised her brows. "What happened?"

"Lack of attention, complacency, apathy. The list goes on and on. Much like the *Vash Nadah* federation itself."

She touched his arm. "You still care a great deal about *Vash* politics, about the future, don't you?"

"Yes." The realization disturbed him profoundly. "I value my heritage," he said quietly. "I cannot abide policies that jeopardize its future." He'd thought himself beyond the ache of guilt, beyond caring. But his reaction to Jas's remark proved he still did. "I'm an entrepreneur," he said flatly. "I don't care to see a poorly operated business when I know it can be run better. Trade lines are breaking down. Where there was once plenty, shortages abound. Who do you think the inhabitants of those planets will blame for their empty stomachs? Heed my words. It is only a matter of time before someone uses their discontent in his favor."

"Someone like Sharron," she suggested grimly.

Rom did not want to sour their time together with bitter memories. "Look over there," he said with forced lightness, changing the subject. "The art museum. And right next door, the library. Both well stocked, and always empty of crowds."

"Empty? Why?"

"Those who come here tend to seek profit, not culture."

She laughed. As he pointed out more landmarks she might find interesting, he mulled over her earlier comment, about how he cared. Perhaps it was not so much caring as it was habit. He'd been raised to view his life on a grand scale—galactic politics, the allocation of resources, the supervision of countless worlds. Even his marriage would have been seen as an alliance. Before his banishment, rarely had something as mundane and insignificant as his personal future crossed his mind. Even afterward, he had thought of his ship, his men.

Until he saw a future that included Jas.

So the jaded trader wants to settle down, eh? The jest in his mind was in Gann's voice, a man who would be pleased to see him do just that. Rom's thoughts raced ahead. He would buy that moon, build the small port he'd constructed countless times in his mind. Jas could join him in the venture. He fought the crazy urge to sweep her into his arms and beg her to be his partner. His lover for life. But what of her children? They lived on Earth. How could he in good conscience lure her to stay far away from them when he could not offer her respectability, or even his name?

"Oh, look!" Jas peeked out from under her hood. "A market."

"Then let us see what bargains await." He dared not meet her gaze until he gained control of his emotions. But his mood lifted as she led the way toward a vendor selling glow-jewelry. Only Jas could make the Depot seem exciting and new.

"They're luminescent," she said, wide-eyed. "All of them."

To the vendor's delight, she gaped at his unimpressive selection as if they were priceless jewels. Loath to dampen her enthusiasm, Rom declined to tell her how common the trinkets were. "Highest quality," the merchant cajoled. Glancing at Rom he conceded wisely, "Lowest prices."

"Ilana would adore these earrings," Jas said. "And I can't leave without getting something for my friend Betty." She fumbled with her waist pouch, where she'd stored her currency cards.

He settled his hand on the small of her back. "Put your money away. I will purchase the gifts. Choose something for yourself, as well. Which bauble shall I buy you?" he asked indulgently.

Her eager expression softened. "I can't let you pay."

"Why ever not?"

"You've done too much for me already."

Rom regretted all he could *not* give her. He removed her hand from her pouch. "Please."

She bit her lower lip and returned her attention to the cheap jewelry. Together they chose Ilana's earrings, a ring for her woman friend, and then a bracelet similar in width to the ones Jas wore. Rom slipped it onto her pale, slender wrist. Angling her arm this way and that, as if the glow-bracelet might look different in what little sunlight seeped through the low morning overcast, she admired the purchase. Then, for the second time in as many minutes, she cast a narrow-eyed glance behind her. Rom hitched her travel bag higher on his shoulder and searched the crowd. "What is it?"

She hesitated before answering. "Nothing, I guess. Just my imagination running wild."

"I've probably made you jumpy with all my warnings." He laced his fingers with hers and coaxed her along. The time he could spare here was diminishing quickly, and he cursed the fact that he could not spend the day with her in bed at the Romjha. Last night's joining had touched him profoundly; she had introduced him to an aspect of lovemaking he had never experienced, one that was deeply emotional—and equally as unforgettable. But the departure slots assigned by the Depot flight authorities were rigidly enforced. With hundreds of vessels coming in and out all hours of the day, a late takeoff could lose him the privilege of ever trading here again. In two standard days you'll have six months with her, he told himself.

He steered Jas into a maze of dank alleyways. Their boots sloshed in unison through oily puddles. Here, an incense shop didn't quite hide the pungent, metallic odor of hundreds of spacecraft hovering just above the low-slung clouds. The passageway opened into a wide boulevard. It was lined with delicate frond-trees, which were imported, replaced every few months as they succumbed to the fumes.

Jas slowed, and he followed her stunned gaze to a beribboned platform floating an arm's reach above the street: pleasure servants advertising their wares. "Hell and back," he muttered. Wrapping his cape protectively over Jas's shoulders, he tried without success to hurry her past.

Fascinated, Jas studied them. "They're dressed identically, every last one of them. They look like gymnasts. Are they athletes?"

"You could say that." Rom urged her along.

One of the women spotted him, and two dozen blond-haired heads swerved his way. He groaned inwardly. They started to beseech him in Basic slang he prayed Jas could not understand, flaunting their small breasts and swaying their hips in a demonstration of sexual positions that made the palace courtesans of his younger days look like amateurs.

Jas gaped at them. "They're pleasure servants, aren't they?"

"That they are."

As they passed in front of the stage, Rom hunched his shoulders in a futile effort to deflect the relentless and intimate invitations. Jas threw him a sidelong glance. "You're causing quite a stir, Captain B'kah."

"It's my appearance," he explained uncomfortably.

One corner of her mouth tipped up. "Yeah, well, you are incredibly handsome."

"I'm *Vash Nadah*."

"That, too."

Clenching his jaw, he explained, "*Vash Nadah* are raised to respect women—and to be skilled lovers. Everyone knows this."

Jas blushed, as he knew she would. Then she linked her arm possessively around his. He grinned at the unconscious gesture, and how she twisted around for one last look as they left the platform behind. Suddenly she said in alarm, "He *is!*"

"He is what? *Who* is what?" Rom's fingers curled around the laser pistol he kept hidden in his cloak.

Jas lowered her voice. "That man there, behind the two traders—he's been following us since the marketplace."

"Keep walking." Rom focused straight ahead. "Tell me what he looks like."

"He's huge," she whispered urgently. "I can't see his face, though. He's wearing a hood."

"What else?"

"A brown cloak, thigh length."

The tension went out of him. "Knee boots?"

She nodded.

"Light brown knee boots? With black soles?"

"Yes."

"A cloak with a double row of stitching down the front?"

"As a matter of fact, he is." She edged aside her hood and eyed Rom suspiciously.

He could no longer hide his smile. "It's Muffin."

Her head whipped around. Then her head snapped back. "Why didn't you tell me?"

"You knew he was my bodyguard."

"Yes, but, well . . . You're right," she conceded. "I just never pictured him following us here."

"Which is his job, one he normally does quite well. I don't know whether to laud you on your commendable situational awareness, or berate Muffin for his lack of stealth."

"Do neither and you'll make us all happy." She peered over her shoulder and, of all things, blew Muffin a kiss. The man hastily tugged his hood lower and faded into the crowd.

Chuckling, Rom said, "when you are alone, he will stay closer."

Her step faltered. "I don't understand what you mean."

209

"Muffin. He will be your bodyguard during your travels."

"Are you serious?"

"Quite."

"But you'll need him at Skull's Doom."

"There I'll have the protection of my entire crew. You're a woman traveling alone. Simply forget that he's here. He has his own accommodations near you. Whatever sights you choose to see, he'll accompany you—somewhat more discreetly, I hope."

They slowed as they entered the gardens of the Romjha Hotel. Rom inhaled deeply and savored the setting. In the ten years since he'd last been to the Depot and passed through these gardens, nothing had changed. Towering fountains filled the air with a cold, crisp mist, softening the harsh edges of the surrounding structures. Birds flitted inside roomy cages, filling the courtyard with song. It was a singular oasis in a gritty, urban port. Yet his stomach twisted into the usual knots.

Jas framed his face with her hands. "Can't I change your mind about coming inside?" He shook his head, and she nodded in understanding. Her voice softened. "Thank you for bringing me here. And for last night." Wonder swam in her gaze. "I won't ever forget you."

At her words, every muscle in his body went rigid. *You'll return here, only to find her gone.* The old fears of abandonment plowed into him: the Balkanor angel, his father, the other *Vash Nadah* families, they had all turned their backs on him without a care. He'd ventured to hope Jas was different. But how would he know for sure unless he allowed fate to run its course? "This is not good-bye," he stated. "I'll be waiting for you in the arrivals terminal in precisely two standard days."

"I know." She flung her arms over his shoulders and stretched up on her toes. "I'll be there."

He brought his mouth down over hers and lifted her against him, drinking in her passion, her faith in him. His absolution.

In that one dizzying, exhilarating moment, nothing existed but the two of them, no pasts conspiring to keep them apart, no old wounds that needed healing. Then an overpowering sense of foreboding chilled him, like a cloud passing over the sun. He gripped her shoulders and slowly pushed her back. He tucked his thumb beneath her chin and lifted her gaze to his. "Two days, angel." His thumb lingered a moment longer; then he swept his cape around him and walked away, leaving his heart behind.

Jas curled her arms around her stomach and watched Rom's long strides carry him away from her, his proud posture that of a king, reflecting thousands upon thousands of years of royal ancestry.

He did not look back.

She watched as he had a brief conversation with Muffin, then disappeared into the crowd. Shaking off a moment of longing, she saw her new protector begin a slow stroll along the pathways, staying well within view. Rom had been sweet to make sure she was looked after, and certainly Muffin was capable.

She carried her travel bag to the nearest bench and arranged her cloak over the cold, wet stone. A light mist was falling. Burrowing into the snug warmth of Rom's cloak, she peered into the birdcage closest to her. There, incredible feathery creatures flitted around their cage. Some had feathers that resembled fur, while the green-spotted ones clinging the wire mesh had curled snouts and six legs.

Fluffy yellow birds scratched for feed on the floor of the aviary. They looked like chicks—cheeped like them, too—and might have been cute if they weren't bald-headed, with gnarled beaks that would make vultures proud. Curiouser and curiouser, she thought. Alice couldn't have found Wonderland much stranger than this.

Gradually the novelty of the birds wore off. Emptiness swamped her, as it had after the crash, as it did after her dreams, something she hadn't once felt on board the *Quillie.* Yet this time she understood the reason behind the desolation: she missed Rom. He'd filled the void inside her as no one ever had. Maybe there *was* something to the concept of a soul mate, what she'd dismissed mere weeks ago as New Age hype. The thought gave her a chill.

Recalling the palm reading Tina had given her in Betty's gallery, Jas unfurled hands she hadn't realized were clenched into fists and stared at the webwork of lines etched there.

There has been heartache and disappointment in your past, yet this pain will continue to make you stronger, strength you will need for your true love.

The prediction reverberated inside her. Without warning, tears swelled, and she bit the inside of her cheek to subdue the impulse to cry.

He will require the full power of your spirit, your faith . . . your flesh.

Not all men were like her ex-husband. Dan and the men in her family had proven that. And Rom. But what if her magical, destiny-driven feelings for Rom shut off, without warning, as they had with Jock, leaving her bereft, while Rom continued to demand what she was incapable of giving him?

Trust . . . believe . . .

Yes. That was exactly what she was going to do. She gathered her things and set out toward the Romjha with a sense of inevitability, of certainty. If her postcrash dreams were the key to figuring out the path her life had taken, then her relationship with Rom was the key to understanding the dreams. Then she could enjoy her time with him with a clear conscience and none of the guilt that had ravaged her life. That alone kept her walking.

From the moment Jas stepped into the vast, open-air lobby, she understood Rom's reluctance to come here. The place was a veritable shrine to his ancestors. Little wonder he'd stayed close to the frontier all these years, far from such incessant reminders of the family that had shunned him.

A lifelike statue of Romjha, the original B'kah, towered above the bustling crowd of intergalactic travelers. It was easily thirty feet tall—and solid gold, she'd bet. Romjha stood with his legs apart, his arms poised and ready for battle. His features were rugged, resolute, and his eyes, looking toward a long-ago horizon, were as perceptive and intelligent as Rom's.

Anger edged aside her awe. Romjha might be the "hero of the realm," as the plaque so plainly stated, but the current B'kah ruler, Rom's father, must be a heartless man. How else could he turn his only son into an outcast? The way she saw it, Rom deserved a statue of his own. He'd saved the galaxy from a sociopath intent on destroying them all. And all his father cared about was Rom's damned sperm count.

"Pardon me." A man wrapped in a long black cloak eased past her and a nearby couple to lay a bundle at the statue's feet. As he meditated in silence, Jas noticed for the first time the other items scattered around Romjha's huge boots. A dish of exotic fruits, gloves, a colorfully embroidered scarf, a scroll tied with a silk ribbon. Charity? Signs of respect? Or had hero worship blended with religion?

Impulsively she twisted off one of her silver bangles and set it on the base of the statue—for good luck . . . and in hopes that Romjha could guide Rom toward some semblance of inner peace.

A clammy breeze swept in from outside the hotel. It ruffled the hem of her cape and tried to lure her hair from the shelter of her hood. Clutching her cloak around her, Jas hoisted her travel bag onto her shoulder and headed across the lobby.

Her instincts prickled, and she slowed. Someone was following her. She peered over her shoulder, half expecting to find Muffin—though she'd already noticed him walking ahead of her. But all she saw was a preoccupied sea of travelers.

Be cautious, not fearful.

She pressed her bag closer to her hip and strode forward. The hotel brimmed with wealth, in contrast to the underlying sense of decay outside. The magnificent floor and much of the furniture were carved from stone the color of caramel, shot through with russet stripes. She veered toward what she assumed was the reception desk, where a clerk dressed in a crisp blue uniform with silver piping was shuffling through a handful of plastic cards that passed for Basic currency. Young, like Zarra, and even blonder, he sported a row of tiny silver squares glued down the bridge of his prominent nose. Skin jewelry, Rom had explained earlier when she'd seen others adorned this way.

"Good morning," she said to get his attention.

He greeted her with a respectful bow. It would be hard getting used to Earth manners again after a year of this. His gaze flicked over her cloak and hesitated on the clasp at her neck. Immediately his manner became more deferential. "Honored lady, how may I help you?" He stooped to peer under her hood.

"A room, please," she stated, tossing the hood back off her head. He drew back, his expression one of curiosity and surprise. She explained dryly, "I'm from the frontier."

As if that explained everything, he relaxed. "Have you a reservation, honored lady?"

"Yes, a standard room." It was what the reporter had stayed in when he was at the Depot, and what she had asked Terz to request from the hotel when he radioed them earlier.

The clerk stored the currency cards he'd been counting in a drawer. "The length of your stay, please?"

"Two days." She handed him a paper card, one of a dozen she'd prewritten with her name in Basic letters. "My name is Jasmine Hamilton."

He bowed again, then busied himself at his viewscreen. Scrutinizing the wafer-thin display, he said, "I have a mountain view, if you prefer."

What mountains? She hadn't seen a thing through the smog. "Fine, whatever you have."

"Your method of payment?"

"Salt." She reached into her waist pouch, withdrawing and handing him one of the vials she'd used to separate her booty into smaller, more manageable quantities. He brought it to a computerized scale, where she was relieved to see him measure out a half teaspoon–sized scoop. It gave her a better idea of how fast she'd spend her salt. The device began beeping, testing for authenticity and purity. After a long tone, it beeped again and dispensed her change in Basic currency, a light blue plastic card, which she slipped into her waist pouch along with the vial. "This is of the highest quality." His voice dropped. "Almost pure."

"It's Morton table salt. Iodized," she confided under her breath. He nodded slowly, and she couldn't resist: " 'When it rains, it pours.' "

"Ah . . . of course." Clearly befuddled, he swiveled his viewscreen so she could see. "Your door code, honored lady."

The four numbers were the closest she'd get to a room key. "Memorize them," Kendall Smith had advised his Earth public. That was what was done here. Repeating the Basic numbers several times in her head, she thanked the clerk and left. "When in Rome," she reasoned, "do as the Romans."

Two days later, after exploring most of the upper floor of the Depot art museum, Jas rested on a bench in a room where the main attraction was a free-form sculpture made from the same alloy as the glow-jewelry Rom had bought her. Recessed lights alternately dimmed and brightened, making different areas of the sculpture come alive. Not all of it was luminescent, she realized after a few fascinated minutes. The artist had ingeniously cho-

sen which parts he wanted to hold the light, and which
parts he didn't, creating absolute magic as the outer illumination rose and died. While she scribbled notes and
sketched, she pondered new techniques she could bring
to her own work. Two women strolled in, the same pair
she'd seen entering the museum shortly after she had.
Jas lowered her pencil. After what Rom had told her,
she hadn't expected to see anyone else here.

The pair sat on the opposite end of her bench, and Jas
returned their warm smiles. The taller of the two was a
patrician-looking woman about Jas's age, with chin-
length hair the color of Rom's. She unfastened her fluffy
gray cloak, opened a sketchpad, and, as her shorter com-
panion looked on, she began to draw. Taking the risk of
appearing hopelessly nosy, Jas craned her neck to see.
"Are you an artist?" she asked.

"Yes," the woman responded with a serene smile.
"My name is Beela. What is yours?" As they went
through the introductions, Jas felt the instant bond she
often did with others in her field.

"My sister Janay is an artist, as well," Beela pointed
out.

Jas glanced from Beela to Janay. *Sisters, hmm? Talk
about the strange inconsistency of genetics.* Janay was
fair, for a non-Earth type, with wide, pleasant features,
whereas Beela's bronze coloring was closer to Rom's.
Beela also shared his long, aristocratic nose and sculpted
cheekbones. Didn't that mean that she, too, was of the
Vash Nadah?

Jas clasped her hands in her lap and smiled. "I can't
tell you how nice this is—meeting other artists so early
in my trip. Painting is my livelihood on my homeworld."

"Earth," Beela said, nodding.

Jas gaped at her.

"Your hair color," Beela explained, fingering the chain of a necklace half-hidden in the folds of her cloak. "It gives you away. My family and I have viewed images of the gentleman from your homeworld. We were very much taken with his appearance. And also by the news that another Earth-dweller followed him here, a woman. After it was discovered, it made big news on your planet." Her smile softened her features, but not her penetrating gaze. "The Depot is smaller than it looks; few actually live here. Word travels fast. Your arrival—it was no secret."

"I see." A flicker of unease shivered through Jas. The idea of others knowing her whereabouts made her uncomfortable. She was glad Muffin was outside, meandering through the corridors, pretending to be interested in fabric art.

Beela slid her hands out of the way so Jas could view what she was sketching. The drawing wasn't rendered in pencil or charcoal as she'd expected, but in a vivid medium resembling pastels: star-strewn black space, where a burst of colors bloomed, concentric rings of bright white fading into shades of yellow, orange, and finally blue and indigo. But what drew her were the ethereal rays of light emanating from the center.

"Riveting," Jas remarked quietly. "It reminds me of water when you throw a pebble into a still pond . . . a deep, dark pond at sunset."

"Sunrise, actually." Janay had finally spoken.

Beela cast her a sharp glance. The woman's fingers darted to her mouth. Lips pressed together, she withdrew a large pad of paper from her portfolio. On the top page was a virtual replica of Beela's drawing. But it was flat and lacked the passion of her sister's.

Jas employed tact as best she could, murmuring words of praise. "Forgive my ignorance in asking, but what is it?"

Beela's aristocratic features came alive. "It is our galaxy's heart. A place the Trade scientists call a domain of cataclysmic violence, a black hole, a hungry monster swallowing mass, light, even time. But that is not the case." Her pale eyes glazed over, and she absently caressed her necklace with her fingertips. "It is the womb from which all life comes. And where all life will return, in the end."

The woman looked to be in rapture. Chills prickled the hairs on the back of Jas's neck. Good Lord, did she herself appear this way to others, too? Driven and slightly demented? She thought of the desert landscapes she had been compelled to create in the aftermath of her dreams, how, locked inside her studio, she hadn't eaten, hadn't slept until the period of furious creativity passed, leaving her depleted but never quite satisfied. The black hole must inspire Beela in the same way the desert affected Jasmine. The insight evoked a sudden emotional identification with the gifted woman. "Do you display your work in a gallery?"

"At our colony. In the mountains above the city. In fact, my sister and I will return there this evening." Beela regarded Jas warmly, toying with the chain around her neck. "You must join us for dinner. The others love to have visitors. Particularly travelers from afar, such as yourself."

With a twinge of genuine regret, Jas shook her head. When Rom returned tonight, she wanted to be with no one but him. "I'm sorry. I'm meeting someone this evening."

"Oh, you must come. You have time. I have something that I *know* will interest you. Please, what could be so important that you can't spare a little time?"

Beela so quivered with urgency that Jas had to press her lips together to keep from chuckling. The woman sounded like the galactic version of a time-share sales rep. "As much as I'd like to, I can't. I'll be leaving the Depot soon." Bowing to her inner judgment, she declined to say more. "Do you have a card, though, a way I can reach you the next time I pass through?"

Beela pressed a glittering, microthin disk into Jas's hand. Not knowing what to do with it, Jas felt more like a frontier woman than ever before. "Your business card?"

"Yes. Data on the colony, and how to get there." Beela lifted the golden chain from her neck and dropped it over Jas's head. "And now, a gift."

Jas protested. "I can't accept this—"

"Bah. I make them at the colony and have many, many more." Beela's motherly tone reminded Jas of Betty. "Keep it, Jasmine Hamilton; meditate on it. May it lead you to the truth."

Which Jas now hoped wasn't a slide show on how to make a fortune selling black-hole merchandise. Thanking Beela again, she wished the friendly but peculiar sisters luck with their ventures and beat a hasty retreat.

Outside, the dreary, overcast sky seemed to envelop her, dampening her mood, and she promised herself a hot bath when she returned to her room, one that would be a thousand times better if she could share it with Rom.

Muffin trailed her into the gardens of the Romjha. Before heading inside, she paused to say hi to the birds. "You guys get cuter every day," she said in English to the green six-legged ones. "Like parakeets on steroids."

They trilled wildly, scrambling over the mesh cage until the entire flock had gathered in front of her. They'd never paid her any mind before. Jas glanced around uneasily to see if anyone else had noticed. "What's caught your eye? This?" She held Beela's necklace toward them. Recoiling, they squawked. Curious, Jas lifted the medallion a little higher. There was an explosion of green feathers. The birds dashed to all sides of the cage, as far from her as possible, where they chirped sullenly, peering at her with accusing eyes.

Perplexed, Jas lowered her gaze to the engraved ornament attached to the flat-linked chain. The piece glowed in the dull light, as if from within. An exotic alloy, she supposed, but still a benign piece of jewelry—if not to birds.

As she walked into the hotel, she slowed her pace in front of Romjha's towering statue to cradle Beela's weighty medallion in her hand, tilting it from side to side, contemplating the way the woman had positioned the sunlike image from her drawing above two hands clasped together in prayer. One man's one woman's. An unsettling recognition flared in her at the sight. Considering all the information she'd crammed into her head recently, she wasn't surprised that she couldn't figure out why. It was a nice piece, though. But too masculine, not to her personal taste. "What do you think," she asked Romjha, "something your great-thousands-of-times-over-grandson might like?"

Blinking, Jas gave her head a shake. Had she not known better, she'd swear the old warrior had just frowned.

Chapter Thirteen

"Great Mother!" Eyes watering, Gann choked on the liquid he'd just sipped. "It tastes like boiled twigs. If you wished me dead, B'kah, I would have hoped you'd choose a more compassionate method than this." He shoved aside the *Quillie*'s cook's first attempt at beer and wiped the back of his hand across his mouth.

Rom helped himself to a serving of the chilled, sour-smelling beverage and raised the glass to the light. "The color isn't bad. Not quite golden, as it should be, but a pleasant light brown."

Gann made a contemptuous snort.

Rom closed his eyes and sipped, rolling the liquid over his tongue before swallowing. "We will keep trying," he said, and poured the remainder of the beer into the sink.

"Be honest with me, old friend. It is not this . . . refreshment that has you rhapsodizing about 'smooth texture, clear, crisp taste, and lingering salubrious effects.' It is the woman."

Rom gave a deep, enigmatic chuckle. "The potential for profit selling beer is staggering. There is nothing like it in the galaxy."

"Evidently," Gann said under his breath. He picked up his playing cards. "I raise you five units." He slid the currency toward Rom. "And one gold chip."

Rom scrutinized the five cards cupped in his palms. Jas had given Gann her deck of cards and taught him how to play various forms of what Earth-dwellers called *poker*. After they left the Depot, Gann had introduced him to the positively entertaining game. It eased somewhat his impatience to reach Skull's Doom, complete his business, and return to Jas.

"I match you," Rom told Gann, keeping all expression from his face as he considered his cards—one depicting a singular red gem, another with a singular black leaf, and three cards with seven units apiece, black leaves, gems, and hearts. An excellent hand, one Gann had called a full palace—for whatever reason. "And I raise you one cube of salt."

A smile tugged at Gann's mouth. With the tips of his fingers, he pushed a tiny white cube next to Rom's wager.

The men presented their hands.

"Full palace," Rom announced.

"Full house," Gann corrected. "But for a B'kah, I suppose the two are interchangeable."

Rom cast him a long look.

"Three of a kind. Your victory." Gann pushed the salt and currency toward Rom. With admirable skill, he began shuffling the deck.

The viewscreen chimed. Terz appeared. "Call's come in for you, sir. Drandon Keer."

"Keer?" Rom gave a laugh of disbelief. "I haven't heard from the man since we left Nanda with that bag full of stolen seedpods. Put him through." The viewscreen flickered. Rom spread his palms flat on the table and leaned forward. "Drandon, you unrepentant space bandit!"

Drandon gave a familiar lopsided grin, his teeth blinding in his now deeply suntanned face. "B'kah. It's been a long time."

"You're damned right it has. You're looking good. I take it growing Nandan silk agrees with you. How's the plantation?"

"Quite profitable. But those pesky Nandans won't give up. Just last harvest they intercepted one of my outbound shipments. I blame them for all this gray hair."

"A familiar refrain. I believe those were your words the day I hauled you out of that Nandan excuse for a prison."

The men shared a laugh laden with memories. The years had mellowed Keer's harder edges. Rom recalled the spunky Nandan princess who'd helped his friend obtain the seedpods. "And how is lovely Jhiara?"

"Very well," Drandon replied smugly. "Three children now. All under six seasons. And you?"

"Still married to my work."

"I'm surprised you haven't found a wife yourself. Surely there's a woman who'd put up with you."

Jas had been gone just two nights, yet it seemed like years since he'd last held her in his arms. "I may have found her," he said casually. "Her willingness to put up with me is one of her many endearing qualities."

Drandon chuckled. After a pause, his smile faltered. "Listen, I've come across something. Something you of all men might want to know about."

The remark didn't surprise Rom. The smuggler–turned–plantation owner—*illegal* plantation owner—was not the type to make casual social calls.

Drandon opened his hand. "One of the seedpod pickers I hired for the season gave this to my wife. Claimed it would bring her to the truth." He held the glinting object toward the screen. "I didn't think so."

Rom shoved away from the table. Every bad memory he had coalesced into the medallion resting in Drandon's palm. *Praying hands, a rising sun. Utter evil.* "Where is the picker now?" he demanded, his heart hammering inside his chest.

"Gone," Drandon answered regretfully. "Before I could squeeze any information from him or the rest of his fanatic pals."

"Whatever you do, don't allow anyone to wear the necklace." Rom pushed himself to his feet. "Lock it away until I see it for myself."

"When will you arrive?"

Rom glanced at the progress display next to the time-teller on the bulkhead. "If I divert now—at maximum speed—I'll be there by morning." He could fly there and still make it back to the Depot by nightfall.

Drandon held up one hand in farewell. "Rom, Gann," he said. "Until then." The screen went blank.

Rom swore under his breath and raked his hands through his hair.

"It may be the same cult," Gann said. "Or a perhaps an imitator."

Rom's gut clenched. "Either way, I fear the darkness has finally caught up with us."

At the arrivals checkpoint Jas stood before a floor-to-ceiling display that showed incoming flights. She scanned the list, looking for the *Quillie*. Disappointment flooded her. They'd posted a seven-hour delay, long enough even to warrant returning to the Romjha. She searched the crowd for Muffin and found him pretending to peruse the contents of a food stand.

Turning, she pushed her way through the travelers and traders wedged into every available inch in the cavernous but stuffy chamber. She made sure that she held her purse close as she squeezed through the doors to the foggy early evening streets. The pungent odor of overheated bodies blended with rocket fumes. Despite the poor air quality, she breathed deep, glad to be outside after almost an hour inside the terminal.

Except for a group of boisterous pleasure servants on display on the opposite corner, the boulevard was almost peaceful. The musical sound of young women's laughter tinkled from behind her. Just as she suspected, Muffin had slowed his pace near the pleasure-servant stage. A few of the more enthusiastic girls had leaped down and were tugging on the big man's shirt. He glanced at her helplessly. She spread her hands and shrugged, and he turned his attention to them, no doubt arranging some late-night entertainment. He'd been following her relentlessly, faultlessly, for two days. Even when she'd tried to shake him, just to see if she could, he'd always shown up moments later. The way she saw it, he deserved a little fun. She was more than capable of walking the few blocks back to the hotel on her own. She turned left at the first intersection, where the pavement narrowed, just as she remembered. Shadows slanted across the frond-trees between her and the street. From the depths of the gap between two buildings, she heard the sounds of a scuffle.

Stay clear of the alleys, Rom had warned. She quickened her pace just as a man bolted out of the darkness. Cloak swirling, he stumbled across her path and fell to the ground. She barely avoided tripping over him.

"Careful! You might hurt someone," she scolded irritably. He groaned, then rolled to his side. "Are you all right?" she asked guiltily, but he didn't answer.

Heart thudding against her ribs, she glanced around for possible help. No officials in sight, and Muffin hadn't yet caught up. Everyone else looked to be hurrying about his or her own business.

She bent forward, then caught herself, not wanting to get too close. Her soldier's instinct urged her to nudge the writhing man with the toe of her boot to get his attention, but she nixed that, too. "Can you walk?"

He moaned pitifully.

"Listen, I'll be right back," she said. "I'll bring help." Something faintly sweet permeated the air, like old incense. It quickly changed into the sharp odor of male sweat. Then someone tugged on the strap of her purse from behind.

"Hey!" She resisted and pulled the opposite way.

The man sprawled at her feet came miraculously back to life, leaping up as a shadowy figure appeared behind her. Jas lurched forward in a running start. Another yank on her purse wrenched it off her shoulder and onto the street with a muffled tinkle of breaking glass—likely her salt vials and a tiny bottle of perfume.

"Help!" she shouted. "Thieves—" A hand clamped down over her mouth. Then a sinewy arm caught her around her waist, pinning her to a strong, wiry body.

Maybe they weren't going to rob her. Maybe they intended worse. They could rape her, or kill her. Terror turned her insides to water. *Inhale . . . exhale . . . inhale.* Grinding her teeth, she fought against it, using everything she had to turn her fear into something useful. No use dying over a few grains of salt.

A robed, shadowy figure rummaged through her purse. The scent of spilled perfume seemed horribly out of place, wafting as it did to her nose. Nearby, one of her lipsticks rolled lazily into a puddle, chased by an unbroken vial of salt.

"You there! Leave her be!" an indignant female voice called out in the misty twilight. More voices joined in, all shouting for assistance. Jas tried to wrest free. But the man who held her shoved her forward, and she hit the wet pavement hard, scraping her palms. The sound of shoes slapping against the wet street came closer, and her attackers fled in the opposite direction. Jas kneeled, panting and tingling with shock.

Gentle hands closed over her upper arm. "Oh, my," a woman said, helping Jas to her feet. "Are you hurt?"

Jas's cheek brushed against a fluffy gray cloak. Her gaze swerved upward. "Beela!"

The woman's austere features softened slightly. "A fortuitous reunion, wouldn't you say?"

The hatch lifted and Rom strode down the gangway, leaving Gann behind to ready the *Quillie* for departure as soon as he returned. This visit to Drandon's silk plantation was not a social call. Although Rom was anxious to see his friend, he had no time to spare. A sense of foreboding continued to shadow him. As soon as he examined Drandon's discovery, he would return to collect Jas. And only when he'd assured himself of her safety would he be able to rest easy again.

Still, the hazy sunshine felt surprisingly good. A humid breeze bore the distinctive perfume of Nandan silk blossoms and left a film of moisture on his exposed skin. He welcomed it. Unlike most of the traders he'd known over the years, he preferred solid ground to the deck of a spaceship. There was a certain permanence to living on a planet, something he was just beginning to realize he missed. The dangers and harsh loneliness of a smuggler's life no longer held the allure it once had.

His friend called out across the landing zone: "Romlijhian!"

Rom waved and increased his pace across the gritty soil. Despite the man's expression of concern, Drandon looked better than Rom had ever seen him. He wore the look of happiness and satisfaction only a good marriage could bring.

A mix of emotions tumbled through Rom. He wanted what Drandon had—a woman he loved by his side, a home where he could put down roots, a stable livelihood. He'd come to believe these things were for other men. But his life was his own now, was it not? Such contentment could be his, too.

Rom grabbed Drandon's forearm in a vigorous shake. The formal greeting dissolved into a warm embrace. Then, gripping each other's shoulders, they regarded each other. For the moment, the reason for Rom's visit was left unspoken.

They stepped apart. Rom scanned the lush, landscaped

gardens, beyond which sat a hangar sheltering at least ten starspeeders. Drandon had never been a man to rely on others for protection. Consequently, it didn't surprise Rom to see him in possession of a well-armed personal fleet. Closer in, a red ball and a worn, toy ketta-cat lay next to the path. Rom smiled. "Where are Jhiara and the children?"

"She took them to the sea. I'm afraid they won't return until tomorrow. We didn't expect your visit." Drandon searched Rom's face. "She'll want to see you."

"As much as I'd like to stay, I can't. Someone awaits me at the Depot."

Drandon nodded gravely. "Come inside," he urged. "At second sunrise the temperature will become unbearable."

They walked toward a sprawling one-level abode built with natural-rock walls and surrounded by shaded courtyards and a wide, wraparound porch—a typical design in tropical climates.

Drandon led him onto the veranda. It overlooked a vast plantation of young Nandan silk trees. Rom admired the view, evidence of Drandon's years of hard work, while a young female servant poured juice into two iced glasses, then left, her slippered feet silent on the flagstone floor. Rom followed Drandon's lead and settled onto one of the wickedly inviting cushions made from Nandan silk. The planet's second sun, a tiny, white-hot orb, peeked above the horizon.

"Over the next hour the temperature will climb twenty degrees," Drandon said. He lifted the lid of one of two ornately carved wooden boxes and handed Rom a dried leaf rolled tightly around what was surely top-grade tobacco. "When it does, we will lower the molecular heat barrier. The humidity here is formidable."

"As bad as on Nanda?" Rom asked as Drandon lit his cigar.

"Worse. Of course, Jhiara loves it, being Nandan."

"And you?"

"Actually, I detest it"—cigar clamped between his teeth, Drandon laced his hands behind his head—"less and less each day."

Rom chuckled. He understood as only another trader could. Success was a thing to be proud of. "Like your wife, the trees love the climate, which is driving your change of heart."

"They grow twice as fast and produce four times as much as those on Nanda." The man's eyes shone. "My grandchildren will live to see this plantation eclipse the production of that entire planet." Suddenly pensive, he shifted his gaze to the rows of lush green trees on the hillsides below. "Or will they?" he asked quietly.

Rom shifted uncomfortably. "Perhaps I can tell you more after I examine that medallion."

With a resigned expression on his face, his friend lifted the lid of the second box, withdrew a lumpy drawstring pouch, and handed it to Rom. "Whether or not the eight families decide to back you, I will. Rest assured, I will fight—"

"I am not here to recruit anyone," Rom said stiffly. "Nor to investigate the possibility of another war. I came for personal reasons. The galaxy is no longer my responsibility."

"Somehow I find it hard to believe you believe that."

Rom let Drandon's remark brush past him. All his life he'd shouldered the expectations of others. No more. He was not the B'kah. He was a simple trader with his own interests at heart. He wouldn't pretend to buoy Drandon's hopes. He might be a hero in Jasmine's eyes, but he didn't care to raise anyone else's expectations simply to end up dashing them.

"I'm here because of my own selfish interests," Rom said briskly. "I don't represent the eight families, or wish to. And the *Vash Nadah* are mired in complacency, so don't look to them for help, either, should the Dark Years come upon us again. Continue to arm yourself and your family. Do whatever you need to keep your own interests safe. Better yet, search out a compatible planet and move there, as far away from the populated regions as you can."

Drandon regarded him skeptically. "Run?"

"It is what *I* plan to do. There is a woman—I care about her a great deal. If your discovery proves to be the shadow of a larger threat, I intend to take her and her family to where they'll be safe." Tamping down on unwanted emotion, Rom untied the drawstring and emptied the purse's contents into his palm. "The Family of the New Day used a depiction of clasped hands below a rising sun. This shows the hands below a nebula, or perhaps a plasma cloud or black hole."

His friend's relief was palpable. "So my picker was nothing more than some fanatic with an interesting bauble?"

"Perhaps." Rom flipped over the medallion. "I suspect he belongs to a group that wants to reclaim the Family of the New Day's former glory. The design is very similar." Rom paused. "Unfortunately, if the *Vash Nadah*'s hold on the Trade Federation continues to deteriorate, I fear we will see more and more individuals like your picker."

He pressed the engraved golden disk between his palms, and a faint tingling sensation crept up his wrists. Startled, he released it. The discovery dismayed him. "This is cast from an empathic alloy, like the original medallions."

"These alloys were banned after the Great War," Drandon pointed out.

"They were." Rom kept all expression from his face as horrific memories threatened to overtake him. "But Sharron had a knack for reengineering banned technologies. This indicates that not all of what he worked toward died with him."

Drandon gestured to the necklace with his cigar. "Isn't it true that empathic alloys were once used to alter brain function?"

Rom nodded.

"So if I were to wear that medallion, someone could make me do their bidding?"

"They might *influence* your behavior," Rom answered. "But they could not control it. Sharron came the closest of all. He possessed some psychic ability—a twisted sense of empathy, you might say—and he used the medallion to enhance this ability. During the war, when we experimented in a similar way with confiscated medallions, we were able to relay suggestions to our subjects' neurons. But actual mind control was never achieved."

Drandon narrowed his eyes. "What *was* achieved?"

"We found that most could deflect the hints we sent, unless they were weakened from sickness or exhaustion. Animals were another matter entirely." Rom slid the medallion near where a Centaurian morning-fly was exploring the base of his glass. It hopped onto the medallion. Then, without warning, the insect rose sharply and slammed itself into the wall.

Stunned, the ex-smuggler contemplated the glittering splotch of moisture left on the stones. "Great Mother," Drandon muttered. "That was quite a graphic demonstration."

"Lesser creatures do not possess the strength of will we do."

"In that, I hope you're right. Just as I pray Sharron took the knowledge of the rest of the banned technology to his grave."

"I suspect he did. From what my men found on his base, it appears he trusted few with his secrets. Only the elders of his sect even knew of the cloning, or far worse, his plans to resurrect antimatter weaponry."

"Antimatter weaponry!" Drandon was uncharacteristically shaken. "During the Great War, the warlords used the like to obliterate entire planetary systems."

"Sharron aspired to wipe out far more than mere systems, Drandon. Had we not stopped him, had we listened to the eight families and dismissed him as a harmless fanatic, he might have followed through with his goal. He wanted to detonate an immense antimatter explosion in the galaxy's core, triggering, he hoped, its collapse. Whether or not that's scientifically possible is debatable, but his group is a doomsday cult on a grand scale. Sharron believed we'd all be reborn into a 'New Day.' "

"With him as God, no doubt," Drandon remarked dryly.

"I must go," Rom said, rising to his feet. Although Jas was safe within Muffin's vigilant protection, in light of what he'd learned today, he wouldn't rest until he was back by her side.

Jas leaned against Beela. Her legs trembled with the adrenaline still pumping through her veins. "I . . . I thought that man was hurt."

Beela sniffed. "I suppose you weren't the first traveler to think so. And you certainly won't be the last." Her two companions, a man and a young woman, collected Jas's scattered belongings and returned them to her muddy purse. Meekly, they handed it to her.

Jas grasped the strap gratefully. "Thank you. Thanks, all of you."

"We were on our way home when we heard your cries," Beela said, gathering her cloak around her. She took Jas by the arm. "It's not wise to be alone after such trauma. Come back to the compound with us. We'll share a light meal and some lalla-blossom tea."

"I don't want to impose," Jas protested weakly.

Beela gave a motherly frown. "You are *not* an imposition. Spend this evening among friends."

"I have to be at the terminal in a few hours. Is it far?"

"In the mountains. But it's only a short transport ride."

"You mean the mountains nobody ever sees?"

"Yes. Above this filthy smog. Close to the heavens, to the stars." Beela smiled indulgently. "I find fresh air enhances creativity and well-being."

Well, Jas thought, that was what Betty had always said. If nothing else, Beela shared her friend's appreciate-the-simple-things attitude, something Jas needed right about now. "Take me," she said. "I'm yours."

Beela gave a curt nod to the others. "We have our own transport," the woman said, steering her toward the smallest of the Depot's three transport terminals.

The young couple fell in behind them. Jas found it odd that Beela didn't introduce them. Maybe they were assistants, apprentices, or possibly servants, below a successful artist's notice. If Beela had her own transport, she was obviously doing well.

In fact, her ship was sleek and unmarked. As Jas strapped into one of the sixteen seats, the air locks closed with a hiss, and seconds later the craft lifted off. She sagged against the headrest, while Beela droned on about how much she would enjoy the visit. Jas hoped Muffin was in bed with his pleasure servant by now and not looking for her. Otherwise she'd suffer the big guy's wrath when they met up later.

Not much more than fifteen minutes later, the transport landed with a resounding thump. Jas followed Beela out onto a windswept plateau on a craggy mountainside. Far below, the city glowed, multicolored and incandescent beneath a blanket of haze. The air was noticeably thinner and colder, lacking the cloying humidity of the Depot itself. Jas filled her lungs. "It's beautiful up here," she said.

"And inside, as well." Beela waved elegantly toward an enormous opening in the rock and said, "Open." The heavy metallic grate lifted on hydraulic pulleys, revealing the glittering interior of a cave carved from walls as shiny and black as obsidian. Jas walked inside, then turned slowly in a circle. Recessed lighting, pinpricks of light in the walls and ceiling, created the appearance of deep space. It was unsettling, making her feel as if she were floating.

Beela continued to sweep forward. Jas almost had to jog to keep up. Snapping her fingers and issuing curt commands, the woman dispatched dozens of men and women on unknown errands. All of them wore similar plain gray tunics, and their eagerness to please Beela was disconcerting. Several cast furtive welcoming glances in Jas's direction, pricking her curiosity. Had she not known better, she might have thought they were expecting her.

Beela ushered her through another door and into an enormous chamber. Taking up most of the space on the back wall was a huge painting of the piece Beela had shown her in the museum the day before. The depiction of the black hole was so vivid, so arresting, that Jas could almost hear within its depths space and time melding into something unimaginable. Then her gaze crept to the other works, and she saw all were replicas of the first. "Did you paint these?"

"Not all. Some were created by my brothers and sisters," Beela said, waving her hand at the group of plainly dressed, bland-faced men and women gathering at the perimeter of the chamber. The hair on the back of Jas's neck prickled. *Brothers and sisters?* These people didn't look anymore like Beela than Janay had. Swallowing, Jas took a second glance at the crowd. It probably wasn't the brightest move, having come here without her own way of getting back to the Depot.

"Please enjoy the paintings," Beela said, pride evident in her voice.

Jas glowered at the nearest. Her unease slipped into exasperation, prodded by her bone-deep exhaustion. Normal, everyday company would have been nice. But no, she'd have to spend the evening with a bunch of zealots when she was tired, irritable, and impatient for Rom's return. God help the first person who tried to engage her in a discussion on politics or religion. She'd probably snap his head off.

"May I bring you some salve?"

Jas realized belatedly that Beela was standing next to her, just a little too close for comfort. Taking a step back, Jas opened her abraded palms. "They *are* sore," she admitted, guilty for thinking badly of Beela when the woman was so accommodating.

The woman turned Jas's hands this way and that. Then she brushed her cool fingertip over Jas's wrist. "So beautiful," she said in a soft, almost reverent tone. "So pale."

Jas gave a nervous chuckle. "And here I am envying your year-around suntan."

Beela continued to clasp Jas's wrists. An awkward moment ticked by. Then she lifted a worshipful gaze to Jas's hair. "Perfect. Black as the Maker's heart."

Jas snatched her hands away. "I beg your pardon?"

Beela blinked rapidly. She took several clumsy steps backward. "I'll get the salve."

Jas watched the tall woman hurry out of the chamber. *Great.* This was going to be one long evening, and she had no one to blame but herself. Since none of the others in the room appeared anxious to talk, she might as well view the artwork. If she was lucky, she'd find something other than the black hole, riveting as it was. Hands clasped behind her back, she wandered across the vast room. Beela's "apprentices" parted for her like the Red Sea. They probably found her hair and skin color strange, too.

On impulse, Jas stepped into a corridor. The rock walls were bare of artwork. The passageway narrowed and led to another, which ended in a wide balcony overlooking the dark, unpopulated side of the mountains. The thick glass doors were sealed shut. "Open," she commanded, just for fun. They remained tightly closed. Apprehension trickled along her spine, and she hastened back the way she'd come. She'd recalled passing at least two comm boxes earlier. If she could remember where one was, she'd call the Romjha. They owned a fleet of transports; surely they'd dispatch one to rescue a stranded guest. That way she wouldn't inconvenience Beela. Although the woman meant well, she was growing spookier by the minute.

Mounted on the wall just to the right of the entrance to the main chamber was a comm box. Jas rummaged through her waist pouch for the comm card she'd purchased for routine calls. Instead her fingers closed around the wafer-thin metal card Rom had given her. She cradled it in her scraped palm, and her heart constricted. *Call him.* Yes, just to hear his voice, to say how much she looked forward to seeing him in a few hours. And to hear him laugh his head off when she told him how she'd gotten herself trapped for the evening in a compound full of loony artists. Grinning, she dropped the card into the slot.

As the machine flicked on, a breeze swept around her ankles, bringing with it a whiff of the incense she'd smelled just before the thieves grabbed her. She whirled around. A body slammed into her, knocking her off balance.

Jas tumbled across the polished stone floor, skidding on her rear end. Sprawled on her back, she gaped at Beela, who was shrieking, "Get the card out! Get the comm call!"

Chaos erupted in the chamber. Apprentices ran toward her from all directions. One dug Rom's card out of the comm box. Jas tried to get up, but someone grabbed her by the hair and wrenched her painfully backward. Her numbness and disbelief transmuted to panic. She flailed wildly, trying to break free, but whoever had grabbed her hair now pinned her arms behind her back.

"I wish you had not tried to do that," Beela said.

Wide-eyed in horror, Jas watched the woman walk toward her, a cloth clutched in her outstretched hand.

Chapter Fourteen

Seconds after the *Quillie* broke free of the atmosphere, the comm call in Rom's front pocket chimed. Relief hit his tense nerves like rain splattering on still-hot thrusters. "Thank the heavens," he said, yanking the device out of his pocket. He lifted the card to his ear. "Jas, your timing is exquisite."

Static hissed on the other end.

"Jasmine?" He tapped the gadget in annoyance. "Hello, Jas?" Silence on the other end resonated with the fear clanging inside him. He met Gann's baffled gaze, then scanned the status page.

CALL TERMINATED AT SOURCE.

Underneath was a twelve-digit alphanumeric code. Rom punched it into the flight computer. Gripping the console, arms braced, he stared at the display. Then he slowly raised his head. "To the Depot—maximum speed."

*   *   *

"What's going on?" Jas cried hoarsely, pumping her legs.

Beela's lips thinned. "Keep her still!"

The apprentice who held her arms tightened his grip until Jas thought her bones might snap. Gasping in agony, Jas stopped struggling. "Why are you doing this?" she pleaded in an urgent whisper.

Beela crouched in front of her. The fanatical determination in her eyes was chilling. "He accepts so few of the treasures I offer him. But he wants you. And has ever since I first spoke of you."

"Who does? What are you talking about?"

"But you made it difficult for me, because you did not wear your medallion. What, did you leave it in your lodgings? Foolish woman! It is for the faithful to wear, not to be left behind." Beela settled the cool, damp fabric over Jas's mouth and nose.

It smelled sweet. *A drug. Don't inhale.* Jas wanted to scream, but somehow she had the presence of mind to hold her breath and press her lips together. Her heart slammed against her ribs, and her lungs burned. Tears stung her eyes. Then grayness tickled at the edge of her vision.

Light-headed, she locked gazes with Beela. The woman's pale gold eyes, so similar to Rom's, held none of his compassion, his humanity.

Jas's lungs felt ready to explode. *Don't breathe.* She knotted her hands into fists and scuffed her boots on the floor. But the elemental instinct to survive was too strong, and she couldn't keep from sucking in a breath. The cloying odor of incense flooded her nostrils and made her dizzy. She saw her mother's face . . . her children's. And then Rom's.

A silent scream of outrage tore from her soul. She wasn't ready to die. Not now, not on the threshold of happiness, of figuring out her life.

A rushing noise filled her ears, crushing her senses and obliterating all coherent thought. And then there was nothing left but darkness. . . .

Consciousness drifted back. Her bruised body ached, and her mouth was dry. She was strapped upright into a seat. Voices filtered through her drugged haze, and in the background, engines rumbled. They were taking her off-planet. She tried to get up, but her wrists were bound. So were her ankles. Fear-laced panic dampened her relief at discovering she was still alive, and a sob escaped her—more to protest her utter helplessness than to broadcast her fear. The voices became louder, closer, more agitated. Someone wedged a tablet under her tongue and it snuffed out the light.

When she woke again, her head had cleared. Although her insides felt strangely empty, considering how brutally Beela's assistants had handled her, nothing hurt. Regardless, she'd best play dead—or whatever state she was supposed to be in—until she understood into what kind of danger she'd stumbled. After being kidnapped, drugged, and transported somewhere, she cringed, thinking of what might happen next.

She kept her eyes closed and attempted to use her senses to investigate her surroundings, as Rom had shown her in the Bajha game. The air circulating around her was cool and dry. She was inside somewhere, sitting upright and untied in a comfortable chair. Whatever she was wearing barely covered her buttocks, because she felt the silken cushion between her bare thighs, which meant—*oh, God*—that someone had removed her bra and panties.

She fought her rising panic. She heard a rustle of fabric, a breath. Apprehension trilled through her. Her stomach tightened with a surge of adrenaline, and her eyelids twitched.

"Ah, she awakens," said a man's raspy voice. Cool, dry fingertips brushed over her cheek. Jas recoiled at the unnerving sensation, then opened her eyes.

An older man crouched in front of her. A shimmering bronze tunic stretched across his broad shoulders, matching the flecks in his yellow-gold eyes. He was amber-skinned and blond, and handsome to the point of being artificial. Coupled with his soft, magnetic smile and hypnotizing eyes, it made him the most charismatic man she'd ever seen. It was just the two of them in a room that was, at most, twenty by twenty feet. Besides the cushion she sat on and the silken rug beneath her bare feet, there were no furnishings, no windows.

And no door.

Terror gripped her. "Where am I?"

"Brevdah Three." An odd rumble marred his rich voice. "Don't be alarmed. You're safe here, my treasure," he said, contemplating her with an insolent air of possession. "My lovely black-haired *gift*."

For the thousandth time since leaving Earth, she wished she'd bleached her hair blond. "Listen, I don't know what kind of arrangement you made with Beela, but it's not going to work." Just her luck the woman was a slave broker, and now this creep thought he owned her. "I'm from Earth."

245

"So I'm told."

"Keeping me here is in violation of the Treatise of Trade."

His smile dimmed. "The Treatise of Trade: ramblings of power-hungry soldier-merchants. Worth little more than the paper it is written on."

She lowered her voice. "Just let me go, and I'll keep things quiet. We'll call it a misunderstanding, all right?" Tugging her embarrassingly short tunic lower on her thighs, she stood. "I'd like my things, please. And my comm call, too. I'll make my own shuttle arrangements back to the Depot, thank you."

"Sit!" He grabbed her wrists, forcing her down.

Terror exploded in white light behind her eyes.

"I do not mean to frighten you," he said.

She nodded, her heart slamming against her ribs.

"It is dangerous for you to be traveling on your own. For your own safety you must obey me."

She took a shuddering breath. His tone, his expression, implored her to trust him. She wanted to—Lord, how she wanted to. But something was missing in his gaze, a quality she was used to seeing in others but could not define. Its absence left her cold. Eyes like this man's would make the devil whimper. "Who are you?"

He appeared genuinely taken aback. "You honestly don't know, do you?"

She regarded him sullenly.

He sighed. "It does not surprise me. You hail from a remote, barbaric frontier world. You would not have been introduced to my teachings. Trillions look to me for guidance." He began to rock slowly back and forth. He was an odd sight, kneeling before her, his beautiful tunic casting bronze sparks on the marble-smooth white walls. "I am the savior," he intoned. "The savior. I am Sharron."

Startled, she blinked. "Sharron's dead."

The man lifted his chin, revealing a crooked, puckered scar on his throat. His raspy chuckle was low and rich, and it went on a few uncomfortable seconds longer than what seemed normal. "I am very much alive, wouldn't you agree? It is my would-be assassin who is as good as dead."

He meant Rom. How dared he assume he was a broken man?

"I know who you are," she said in a sneer, her voice quavering with repressed rage. "I know about the war you started. And the people you killed." *How* she knew, she kept to herself. If she revealed her relationship with Rom, it might place him in danger, and she'd be damned if she'd allow this monster to attack him again. "The *Vash* put women on pedestals. But you see them as breeding machines. You choose which women bear children, and with whom."

"Analytical procreation," he replied. "To give society strength and purpose. It is not all that different from any other culture."

Her voice was flat, cold. "I'll never submit to you."

Sharron snatched the heavy medallion she hadn't realized was draped around her neck. It was identical to Beela's gift. Holding the necklace in one hand, he settled back on his haunches and stroked the disk with his fingertips. Inexplicably, desire flooded her. Unable to block the baffling sensations, she went rigid.

"You feel it," he said in a rich, husky whisper.

Jas made a small sound of dismay.

"You feel *me*," he murmured. "Do not deny it. We

are intertwined, you and I. Our souls have known each other—have desired each other, have *sought* each other—since the birth of time."

She shook her head. He raised one pale brow. "Tell me, then, why did you leave your frontier world, Earth?"

She gritted her teeth against the heat pooling low in her belly. "I don't know."

"Ah, but I think you do." He smiled his enigmatic smile. "You came here in search of something, didn't you? A quest to find, and define, what was missing in your life."

She froze.

"You were empty, all used up, dissatisfied, but not understanding why. All you knew was that you were missing something, your other half . . . me."

Jas tried to rail against his suggestions, but her words drained away before they streamed from her mind to her mouth.

"And so you journeyed to the stars because *I* called to you," he continued softly. "Because I needed you."

Nausea and disbelief clogged her throat. She swallowed hard to fight the tears stinging her eyes. He *couldn't* be why she'd left home.

Or was he?

No. It was a trick even the most amateur palm reader knew: making guesses about her past and then using her reactions to fine-tune them. But somehow the medallion was aiding him, and that frightened her. Frantically she tried to conjure Rom's face, but all she saw was her handsome captor.

Sharron.

Doubt swamped her.

"With me, my treasure, you are complete." He leaned

toward her. Her lips parted of their own accord. She moaned softly, stiffening when he brushed his mouth over hers. "You resist me," he rasped, his breath warm against her. "Your will is strong." Abruptly he let the necklace fall between her breasts. The fuzziness lifted from her mind, along with her disturbing, contradictory feelings.

"I must dissolve that will so that it does not keep us apart," he muttered as if to himself. "Yes, the purification shall commence. By the second moon's rise, you will be ready. Then you will welcome my seed and we shall bring the galaxy to a new day. A new beginning."

Her face heated with anger. "Is that what you call murdering women in your cult after they give birth?"

In the space of a heartbeat, he grabbed the medallion she wore and yanked her face close to his. His feline eyes narrowed into ocher slits. "I don't murder them. I give them *life*. Eternal life."

To her horror, his indignation flowed into her. Her muscles refused to heed her urgency to push him away, while his thoughts mingled with hers, like tendrils of toxic smoke. She wanted to gag. His mind was fragile, diseased, yet keenly intelligent, humming with a predator's single-minded purpose. She recoiled from its coldness, its utter absence of compassion.

"It is what I shall give you, my treasure," he whispered against her lips, caressing the medallion, his knuckles grazing her breast. "Eternal life. You will be delivered to the galaxy's beating heart, secured to an extraordinary and unjustly maligned little innovation called an antimatter bomb, and once there you will bring us *all* to the new day."

Almost reverently, he brushed the back of his hand

over her cheek. "Let the purification begin!" he called to the far wall. The marblelike surface wavered like a sheet drying in the wind; then it split, revealing a darkened hallway outside.

Sharron's cloak swirled around him as he strode to the rippling opening and stepped through. The wall snapped shut behind him, as featureless as it was before.

Jas bolted off the cushion, yanking on the hem of her microtunic that might make a hospital gown feel like full-body armor. She smoothed her hands over the wall's slick surface. What was the trick? Hand recognition? A voice command? "Let the purification begin!" she repeated. Nothing. Her hunt for seams in the wall became feverish. "Hey! Let me out!" She pounded her fists on the cold, unyielding surface. Something thumped between her breasts. The necklace! Disgust tightened her insides. She grabbed the weighty ornament, felt a tingling worm its way up her arm. As she lifted the medallion over her head, an overwhelming sensation stopped her.

No, you must not. . . .

She stared at the disk, confused. Then she tried again.

Must not . . .

Quivering, she tried to yank it over her head. This time her arms shot out to the sides. Bewildered and disoriented, she struggled to get rid of the medallion, but every time she did, her body rebelled. She felt like a marionette, except that the contradicting commands were coming from *inside* her. "What's happening to me?" she demanded. A piercing alarm began to blare. It shrieked on and on, a knife slashing her sensitive eardrums, bringing pain beyond her imagination. She slapped her hands over her ears and screamed.

The volume rose with her hysteria, like dirt sucked into a tornado. She sagged to the floor, writhing and crying out until her voice had faded to a ragged whisper.

Three abreast, Rom, Muffin, and Gann walked briskly into the glassy-walled cave. The sound of their footfalls echoed off the obsidian walls.

"Hell and back." Scouring Jas's hotel room, they had found a medallion just like the one Drandon's seedpicker had flaunted, that and a locater card that Rom hadn't recognized. They had followed the directions on the card—of a person named Beela—directly to this compound. Rom had kept alive the hope that he'd finally find Jas here—or at least an individual who could be forced to reveal her whereabouts. Now his confidence faltered. The cavernous hall was littered with the signs of habitation—scraps of paper, books, a cloak. But it was eerily empty of people.

"They left in a hurry," Gann said, righting a *tock* cup.

Rom crushed his hands into fists. "To where? The card listed a dozen other possible locations. By all that is holy, if she's not here, how will I find her?"

His men judiciously maintained their silence. Muffin— brought low by guilt—strolled away, peering at the floor, searching for signs of a struggle, while Gann knocked the repulsive paintings from the wall, one by one, looking behind each for hidden panels or compartments.

They looked like a couple of rookie Trade Police, Rom thought. Frustration vibrated inside him. This was not the way to proceed. The compound was deserted; any fool could see that. By now the Family of the New Day had taken Jas off-planet, to any one of countless worlds. Were they as unspeakably evil as when Sharron had led them? Or were they merely fanatical artists? Regardless, they'd taken her against her will.

But to where?

Rom turned in a slow circle. Reaching deep, he silently evoked Romjha, the ancient warrior whose blood he shared.

Guide me.

Rom shuddered and closed his eyes. Using the lessons drilled into him from birth, he embraced the eons-old legacy he'd fled, the ancestry that filled him with both pride and pain. "Guide me," he whispered.

Only this once.

Only to keep the woman he loved alive. "I will find you, Jasmine," he chanted under his breath. "I *will* find you."

His senses gathered . . . coalesced . . . until every pore in his body thrummed. He moved beyond the physical, transcending time. He became thoughts and feelings and dreams, while memories swept over him like a restless sea.

He lost track of how long he stood there, motionless in the middle of the vast, barren chamber, but when he opened his eyes, it was with the supreme confidence of a hunter.

He would find her.

"Muffin! Gann!" The men met him at the perimeter of the room. "To the ship. She is not here." Pistol drawn, he led them into the shadowy corridor.

The siren soared to an agonizing pitch, wailing on and on. Fearing she'd lose consciousness and render herself helpless, Jas fought to sweep the choking terror from her mind, succeeding in calming herself only fractionally. The alarm diminished in kind, but she hadn't changed the pressure of her hands over her ears. Was it coming from within her head? Writhing on the cold floor, gasping in pain and panic, she uncovered her ears just slightly. The horrific screech remained unchanged. It *was* coming from within her! Her fear skyrocketed. So did the brutal siren.

It's feeding off your panic. The thought—her own— cut through the chaos. *If you don't control yourself, it'll get worse.*

Panting, shaking uncontrollably, she wrapped her arms around her stomach and bent forward, gritting her teeth, her damp forehead pressed against the rug. *It's okay; it's okay,* she told herself. Terror nearly overwhelmed her fight to save her sanity. Every time her anxiety spiked, so did the high-pitched howl. How much time passed, she hadn't a clue, but when she finally calmed herself, the wailing ceased.

She pushed herself up on quaking knees. After a few moments she stood, using the wall for support. Sharron must have known this would happen, that the medallion would feed off her emotions and magnify them, a feedback loop of some sort, designed to shatter her mind. This room must have equipment rigged to facilitate that. The knowledge nauseated her. Had she not figured out how to fight back, she'd likely be a compliant zombie by now, "purified" like the rest of his subjects—save Beela.

She had to ditch the medallion. Could she do it now? And if she did, how would she hide the fact from Sharron? If he discovered it missing, he'd likely immobilize her to keep her from trying again. Then she'd be at his mercy—something she was now certain didn't exist.

She studied the necklace. The charm was connected to the chain by a link—one easily wrenched open. Hope flared inside her, chased by a mental buzzing. She immediately tamped down on her response and the buzzing stopped. It reacted to feelings, which meant she'd have to blunt all emotion, good and bad, to keep her mind unfettered.

She glanced nervously around for hidden cameras, forcing a vacant expression onto her face in case her activity might alarm her keepers. In one swift motion, she tore at the link. It opened, the disk plopping into her trembling hand. She sat on the couch, pretending to clutch her stomach, and furtively slipped the medallion under the cushion. Feeling a wave of triumph rush through her, she tucked the bottom of the chain into her bodice. Now all she had to do was pray no one checked.

As discreetly as she could, in case anyone watched, she faked a limp, searching the small room for anything that could be used as a weapon. Nothing. Too nervous to sit, she paced. Sharron would summon her when the second moon rose, however long that was. What was he going to do to her? Rape her repeatedly until he got her pregnant? And what was that he'd said about a bomb?

She stepped faster to quell the fear chilling her insides. She'd never felt so afraid—or so alone. If only Rom knew she was here.

But he didn't.

Jas gave her head a curt shake. A plan, she told herself; she needed a plan. She had been a soldier once, trained for such situations. Sharron must assume the medallion had turned her mind to Jell-O by now. Naturally she'd show him what he expected to see, pretending to be obedient, and then give him the surprise of his life.

A popping noise brought her to a halt. Three of the four walls morphed into blisters that swelled, then ruptured. The gaps revealed a virtual army of Sharron's gray-cloaked minions. Jas's heart sank. It was time. The second moon had risen.

Chapter Fifteen

Jas followed her captors into a darkened corridor. Fresh air washed over her bare arms and legs, cooling the perspiration prickling her skin. Somewhere a door or window must be open to the outside, to freedom. Longing tightened her chest, but she kept her head bowed in the manner of a meek convert. Patience was the key, she reminded herself. That was how she'd escape.

Using her peripheral vision, she took in as many details as she could. The glassy black walls and floor shimmered in the light of laser torches. There were plenty of doors similar to those on the *Quillie,* but they were all sealed.

Again she turned her attention to the floor, unable to shake the bleak sensation that these dozens of somber, drably clothed zealots were leading her to her execution. What a strange and awful turn her life had taken. A month ago she had been a divorced mother of two whose biggest fear was going on a date. Now look.

But she didn't regret the past few weeks for a minute. She'd never lived so fully, so completely. Anger blazed, and she clenched her jaw until it ached. It wasn't her time to die—she knew it in her soul—and she sure as heck wasn't going to make it easy for Sharron to kill her. *Hell no.* She'd fight until her last breath. That was what Rom would do if he were in this situation.

Rom . . . She bit her lip to keep it from quivering. Even out of sight the man made her emotions gush to the surface. A shame they had never had more time together—more than that one beautiful night.

The slightly built man she guessed was in charge gestured into a cavernous, empty room. "You go," he whispered. A viewscreen dominated the wall opposite the door. The screen was blank, but not in the silvery standby mode she was used to seeing. She was being covertly observed. The knowledge brought her to a halt.

Her escort peered questioningly at her from beneath his hood. "You go," he repeated under his breath.

Mute, she stepped inside. A plush mattress was mounted in the exact center of the room, like the prized showpiece in some nightmarish gallery. It was draped in shimmering white sheets as deceptively lovely as a moonlit arctic night.

Her escort poked a gloved hand at the bed. "Gown."

She followed his finger to a dress arranged on the coverlet, made from the same glittering material.

"Put on," the little troll insisted.

Jas ground her teeth.

"Put on—"

"I need privacy," she said, stalling for a way to investigate the room without the guards looking over her shoulder.

"I stay."

Pointedly turning her back to unknown pairs of eyes, she traded her tunic for the sparkly white sleeveless dress, and gave the hem a single impatient jerk. The dang thing was as short as the tunic. Fortunately the neckline was just as high, hiding the fact that she'd removed the medallion from her chain.

The short zealot collected her discarded clothing and backed toward the entryway. "Lie down," he said. "On back."

Great. She shot a weary glance at the viewscreen, and reminded herself for the hundredth time that her escape plan depended on a convincing performance of docility and compliance. If she tried to run or fight the guards, they'd bind her arms and legs, rendering her completely helpless.

Only after she had settled onto the soft mattress did the double doors slam closed. Then a grating noise rumbled from behind them. A bar or something similar was being used as a lock. Old-fashioned, compared to her previous quarters, but just as effective.

Laid out like a human sacrifice, she stared at the ceiling. It was decorated with a starkly realistic painting of the galaxy's core. Streamers of white and yellow and red fanned out from its center, reminding her of a bloody cracked egg. She swallowed and glanced away.

The silence, the waiting, became oppressive. Her arms and legs trembled. *A wonder that I have any adrenaline left,* she thought glumly. To keep fear at bay, she went over her plans. First she'd feed into Sharron's fantasies. Then, as soon as he reached a vulnerable state of arousal, she'd ram her knee into his groin for all she was worth. Then she'd finish him off. She had been trained in self-defense in the air force, and although she hadn't practiced the moves in nearly two decades, she knew that the heel of her palm could still shatter a nose, and that knuckles rammed into a throat could crush a trachea. Even if she didn't kill Sharron outright, with the dazed state of his followers, she had a chance of escaping before he recovered. Not being a mindless zombie would give her a mental advantage over them all, she hoped with a quick morbid laugh.

The bar outside the door rattled. Her chest squeezed so tightly that she could hardly breathe. A breeze suggested that the doors had opened and closed. Thuds of booted feet stepping toward her confirmed it.

Sharron had entered the room.

She lifted her head to peek at the cloaked, hooded figure approaching the bed. *Patience.* Her only hope lay in accuracy, in surprise—and timing.

The cult leader paused to scrutinize the viewscreen, as if he liked performing in front of an audience and wanted to make sure the camera was running. *Creep.* She braced herself when he resumed his confident strides. Without a word, he lowered his big frame to hers. Cool cloth billowed around her, the scent of burned incense concealing his punishing physical strength. The terror of being raped destroyed her fragile calm, and she plowed her left knee into giving male flesh.

Sharron's breath exploded in a hearty *oomph.* "Great Mother—" he said in a gasp.

Yes! She'd done damage. She jerked her thumbs upward, aiming for his eyes. But he snatched her wrists and used his body to squash her into the mattress like an unrepentant bug. She instantly regretted her too-early, fear-driven attack. Bucking, she twisted under his weight. One leg came almost loose, but he pinned her with his muscular thighs. Finally she wrenched a fist free, throwing her weight into the swing.

"By all that is holy," he whispered loudly. "Jas, it's me."

Her arm froze in midair. "R-Rom?"

Familiar golden eyes peered at her from beneath the rumpled hood. Joy exploded in her heart. She flung her arms around his shoulders, and his mouth came down hard over hers. Molding herself to him, she shuddered with the raw emotion in his fierce, passionate embrace.

He clamped her head in his big hands and groaned, the sound vibrating in her chest. But just as she lost herself in his kiss, he seemed to remember where they were and abruptly pulled away. Love and worry pierced his gaze.

And pain.

"I hurt you." She twisted her hands in the fabric of his cloak. "I thought you were him—Sharron. He's alive, Rom. *Alive!*"

"I know," he whispered, and pressed one finger to her lips. "The viewscreen. It may or may not be transmitting."

"But how did you get here?" she mumbled anxiously. "How did you find me? Did he see you?"

"Answers later." He regarded her solemnly, stroking warm fingers over her face. His eyes were liquid gold, molten. "I didn't know if I'd ever see you again," he said in a thick whisper.

She brushed her knuckles over his cheek, simply nodding, while she held her breath to stave off tears.

"We have little time." Rom eased his weight off her and again became disciplined. "Sharron and his elders are in the prayer chamber. I hope they'll be there for some time yet. If we're going to get out, we have to do it now."

"Tell me what to do."

He clasped her hands in his and helped her to her feet. "I need you to play religious convert." He produced a wadded gray cloak. "Think you can?"

"Oh, yeah." She shakily smoothed back her hair. "I've become a regular Greta Garbo."

He cocked his head questioningly.

"Watch." She demonstrated the meek shuffle that had kept her alive so far. His eyes gleamed in silent approval as he handed her a pair of slippers. Earning the respect of this seasoned warrior was a compliment like no other.

Swiftly they fastened the garment Rom had brought with him over her white dress, arranging the hood over her hair. He withdrew a laser pistol from the folds of his cloak and peered into the corridor. "Clear," he said, beckoning her into the deserted hallway. "Now up."

"Up?" she asked blankly. She'd assumed they'd bolt down one corridor or the other.

He poked his gun in the air. A skylight-sized opening gaped just above their heads. "An access panel to the ventilation system," he said.

A hand thrust out of the hole. Jas jumped backward. Thick fingers wriggled invitingly, and her gaze tracked up a muscular forearm to the galactic version of a big blond Swede. "Muffin!" she choked out.

"Up we go." Rom slapped his hands around her hips, hoisting her into his bodyguard's grasp.

Muffin pulled her into a narrow, gloomy passageway.

She scooted backward in the air duct, allowing Rom room to climb in after her. He kicked up a snowy layer of dust while he refastened the panel over the opening. She muffled a sneeze.

Rom rotated in the cramped space and let Muffin take the lead down the dusky tunnel. Rom fell in behind her. The metal flooring abraded her knees, and she tripped on the hem of her cloak several times as they navigated through what seemed like miles of ductwork.

"I was in the middle of calling you when they drugged me," she said.

"Thank the Great Mother. That's how I knew something had happened. I found your travel bag and your tube of paintings at the Romjha. Wherever you were, I knew you were there against your will; you'd never willingly leave your artwork behind. When I found that woman's card I guessed what had happened."

Beela's card! "Thank God for that. Who else is with you?"

"Zarra's outside," Rom said. "He's guarding a couple of borrowed starspeeders. I wanted to bring Gann and the others, too, but couldn't risk a large group."

"Three's still a good number. Do you have an extra gun? I'll cover you and Muffin when you go after Sharron."

"I'm not going after Sharron."

Incredulous, she shot a glance over her shoulder. "His death was what made your exile bearable. How can you leave here and live with yourself knowing he's still alive?"

His reply was barely audible above sudden whirr of the air through the ducts in which they crawled. "When I came here and learned Sharron still lived, the craving to avenge my brother was unimaginable. But I had a choice, a choice between you and Sharron. I chose you."

"He has antimatter bombs."

That met with a few seconds of silence.

"The braggart's still glorying in his empty threats," Muffin remarked to Rom. "He doesn't have them. They're too complicated for anyone to reconstruct."

Jas persisted. "He said he'd strap me to one and send me to the center of the galaxy."

Rom's tone was hard, edgy, and not to be contradicted. "Whether or not Sharron's tinkering with antimatter isn't our immediate concern. Getting out of here is. Now listen closely. Our starspeeders are parked outside the compound. If we get separated, go out the front entrance and head for the trees. It's below freezing, but you won't be outside for long. You'll see one peak that's higher than the rest. Head for it. Keep going until you see the ships. If all goes as planned, Muffin and Zarra will take one and we'll take the other. But if anything should happen to me, you go with them."

"No way am I leaving without you."

"Oh, I think you are." He gave her rear a not-so-gentle shove. "Now move."

"Boss me around all you want," she whispered threateningly, "but I don't plan on leaving unless you're with me."

"Trust me, angel, I don't plan on it either." His matter-of-fact statement radiated so much confidence that she smiled despite her anxiety. "Sharron has accrued a considerable space force here—formidable fighters. He'll send them after us. The more lead time we have the better."

They rounded a corner and the passage constricted,

brushing the tops of their heads. Muffin stopped abruptly. Jas collided with his wide rear end, and Rom plowed into her from behind. Suave covert operators they weren't—on the outside, at any rate.

Muffin took a tool out of his cloak and used it to pry open a panel. He lifted it high enough to peer into the torchlit corridor below. The sound of distant monotone chanting sent chills careening down her spine. "All clear," he whispered in a deep rumble. He braced himself above the opening, paused, then dropped with surprising catlike grace to the floor. He flattened himself against the wall and withdrew his gun from his cloak.

Jas hesitated. The hallway below was deserted, but at any time someone could walk by and see them. As if sensing her fears, Rom said quietly, "The worst is over. The front entrance is but a hundred paces from here. We'll soon be free."

She blinked perspiration from her eyes and jumped.

As her feet hit the floor, all hell broke loose. Doors slammed, men shouted. A high-pitched siren blasted out of vents in the ceiling . . . and this one was not in her mind.

Rom snatched her hand. "Run!" She stumbled in tow, then regained her footing as they turned the first corner. The corridor turned on an L to the right. Muffin had disappeared. Fifty paces ahead a door framed a frosty wooded landscape below a leaden sky. But a hooded figure stepped in front of them, neatly blocking their escape.

Swathed in a bloodred robe, this New Day cultist's movements were clean, not sluggish as the others' had been. The zealot waved a strangely shaped rifle in the

264

air and the alarm ceased. "I had heard that my master's gift was cavorting with a *Vash* gentleman," said a familiar female voice. "Only I had no idea it was you, Rom B'kah."

"Oh, damn," Jas blurted. "Beela. She brought me here."

"Don't make eye contact, and don't speak," Rom said under his breath. Deftly reaching inside his tunic, he withdrew his laser pistol.

Beela's trigger finger flexed. Ice-blue energy coalesced on the muzzle of her gun. "Prudence dictates that you halt and drop your weapon."

"Move aside," Rom replied, equally calm. He slowed his forward movement, tightening his grip on Jas's hand as he took aim. In one smooth motion, Beela swept off her hood and swerved the muzzle of her long, pointy weapon to Jas's head. Jas's already pumping heart lurched, pounding impotently behind her ribs.

Beela's sculpted features eased into a winning smile that never reached her eyes. "Need I remind you that proton rifles are exceedingly messy?"

A profound look of pain tightened Rom's features, chased by a flicker of indecision. His knuckles went white as he gripped the butt of his pistol. Then his expression blanked like a skilled poker player's.

He kept his pistol aimed at Beela.

Beela's weapon remained pointed at Jas's head.

The air felt ready to shatter. Jas swallowed against a surge of nausea. She hoped Rom knew what he was doing.

Beela's attention settled on Jas. Her cold, sharp eyes glinted like chipped diamonds. "You should not have run away."

Rom squeezed her hand in warning. "She didn't run. I took her."

"The master must not find his bed empty," Beela went on. "Return to your room." For the first time, the woman sought her compliance through the medallion. Jas sensed her trying to influence her thoughts as Sharron had.

Jas lifted her chin and stared back. Beela's photon rifle shook slightly, her gaze tracking down to Jas's neck where the empty chain dangled. "Where is it?" she asked. Nostrils flaring, the woman snatched for the collar of Jas's cloak. Rom's forearm arced upward.

A loud crack echoed somewhere behind them. At the same time, greenish blue sparks ricocheted off the walls as Beela's photon rifle discharged. The air was forcibly sucked from Jas's lungs. She staggered backward, half-blinded. Arms came out of nowhere to catch her just as her knees buckled. Muffin! The stench of something like an overheating car radiator burned her nostrils.

Clutching her side, Beela wheeled on them. "The Family will bring the truth to your homes, to your children. We will bring war to you, B'kah, as you did to us. We *will* triumph, and the new day will dawn." She lifted her rifle, but another burst of light silenced her, slamming her into the wall. Sagging to the floor, the woman regarded them with an expression of almost childlike surprise. Lacy smoke drifted up from her neck and shoulders, and Jas couldn't help but feel a brief sadness for all those caught by Sharron's power.

A steady red light above the exit began to blink. Then the thick metal plate anchored to the ceiling shuddered. "Door's closing!" she yelled.

They bolted for the exit. "Go!" Rom shoved her through the swiftly narrowing opening. Muffin dove through with her. Scraped and bruised, she tumbled alongside him over frozen dirt. The door thudded shut.

"Where's Rom?" she shouted. "He didn't make it!"

A small, intense explosion blew apart the door, and Rom staggered out. He snatched her hand and off they went. The cold air stung her eyes, making them water. Snowflakes pricked her cheeks like needles. Over her uneven breaths, she heard the unmistakable rumble of engines roaring to life. A pair of ships soared overhead, then another. *Sharron's fighters.*

A snow-covered peak loomed, but Jas lost sight of it as they entered a grove of dizzyingly high coniferlike trees. Pinecones the size of Volkswagens littered the forest floor, slowing their progress. Sharp relief pierced her when she spotted a pair of sleek ships ahead.

Zarra ran out from where he was standing between the starspeeders. He tensed, abruptly raising his pistol. "Behind you!" He began blasting away at their unseen pursuers.

Beams of light exploded past. Rom and Muffin wheeled around and returned fire. Projectiles pinged off the closest starspeeder's hull, and blinding threads of energy sliced off tree branches. Jas clutched for a holster she wished was there.

A startled cry tore through the chaos. Turning, she saw Zarra fly backward. "*Zarra!*" she screamed.

Rom caught her arm before she could run to the fallen young man. "Inside!" He thrust her into the speeder's snug interior. The craft had accommodations for a small crew, but was by no means spacious.

"Muffin's got Zarra?"

"Yes!"

She breathed a prayer. The kid had nine lives.

The hatch snapped shut behind them. She barely made it into one of two pilot seats in the cockpit before Rom fired the thrusters and yanked back on the yoke. The craft's nose lurched skyward, slamming her into her seat. They broke free of the atmosphere. There was no gravity generator on this small ship, and her hair floated around her face.

"Bandits, six o'clock high!" she shouted as the display in front of her lit up in warning. With the onboard computer providing split-second timing and protection from immense forces of acceleration, Rom jammed the controls left. The stars outside spun in a stellar kaleidoscope, and the long-forgotten rush of flying combat trilled through her. This was space, not the sky, but the sensations, the maneuvers, were the same.

Rom fired. The first enemy ship burst into green and white fireworks. Chunks of debris thudded against the shield across the starspeeder's hull. More fighters appeared on the viewscreen. Muffin immediately took out two, but the others veered in formation, heading their way.

Rom swore under his breath as his fingers danced over the console. "The missile uploader's jammed."

"What do you mean?" she blurted.

"Unless I fix the blasted thing, we can't fire back." Rom unstrapped himself.

"Where are you going?"

"Belowdecks. To the missile bay." He squeezed past her seat. "I think I can fix it manually."

Jas gaped at him as he floated to a hatch in the floor and opened it. "Who's going to fly?"

Rom winked at her.

"You're crazy! I haven't flown combat in twenty years!"

"Worry about that later." His head dipped out of sight.

"Damn you, B'kah." Jas whirled back to the controls. Steadying herself, she lifted her gaze to the starfighters in pursuit and curled both hands over the yoke.

Chapter Sixteen

"Off my tail, you bastard!" Jas dragged Sharron's relentless pilot through maneuvers designed to bleed off his energy and slow him down. But it wasn't working. Thrusters capable of light speed far outperformed the jet engines she was used to, and the starfighter stayed in her six o'clock. At most, her tactics kept him from firing, giving Rom the precious minutes he needed to repair the uploader.

"Blasted thing's up and running," he said, pulling himself to his seat.

WEAPONS READY blinked on the status screen. When Rom didn't immediately grab the controls, Jas understood what he wanted her to do. She rolled the speeder upside down and pulled hard on the yoke. Head-to-head with the pursuing ship, she fired. A blinding flash blotted out the stars. "Yes!"

"Well done."

"Thanks." It was nice to see she hadn't lost her touch.

Rom took control of the speeder. Muffin's ship streaked past, trailed by a swarm of enemy starfighters. Half the squadron broke off the chase and headed their way. Her mouth went dry. "There must be twenty of them!"

"Hang on." Rom pushed the thrust lever forward, and the stars elongated into streamers. A moment later they blasted into deep space.

"Light speed?" Jas asked when she felt her heart slow down.

"Yes. They can't track us through hyperspace if we don't transmit coordinates."

"What about Muffin and Zarra?"

"They made the jump when we did. As briefed."

"So it's over. We're safe." She relaxed a fraction.

The lines bracketing his mouth deepened. "Not yet. We jumped to light speed blind. There's no quicker way to kill yourself." Visibly bracing himself, he slowly brought the thrust levers out of maximum. "Because you never know where you'll come out on the other side."

"Watch out!" Jas reared back in her seat as one of hundreds of jagged boulders tumbled past. "We're in the middle of an asteroid field!"

Rom swerved the ship left, then right. She clamped her hands over her armrests and simply hung on. They were almost out when one of the huge rocks hit. The hollow thud vibrated through the ship. The maintenance status panel began scrolling out a list of systems affected and in need of repair. "Help me find a place to land," he said evenly.

"What are we looking for? A flat top?"

"Flat." He lifted his shoulders. "And wide, I suppose."

"You *suppose?*"

He gave her a sideways glance. "Never had the occasion to land on an asteroid."

She bit back a groan.

Rom rolled the starspeeder. An asteroid careened past, scraping the underside of the ship.

She should have been terrified, but she wasn't. She'd never trusted anyone as much as she trusted Rom. An hour ago he'd saved her life, and, she didn't doubt he'd do it again.

They spied the immense platelike asteroid at the same time. Craters pockmarked the hulk, which was rotating slowly like a fallen leaf on a pond. Rom aimed for it. "Hold on."

The landing was noisy, bumpy, and short. The starspeeder skidded over a shadowy, meteorite-strewn plain, then into a shallow embankment. One last jolt threw them against their shoulder harnesses.

Jas sat perfectly still, half expecting the final blow. "We made it," she said tentatively, glancing around.

Rom unstrapped. There was just enough gravity from the asteroid to keep him planted on the ground. Bracing himself on her armrests, he leaned over her.

"We're alive," she whispered. "*Alive.*"

"I fear I frightened you."

"I don't understand."

"In the compound. I didn't drop my weapon as ordered."

"Rom—"

He held up one hand. "It was a risk. But not one I made because I took your life lightly. My senses told me that *Vash* traitor would step on her own toes—given enough time."

"You called her bluff," Jas said. Rom shook his head in bemusement at the statement. "It's the hallmark of the best poker players," she explained. "Unflappability. Poker is an Earth card game."

He almost smiled. "Yes, I know of it."

"Beela wanted you to believe she held better cards. But she didn't. You knew, but you didn't show it. You forced her to play her weak hand, and she folded. You were brilliant."

When relief suffused his handsome face, all at once she realized how worried he'd been that she thought he had risked her life unnecessarily. Profoundly touched, she reached up and framed his face with her hands. "You're the most incredible, the most selfless man I've ever met. I don't understand how or why we ended up together, only that you bring me so much joy."

He grasped her head in his hands, then lowered his mouth to hers. Jas grabbed his cloak and deepened the kiss, straining against her waist and chest straps to pull him closer. Desire more powerful than anything she'd ever thought possible consumed her. Driven by an almost primal need to mate with him, she became the aggressor, fumbling with the fastenings of his cloak. When they wouldn't come loose, she wrenched them open with a sharp hiss of torn fabric.

"I want you," she said in a gasp. To refute Sharron's claim she belonged to him, to erase Jock's mocking words, to obliterate every lonely year in between. "Anywhere, the floor, the seat, I don't care. I just want you."

The stoic control that was such a part of him vanished. With hurried fingers, he unbuckled her harness and hauled her toward him. His hands closed firmly over her buttocks, pulling her hard against him. His kiss was possessive, demanding, and there was nothing gentle or reserved in his touch.

His caresses became rougher, but so did hers. She threw their cloaks to the side, yanking off his shirt as she pulled him backward into a narrow bunk. In the light gravity, they fell onto the mattress in slow motion, as if they were underwater. Dazed by her urgency to join with him, Jasmine let her hands tangle with Rom's in a race to free him from his trousers. Her short dress billowed to the floor. Warm, callused palms slid under her rear. And then, in one swift, incredibly deep thrust, he raised her hips and drove into her.

She cried out, her toes curling. He moved atop her, his body heavy on hers, his entry burning where he'd stretched her. But as she pushed her hips against his, the sting throbbed into sweet, aching heat.

He rocked against her, his mouth and his hands hungry and possessive. She clung to him, her fists clenching over the heaving muscles in his back, her cries of pleasure cut short as he ground his mouth over hers in a raw, savage kiss.

This was nothing like the lovemaking they'd experienced on the *Quillie*; it was a frantic, desperate mating fueled by adrenaline and a thousand emotions she could not define. They crashed together in a wild, primitive bond, an extraordinary celebration of survival. And when his powerful body stiffened, then shuddered, liquid heat filled her, triggering a sharp, exquisite climax.

They collapsed together, limbs intertwined.

Rom's head sagged forward until his wet forehead grazed her breasts. Savoring the delicious tremors coursing through her, she sifted lazy fingers through his damp hair. Long moments passed before either was coherent enough to speak—or think.

He lifted his head. "What have I done?"

She smiled and her lids drifted half-closed. "Made me about the most thoroughly loved woman in the universe."

Great Mother. Rom rolled away in self-loathing. Jamming his fingers through his hair, he sat on the edge of the bunk. By all that was holy, she was an unschooled frontier woman and he'd all but raped her. "I am an animal."

"Mmm. An incredibly delicious animal, at that." Jas climbed to her knees and wound her arms around him. His heart sank as she made a small snarl.

"A warrior does not give in to his own needs before those of others."

"Wait—the way we just made love bothered you?"

"That was not lovemaking," he said crisply. "It was primitive and undisciplined."

"And"—she slid her slender arms around his chest to rest her cheek on his shoulder—"incredibly wonderful."

Her soft, warm breasts pressed against the taut muscles in his back. He wanted nothing more than to lean into her embrace, to close his eyes and lose himself in her gentleness, her generosity of spirit. "I needed you," he offered lamely. "My only thoughts were of how much I wanted you. I lost control."

"Ah," she said quietly. "The real issue."

"It is inexcusable."

Her fingertips skated lightly over the scar on his chest. "That's what you were taught."

"Since birth."

"I can't see that applying to sex."

"*Vash Nadah* children receive instruction in the art of lovemaking from their earliest years."

"Instruction?" she blurted, aghast. "What kind of instruction?"

"Discussions, the answering of questions by teachers experienced with the curiosity of youngsters. Nothing on the physical level until the teenage years—and then only for the males." Memories washed over him, the perfume worn by the palace courtesans. Odd that he would remember the scent but not the bodies.

Jas's fingers faltered over his scar. "So you had sex lessons when you were a teenager?"

"Yes. Until a *Vash Nadah* man marries, he is allowed as many women as he pleases. The purpose is to gain skills designed to bring his partner pleasure, ultimately to strengthen a marriage. 'The foundation of society is family. Sexuality enhances spirituality.' It is written in the Treatise of Trade, which is an integral part of our culture, and our faith."

"I'm not criticizing any of that. And I'm by no means an experienced woman when it comes to sex. But knowing I can let go when we're together . . . it's the beauty of our lovemaking—losing control without the fear of losing myself. It's exhilarating, like falling when you're certain someone will catch you. I want you to feel that way with me. It doesn't have to extend to other parts of your life if you don't want it to. It can be something beautiful and special just between us."

He leaned back into her arms and closed his eyes. "Here I saw my loss of control as dishonoring you, while you consider it a compliment." He smiled at the absurdity of it all. "Ah, Jasmine. It won't be easy turning off the teachings of a lifetime."

At his words, she swept tender kisses along his jaw. "I love you, Rom. It scares me to death, but I do; I truly love you with all my heart."

He twisted around and pulled her onto his lap. Gruffly he said, "I love you. I've waited a lifetime for you." Joy lit up her face. Tasting salt and sweetness, he kissed her with a depth of tenderness that was new to him, wanting to convey without words the profound emotions she evoked in him. Never had he felt closer to another.

"The idea of being stranded with you is awfully appealing," she said when they moved apart. "We'll have to talk—about Sharron, about a lot of things. But for now, I hope we're not in a rush to repair this thing."

"The only thing I want to repair is lost time." He wrapped his arms around her waist and tossed her onto the bunk. Though the menace of Sharron's survival and Beela's threats remained, for a brief moment his heart felt as light as Siennan mist. "I say it's time we took advantage of the fact that we're temporarily marooned."

"Fast and furious," she asked teasingly, "or slow and sweet?"

He gave a deep chuckle and gathered her close. "On that, angel, you'll simply have to trust me."

All through the night he loved her with skill and tenderness. As the hours melted one into the next, he introduced her to erotic forms of lovemaking far beyond her experience, bringing her pleasure beyond her imagination. Her fragile sexual confidence bloomed.

When they finally rested, Jasmine whispered, "I didn't

think I was capable of this." She was a real woman again—a normal woman who could give and receive intimate pleasure. Maybe it was because this time she'd chosen a man, instead of a boy masquerading as one. Rom filled the emptiness inside her as no one ever had, and she wanted to see where the relationship would go. But with light-years separating her from her children, from her family and friends, how could she with a good conscience consider staying in space longer than the time she'd planned?

As if sensing her disquiet, Rom wordlessly embraced her, his fingertips wandering over the contours of her back.

Lost in thought, she snuggled against him.

"Lights," Rom said after a while. "Setting dim." Only an overhead light in the bunkroom glowed faintly as they lay twined together, no barriers between them.

Rom wondered what his father would say if word reached the palace reporting that his erstwhile heir was consorting with a once-married, midnight-haired frontier woman with no knowledge of the Treatise of Trade—a mate who would have been absolutely the wrong choice in his former life. No doubt Lord B'kah would denounce him as he had before, iterating to all that his son lacked discipline, that he was impulsive, and that he cared nothing for the foundation of their society. What better way to prove the old man right than by openly taking Jas Hamilton as his lover?

But the very thought of using her induced a shudder of self-loathing. Jas did not belong in a pointless game of spite. She belonged in his arms, warm and sated, while his ship traversed the eternal night of endless space.

Your life is your own now, he reminded himself. Yes, he could be with whomever he pleased. Wrapping his beloved in the protection of his strong body, he let her quiet breathing lull him to sleep.

"Zarra's dead."

Dead. Too shocked to speak, Rom shifted his gaze from Gann's face on the viewscreen to the meal he'd been sharing with Jas before being hailed by the *Quillie* in what he presumed was a routine call to set up their rendezvous.

"*Oh, God,*" Jas murmured in her language, dropping into a crouch next to Rom's chair, her hand resting on his thigh.

"He got to his feet as soon as he went down," Gann explained, his words, Rom suspected, as cautiously chosen as footsteps in a nuclear minefield. "The boy even boarded the speeder on his own. But the blood loss was too severe, too swift—there was nothing Muffin could do. He . . . died a warrior, Rom."

Rom stared fixedly at his half-eaten stew. *Another futile death in this undeclared war.* The realization echoed inside him, until the desire to avenge Zarra boiled over. His knuckles turned white, and he expelled a hiss of air. The spoon clutched in his fist cracked in two, as surely as he wished to snap Sharron's neck.

"Rom?" Jas whispered. Her hand slid over his, warm and reassuring, but he did not, *could not*, release his grip on the broken utensil. The urge to weep was as powerful as his murderous desire to return to Balkanor immediately and kill Sharron. But when he lifted his eyes to Jas's face, and then Gann's, and saw in their expectant gazes the willingness to follow him back to Brevdah

Three against all odds, he shuddered. He would not risk them. Not for a fight that was no longer his.

Rom fought to keep his voice steady. Stiffly, he addressed Gann. "I want you to take the Quillie to Skull's Doom." He knew from long experience that the best way to keep guilt and grief at bay was an exhausting schedule. "Finish our transactions there," he said. "After that, head to Karma Prime and sell our salt as originally planned."

As if Gann worried Rom planned to seek retribution against Sharron on his own, the man's head swerved to Jas. "And you? Where will you go?"

Jas waited for Rom's answer with a steady, unwavering gaze. Her eyes softened with understanding and relief when he replied quietly, "To regroup."

And to somehow find a way to atone for yet another death.

Rom's anguish throbbed into impotent wrath. Each time he confronted Sharron, the monster took someone he cared about. Only this time, he wasn't alone in the aftermath. Jas shared in his mourning, sustaining him with her tenderness and unconditional love, and he was almost relieved when his grief finally dulled into the soul-deep regret to which he'd grown accustomed.

Over the next few days he would busy himself getting Drandon Keer's starspeeder fixed enough to fly. Once off the asteroid, they would fly to the Gorgenon system, where he knew of a mechanic. When the starspeeder was up and running, he and Jas would take a day or two for themselves, to mourn. Nearby, was a planet famous for what was one of the strangest diversions in the known galaxy.

*   *   *

"Oh, my God, Rom, giant snails!" Jas blurted, clinging to a thick branch for all she was worth.

He pried her left hand off the tree they were perched in and pressed it to his lips. "I thought you couldn't wait to ride them. In fact, I recall you asking me questions for a good hour about the first time I came here."

"Anticipation and reality are two different things," she teased back. In truth, though, she was enjoying herself. The respite was welcome after the intensity of their ordeal.

Ceres was enchanting. The climate was temperate and humid, like Hawaii in January, making it ideal for camping. The boulder-strewn glade Rom had chosen in which to pitch their tent was safe from the snails' nightly path—or so he insisted. High above, the trees leaned into each other, their fronds lacing together to form a canopy that muted the daytime sunshine and tinted it green. If only the real universe and its demands—the threat of Sharron, her family waiting for her on Earth—didn't claw at the edges of this brief idyll. She could easily go on like this with Rom forever, living like nomads, moving on when they felt like it. Or simply staying put for a while, as they had during those days on the starspeeder, when time had blurred in a sensual haze. They'd found escape and solace in each other.

Another snail hissed past. Jas gripped the tree. "They're as big as houses."

"And harmless, gentle creatures. Ceresian mollusks are found nowhere else but here. If you pass up this chance you'll regret it the rest of your life." Rom's golden eyes glinted in the dark, starlit night. "But if you'd rather, we can return to the tent. A game of cards, perhaps—"

"Quiet. I'm mentally preparing myself, that's all." Jas set her jaw and peered down at one of the monsters gliding by. Its scarred brown shell glowed in the light of a rising moon, which made the slime on its bumpy skin shimmer. It scraped over the forest floor with a snapping of twigs, its two antennae waving from side to side. Her heart thudded in her chest, and adrenaline made her hands sweaty.

In the distance she heard another couple's laughter as they dropped out of their tree to land on one of the mollusks. People did this all the time, she reminded herself. The goal was to ride the creatures to their feeding area near the sea, and enjoy the view their height afforded.

"I say we take this one here," Rom said. With his chin, he motioned to an approaching brown hulk.

The snail thumped into the tree behind them, jarring it as if it were a fragile twig. She took a steadying breath. "Okay. Let's do it."

"On my call we drop onto its back."

"And then it's 'ride 'em, cowboy.' " The creature's antennae veered her way. Jas shrank back. The thing was probably plotting a round of snail rodeo. Or were snails too dense to tell if you were intimidated, unlike horses and big dogs? She hoped so.

Rom shifted position. "Ready?"

She gulped. "As I'll ever be."

"Three, two, one—*go*."

Her stomach soared up to her ears as she plunged from the tree. She hit the snail hard and scrabbled for a handhold. The cool, moist shell smelled like wet leaves, and the texture was similar to that of a coconut husk, making it easy to grip. Rom helped her crawl to the hump near the snail's undulating neck. The surface was wider and flatter than she'd thought, giving them room to spread out. They held on to the shell's rim, sprawled on their stomachs, side by side. As it crested the hill, the snail swayed slightly, like a gigantic elephant. Silent, they watched the landscape move slowly past. Two moons rose and another set. Ahead the sea gleamed like a treasure chest of pearls.

"What do you think?" Rom asked, the white teeth of his grin visible in the dark.

She laughed in delight and relief. "It's beautiful!"

Rom wound his arm around her shoulders and drew her close. *"You're* beautiful." He nuzzled her ear, then settled his mouth over hers in a warm and sensual kiss.

She risked letting go of the snail shell with one hand to sift her fingers through Rom's clean, silky hair. He deepened the kiss. The excitement of the ride and her seemingly nonstop desire for him spiraled into an explosive mix. Almost giddy, she followed the line of his jaw with breathless, nipping kisses. He responded with the familiar sound he made in the back of his throat whenever she aroused him.

"If you continue doing that," he said, caressing her breast, "you're going to find yourself being made love to on the back of a snail."

"Hmm. Have you?"

"Have I what?"

"Made love on a snail?" She worked her thumbs into the waistband of his pants. "Or will I be the first?"

He forced her onto her back. "You know the answer," he said, seizing her mouth.

Joy shot through her. She was first with him, always first. She wrapped her arms over his shoulders and kissed him passionately. His rich masculine scent blended with the fragrance of damp earth.

Rom's movements became more earnest. His boots scraped over the shell's uneven surface, and she felt him unfastening his trousers, nudging her thighs apart with his knee. She was wearing stretchy pants under a tunic, and he easily tugged them to her ankles. Her legs fell open to the cool evening air. And then he filled her with his thick heat. *"Omlajh anah,"* he murmured. *"Inajh d'anah . . . "* Gripping the shell's rim above her head, he anchored her with his body, rocking slowly.

Her eyes found the starry sky above, and she spiraled higher, soaring in the magic of his touch. The ocean breeze cooled her perspiring skin; the swaying of their bodies mirrored the snail's unhurried gait. Timeless. Eternal. She teetered on the line separating conscious thought from pure sensation. Her pleasure tightened, became exquisitely focused. She couldn't breathe, couldn't think, and she arched into Rom with a soundless plea for release.

He caught her moan with his mouth, kissing her until they found heaven together, limbs entwined, souls meshed, joy resonating between them until only the sound of their labored breathing filled the night.

In the tent the next morning, dawn seeped through the canopy of trees and past the thin membrane of their shelter. Unable to sleep, Jas watched the filmy blue light caress Rom's sleeping face, softening his patrician features. By all appearances, he was a happy man. But she knew he privately tormented himself over Zarra's death, and questioning whether Sharron would eventually attack the *Vash* homeworlds. The eight ancestral planets were critical, and surely his first targets. If the worlds were decimated, it would break the back of the *Vash Nadah* federation. Without a central government, there would be carnage, turmoil, a battle for control.

What would happen to Earth in such a collapse? The thought chilled her. Without a space fleet, her planet would be helpless in an interstellar war. Not to mention all the other planets that might be destroyed.

No political system was perfect, certainly not the *Vash Nadah,* but the alliance of ancient families was all that seemed to separate the galaxy from the terrifying, lawless place it had been eleven thousand years ago. The realization unnerved her, pricking her soldier's instinct to defend. It was time to do something about Sharron.

Chapter Seventeen

"You're safe; the rest of my crew is safe," Rom said as he paced the length of their small tent. "I'm not going to jeopardize that by heading off on a revenge-driven crusade."

"I'm not suggesting you do this alone."

"I want no part of galactic politics."

But other than appealing to the *Vash Nadah* rulers for help, the same men who had turned their backs on him decades ago, he had no way to drum up the kind of support he needed to wipe out the Family of the New Day and their illegal weaponry. He just wouldn't see that. Composing her thoughts, Jas tried to come up with enough justification to change his mind. "You're not facing the same enemy you did twenty years ago. Tell them *that*. Beela's involvement with the group is significant. It means Sharron's now recruiting highborn *Vash*. That means he's gained credibility, and that's going to bring him more powerful, more influential followers."

"The presence of that highborn *Vash* woman disturbed me," Rom affirmed.

"It *shocked* you. I was there. I saw it in your face."

Dryly, he said, "I've been living in the frontier. I haven't kept up with which royals have fled courtly life and which ones haven't. Certainly *Vash Nadah* intelligence has kept track. They undoubtedly are aware of the Family of the New Day."

"But not that Sharron's alive."

"Perhaps. Or maybe they've chosen to ignore that fact."

"Idiots." She shoved their extra clothing into a waterproof sack, snatched the sleeping bag, and rolled it up with furious, jerky movements. "The Family of the New Day's not a cult anymore. It's a full-fledged revolution."

"I know this, Jas—"

"Beela said they'd bring the war to us, to our homes, our families!"

"Boasting is the bread and butter of zealotry."

She whirled on him. "Do we take that chance?" she implored. "Do we have the *right* to take that chance?"

Uncertainty etched weary lines on either side of his mouth. Hands clasped behind his back, he halted in front of the open tent flap and stared outside. After long moments of promising silence, he said, "It would take an immense army to locate and destroy his military storehouse."

"Then we'll raise one. Look, you said you never had proof of his evildoings. Well, now you have me. I'll tell them about the medallions, the antimatter bombs, the fun he planned for me after I had his baby. Put me in front of the Great Council—"

287

"Galactic politics." Rom spat the phrase as if it were a swear word. "Give me the distant frontier, where a man can carve out his own fortune."

And where he could exist far from the reminders of failure that had dogged him all his adult life.

An acute, wistful longing overtook her. She could give him what he wanted, and gain happiness for herself at the same time. Earth qualified as the frontier. They could settle there, live out their lives pretending the galaxy wasn't teetering on the brink of war. But even as she worked up the nerve to invite him home, the mere thought of confining this larger-than-life hero, this once-heir to the galaxy, to her ordinary suburban life in Scottsdale, Arizona, kept her from doing so.

Frustration boiled inside her. She snatched a towel and a packet of soap. "I'm going to the spring to bathe." She prayed she could sort out their dilemma.

Early morning was beautiful on unspoiled Ceres. She wore a pale green dress, one of the outfits she had bought while waiting for the starspeeder to be repaired, a slim, ankle-length garment in a giving fabric designed for space travel. The plush and cozy cloth reflected the dawn light in the slightest of shimmers. It had rained for a while after they'd returned to the tent last night. She remembered listening to the drops drumming on the roof. But it had stopped while they were sleeping, and now only occasional plops of water fell from the tall trees.

She hugged her arms to her chest, inhaling air thick with the rich essence of dampness and plants. But the splendor of the forest brought her no peace. She thought of Rom, the grief and loneliness he'd suffered for so many years, after losing his family as a young man. He'd sacrificed more than anyone had to see Sharron dead.

She couldn't blame him for not wanting face the trauma of loss all over again. Could she?

Head down, she marched into the woods. Runoff water from daily rains had carved a narrow path to the spring. But the boggy ground kept her from walking as fast as she would like. Supposedly the snails were now slumbering in their burrows, but she'd rather not meet up with one alone.

A flock of scarlet birds flitted overhead. She turned to watch them, and her flimsy sandals skidded atop a flat boulder made slick with ooze. She fell hard. Feet swerving out from under her, she yelped and slid like a drunken sea otter into a puddle of stagnant water. Sour-smelling muck splashed onto her face and hair. She spat, wiping the back of her hand across her splattered nose and chin. Silver eddies caught her eye as she wobbled upright, microscopic creatures swirling like glitter in the storm she'd created. Amazing, even the algae were gorgeous in this Garden of Eden.

Where the spring formed a small, tepid pool, the water was clean and clear, with a silt-layered bottom as silky as baby powder. After bathing, she leaned against a sun-warmed boulder and squeezed excess water from her dress and hair. Her toes curled in the spongy, moss-covered ground, where dappled sunshine danced. She looked forward to bringing Rom to the spring. He loved water, having grown up on a desert planet where water was considered a luxury, even for a privileged family. They'd spend the afternoon together, relaxing, laughing . . . making love. Low in her belly she warmed with the thought. Sensuality was an integral part of her personality, and probably always had been, something she was beginning to see as she learned to express that passion physically, rather than confining it to a paintbrush.

The warmth changed to a vaguely unsettled twitching in her stomach. What she needed was some *Vash* breakfast stew—and the good-morning kiss she'd forfeited to argue about Sharron. She headed back.

Savory scents met her at the top of the rise. Lost in thought, Rom was stirring the contents of a pot bubbling on a rack over a laser fire. Her stomach rippled with hunger, then a faint nausea. Absently she rubbed her belly as Rom scooped food into two bowls and joined her on a fallen log. She dragged a piece of flat bread through her stew, hoping to rouse her appetite. But her stomach protested, making her skin feel warm and clammy. She set the bowl down.

"Lost your appetite?" Rom inquired. "Now you know why I don't care to argue before breakfast."

"No, it's not that."

Thoughtful, he regarded her. "You hardly ate last night, either."

"Because I was nervous about the snails. This is different." She took several gulps of air to quell her roiling stomach.

"Nauseated?"

She nodded.

Eyes softening with curiosity and concern, he pressed his palm to her forehead. Then he strode into the starspeeder, returning with a bag of medical supplies, dozens of drugs, biochemically and genetically engineered to cure almost every ill imaginable. She'd learned that, because the medications were so effective, most who lived in the central part of the galaxy saw doctors only for severe injury and surgery.

Rom sprayed a scented mist under her nostrils. When

she inhaled, her abdomen knotted up, as if someone had punched her in the gut. She shot to her feet and ran to the bushes, her hand pressed over her mouth. She fell to her knees, almost blacking out. Her stomach heaved in great spasms until she was left empty and shaking. She was vaguely aware of Rom's presence behind her, his hands smoothing her damp hair away from her face and neck. Sitting back on her haunches, she closed her eyes and panted.

"The worst is over, angel," he assured her, lifting her to her feet. Her legs wobbled, and she leaned against him as he led her away from the underbrush to a blanket he'd spread over the dirt near the fire.

Her stomach muscles unclenched. After a few uncertain moments, she ventured, "I think the drug's starting to work." But queasiness enveloped her as soon as she sat. "Maybe not."

"The drug acts more swiftly with some individuals than others. It'll catch up." Rom eased her backward, settling her against his chest and within the cradle of his thighs. Her damp dress felt horrible, though it hadn't bothered her before, but she was too unmotivated to change or ask him for help.

"Any better?" he asked.

"No . . . it's . . . not helping."

He misted her again with the medicine. "Inhale . . . hold it. That's it. Now let it out slowly." Her pulse pounded in her ears. Rom's wide palms circled over her lower belly. "Perhaps it is something you ate."

"We had the same meals, though." Another queer spasm gripped her middle, and she closed her eyes. "I wonder—it could be too early, I know, but . . . I could be pregnant."

291

His hands froze.

Embracing the idea, she said wistfully, "I was so sick with the twins. For months."

His breath caressed the side of her throat. "But Jasmine, I can't—"

"Yeah, well, that's what you were told. In a diagnosis made years ago. But how do you know it's still true? Every woman you've slept with since took precautions against pregnancy, right?"

"Yes, but—"

"It's been some time since we first made love—without protection—and I'm late." She stopped to pant so she wouldn't have to dash to the bushes before she finished. "What if your sperm count's come back? All it takes is one."

"Jasmine—"

She turned slightly. "But what if?"

His hands fanned protectively over her abdomen, his signet ring sparkling in the sunshine. "Jas . . . to father a child, *our* child—" He swallowed and held her tighter. "Long ago I'd accepted that such riches would never be mine." His voice held enough pain, enough hope, to bring tears to her eyes.

In that defining moment, she saw her reservations about remaining in space for what they were: she'd believed her family and friends couldn't exist without her because it was a built-in excuse to flee happiness, to flee Rom's love, for fear of being disappointed again. Accepting that, she allowed a future she hadn't contemplated to unfold in her mind's eye: Rom, the seasoned warrior, cradling an infant in his muscular arms; then herself, breastfeeding after all these years.

"Can you see us as new parents?" she asked, laughter in her voice. "At our age?"

"Nonsense! We're in our prime." Rom pushed aside her damp hair and pressed his lips to the side of her throat. "*Vash Nadah* delight in large families. We'll have more after this one."

A hot-cold sensation spilled into her middle. Prickles of nausea quickly turned into needles scouring her insides, but she couldn't take the deep breaths necessary to blunt the pain. A hiccup slashed at her insides. She winced, touched quivering fingertips to her lips, and her hand unfurled into a blossom of glistening crimson blood.

She wasn't pregnant; there wasn't going to be a baby. And she might not live to try again to make one. Along with skyrocketing fear, the unspoken understanding flickered between them.

He hoisted her into his strong arms. She must have passed out for a few seconds, for when she came to, she was on her knees, puking her guts out in the bushes.

Rom waited until Jasmine lifted her head, then dabbed her mouth with a soft towel. Foreboding consumed him. She was bleeding internally—the color had already leached from her lips.

Aboard the starspeeder, he settled her into the bunk. "Try to remember. Did you nibble on something at the spring?" He leaned over her. "Fruit? A blade of grass? Anything at all?"

Her brows drew together. Between what appeared to be spasms of extreme pain, she managed, "Puddle . . . fell. Swallowed water."

His anxiety spiked. Parasites. Voracious parasites existed that could consume internal organs in the space of hours. He tucked her in bed, bolted out the door of the starspeeder, and tossed their camping gear in the cargo hold. Then he blasted out of Ceres for Gorgenon Prime, the planet where they'd had the starspeeder repaired, and the only one in the system with a doctor.

With the coordinates entered into the navigation computer, he floated in zero gravity back to the bunk, hunkering down by Jas's side. Inventorying his medical kit, he grabbed a pain-blocker and an antiparasitic. They would buy him time, of which instinct told him he had precious little. He fitted the pain-blocker patch below her jaw, then slipped a paper-thin antiparasitic disk under her tongue. "This will help until we get to the doctor," he said, brushing his knuckles over her cheek.

Her midnight hair floated around her head like a halo. Her lips had taken on a bluish tint, and her skin was turning gray. Between breaths, she moaned.

Rom felt helpless, and he detested it. Even if he reached a physician in time, the damage done by then might be extraordinary. By all that was holy, he had no business taking her to Gorgenon Prime. She needed a *Vash Nadah*–trained surgeon, not the run-of-the-mill practitioner he'd no doubt find there. *Vash Nadah* physicians were the best doctors in the galaxy. But he might as well wish for a magic wand. Those renowned, highly skilled individuals were raised from birth to treat the eight rulers and their families—and served them exclusively.

He was one of them, was he not? One of the eight, the once-scion to the B'kahs. No matter how thoroughly his past deeds had sullied his family name, that simple fact remained—blood was blood.

Hand over hand, he propelled himself back to the cockpit and consulted his star map. His mind buzzed with possibilities, while hope thrummed in his veins. Mistraal . . . yes. The ancestral planet of the family Dar was but a day's journey at maximum speed. It was also his brother-in-law's home, a man he had once considered his close friend.

A man he hadn't spoken to in twenty years.

Not that Rom's life spent on the fringes of civilized space had facilitated familial contact, if Joren had cared to try . . .

He rotated in the chair to face the bunk. Aside from surrendering what little personal pride he had left, showing up on a *Vash Nadah* homeworld looking for help was in flagrant violation of the mandate that had transformed him from heir to the throne, to outcast. Not to mention that it would amount to outright groveling. But resolve fortified him at the sight of Jas's pain-etched face. The planet Mistraal was his best chance, perhaps his only chance, at finding a surgeon with the skills to save her. *If Joren Dar's starfighters don't blast me to cosmic dust first.*

Willing that dismal prospect from his mind, Rom reached for the navigation console and entered the co-ordinates for the desolate, windswept planet Mistraal.

Pushed to maximum speed, the starspeeder shook. Stars stretched to impossible lengths across the forward viewscreen, while Mistraal, a tiny pinprick of light, crept across the navigation display. Rom had kept up the grueling pace all day, while Jas grew slowly colder, weaker.

By now she would have been under a doctor's care

on Gorgenon. Instead she was dying on a thin-sheeted space pilot's bunk. As in poker, the game her people so loved, he had to bet everything on what he could not see. All he could do now was pray that when fate's hand was revealed, the cards were in his favor.

"Unidentified starspeeder, this is Mistraal Control!"

Rom jolted instantly alert.

"You are entering protected space," the controller barked. "State identification."

"Starspeeder, all-purpose class-type M, registration number 18693, M-2A."

"State intentions."

Rom spoke slowly, evenly. "Request permission to land. Medical emergency. I repeat, medical emergency."

"Pilot identification," the controller demanded.

"Romlijhian B'kah."

"Er . . . say again?"

"Romlijhian B'kah." A telling silence followed, and he pictured the conversation that must surely be taking place in the control pod.

Another controller took over, a bit more experienced, as evidenced by her sterner, confident voice. "State pilot identification."

Rom spread his hands on the console and replied. He must have come within interrogation range, for a string of lights then danced across his forward computer panel as Mistraal extracted the information they needed to authenticate his claim.

The sparkles winked out. Minutes of silence dragged into almost half an hour. Then icy shards of dread began to chip away at his confidence. He floated out of the chair and stretched his cramped muscles. He looked back toward Jas. "Patience, angel. Simply a minor bureaucratic snarl. Nothing's changed in the years I've been gone."

The lightness of his tone did not transfer to his heart. He'd gambled that his sister's husband wouldn't turn him away. But what if the years had eradicated what loyalty might linger from friendship and family ties? Joren Dar could refuse him entry.

Easily. Or what if Joren was dead?

Then what?

Perspiration needled his forehead. The other *Vash Nadah* worlds were too distant to be of any use. If Joren turned him away—and he'd be well within his rights— Rom would be forced to take his chances on some forsaken planet. And Jas would die; he knew it as surely as he breathed.

"Attention 18693, M-2A—this is Mistraal—do you read?"

He shoved himself into the chair. "Go."

"You have permission to land. Proceed to checkpoint alpha."

"Copy," Rom said on a sharp exhalation. "Checkpoint alpha." Grabbing the thrust lever, he eased the craft into the landing protocol.

Fatigued to his very bones, Rom cradled Jas in his arms and strode through the hatch of the starspeeder into a vast anteroom. *Remember that you are a B'kah. The blood of Romjha runs in your veins.* He squared his shoulders and lifted his chin. As his boots echoed off the floor of flawless white crystal, he instinctively searched the group assembling in the chamber for a familiar face, but found none.

"Summon your surgeon," he told the openly curious

palace dwellers, using the most authoritative voice he could muster in his depleted state.

Two men nodded and ran from the room. Irritated, Rom watched them go. Hadn't he transmitted on arrival that he needed a doctor to meet him? Why wasn't one here waiting?

"Rom—it *is* you!"

The familiar, breathy voice cut through the crowd. He steeled himself as the gathering parted for his sister. Melon-hued silk breezed behind her as she hurried toward him. Her hair was piled ornately on the top of her head and partially hidden beneath a filmy veil. Swept back from her face, the style revealed the elegant features of a woman—not the girl he once knew.

He felt a rush of homecoming, a sense of years wasted. Somehow he kept control of his emotions, a far more difficult task now that he'd grown accustomed to revealing them to Jas. "Di—" he said lamely, using her childhood nickname as if days instead of years had passed since they'd last seen each other.

Tears welled in her eyes. "They told me it was you. I was afraid to believe—but by the heavens, you are actually here." She slid one warm, smooth hand over his cheek and traced the contours of his face.

He caught her hand. "Never have you been far from my thoughts."

"Nor you from mine," she whispered.

Her expression of unqualified joy told him what he'd dared not hope. The love between them had survived their years apart.

Swallowing hard, he forced himself to focus on the reason he was here. "Is your surgeon on the way?"

Her gaze veered to Jas, whose hair tumbled nearly to

the floor. "Yes." Clearly taken with Jas's startlingly exotic appearance, she asked, "Who is she?"

"My *a'nah*." The words slipped out without forethought.

His sister peered at Jas with heightened interest. Unconsciously Rom hugged Jas more tightly to his chest. Though not formal, the title "wife-without-spoken-vows" would give Jas much-needed status in a society that revolved around rank and family.

He would simply explain everything when she awoke.

"You summoned my surgeon," Joren called out as he caught up to his wife. His ceremonial robes swirled around his tall, muscular frame as he halted beside her. "The woman is ill?"

"Yes," Rom replied uneasily, unable to tell from Joren's guarded expression what the man thought of his arrival here. "Parasites. The most incredibly voracious species I've seen. My antiparasitic had little to no effect." Desperation slipped into his voice. "I fear that if she is not treated immediately she will die."

Joren flicked his hand and more men ran off, presumably to speed the surgeon's appearance. "I was not informed of the seriousness of her condition. Bello!" he shouted. "Bring the senior controller to me immediately. With the feeble excuse on the tip of his tongue as to why I was given incomplete information." When the man fled the chamber, Joren muttered, "Unlike my space controllers, my surgeon and his staff are the best the galaxy has to offer. We will make the woman well."

"His *a'nah*," Di supplied pointedly.

The couple exchanged glances. "Your *a'nah*, then. She is welcome here." He sought and held Rom's gaze. Two decades of misgiving shone in his eyes, along with unequivocal regard and love. "As are you, my brother," he whispered.

Rom's throat closed painfully. He extended his right hand, despite his hold on Jas, and Joren grasped his forearm in the traditional familial greeting.

There was a commotion. The crowd of palace onlookers separated to allow a green-robed surgeon and his entourage past. A knot of capable assistants eased Jas onto a gurney. Rom and Joren accompanied them out of the vast antechamber and into a maze of well-traveled corridors. Everyone he passed stared, openmouthed. "The B'kah," some whispered.

Under his breath, Rom said, "You've taken a great personal risk by allowing me to stay. There'll be consequences when the others find out."

"I don't care a scarran's seed about—"

"Just save her, Joren," Rom interjected, his voice pleading and low. "That's all I ask. Save her and I'll trouble you no more."

A chime woke Jas, but the healing fragrance of Siennan incense was what finally coaxed her to open her eyes. It took a while to absorb where she was. The enormous bedroom was suffused with the soft glow of laser-candles. Three walls were carved from an opaque, almost luminescent material resembling white crystal, while the fourth was entirely open to the outside, a terrace overlooking a vista of desolate steppes awash in muted hues of ocher, pumpkin, and beige. Lush cushions and wall hangings kept the spacious chamber from feeling cold.

Floating on a sense of well-being—of having healed—she decided that Rom must have found a doctor, and a fine one, too, judging by the quality of her surroundings.

Another crisp *ting* of metal hitting a bell interrupted the silence. She rolled to her side. Her insides felt battered and tight, as though she'd done too many sit-ups— a *thousand* too many.

Across the shadowed room, a broad-shouldered form knelt before an altar. His powerful body was bowed humbly as he tapped his prayer wand against an ancient-looking engraved bell.

Sending his prayers to heaven.

Her throat squeezed tight. "Rom," she called huskily, lifting one hand. He whipped around and met her gaze. His expression revealed his stark relief and the intensity of his emotions. If there was any doubt that he loved her the way she loved him, it evaporated in that moment.

He strode across the room and eased himself next to her in bed, carefully and tenderly, as though she'd break if he moved too fast. He slipped his arms around her and murmured against her hair, "So how do you feel, angel?"

"One hundred percent better." Contentedly she tucked one hand inside his loose silken shirt to savor the heat of his skin. "How long have we been here?" she said softly. "And what did they do to me?"

"Three days. During which you underwent abdominal surgery and tissue regeneration."

"And I feel this good?" She hesitantly felt for scars and stitches. Her stomach was tender and a bit puffy, but as smooth as before. "Amazing."

He brushed his lips across her forehead. "The surgeon is a master. Among the best in the galaxy."

"Like this hospital, no doubt." The bedroom resembled her suite at the Romjha Hotel, only it was three times as big and decorated on a more opulent scale. Wealth and good taste infused every fixture in the room, many of them works of art in their own right. "Where are we—Gorgenon Prime?"

She felt the muscles in his back tighten. "No. Mistraal."

She peered down at him. "We're on Mistraal? A ruling *Vash* homeworld?"

"Yes. The Dar Palace."

She searched his shadowed face for confirmation that he was joking.

"Gorgenon Prime did not maintain the facilities necessary to save you. Here, they did." He reached up and cupped her face with one warm, dry hand. "Joren Dar is my brother-in-law."

Words eluded her. The enormity of what Rom had done for her hit her hard. He hadn't wanted to go home, to involve himself in *Vash* affairs, even with Sharron's threat weighing on his conscience. Now here they were. "Did you tell them about Sharron?"

"Only Joren. We spoke yesterday."

She leaned toward him. "And?"

"He was shocked to hear Sharron survived. But even more so when I told him illegal weaponry is involved. I told him this is bigger than we thought, that all we value as a society is at stake. Now Joren is meeting with his advisers and intelligence officers to see if more can be learned."

Thoughtfully, she said, "So *Vash* intelligence didn't know about the Family of the New Day after all."

"They do now. At first light we'll leave. The starspeeder is packed with supplies and ready to go."

She pushed herself up. Her robe fell open and she

clutched it closed, pressing the sumptuous, satiny blue cloth to her breasts. "I thought this was your sister's home."

"It is, but—"

"Did you tell her your plans?"

"No, but—"

"Good," she said with a sigh. "It'd be beyond me how a woman who hadn't seen her only brother in years could let him walk away after a three-day visit."

"Jasmine, we will leave at sunrise. I've already told them what I know. I have no place here."

"Phooey," she snapped. "This is *family*."

"My presence here places my brother-in-law in an awkward position, should the ruling council find out."

"*That's* politics. There's a difference."

He heaved a weary sigh. The entry door banged open and the melodic sound of children's laughter spilled into the room. "*Tajhar Rom, Tajhar Rom!*" Half a dozen bronzed, golden-eyed cherubs scampered to the bed, belting out shrieks of joy as they tugged on Rom's shirt.

"Who invited you into my bedchamber?" he demanded playfully as he bounded out of bed. "You will pay for this act of impudence." He grabbed the two littlest ones, a boy and a girl, and tossed them onto the floor cushions, tickling them into fits of squealing giggles, while the older four danced around him, vying for attention.

"*Parjhonian, Entok, Jon . . . Theea et Preejha.*" A tall, graceful woman clothed from head to toe in white silk burst through the open doors.

Jas's heart leaped. She was a female version of Rom. She had the same gorgeous sculpted features, dark-lashed pale eyes, and nutmeg-hued hair, which she wore braided and coiled on the top of her head.

The woman shooed the children away, her bracelet-adorned arms gesturing wildly as she scolded them in a lyrical and expressive tongue that had to be Siennan. After herding them outside, she shoved the double doors closed and slumped against them. Her golden eyes brimmed with wit and intelligence—and a good deal of curiosity as she gave Jas a thorough once-over. Switching to accented Basic, she said, "My heart sings to see you up and well," before launching into a rather flustered apology for the children's intrusion.

Jas protested. "Six children, and there can't be more than a year separating them. Frankly I don't know how you do it. I had my hands full with two."

"Ah, but my three are much older. Those ruffians are my nieces and nephews." She regarded Jas, then Rom, her gaze brimming with affection.

Rom introduced the women with a gracious sweep of his hand. "My sister, Dilemma Dar. Di, we call her."

Jas choked back a small sound of amused surprise. *Dilemma—how apropos.* Extending her hand, she said, "I'm so glad to meet you." With a challenging glance in Rom's direction, she added, "I *do* look forward to getting to know you better."

Predictably, his expression darkened. Oblivious, Di told him cheerily, "Everyone's gathering in the dining hall. You'd best help your wife prepare for the evening meal."

Jas gaped at him. "Your *wife?*"

Rom groaned.

"You're . . . *married?*" she asked incredulously.

"There isn't a wife," he assured her.

Dismayed, Di cried out, "But you said—"

"I meant that Jas is my wife."

Jas's mind spun. "Would someone please tell me what is going on?"

Appearing sheepish, Rom crouched at her side. Taking her hand in his, he gave her a lengthy and convoluted explanation of the term *a'nah,* and why he'd thought it would benefit her. The emotional benefits were less clear. He hadn't mentioned a desire to make the arrangement legal.

And why would he? she thought, gazing around the spacious room, the silk carpets and gold-inlaid mosaics, walls that reflected light like an iced-over pond. The place was a castle. In *Vash* circles marriages were alliances between mighty families, not love matches with divorced housewives from backwater planets like Earth.

She gave a small, disappointed sigh.

Di's eyes sparked with mischief. "Dear brother, I rejoice. With your infinite charm, you have convinced this lovely woman to be your *a'nah.*" She melted his narrow-eyed, big-brother frown with a sweet smile. "Do escort her to dinner—if she feels up to it." Nodding at Jas, she left the room in an elegant sashay.

When the door closed, Jas folded her arms over her chest.

Rom spread his hands. "What?"

"She loves you. And you love her."

He sighed.

"Still, we're leaving."

He walked away from her, twisting the signet ring on his finger. "If I stay, I fear I'll be forced to choose between you and my involvement here."

"You won't. Not if you convince the *Vash Nadah* to take over the fight." She gathered her robe around her and climbed out of bed, wincing as she did so. "Listen to me. Even if you don't want to get involved with what's going on with Sharron . . . life's too short—if we get a day of happiness, or a week or month or year, we need to grab hold of it, because tomorrow's not promised to anyone. Stay a little longer, Rom. Please." She grasped his upper arms. "Just to recapture some of what you and your sister lost."

Rom closed his eyes to steady himself. In the sudden silence, a bowl of incense popped and hissed, and hushed voices emanated from outside the room. The heat of her skin brought to him her sweet fragrance, the scent of freshly laundered bed linens, and the faint tang of medicinals.

He opened his eyes to find her watching him worriedly. "We will stay here awhile longer," he said to her obvious relief. He knew not the consequences of his acquiescence, but something within him hinted it was what destiny had planned all along. "Meanwhile, I'll not squander the opportunity to talk my people into seizing the gauntlet, even if it requires my throwing it at their feet."

"If you think the *Vash Nadah* are stubborn, wait until you see me in action. They won't be able to deny us."

Dryly, Rom said, "An exile and an Earth-dweller conspiring to break down eleven thousand years of galactic pacifism. Should be interesting."

Jas didn't let his sarcasm deter her. Obviously the thought of participating in such an undertaking electrified her. "This is a campaign of good versus evil in its purest form. It's an adventure more ambitious and meaningful than any I've ever imagined." She took a breath to calm herself. "You won't be alone in this. I'll be by your side every step of the way."

Rom covered her shoulders with his hands and moved her to arm's length. "You'd do this for me."

Her voice softened with love. "I'd do *anything* for you."

Her devotion, her absolute faith in him, filled him with wonder. Others had abandoned him—but not her. Sliding the pads of his fingers along her jaw and under her chin, he tilted her face up. "Ah, Jasmine, I bless the day the Great Mother brought you to me, and every day since that She has allowed you to be with me."

Moisture glistened in her eyes. It seemed his admission had caught her off guard.

He gentled his tone. "I am grateful to you, Jas. For your purity of heart, your spontaneity, the way you make me laugh. And that, in my darkest hours, you've always admired me for what others disdained in me." He grazed his knuckle over her cheek. "Sometimes we don't say aloud all that we feel inside. Then the chance is lost and the words never said."

"You sound like you're saying good-bye," she whispered.

"Bah! I'm merely expressing what is in my heart. I want a simple life, a life with *you*. Somewhere, anywhere I can keep you safe, you and your children. Your entire family if need be, mother, father, sisters—"

She flung her arms around him in an impetuous hug. His hands crept under her robe and up her bare back. Holding her close, he was loath ever to release her. Twenty years before, her appearance had signaled the end of life as he'd known it. Now that his "angel" had led him full circle back to the *Vash Nadah*—and his traditional obligations—he couldn't help wondering how many more moments like this they had left.

Chapter Eighteen

Word that the legendary B'kah had taken up residence at the palace spread quickly, bringing *Vash* diplomats and members of the great council to Mistraal in never-before-seen numbers. The Dar compound was jammed with would-be crusaders. More arrived every day. When Rom last checked in with the *Quillie*, Gann stated that they, too, were on their way.

But despite relentless lobbying to amass a force large enough to hunt down and destroy Sharron's bases, Jas was sorry to see that their efforts netted them but a handful of true allies. Ever careful to defer to those in power, Rom was disinclined to do more than meet with the visitors in private audiences, always insisting that he had not come here to involve himself in *Vash* politics. But the longer they stayed, the more involved he became, until finally he bowed to Joren's urging to give an address.

Susan Grant

Since Rom was banned from setting foot on the Wheel, the vast structure housing the Great Council when in session, he agreed to speak at the palace. Jas worked doggedly with him on its content, hoping it would be the catalyst they needed to spur the *Vash* into declaring war against Sharron. Unfortunately, the villain hadn't helped their cause by virtually disappearing in the weeks since they'd fled his compound.

"While you were in the exercise chamber this afternoon," Rom said, venting his frustrations one evening while she dressed for dinner, "a group of council elders took it upon themselves to inform me that my implication that Sharron possesses and intends to use forbidden technology is merely conjecture—and thus not worthy of their concern."

"What did you say?"

" 'Do we have the right to take that chance?'—the very question you asked of me on Ceres. But they want proof, proof that the forbidden technology exists. And that is the one thing I cannot give them." He walked to their bed and settled tiredly onto the coverlet, wedging a pillow behind his head. "Sharron has always been too clever to allow that proof to become known."

His fatigue and frustration troubled her. "Joren supports you. So does that plantation owner, Drandon Keer. They don't need proof."

"No, but they are friends."

"Friends with influence and money."

"Resources are useless without unity." He stared at the ceiling. "Perhaps if the B'kahs would come, true headway might be made."

"Your father." Jas tried to hide her distaste for the man. Even now he was blocking Rom's efforts. Her fingers stiffened as she twisted her damp hair into a chignon. Fumbling, she made a conscious effort to relax them in order to put her hair up. "This is more his responsibility than yours. He's the one who didn't help in the first place. And he and the other elders are the ones who've mismanaged the trade routes and given the Family of the New Day the chance to come back, not you."

"When my father should have devoted his time to the Great Council and left the day-to-day mechanics of ruling to a son, he had to do two jobs. It is hard to do them both well."

His calm impartiality surprised her. "You're making excuses for him. I don't know if he deserves it."

"We've all made mistakes," Rom quietly conceded. "Perhaps I'm finally beginning to understand that."

A series of resounding booms rumbled through the palace, coming closer and closer until a startling *whoomph* blasted behind her. Air swirled past her ankles. She spun around. "The shields?"

"Yes. They'll stay in place over every portal until the wind velocity drops to normal levels."

The *Tjhu'nami.*

She peered out beyond the terrace to the endless savanna. A ten-foot-thick clear barrier was now in place. Beyond it, the long grasses were completely flattened. She could feel, but not quite hear, a constant rumbling—the receding tide of air before a distant monstrous wave.

Deadly windstorms made Mistraal the most inhospitable and forbidding of the eight *Vash Nadah* homeworlds. By midnight—nights here were half as long as Earth nights—the *Tjhu'nami* was anticipated to reach an unimaginable eight hundred knots. Worse, the storm would pass directly over the palace and Dar City, home

311

to the planet's entire population. Shuddering, Jasmine rubbed her hands up and down her arms. Ever since the weather station on the huge space-city orbiting Mistraal had issued its warning, she'd been as agitated as an apartment-bound cat that sensed an earthquake was imminent, but could do nothing more than dart from couch to chair to coffee table.

"My ears are popping," she said, tearing her gaze from the once-soothing vista.

"So are mine. The atmospheric pressure's plunging. Dar City will literally close down within—" Sitting up, Rom glanced at his watch. "Well, now. It looks as if we already have. Total communications blackout—for at least a day."

She thought of the envoys crowding the palace—relentless in demanding Rom's time. And those in the space-city high above the planet. "That means no one can fly out, unless it's an emergency."

"Nor in, either." Mischief glinted in his golden eyes.

She matched his devilish grin. "Poor politicians, stuck in orbit. What a shame."

"For them, perhaps. For us, a temporary respite I say we celebrate." He swung his legs off the bed and extended his hand. "Allow me to escort you to dinner, angel."

The Dar Palace was a galactic version of medieval splendor—with all its idiosyncrasies. Dinners were communal banquets shared with hundreds of others in the largest room Jas had ever seen. Massive columns of white marble supported a dome resplendent with hand-painted scenes of an alien sea, replete with creatures she'd not find on any Earth shore. The ceiling was so high that moisture collected there in diaphanous ribbons of mist, imparting the dreaminess of a mermaid's underwater castle.

Rom led Jas past tables laden with fragrant delicacies. Sociable men and women, descendants of those who had attended the Dars for eons—a sought-after position among the merchant class—served hot and cold dishes of every description, liqueurs, wines and juices, casks of salt, the best the galaxy had to offer.

As the wind slammed hurricane fists against the shielded windows that spanned the height of the room, the very air drummed with the tempest. Yet musicians played, Bajha aficionados regaled each other with tales, and children squirmed and giggled, while sinewy, downy-haired ketta-cats prowled under the tables, looking for scraps.

As usual, they sat with Joren and Di, their children, and assorted powerful and influential members of the Dar clan. Since most spoke Siennan, except when addressing her, Jas was immersed in the tongue. The language was difficult, but gradually she was learning to communicate. She was thankful that tonight the conversation centered on lighthearted subjects, perhaps due to her and Rom's obvious exhaustion in the wake of preparing for his address, and their consideration of it. The Dars were family, after all.

"The Earth beverage, sir." A young man sporting a double row of silver triangles down his nose handed Rom a flask of wheat-colored liquid crowned with a layer of white foam. Then he bowed and backed away.

Rom grinned. "Beer."

Protests and groans met his announcement.

"A different recipe this time!" he shouted over the

noise. "The cooks assure me that it will win your stomachs and your hearts, as Jas's precious supply won mine. Give me your glasses."

All within reach reluctantly thrust out what clean cups they could find. Rom splashed beer into them one by one. Foam bubbled over onto the tablecloth, spreading in dark circles over the holographic pattern.

As Rom poured the last of the beer into her goblet, Jas remarked, "At least it's the right color this time."

He sniffed. "The aroma is promising, as well." He raised his goblet high. "Let us drink!"

Jas nearly gagged when the bitter liquid hit her tongue. Fingertips pressed to her lips, she glanced around, desperate for any alternative to swallowing the stuff.

"Romlijhian!" Joren bellowed, slamming his glass down.

Jas squeezed her eyes shut and swallowed.

Rom dabbed at his mouth with a napkin. "Yes, brother?"

Mirth danced in Joren's watering eyes. "Be warned, if I ever see this beverage at my table again, I will happily and quite unceremoniously bathe you in it!"

Laughter erupted. Rom waved his napkin like a flag of surrender. Then he dipped his head to Jas's ear. "You say your friend Dan Brady maintains an Earth establishment devoted solely to the creation and distribution of beer?"

She smiled. "Well, he serves solid food, too."

"We'll partake of both, naturally, but the beer is what intrigues me." His mouth tipped crookedly into a roguish grin, reminding her that he was still a rebel smuggler at heart. "Red Rocket Ale," he said, pronouncing it *Redeh*

Rockeet Ell. "I still have in my possession the trade agreement you brought with you from Earth. I believe it grants me an exclusive arrangement."

She slid her arms around his waist. "You know, I have the feeling you're going to make Dan a very wealthy man. B'kah and Brady—purveyors of beer to the stars."

He threw back his head and laughed.

Oddly, his delight tugged at her heart. "I haven't seen you do that in . . . I can't remember how long."

"What? Laugh?"

She nodded. "It's wearing on you. The stress, the long hours. I realize we're racing against the clock, but if you don't take a break, you'll burn yourself out."

He turned pensive, drumming his fingers on his upper arms. Then his golden eyes sparked almost boyishly. "Let's go flying."

She reared back. "Are you serious? Where? When?"

"Patrol—each in our own starfighter. It's more a tradition than a necessity, but after a storm passes, the Dars launch ships to survey damage to the palace—if any— and to symbolically reestablish contact with the space-city. No doubt the space chief has already chosen pilots for the mission, but surely he'll be amenable to a little, ah, rearranging."

She smiled and squeezed his hand. He was doing this for her, to cheer her and alleviate her concern. No matter what his condition, he always put her first. *The good of the people outweighs the desire of the individual.* It was what he was taught as the young heir to the throne.

She considered that, and then all the people who had flown here to hear him speak. They were looking to him for leadership, and she couldn't help wondering what that would someday mean for their relationship. But for

315

now, for the space of this one flight he wanted to arrange, he was hers.

"Auxiliary boosters."

"Check," Jas said over the comm linking her vessel to Rom's.

"Life-support system."

"Check."

"Weapons systems," Rom finished.

"On-line."

Jas glanced at him across the shadowy hangar. Supposedly she wasn't "seeing" him at all.

"Let me see if I understood you correctly," she asked. "My windows aren't really windows?"

"Correct. They're viewscreens, simulating exactly what you'd see if they were transparent. Only they're better than transparent. The onboard computer compensates for any decay in visibility."

Cool, she thought. Except for her brief stint at the controls in the *Quillie* and the starspeeder, she hadn't piloted anything in decades, and certainly not a craft this automated. Even the seat she was strapped to was "smart." Capable of reacting faster than any human brain, and certainly *her* brain, it provided protection and guidance in situations ranging from interstellar combat to the far more mundane task of shielding her from the tremendous accelerations required for space flight.

Lowering her black visor over her face, she gave Rom a thumbs-up.

"Patrol One's ready," Rom radioed to the space controller, who sat in a pod just outside the cavernous shuttle bay.

"Cleared to launch," the controller replied.

Jas gave a silent cheer as the shield in front of her vibrated, then slowly lifted. Dried leaves and grasses whirled inside the bay, borne on the wind of the dying storm. Spread out before her were endless plains below a dust-yellowed sky. As in her fighter pilot days, she sat poised like an eagle about to take wing.

In a burst of energy, Rom's starfighter departed first. Three seconds later, she flipped on the thrusters. G-forces pressed her into her seat, bringing on a fleeting twinge of pain in her abdomen, where she was still healing.

Clearing the hanger, she aimed the craft's nose at the sky. Though piloting the starfighter wasn't difficult, she saw she wouldn't have the same ease she'd acquired in her F-16.

The storm was ebbing rapidly, but turbulence shook her starfighter in uneven jolts. Hampered by oversize engines and stubby wings, the craft was designed for space rather than the atmosphere, but it was smaller, more advanced, and more heavily armed than the starspeeder Drandon had loaned Rom. For a society that abhorred conflict, the *Vash* certainly put a lot of effort and expense into their weaponry.

Within moments she joined Rom in formation. Side by side, several hundred feet apart, they soared over the prairie, searching the sprawling palace below for damage. Finding none, Rom said, "Onward to the space-city," and took them higher, through the atmosphere, until stars took the place of the rising sun.

Space. A rush of freedom swept through her, and she suspected Rom felt it, too. Turning the heavens into a glittering carousel of stars, he led her through a series of practice maneuvers, careful not to heap too much strain on her tender stomach.

"Patrol One, this is Mistraal Control," said a voice in their comm.

"Go ahead," answered Rom.

"Unable to establish contact with the space-city. When you arrive, have the controller initiate comm from their end."

At first the exchange puzzled Jas. How could they be cut off? Forty thousand citizens made their home there and on the mining colonies. The controller's problem gave her an insight into the differences between the way Rom's people and hers on Earth had developed. The *Vash* had perfected star travel and built space-cities, yet the Dars couldn't compensate for something as simple as atmospheric turmoil disrupting space-to-planet transmissions.

Rom acknowledged the call, then moved his craft close to her left wing. Cockpit to cockpit, she waved him off. "You're taking a chance, space cowboy," she said when he stayed put. "This is no F-16. No guarantees how steady I can keep this thing."

"So why wouldn't you dance with me last night at dinner?" he asked, immune to her warning.

She gave an incredulous laugh. The question was the very last one she expected in the midst of flying patrol. "It was the promise song, that's why."

"We're an unmarried couple. That is the only requirement to perform it."

"Unmarried couples intending to legally wed."

"When I request the song again tonight, will you dance voluntarily? Or will I have to toss you over my shoulder?"

She snorted. "I dare you." Something told her that shoulder tossing wasn't an everyday event in Joren's palace. "We'll be the oldest ones out there by twenty years. But you, I take it, as family rebel are tired of such details?"

He sighed. "More than you will ever know."

The airless, frigid chasm of space sat between them like an unwelcome chaperon, magnifying their sudden silence.

From his cockpit, Rom wished he could see past Jas's visor, wished he could read what was in her eyes. "My decision to make you my *a'nah* was impulsive. It is not at all what I wanted for us, but I haven't a choice. I have no title, few resources." And if he joined with a non–*Vash Nadah* woman in an unapproved, unarranged marriage, it meant giving up his secret hope of reclaiming his father's favor.

His stomach muscles tensed. Well, he thought. He'd finally admitted it. But with the admission came a harder realization. If the man wished to see him, he would have done so already. But in its own way, that, too, was liberating.

"By all that is holy, Jasmine, we ought to be wed. Lawfully. Alas, I have spent a lifetime dreaming of the impossible, wishing for what cannot be—"

"Why can't it?"

Because he never imagined such a decision was his to make. The concept shook him. His life was his own now, was it not? He was not the B'kah heir, would never be again. They'd leave soon to visit Earth, and after that . . . well, they had yet to discuss it. Of course, there was the question of whether she'd actually consent to any arrangement . . .

His words rushed out like a nervous youth's. "We would need authorization—I've no official title, you see. But then, you are not *Vash Nadah*. However, there are different restrictions for the frontier, looser restrictions. The Treatise of Trade states—"

"Rom."

He stopped himself midsentence.

Her voice was husky, a soft caress. "Are you asking me to marry you?"

With the computer maintaining the fighter's speed, Rom gripped the control stick with one hand and lifted his other, pressing it to the window facing Jas. "Yes." Silent, she raised her hand, fingers spread wide, as if overlaying her palm with his. He reached out with his senses until he could almost feel the heat of her skin coursing up his arm.

Tenderly, he asked, "Well? What say you to a lifetime formally bound to a space drifter with nothing to offer but a cargo ship and a bad reputation?"

Jas had no chance to respond. Out of nowhere a hunk of jagged metal hurtled toward them. She banked right and he veered left. The debris tumbled between them.

"Asteroids?" Jas asked tightly.

"No." He checked his viewscreen. "It was an outlying buoy. One we would have used to set up a comm link with the space-city." He searched ahead for the other buoys. "That's odd. I can't find anything."

"Let me try." She input the coordinates he gave her into her viewscreen. "It looks like more debris."

He initiated a diagnostic on his ship and Jas's, certain he'd find a malfunction explaining it all. But he found no glitches, only an empty viewscreen. The back of his neck prickled. Where was the space-city? Surely he'd have seen it by now—the sparkling lights on the immense central cylinder, the majestic spokes radiating outward. But nothing seemed to be out there.

Impossible. Something that huge simply didn't disappear.

They blazed over the curve of the planet and into a sea of wreckage. *Great Mother.* Their starfighters looked like specks compared to the chunks of solidified slag whirling past. But the smaller items were what riveted his attention: a broken chair, a shoe. He fought a surge of nausea.

"What's happened?" Jas asked.

"The space-city...the mining colonies—they're gone." Unable to fathom the immensity of the devastation, he listened to his own words with disbelief. Not since the Dark Years had there been such an atrocity.

Forty thousand people. Dead.

It was Sharron's doing! He'd sent his minions after Rom as he'd promised, a brilliant hit-and-run above the cloak of the *Tjhu'nami.*

As his ship's computer scoured the area, searching for signs of life, Rom envisioned the bleak future awaiting them if nothing was to be done about this attack. One by one, the ancestral homeworlds would fall. Over time billions would defect to the Family of the New Day out of fear as the balance of power shifted. All because the *Vash* federation was too mired in tradition to act.

He swore under his breath. No, such a future would not come to pass. Not as long as the blood of Romjha beat within him.

With the exigency to retaliate singing in his veins, he punched the flashing red light that was a direct link to

Mistraal's planetary security. "Get your asses up here. All available fighters—"

Jas shouted, "Bandits—two o'clock!"

A surge of adrenaline readied him for combat. His gaze tracked to his viewscreen, to several cruisers and a contingent of smaller vessels speeding away from them. He enhanced and magnified the image until he discerned the symbol emblazoned on their sides.

A blazing sun above two clasped hands.

The Family of the New Day.

"Rom, they're almost out of range!" Jas yelled.

One glimpse of her, still flying valiantly off his wing, plunged him into soul-wrenching indecision. She was a worthy combatant, but never would he willingly place her, or any woman, in jeopardy. Yet what of his brother Lijhan, and Zarra? Hadn't he lost them because he had left them behind?

"Jas—" A sound of anguish rumbled in his throat. The last of the enemy fleet was about to jump to hyperspace. If he lost them, he'd never discover their home base. "Turn back."

I loved you, Inajh d'anah, he said silently.

Sweat and remorse burned his eyes as he sped away from her. Sharron would pay for the carnage he'd wreaked; *this time* Rom would see it through, even at the cost of his own life.

But not Jas's.

He'd ensure her safety by snatching the enemy ship's coordinates, jumping with them to light speed, then trailing the bastards until they dropped back to normal space. By the time they engaged in battle, Jas would be light-years behind, enfolded in the protection of the Mistraal space force.

Accelerating to catch the retreating ships he armed his weapons. "Sharron, I will find you!" he roared into the blackness of space.

"Romlijhian, is that you?"

A raspy voice invaded his comm.

Rom froze. A muscle jumped in his cheek. The man had sensed him. Fighting for composure, he extended outward with his senses, searching the enemy fleet. Sharron was among them—but in which ship? He reached farther. *There*. In the one remaining cruiser: irreparable, desolate coldness honed by intense self-absorption.

"Join me, Romlijhian."

Rom blocked out Sharron's entreaty, pushed his starfighter as fast as it would go.

"Things have changed considerably since Balkanor. Then you were a naive young man driven by misplaced heroics. Now you are adrift without family, without power. But you can have those things back. I can give them to you." Sharron's voice was gentle, so very reasonable. "Walk with me, Romlijhian. Let me save your soul."

Revulsion choked Rom. "Save *this*."

He fired what he intended to be a preemptive strike before achieving light speed. But Sharron's cruiser slowed—because of Rom's offensive, or simply in impatience to retaliate, he didn't know, but he had no time to worry about it.

Rom blew past. Sharron's cruiser fired. Rom yanked his starfighter into an evasive maneuver, banking away from the pursuing missiles, his onboard computer expelling chaff and decoys in the ship's wake. The first missile spent itself on a decoy. The second got "smart," and exploded in a blinding sheet of energy. Rom's shields protected him, but the impact rammed him against his harnesses. The stench of something burning seeped into his air supply. Warnings flashed on the control console: HULL INTEGRITY 64 PERCENT, PLASMA LOSS NUMBER TWO THRUSTER, EQUIPMENT BAY FIRE. Somehow the damaged starfighter stayed intact. But it was leaking fuel, losing thrust. He shoved the good thruster to maximum power. *Go, go, go!* But the starfighter shuddered and dumped most of its velocity. Sharron's cruiser wheeled slowly around and headed toward him. *To finish me off.*

"Crush the darkness!"

Startled, Rom jerked his attention away from the cruiser.

A starfighter streaked past. Great Mother—it was Jas! Uttering a war cry he'd shared with no one since . . . the Balkanor angel.

Rolling inverted, she let loose a deluge of missiles, hammering away at the cruiser and the fighters that hadn't yet made the jump to hyperspace. One of the smaller ships burst apart, the explosion damaging another too close by. Hurtling away, its wreckage glanced off the shield on the cruiser's underbelly.

"The next shot will be between the eyes, *pal*," he heard her scream into her comm. "*Between the eyes!*"

Rom sensed Sharron's surprise, and then his outrage. He'd kill her.

"Jas!" Rom shouted. "Egress, egress now!" *Don't die in my place,* he beseeched her silently, desperately. *Turn back.*

No! I won't leave you this time.

He heard her response in his mind—as she'd no doubt heard his. *But how?* He obliterated the thought even as he formed it. If he distracted her from her task, they were as good as space dust. There would be time for questions later, *if* they survived.

Their two starfighters were no match against a heavily armed cruiser, but a tenacious assault could very well keep Sharron from making the leap to hyperspace. And the longer they occupied him, the greater his and Jas's chances of receiving reinforcements. Panting from exertion, Rom blinked sweat from his eyes. Victory depended on him and Jas. This time he had no choice. Together, they must fight.

Perhaps, he thought, that was what the Great Mother had intended all along.

"Crush the darkness!" he roared, his senses unnaturally acute, heightened by shock and proximity to death. Jas's thoughts, her fear and exhilaration, ebbed and flowed with his, mirroring the eerily beautiful dance he remembered from Balkanor. They blasted away at the cruiser's defenses and most of the weapons the enemy ship hurled at them. But they took hits, hard ones, damaging their shields. Rom's hopes of getting Jas out of this alive eroded. They were weakening. They couldn't go on much longer.

Abruptly Sharron's four remaining starfighters detonated in front of them. The intense display of pyrotechnics made lights dance before his eyes.

Rom whooped. "What a shot!"

Jas gasped. "Try to warn me next time."

"That wasn't you?"

"I thought it was *you!*"

Rom jerked his attention to his viewscreen. The *Quillie* was screaming toward them from one quadrant, and

Mistraal's fleet from the other. "Looks like we have company."

"Woo-hoo!"

In moments, the engagement escalated from doomed skirmish to an emotionally charged battle. The odds were even. Missiles were exchanged. Relativistic bomblets. Deadly smart-dust that detonated on impact. Someone's shot—his? Jas's?—tore though the already weakened cruiser's hull. The trillidium surface peeled back like fish skin, exposing its inner core. The cruiser erupted into a glorious blossom of energy so intense it seemed to ignite space itself.

Rom stared at the fireball long after it dwindled into tiny, unsurvivable bits. Then he tipped his head back against his seat, his muscles shaking with relief and exhaustion. He had lived this moment once before, on Balkanor, when he thought he'd killed Sharron. Only this time he knew it was true. The coldness, the *evil* he'd sensed during the battle, was gone.

Sharron had ceased to exist.

Once back at the palace, Rom was swept into the shuttle bay's antechamber along with a sea of disheveled, exhausted soldiers, men whose battles were ordinarily confined to the Bajha arena. But numbing grief had already subdued their triumph. Forty thousand people were dead.

He pushed his way through the crowd until he found Jas. She cried out and ran into his arms.

He lifted her to him, finding her with his mouth, shuddering with the raw emotion in their all-too-brief embrace. As the crowd jostled around them, he clamped his hands to either side of her face and gazed intently into her eyes. "You remembered. You remembered Balkanor."

"Yes," she whispered, her eyes shimmering with tears. "When I realized it was Sharron out there, and you were about to face him alone, my thoughts . . . *imploded.* I don't know how else to describe it. Words came into my head . . . images."

She paused to take a breath. "*You're* the man in the desert; it was *you* I always searched for, but couldn't find. Because I never meant to leave you there, wherever it was we were. Never. Do you understand? I was taken from you when I was rescued—when I woke up after being unconscious. My God, after all these years, the dream finally makes sense. My life makes sense."

He closed his eyes as she swept kisses along his jaw. The old memories overtook him then, swirling like grit in a sudden sandstorm, recollections of his first year of exile, how his obsession with the Balkanor angel had enabled him to dig in his heels when loneliness and guilt had pushed him to the precipice of despair. *I never meant to leave you.*

"If only you knew what those words mean to me, *Inajh d'anah,*" he whispered. Not trusting his emotions, he caught her around the waist, pinning her to him as they merged back into the crowd of returning pilots.

The massive doors to the dining hall slammed open. *"Ajha, ajha!"* Exclamations of shock and surprise preceded them into the enormous chamber, where Joren awaited them. Music hushed. Plates crashed to the floor.

Rom released Jas and walked to his brother-in-law.

"Is it true?" Joren demanded.

"Yes. The orbital city, the mining colonies, all gone."

There were gasps and muttered prayers.

Rom raised his voice. "It was deliberate, premeditated."

Joren recoiled, as if the concept was too grotesque to contemplate. "Go on."

"Sharron used the *Tjhu'nami* to cloak his attack."

"And now he's dead."

"Yes," Rom said. "The surviving ships jumped to hyperspace."

Joren swore under his breath. "Now we've lost them."

"No, we haven't, my lord," a new voice said.

Intrigued, Jas glanced over her shoulder. Gann stepped past, Muffin behind him. They looked rumpled and worn out. Gann's forehead was bruised, and he was favoring his right ankle. Unconsciously she pressed her palm to her sore stomach.

Gann straightened under Joren's scrutiny. "Gann of the *Quillie,* my lord, inbound from Karma Prime to see Rom B'kah."

"You had help?" Joren prompted.

"Yes. A cruiser. Class-six. They picked up a distress call from one of the mining colonies, as we did, and came straightaway. We both detected the enemy vessels as they transmitted coordinates to make their jump. Had but seconds to decide—the class-six was the better ship to track them out of the system, so I brought the *Quillie* here. We came in as the battle was under way."

"So the cruiser's trailing them?" Joren asked.

"Yes, my lord."

Rom drummed his fingers on his upper arms. "A

class-six. I wonder who they are. Merchants, you suppose?"

"No. *Vash Nadah*." Gann appeared uneasy. "Rom, it was a B'kah ship."

Chapter Nineteen

Visibly shaken, Rom stepped toward the exit. "We shall discuss this privately." Joren, Gann, and Muffin trailed him, along with several guards. Jas hung back for a heartbeat. Di and the other women appeared stricken, but none seemed remotely interested in following. In that moment, the culture gap between them seemed enormous. She ran into the corridor as Rom spun around, clearly looking for her.

He waited until she caught up. "We have fought side by side since the beginning. We won't stop now." Pointedly, he settled her hand over the crook of his arm and resumed his long strides.

They entered a room with two conference tables arranged in concentric circles. Then the visiting diplomats—those who had been lucky enough to be in the palace and not the space-city—filed in, their shoulders bowed as if they bore lead weights. Soon the room was

filled to overflowing. Jas edged toward a window to inhale fresh air. The pale blue sky was streaked with con-
trails. Ships that had weathered the storm in underground
hangers were soaring beyond the atmosphere to view the
aftermath of the attack, while communications personnel
hunted for signals sent back from the B'kah ship trailing
the surviving attackers.

The day wore on. After a brief visit with the Dars'
surgeon to treat her reinjured abdomen, Jas returned to
the conference room.

Rom brooded, sitting by her side, while officials who
ran palace intelligence came and went, asking them
questions and entering the data in their handheld computers. Some gazed at her with a mixture of curiosity
and awe. News of her decisive role in the battle had
spread.

"Lord Dar, sir!" A strapping young man entered the
conference room, gripping a starfighter pilot helmet in
his hands. He bowed in front of Joren. "Wing Commander Ben e' Dar requests permission to speak."

"Proceed," Joren said.

"Our tests indicate that antimatter detonations indeed
destroyed the city."

Several gasps emanated from the crowd.

"An entire city." Joren peered around the room. "And
dozens of ships carrying respected members of our Great
Council. All killed in a cowardly terrorist attack carried
out with banned weaponry." Joren glanced at Rom. Jas
saw a silent signal pass between them. Then Rom nodded curtly and addressed the group.

"Sharron vowed he'd bring his war to the *Vash* homeworlds. And he has. Yes, he is now dead. But his people
will carry out his wish to destroy us all."

Susan Grant

The diplomats and surviving Council members began to murmur among themselves. Joren silenced them. "They are more ruthless and more relentless than we ever grasped. It is time we paid heed to Romlijhian's warning—one he gave us twenty years ago. This man owes us nothing. This man has every right to leave us to our closed-mindedness, our stubbornness in not acting intelligently to end such an appalling threat. But he has not."

Joren's black-and-gold tunic shimmered as he faced Rom. "You are the heir of the exalted Romjha, our light in the dark. We await your orders, Lord B'kah." He fell to one knee and bowed his head. One by one, others, though not all, followed suit.

Jas gripped Rom's warm hand. She expected him to rise, but he remained seated for taut moments, twining his fingers with hers, as if letting go indicated his acceptance of the leadership role Joren offered. *A choice. He said he'd have to make a choice.* She stared at their clasped hands, then shifted her gaze to the men crouching humbly and expectantly before Rom.

This was his true calling, she acknowledged inwardly, his birthright. Her relationship with him paled in comparison to this galactic Pearl Harbor, to these people and their inexorable pull on him. Rom was merely her lover, but he was their king. And they had every right to take him from her. She forced open her grip on his fingers.

Rom brought his mouth to her ear. "It is time to offer the gauntlet once more. Pray this time they take it." He stood, proud and tall. "Lord Dar—"

"One moment, my lord," the young pilot said, this time addressing Rom. He was gripping his helmet so hard that his knuckles were white. "I have news of the

B'kah cruiser. They followed the enemy out of hyper-space, then to what we think is their center of operations. Their arsenal there—it boggles the mind."

"Where is it? Do they know?"

"Yes, sir. Balkanor."

"Balkanor," Rom said on a harsh exhalation. Jas looked at his face anxiously. What he'd feared most had happened: the years had allowed Sharron to transform Balkanor into a womb of illegal weaponry. "What of the cruiser?"

The pilot lifted his chin. "The signal was lost. We haven't been able to raise them since. I . . . we think the ship was destroyed, my lord."

There was a small commotion near the doorway. Then the group parted for Di, tight-faced and cloaked in an uncharacteristically somber garment. Her chest was rising and falling rapidly. "Romlijhian, a call came for you on the private channel." Her voice shook. "It's Father. He's summoned you to the Wheel."

From the viewport in the luxurious Dar cruiser, Jas could see their destination. Lit from within, the tiny disk rotated slowly, like a lost toy among the stars. But as they neared the Wheel, it grew in size until it was staggeringly huge. A million winking lights; spokes as wide and tall as the Empire State Building. It was a marvel of construction, even for a society that had achieved light-speed space travel eons ago. "Five thousand years old . . . incredible."

"Much history has transpired here," Rom said, his arms snug around her waist. She set down her mug of steaming *tock* and leaned back into his embrace. They watched in exhausted silence until their cruiser docked in one of the thousands of bays. They'd been traveling for three days, sleeping little while they prepared the address Rom hoped to deliver to the Great Council—and his father.

The elder B'kah had not yet contacted Rom during their journey to council headquarters, nor forwarded any messages other than the mysterious summons he had sent Di. What pressure Rom must be feeling, Jas thought, not knowing whether his father had brought him here to laud him or humiliate him. All she knew was that the tyrant had better not cross her path, unless he wanted to hear how she regarded his treatment of his son.

The cruiser shuddered, then stilled. She tried to sound lighthearted. "Well, this is it. We're here."

Rom rested his hands on her shoulders, turning her to face him. Long, silent moments slipped by as he observed her somberly. She came up on her toes to kiss him lightly. "A grain of salt for your thoughts," she coaxed.

He seemed to choose his words carefully. "I have given much thought to us—to our shared vision, and to why you returned to me. The Great Mother gave us this time together"—his fingertip traced her lower lip—"not for love, or the happiness you have brought me in such abundance, but to light my path to the destiny She has chosen for me."

The hairs on the back of Jas's neck tingled. "You're scaring me," she whispered.

His pupils darkened within his pale gold irises, and he smoothed both palms over her hair, slowly and with care, as if memorizing her. "Your Earth world with its riches brought me back from the frontier. Then you were captured by the Family of the New Day, giving me the chance to rescue you and discover that Sharron was still alive. Then your sickness led me back to the fold of my family—something I swore I'd never do. Now we are here. The Wheel, home of the Great Council."

She sagged against him. He rested his chin on her head.

"By coming back to me, you have allowed me this chance to convince the *Vash Nadah* to mobilize for war and defeat the revolution. And perhaps"—his voice tightened—"the opportunity to reconcile with my father. But Jasmine, I fear that since your task is complete, you will leave, as you did before. Even if it is not of your own choice."

She reared back, her chin jutting high. "Magic may have brought me to you, or destiny—or God. But love is why I stayed. Do you understand that? I love you. I will never leave. *Never.*"

His gaze softened with his love for her, blunting the anguish she saw in his golden eyes. He opened his mouth to speak.

"Brother, the Council awaits you in the great hall," Joren interrupted, walking toward them.

Jas slid her hand down the side of Rom's face, over his cheekbone and the faint prickles of his beard. "We've worked on this speech long and hard. It's terrific. I'll be there, listening, praying." She swallowed. "You'll be wonderful."

He kissed her on the forehead, then her lips, before he took her by the hand. They followed Joren out of the cruiser and into the rather intimidating confines of the Wheel. Gann and Muffin brought up the rear, overtly protective in the way they scanned the crowd. Jas didn't

335

doubt either man would hesitate to beat to a pulp anyone who tried to hurt Rom.

Several dignitaries met them on the way, taking Joren and Rom with them, as she'd been told to expect. The men had been assigned seating near the immense stage. Had she been Rom's legal wife, she would have sat at his side. She thought of Di, who had stayed behind, torn between her religion's dictates against war and the necessity she now saw for it. For her, the ageless terror of seeing loved ones killed in battle, even if their deaths were to save them all, had left her all but paralyzed.

Jas, flanked by Gann and Muffin, entered the anteroom of the Great Council Hall. People turned to stare at them. What an odd sight they must make, she thought wryly, a woman with peculiar black hair and fair skin escorted by two hulking men dressed like escapees from smugglers' prison. As if reading her thoughts, Gann kept his hand lightly and reassuringly under the crook of her arm. His voice was gentle. "Are you doing all right?"

Her stomach squeezed tight. "Yeah. How about you?"

"More exhausted than after a match of Bajha with B'kah." She smiled at his remark. "In here," he said. They found seats in the rear of the darkened auditorium. He helped her tune a translator imbedded in a console in front of her so she could listen to Rom's Siennan words in Basic, in which she was far more fluent.

Eight massive thrones graced the right side of the stage. From the left, eight immaculately robed older men marched to the chairs. The tall, broad-shouldered gentleman who led them had the confident stance of a warrior, a familiar lean gait. Jas's heart skipped to a stop.

Rom's father.

Though his facial features weren't similar—Rom must

resemble his mother—his body and that of his son's were nearly identical. Fascinated, she watched a silver-trimmed indigo cape billow around the man's long legs as he sat. The other seven followed, dominolike, in what Jas guessed was an order based on family ranking. The hiss of applause began at the front of the immense hall, spreading slowly to the rear.

Then Rom took the stage, walking resolutely to a crystal lectern. Seeking eye contact from those within the audience, he gripped the podium, his knuckles white—not with anxiety, Jas thought, but with passion. This was the opportunity he'd wished for so fervently twenty years ago and never achieved: the chance to convince the stubborn, peace-loving *Vash Nadah* to go to war.

"I am Romlijhian B'kah," he announced. He inclined his head toward the eight leaders, then faced the audience. "I have been invited to address you because I have experience with a revolution begun by a group called the Family of the New Day." His self-assured voice boomed, filling the hall with its power. "Five standard days ago, the Dar homeworld was suddenly and deliberately attacked by these revolutionaries. They annihilated a space-city, home to forty thousand, as well as five mining colonies, several honored members of this Great Council, and countless assembly politicians and diplomats. Then, without provocation, the Family of the New Day fired upon and destroyed a class-six cruiser in the B'kah fleet." His hands opened. "We are in grave danger."

Exhaling, he paced across the stage. "To fully comprehend that danger, the future we face if we do not take action, we must try to understand our turbulent past. Not

337

simply in the manner in which we learned Trade History
as youngsters, but with a more critical eye." He clasped
his hands behind his back and faced them. As he re-
counted the Dark Years preceding the Great War, Jas
fell fully under his spell, barely breathing when he described in sickening detail the outcome of massive antimatter weaponry detonations.

His voice was low and earnest. "It is difficult to imagine a war so terrible, comprised of acts so heinous, that
its psychological aftermath impelled warriors bred for
battle to lay down their weapons . . . forever. But that
they did. 'Peace for all the time,' they decreed, and in-
corporated that covenant into our holiest of documents,
the Treatise of Trade . . . so that we would never forget.
But—I ask you—did they honestly intend that we maintain that peace in the face of evil? *At any cost*?"

The crowd reacted first with silence, then with uneasy
grumbling, a reaction that seemed to please Rom. His
voice soared as he likened Sharron to the warlords who
had brought civilization to the brink of annihilation
eleven thousand years before. "Their leader is now dead.
But his soldiers will carry on without him—many of
them *Vash Nadah*. Those who do not believe me—look
at the data! Even now, your intelligence reports reveal
that they are preparing for another attack. Where will
that be? When? How many more lives must be lost before we wage war against this monstrous threat, this
strengthening evil unsurpassed in our time? We must
fight as one to defeat them. I do not mean one family . . . or three. But all eight. Unity is victory." He
slammed his fist into his hand. "And without victory
there is no survival!"

Jas glanced around in the darkness. Some assembly

members were shouting, some weeping. Several stormed out. But most were listening in rapt silence. Rom's father, ensconced in his gilded throne onstage, scowled. The man's hands were spread on his knees, his muscular arms braced, his eyes downcast. He was either deep in thought or angry as hell.

Shoulders rigid, Rom faced his father and the other seven kings. "Honored members of the Great Council. You, the Eight, are leaders entrusted with the sacred power and vision of the ancient warriors. Your onerous responsibilities often force you to make complex choices—but none, I believe, as painful as the decision you must make today." Pointedly, he sought and held his father's gaze. Silently Jas cheered for Rom. In all her life she had never known a man with more guts.

Rom's voice rose, just as they'd practiced. "I ask that you declare war against the Family of the New Day, to defend the galaxy whatever the cost, never to surrender, even if battles are to be fought on the very home planets that protect our children. I ask that you carry on the struggle, for as long as it takes, until the Great Mother deems us worthy to liberate the galaxy from this utter, merciless evil." Rom regarded them for endless heartbeats, then bowed and backed up several steps. "Crush the darkness!" Fists clenched, he walked off the stage.

Applause erupted with the suddenness of a downpour. "B'kah, B'kah," some began to chant. "Unity is victory!"

Pride and apprehension tumbled through her, and goose bumps pebbled her arms. She clapped her hands until her palms stung. Quietly, she remarked to Gann, "He's reclaimed his role as leader."

He whispered in her ear. "Whether he wanted to or not."

She reached for his hand and squeezed it.

The applause abated only after the assembly members stood. Jas, Gann, and Muffin filed out a side entrance. She glimpsed Rom near the far wall of the anteroom, on the other side of a throng of eager admirers. He was glancing around, as if looking for her. She tried to push her way through the crowd, but it was slow going, particularly with everyone gaping at her—and her hair. She should have worn a cloak with a hood.

When she next checked the place Rom had stood moments before, it was empty. "Do you see him?" she asked Muffin, who towered over the crowd.

The big man craned his neck. "He took the center corridor. Lord B'kah was with him. And the other seven."

They jogged to the spot where Muffin had seen the men disappear. By the time they got there, formidable-looking security guards had blocked the hallway. Their laser pistols glinted ominously. "I need to see Romlijhian B'kah," she said breathlessly.

Muffin's shadow fell over them. The soldiers braced themselves.

"I'm Rom B'kah's *a'nah*," she explained. "He's expecting me."

The men glanced at each other. The shortest of the trio spoke, his demeanor polite but firm. "They are in council. No one is permitted inside. No wives." He lifted his uneasy gaze to Muffin. "No one."

She released a worried breath. Gann placed his hand on her shoulder. "Come. I'll buy us all a drink. We have no choice but to wait."

* * *

Loud voices echoed from across a vast plaza, where Jas
huddled at a tiny al fresco bar with Muffin and Gann, a
bowl of shimmer crackers between them. Real grass
grew along brick sidewalks lit by laser-lanterns. A dome
above let in the glow of trillions of stars. Several glasses
of mogmelon wine warmed her belly, muting her nerv-
ousness, but at the sight of Rom marching her way,
trailed by *Vash* starfighter pilots and intelligence officials, her pulse jumped all over again.

She pushed away from the table and stood, smoothing
the long silken sleeves of her gown. Rom's face was
shadowed. He wore his mask of indifference, hiding his
true emotions, though the glint in his eyes told her that
something significant had transpired in the meeting.

He didn't slow as he swept past. Grabbing her by the
elbow, he propelled her away from the table. She
glanced over her shoulder at the veritable army pursuing
them. "Who are they?"

Rom whirled on his entourage. "Go." When the men
hesitated, he beseeched them, "I ask for privacy now. I
will be at the appointed place at the appointed time."

The men halted by Gann and Muffin, and Rom resumed his punishing pace. Jas followed. They were practically jogging across the plaza. A warren of dark,
narrow streets loomed ahead, lined with stores and what
appeared to be private residences. He chose the second
alleyway, as if he knew exactly where he was headed.
"Where are we going?" she finally managed, gasping for
air in the Wheel's thin atmosphere.

"Down below," he said. Metallic cobblestones clicked
under their boots. The structures were built so close together that they blotted out the stars above. The air

reeked of overworked computer equipment, cooking meat, and something sour, like standing water. The cobblestones turned into stairs that descended into the bowels of the ancient space station.

Rom steered her off the main path, urging her along until they were wedged between a wall and a trash receptacle of discarded machinery and rotting food. She peered around nervously, and her mouth quirked. "Nice part of town. Mind telling me what's going on?"

He pressed his lips to the sheen of perspiration on her forehead. "I must leave you."

She went rigid and pushed away. "When?"

"Now. Tonight." He swallowed. "They await me at the docks."

"Who? What's happened?"

"There was another attack," he said grimly. "On the Lesok homeworld. The Family of the New Day's forces have returned to Balkanor to rearm. Then they will strike again. Only this time we will not allow it."

"*We?* You've convinced the *Vash Nadah* to fight back?"

"Yes." Rom saw triumph spark in her eyes. "And they chose me to lead the attack."

The blood drained from her face. "I thought . . . I thought you were throwing them the gauntlet. If you did, they tossed it right back."

"I have the best chance of sneaking into the New Day headquarters undetected. I've seen their ways—and I've been to the planet. Their weapons lab and storage are deep under the planet's surface. Only I know the landmarks to find the entrance, the system of underground tunnels to get there." He thought of the dank cells where

Sharron had tortured his prisoners. "I'll be able to get my men in before anyone knows we're there."

Like a true warrior, she bravely absorbed what he had said. But her voice was huskier now, betraying her fear. "How long will you be gone?"

"I'm not coming back, angel."

She gasped, lifting a trembling hand to her mouth.

"Jas, I can get my team in, but I will not be able to get us out."

"You don't know that!" Her eyes glistened with unshed tears.

He felt such pain that he could not describe it, would not share it with her. "The security measures in place at the cult headquarters are extraordinary. Even if we are successful, there is no way we can escape." An image flashed in his mind of the group of men who comprised the Wheel's elite guard, the best-trained warriors of the *Vash Nadah*. When he'd put forth the plan, no one brought up their nonexistent chances of success. Without hesitation, they were ready to follow him into a battle they couldn't possibly survive. "Jasmine, I *have* to do this. I have to finish what I started."

Weeping quietly, she wrapped her arms around him. He held her tight to his chest, each one of their heartbeats marching closer to the moment he'd never see her again.

"I am going to ask you to do something I fully expect you to decline," he said. "I will not blame you if you do."

She tilted her face up. "Anything," she said shakily. "You know that."

"When we flew patrol, I asked you to be my wife.

343

You were interrupted before you gave me your answer." They leaned into each other. He murmured his words against her hair. "I need to know what you intended to say."

"Yes," she whispered. "It was yes."

Joy and remorse rocketed through him with the awareness that this was both the best and worst moment of his life. "Then marry me tonight. Consent to be my wife. It is for selfish reasons only that I ask, a dying man's wish—"

"Stop it! You're coming back. You know it, too, or you wouldn't bother marrying me."

He sighed. "That is not the reason. In my religion, a man and woman must be legally wed in order to live together in the ever after. By all that is holy, Jasmine, we deserve eternity since we cannot have now." He gripped her upper arms and moved her backward. "All I can offer is my family name, but it is something I value more than the rarest of jewels."

Jas bit her lip until it stung. Rom was heir to an an empire that defied imagination. A king did not choose his life's path. His obligations came before personal wishes. Deep down, she'd already acknowledged that; only now had she finally accepted it.

"Rom, my love, if I could give you one thing in this universe, it would be happiness." She wiped the back of her hand across her face, wiping away her tears. "Let's find someone who can marry us."

She saw the answering moistness in his eyes when he caught her hand and tugged her away from the wall. Her boots skidded over the cobblestones, which had become slick from condensation dripping from high above. Rom answered her unspoken question. "The people who live here are descendants of those who built the Wheel long ago. Not all are *Vash,* and the customs they practice are often ancient—and unapproved. But because of the sacrifices their ancestors made in building this space-city, we look the other way." He slowed his pace, turned right, then followed the path to a dead end. Chimes tinkled as he pushed open a door leading down a dark and narrow flight of stairs. The air was muggy, warmer, and scented thickly with incense.

"Who told you about this place?"

"I asked one of the guards. He told me where to come."

They entered a cramped sitting area. A single laser-lantern hung from a wire tied to a metal beam in the ceiling. It spun in crooked circles, casting dizzying slashes of amber light across the walls and floor. "This counts as a legal ceremony?" she ventured doubtfully.

"Among the *Vash Nadah,* no. But it will be recognized among the merchants and in all the known worlds, including the frontier. And in my religion."

"Ah, ah!" An incredibly short, plump woman scurried into the room. The top of her head barely reached Jas's hips. "He told me you come." She propped her hands on her waistless form and leaned back, gazing in admiration at Rom, then at Jas. She gave a quick satisfied grunt, her pale eyes sparkling in her seamed face. "I will do for you. Ah, yes, I will do."

Despite the grief choking her, Jas exchanged smirks with Rom. The little woman reminded her of a chirpy little sparrow. But Jas's brief amusement faded as soon as she saw the altar. Weddings were supposed to be times of joy—not of sorrow. She ground her teeth together. The bird-woman flitted around them, indicating

345

that they kneel before a table littered with smoldering candles—real candles—and pots of fragrant bubbling oil. Rom hunkered down at her side. His warrior's body pressed against hers, lending her his warm strength. The woman performed a curious, slow little dance, her face scrunched closed in prayer, while she raised two candles above her head, one in each pudgy hand. Then she offered a candle to Jas. When she took it, the woman gave another to Rom.

"Today the blood of the B'kah and the Hamilton are joined," she recited in a singsong voice. "Two are stronger than one." She waved her fingers, indicating that they were to touch the candles together. Jas's hand shook. She gazed into Rom's shadowed face. Quivering candlelight imbued his bronzed skin with an amber glow. She held her breath as they brought the wicks together. They sparked, then surged into one tall flame, and the reflection danced in Rom's eyes.

While they held the candles together, the woman leaned closer, inspecting the flame. Then she cupped her gnarled hands over the candles. Her eyes took on that faraway, wisdom-of-the-ages look, reminding Jas of Tina, the elderly New Ager who'd once read her palm. "Very fortunate," the little sparrow whispered. "Yes, good future . . . long life . . . many descendants. Your progeny will travel to many worlds."

Jas averted her eyes. Apparently psychic abilities were not this ancient's strength.

"All done," the woman called out cheerily.

"One moment," Rom said. "I want her to have this." He twisted off his treasured signet ring and pushed the chunky band onto Jas's left index finger. "Take my ring."

Touched profoundly, Jas clenched her hand until the ring pinched her flesh. Then she crushed her fist protectively to her breasts. Solemn and silent, Rom leaned forward and kissed her, his mouth sweet and warm and tender. "I love you," they whispered to each other.

The woman plucked a handheld computer from the folds of her dress and punched several keys. Entering the event in a galactic database? Then she spread a comfortably normal-looking piece of paper and two pens on the table. Unable to make out the runes, Jas let Rom guide her hand to the proper place to sign. Then they were back out in the filtered and thin night air.

Jas tried not to dwell on why Rom was in such a hurry, striding through the underground village and uphill to the docks. It was more crowded in the main part of the station. People who passed them made their support of Rom known: "Unity is victory!" "Without victory there is no survival!" The words had become the new battle cry to defeat Sharron's uprising.

Ahead were the docks. Outside an enormous battle cruiser waited, its gleaming hull glowing in the Wheel's reflected light. Soldiers lined both sides of the corridor leading to the hatch. They watched her with tender understanding, having already bidden good-bye to their own wives. Joren, Gann, and Muffin stood off to the side—with Rom's father, stoic in his resigned despair, his face drawn. He pointedly sought eye contact with her and nodded, giving her his silent respect, but making no move to steal what little time she had left with his son. With sudden clarity—and surprising empathy—she realized how much pain he must feel at losing the same child twice.

Ten feet away from the onlookers, Rom stopped and

drew her close. Jas felt sluggish, numb, as if she were trapped in a nightmare. Tomorrow Rom wouldn't be with her, but now he was. She hugged him with all her might, laying her head against his shoulder as she closed her eyes.

"Be happy," he whispered.

She pushed away, trembling, and dragged her fingertips down his cheek. "Come back to me."

He swallowed hard. Haltingly, he began to speak in English. "Jasmine Boswell Hamilton B'kah. I . . . love . . . you." Then he kissed her, drawing away slowly.

When she opened her eyes he was striding up the gangway into the ship. The soldiers followed; then the hatch snapped shut. Somehow she managed to keep her composure through the rumbling of thrusters. As the ship streaked away, she felt suddenly faint. Joren and Lord B'kah blurred. She wobbled and Gann steadied her, escorting her away quickly, protecting her from questions and condolences with his large frame. He brought her to a room. His quarters? Hers? She didn't know . . . or care. She began to shake. Gann caught her before she crumpled to the floor. He propped his back against the wall and supported her crosswise across his lap, holding her to his chest. Shoulders heaving, she cried until it hurt. Sometime later, how much later she didn't know, she heard deep voices. Muffin. Gann. "Have news . . . Balkanor is destroyed. . . . No survivors . . ."

My God. Rom was dead.

He was never coming back to her.

A low, keening cry tore from the depths of her soul. Gann hugged her while she wept anew—for Rom, for her, for all they had lost, and for the sacrifice he'd made for his people. When she finally collapsed into exhausted sleep, she did so protected by her star king's loyal knight.

Chapter Twenty

"Three hundred and fifty thousand—yes, that's the sale price." Standing on the rear steps of the Rivas-Blackwell Gallery, a cordless telephone pressed to her ear, Betty glanced questioningly at Jas.

Not now, Jas mouthed. Her Range Rover took up Betty's narrow parking space and half the one next to it. She sought refuge behind the mechanical hulk, slipped on a pair of dark sunglasses, muting the surrounding sun-splashed maze of narrow alleys and fountain-filled courtyards, and unlocked the trunk. Rom's heavy signet ring—her wedding ring—swung beneath her blouse on its long chain. The familiar way it thumped between her breasts had become as reassuring and essential as her heartbeat.

"Fabulous. I'll have it shipped Tuesday." Betty rounded the corner near the hood. "Pardon? You'd like to speak to her?"

Jas quickly buried her head and shoulders in the trunk.

"She's still in Washington," Betty improvised. "But I'll let her know you called."

Jas pantomimed a thank-you. The artwork she'd created on her space travels had found a market—a lucrative market—and she was grateful for the success, but as for chatting with buyers and fans, some days were better than others, and today was not one of the good ones. A week of translating Basic to English for the Senate trade hearings had worn her out. Regardless, she'd eagerly volunteered to repeat her duties as freelance translator in two weeks for the United Nations. The ache inside her wasn't as sharp when she kept busy, unlike those devastatingly lonely first months home when she'd lived as a recluse in the guest cottage on Betty's forested property.

"I thought you were going directly home after the airport," Betty scolded, hanging up the phone.

"I did—for all of five minutes." Jas hoisted a carton of art supplies she'd purchased in Scottsdale and laid it on the pavement. "But Ian was gone who-knows-where, and the house felt too darn empty. So here I am, on your doorstep again. I'll cook dinner."

Betty suppressed a smile and moved aside a paint-speckled tarp covering canvases in the back of the Range Rover. "I'll let you cook. But only if you have something finished for me—" The woman sucked in a small breath, as she saw one of the paintings. "Oh, hon . . ."

Jas's face heated, and she rose to her feet. "It's Rom," she said slowly. It was the cherished work she secretly carted around with her.

Betty studied her intently. "Has anyone else seen this?"

"Only him. When I first painted it." Jas stared at the lovingly applied daubs of pigment that depicted Rom sleeping in their bedroom on Mistraal. He was sprawled on his stomach, arms flung above his head, bedsheets and discarded clothing twisting over and under his long, muscular legs, barely covering his buttocks. Marigold yellow, dusty rose . . . bronze leaf and cinnamon—the light of Mistraal's savanna flowed over his sculpted back, highlighting his smooth skin, and glinting golden where his beard stubble caught the first hints of dawn. Jas closed her eyes, remembering how the cool, fresh air had flooded the chamber that morning, waking Rom, the way he'd rolled onto his back and given her his sleepy, sexy smile.

"I like the way it makes me feel," she admitted in hushed tones. "So I keep it close by."

Awe tinged Betty's voice. "By far it is your best work." She returned the painting to its hiding place, respectfully tucking Rom away as if he were a treasured remnant of history, a long-dead warrior.

Jas ground her teeth. Frustration at the unfairness of it all turned her constant heartache to anger. "The *Vash* triumphed—because of *him.*" The invasion of Balkanor had been devastating for both sides, and the sparse details of the ensuing war were only now making their way to Earth. She slammed the trunk closed. "He saved his people, Betty. He should be alive to savor his victory."

Betty spoke with patience and empathy. "I know it hurts, Jas. It will for some time yet. But you are stronger now than before you left. And maybe more content."

Jas shot her a startled glance.

"You took a risk, Jas. You defied expectations, and

you traded mediocrity for the unknown. In return you found self-respect . . . and true love."

Jas held her friend's wise gaze. "I suppose I'll have to keep telling myself that," she whispered.

The distant thunder of motorcycles sliced through Sedona's perfectly still late-afternoon air. "It's Ian," Jas said, her mood lightening. Two Harleys roared into the parking lot. Her son lifted his visor and waved. Both riders looked dusty and tired, as if they'd been riding for hours.

Betty raised a brow. "Who's his friend?"

"Haven't a clue," Jas murmured. The helmeted stranger swung one long leg over his seat and stood. His leather-clad, athletic body elicited a shiver of desire, something she hadn't felt since Rom. She shoved her hands deep in the pockets of her jeans. "Here to see Sedona?" she asked him as casually as she could manage.

"No"—he removed his helmet—"I am here to see my wife."

At the sight of his golden eyes and tousled nutmeg hair, Jas's emotions whipped into a maelstrom. "Rom!" She choked. Her vision tunneled. Suddenly there wasn't enough air to breathe. Gasping, she sat hard on the curb, spilling the contents of her purse. Black spots whirled in front of her eyes as she watched her lipsticks roll down the asphalt slope. Then the spots turned to blobs that blotted out her vision, and someone was shoving her head between her legs.

When she came to, she was lying on her back on the pavement. Shivery hot and vaguely nauseated, she opened her eyes. Rom was crouching over her. He looked stricken as he smoothed her hair off her forehead. "I apologize for shocking you so" he said in Basic.

She squeezed her eyes shut. Upon opening them, he was still there. She made a small cry and flew upward, nearly knocking him backward. His arms locked around her. She hugged him as hard as she could, her kisses frantic, landing everywhere but his lips. He steadied her by pressing his wide palms to either side of her face, then covered her mouth with his. His kiss was deep and utterly tender. Dizzy, she sighed, and he lifted his head, regarding her with moist eyes. "Oh, Rom . . . oh, my love," she whispered fervently. Their mouths came together, this time hungry and fierce.

As the reality of his appearance sank in, her relief slid into disbelief. How could he be alive and she not know it? She tore her lips from his. "The war was over months ago," she said in a gasp.

"I came as soon as I could. I was wounded early in the invasion, then captured. I was as good as dead by the time I was rescued and brought home."

"Why didn't I know? I thought there were no survivors. Why didn't anyone tell me?"

"I asked my father not to."

"What!" she blurted, incredulous.

"I was in a coma. I woke blind and unable to move my legs. I didn't want you to feel obligated to a husband who was unable to protect you."

She took a closer look at him. Beneath his black leather jacket and chaps, he was thinner. The hollows under his cheekbones were more pronounced. Her heart twisted, and her joy boomeranged into white-hot fury. She slammed her fists onto his chest. "You had no right to make that decision alone. I'm your wife. I should have been at your side." She was crying now, speaking half in English, half in Basic, pummeling him with her fists. "I've been going through hell—"

He caught her wrists in his big hands. "Jasmine, listen to me."

"—bawling my eyes out every night!" She tried to scoot backward, but he held on to her wrists and came up on his knees. She shoved away from him, landing on her rear, her legs sprawled on the pavement. Her voice shook. "I thought you were dead."

His eyes were tortured, sorrowful. "I know, angel."

She crawled back into his arms, and he clutched her as if he'd never let go. "Why didn't you call?" she demanded, her tone softer.

"You are so good at heart, Jas, so loyal. I feared that the very qualities I admired in you would bind you to me . . . whether or not I could be a true husband to you."

She rested her cheek against his shoulder. The scent of dusty sun-warmed leather mingled with his clean, masculine scent.

"My father brought me back to Sienna to recuperate. As I mended, so did our differences." He compressed his lips. "It has not been an easy road. We are both hardheaded men."

She huffed. The ends of his mouth lifted in the barest hint of a smile. But it faded when his eyes flooded with obvious pain. "By all that is holy, I miss you, Jas. I *need* you. 'Don't fear happiness,' you told me on Mistraal. Those words came to haunt me day and night, until finally . . . *finally* I saw that I'd fallen back into my old ways—the ways of my father, and those who preceded him. My warrior's stubborn pride in not contacting you was the same unenlightened adherence to tradition that made the *Vash Nadah* brittle. That's why we nearly shattered with our first true challenge—a blunder I vow not to repeat." He gripped her shoulders. "I will begin by addressing the custom of arranged marriages for rulers. I hereby choose love instead.

"Come home with me to Sienna," he beseeched her, "so that we may wed formally. But be warned—the ceremony lasts six days. And not all is feasting and merrymaking. There are passages from Treatise of Trade to memorize, rituals to perform—"

"Rom." She framed his face with her hands. "No matter how many times and how many ways you propose, my answer will always be yes."

He stood, pulling her into his arms. A teary smile graced Betty's face while she applauded. Sniffling, Jas introduced them, then peered at her two road-weary motorcyclists. "Now why don't you gentlemen explain where you've been?"

The men exchanged glances. Ian spoke first. "Rom called before you got home—yesterday morning, early— and left about a million messages on the machine. He couldn't figure out why you wouldn't answer him—why you kept saying the same thing over and over every time." He grinned affectionately at Rom. "Mr. High Tech's first encounter with an answering machine."

Rom hooked his thumbs in the waistband of his snug jeans and shrugged.

"You understand English?" Jas asked.

"Most," Rom answered in kind. "Speak is much hard . . . hard*er*."

"So I star-69'd him, called him back, then told him you were in Washington and that he ought to come over.

The next thing you know I was teaching him to ride. I knew you weren't coming home until today, and, uh, we ended up camping overnight in the canyon." Ian shrugged guiltily. "We should have called."

Rom grazed his knuckle along her jaw. "My wrong. I ask Ian for time to know me more, so he will allow me to be husband to his mother."

Before she could say anything, Ian piped in. "It was a great trip. We talked. Most of the night, actually." Again he cast Rom an admiring gaze. Her joy-filled heart skipped a beat. They'd become confidantes.

"After I graduate," Ian went on, "he's going to teach me the family business."

"The 'family business'?" she repeated numbly, her mind reeling.

Rom replied in Basic: "Ian is my stepson. A good and loyal lad whom I'd be proud to call my heir, should he desire such an onerous hallmark. But you and I will talk further on this topic another time." He unsnapped the saddlebag on his bike and tossed her a leather jacket, helmet, and boots. "Tonight we will sleep in the desert, under the stars. Our long overdue wedding night."

His gaze turned dark and sexy, and anticipation trilled through her. "Then tomorrow, or maybe the next day," he added pointedly, "we will travel to see your daughter. But first we will celebrate." He raised the lid of a cooler just high enough for her to see the glint of ice chips and bottles. "Red Rocket Ale," he said with a wink.

She threw her head back and laughed. He grabbed her around the waist and spun her around. When her feet touched the ground, he murmured into her hair, "I apologize for the pain I caused you. I admit I have much to learn about being a husband."

She smiled through her tears and hugged him back. "Don't worry, Rom. You'll have a lifetime to get it right."

SUSAN GRANT
ONCE A PIRATE

Andrew Spencer sails the seas seeking revenge, and there are very few merchants' treasures that he hasn't given a jolly rogering. But on this particular voyage, he finds his task harder than usual. As a brown-eyed beauty is hoisted from the waves, he finds his pirate's soul plundered from without and a fiery need conjured up from within.

The freak storm that causes her plane to go down in the Atlantic sends fighter pilot Carly Callahan's life spinning out of control as well. Pulled from the freezing ocean, she finds herself in the hot embrace of an Adonis. But his eyes are cold and hard, and the man's burning lips swear she is someone else before he claims her as his own. Carly knows she has one chance to go home, but there is so much to see and feel here—and the best is yet to come.

__52364-7 $4.99 US/$5.99 CAN

Dorchester Publishing Co., Inc.
P.O. Box 6640
Wayne, PA 19087-8640

Golden Man

Evelyn Rogers

Steven Marshall is the kind of guy who makes a woman think of satin sheets and steamy nights, of wild fantasies involving hot tubs and whipped cream—and then brass bands, waving flags, and Fourth of July parades. All-American terrific, that's what he is; tall and bronzed, with hair the color of the sun, thick-lashed blue eyes, and a killer grin slanted against a square jaw—a true Golden Man. He is even single. Unfortunately, he is also the President of the United States. So when average citizen Ginny Baxter finds herself his date for a diplomatic reception, she doesn't know if she is the luckiest woman in the country, or the victim of a practical joke. Either way, she is in for the ride of her life . . . and the man of her dreams.

___52295-0 $5.99 US/$6.99 CAN

Virtual Heaven

Ann Lawrence

The warrior looms over her. His leather jerkin, open to his waist, reveals a bounty of chest muscles and a corrugation of abdominals. Maggie O'Brien's gaze jumps from his belt buckle to his jewel-encrusted boot knife, avoiding the obvious indications of a man well-endowed. Too bad he is just a poster advertising a virtual reality game. Maggie has always thought such male perfection can exist only in fantasies like *Tolemac Wars*. But then the game takes on a life of its own, and she finds herself face-to-face with her perfect hero. Now it will be up to her to save his life when danger threatens, to gentle his warrior's heart, to forge a new reality they both can share.

___52307-8 $5.99 US/$6.99 CAN

Dorchester Publishing Co., Inc.
P.O. Box 6640
Wayne, PA 19087-8640

Please add $1.75 for shipping and handling for the first book and $.50 for each book thereafter. NY, NYC, and PA residents, please add appropriate sales tax. No cash, stamps, or C.O.D.s. All orders shipped within 6 weeks via postal service book rate. Canadian orders require $2.00 extra postage and must be paid in U.S. dollars through a U.S. banking facility.

Name_____
Address_____
City_____State_____Zip_____
I have enclosed $_____ in payment for the checked book(s).
Payment <u>must</u> accompany all orders. ❑ Please send a free catalog.
CHECK OUT OUR WEBSITE! www.dorchesterpub.com

A Case Of Nerves
Angie Kay

Standing on the moors of Scotland, Alec Lachlan could have stepped right off of the battlefield of 1746 Culloden. Decked out in full Scottish regalia, Alec looks like every woman's dream, but is one woman's fantasy. Kate MacGillvray doesn't expect to be swept off her feet by the strangely familiar green-eyed Scot. But she is a sucker for a man in a kilt; after all, her heroes have always been Highlanders. Wrapped in Alec's strong arms, Kate knows she has met him before—centuries before. And she isn't about to argue if Fate decides to give them a second chance at a love that Bonnie Prince Charlie and a civil war interrupted over two centuries earlier.

___52312-4 $5.50 US/$6.50 CAN

BELOVED WARRIOR
JUDY DICANIO

Jennifer Giordano isn't looking for a hero, just a boarder to help make ends meet. But Dar is larger-than-life in every respect, and as her gaze travels from his broad chest to his muscular arms, time stops, literally. Jennifer knows this hulking hunk with a magic mantle, crystal dagger, and pet dragon will never be the ideal housemate. But as the Norseman with the disarming smile turns her house into a battlefield, Jennifer feels a more fiery struggle begin. Gazing into his twinkling blue eyes, she knows she can surrender to whatever the powerful warrior wishes, for she's already won the greatest prize of all: his love.

___52325-6 $5.50 US/$6.50 CAN

Lord of The Keep
Ann Lawrence

He has but to raise a brow and all accede to his wishes; Gilles d'Argent alone rules Hawkwatch Castle. The formidable baron considers love to be a jongleur's game—till he meets the beguiling Emma. With hair spun of gold and eyes filled with intelligence, she binds him to her. Her innocence stolen away in the blush of youth, Emma Aethelwin no longer believes in love. Reconciled to her life as a penniless weaver, she little expects to snare the attention of Gilles d'Argent. At first Emma denies the tenderness of the warrior's words and the passion he stirs within her. But as desire weaves a tangible web around them, the resulting pattern tells a tale of love, and she dares to dream that she can be the lady of his heart as he is the master of hers.

___52351-5 $5.99 US/$6.99 CAN

Dorchester Publishing Co., Inc.
P.O. Box 6640
Wayne, PA 19087-8640

Please add $1.75 for shipping and handling for the first book and $.50 for each book thereafter. NY, NYC, and PA residents, please add appropriate sales tax. No cash, stamps, or C.O.D.s. All orders shipped within 6 weeks via postal service book rate. Canadian orders require $2.00 extra postage and must be paid in U.S. dollars through a U.S. banking facility.

Name_____
Address_____
City_____ State_____ Zip_____
I have enclosed $_____ in payment for the checked book(s).
Payment <u>must</u> accompany all orders. ❏ Please send a free catalog.
CHECK OUT OUR WEBSITE! www.dorchesterpub.com

AN ORIGINAL SIN
NINA BANGS

Fortune MacDonald listens to women's fantasies on a daily basis as she takes their orders for customized men. In a time when the male species is extinct, she is a valued man-maker. So when she awakes to find herself sharing a bed with the most lifelike, virile man she has ever laid eyes or hands on, she lets her gaze inventory his assets. From his long dark hair, to his knife-edged cheekbones, to his broad shoulders, to his jutting—well, all in the name of research, right?—it doesn't take an expert any time at all to realize that he is the genuine article, a bona fide man. And when Leith Campbell takes her in his arms, she knows real passion for the first time . . . but has she found true love?

___52324-8 $5.99 US/$6.99 CAN

THE Last Viking

SANDRA HILL

He is six feet, four inches of pure unadulterated male. He wears nothing but a leather tunic, speaks in an ancient tongue, and he is standing in Professor Meredith Foster's living room. The medieval historian tells herself he is part of a practical joke, but with his wide gold belt, callused hands, and the rabbit roasting in her fireplace, the brawny stranger seems so... authentic. Meredith is mesmerized by his muscular form, and her body surrenders to the fantasy that Geirolf Ericsson really is a Viking from a thousand years ago. As he helps her fulfill her grandfather's dream of re-creating a Viking ship, he awakens her to dreams of her own until she wonders if the hand of fate has thrust her into the arms of the last Viking.

___52255-1 $5.99 US/$6.99 CAN

Rejar

DARA JOY

Lord Byron thinks he's a scream, the fashionable matrons titter behind their fans at a glimpse of his hard form, and nobody knows where he came from. His startling eyes—one gold, one blue—promise a wicked passion, and his voice almost seems to purr. There is only one thing a woman thinks of when looking at a man like that. *Sex.* And there is only one woman he seems to want. *Lilac.* In her wildest dreams she never guesses that bringing a stray cat into her home will soon have her stroking the most wanted man in 1811 London....

_52178-4   **$5.99 US/$6.99 CAN**